THE MAN WHO LIVE

THE MAN WHO LIVED TWICE

DAVID TAYLOR

Matador
9 Priory Business Park,
Wistow Road, Kibworth Beauchamp,
Leicestershire. LE8 0RX
Tel: 0116 279 2299
Email: books@troubador.co.uk
Web: www.troubador.co.uk/matador
Twitter: @matadorbooks

ISBN 978 1788036 139

British Library Cataloguing in Publication Data.
A catalogue record for this book is available from the British Library.

Printed and bound in the UK by 4edge Limited
Typeset in 11pt Bembo by Troubador Publishing Ltd, Leicester, UK

Matador is an imprint of Troubador Publishing Ltd

To my grandchildren Thomasina, Kit and Evelyn

'*Hate the sin, love the sinner.*'

Mahatma Gandhi

THE MADISON PAPERS

It was a ridiculous mission. No more than a token gesture. He knew that. To attack a city you couldn't hope to hold was the height of folly, especially when that city was the capital of an ambitious nation of seven million people. There would be far-reaching consequences, impossible to predict.

Major General Robert Ross felt he had gone far enough. He had doubted the wisdom of moving his troops so far from their ships. His expeditionary force of 4500 infantry and marines had travelled deep into enemy territory and scouting reports had established that a much larger army of 7000 men was waiting less than a mile away, ready for battle.

'Couldn't be better, Ross. They are there for the taking and no mistake.' He could hear the contempt in Rear Admiral George Cockburn's voice. The man was pig-headed, insufferably arrogant. Sent to America with a small fleet to blockade ports and harbours in the Washington region, Cockburn had tactical responsibility for this British task force incursion and he was asking, nay demanding, that Ross attack the capital. The hawkish admiral was not alone in wanting to engage the enemy. The men were spoiling for a fight. Giving Brother Jonathan 'a good drubbing' had become an article of faith for British soldiers as this miserable colonial war dragged on into its third year.

Sweat poured down the general's cheeks as he squinted through his spyglass at the enemy lines drawn up on the west bank of the Potomac River. They had the weight of numbers and were on ground of their own choosing. Ross thought of Burgoyne at Saratoga and Cornwallis at Yorktown in the Revolutionary War. Another humiliating British defeat on American soil seemed inevitable on this hot August day in 1814.

1

Or was it? His body stiffened. The Americans had had a week's warning of his advance on Washington and yet their dithering commander Brigadier General Winder had failed to blow up the bridge at Bladensburg, which was the best way of crossing the river. Tactically too Winder had got it wrong. While possessing greater firepower and the territorial advantage of the semi-wooded hillside, Winder had left too big a gap between his frontline artillery and the rest of his army. And there was something else in Ross's favour. The American militia were clearly raw recruits, a ragtag collection of farmhands and office workers, brave enough no doubt, but not real soldiers tested in the heat of battle. Create panic in their ranks and they were likely to cut and run.

Ross touched the unhealed scar on his neck, thinking of past battles. Unlike their homespun adversaries, his three brigades consisted of combat-hardened veterans, trained in the Napoleonic Wars to march toward the sound of the guns, drilled to reload a musket in fifteen seconds. There was no danger of them fumbling a cartridge or losing a ramrod. They may be the dregs of society, wharf rats and petty criminals, but they were ferocious fighters. Perhaps Cockburn was right after all. Attack was the best policy. Here was the perfect opportunity to strike at the heart of the enemy's power. Defeat Winder and the road to Washington was clear.

'Right then,' Ross muttered, spurring his chestnut thoroughbred forward. 'Major Smith, present my compliments to Colonel Thornton and ask him to take the 85th across that bridge.' The words were spoken casually but there was tension in his voice. He was crossing the Rubicon. Should this military action fail, his career would be over.

He summoned his aide-de-camp, 'Take a note, Clarkson. "Noon, August 24th, decision taken to attack American army at Bladensburg. Perceived weaknesses in enemy strategy and tactics will prevent them from reinforcing the critical battle and lead to their eventual rout.'"

'You've seen this many times, I suppose sir?' One of the general's junior aides, who had never fought before, was trying to steady his nerves.

'Aye, so I have,' Ross replied. 'The first bit is the worst.'

They watched the 85th Light Infantry filing down the hill towards the bridge. In their red coats, white trousers and stovepipe shakos they made an easy target. Seeing their approach, the Americans whooped and hollered and began to fire their six-pound cannons. The first ball fell fifty yards short, ploughing up earth and stone before bouncing over the heads of the advancing soldiers to tear through a dogwood copse. The next ball overshot its mark and ricocheted off a wall. Soon the American gunners would find their range but the Buckinghamshire regiment continued to march at double time without a word being spoken.

'Look at our men,' said Ross's admiring aide, 'silent as the grave and orderly as people at a funeral.' The general thought this an odd thing to say: too prescient to be appropriate.

As the first British soldiers reached the bridge they were greeted with a furious broadside from a gun battery two hundred yards away. Crowded three abreast on the narrow walkway, the front line fell under this devastating barrage. A round shot hit the bridge, plunging wickedly through the exposed ranks, carrying off a young man's leg and cutting swathes of bloody flesh, and yet still they came, stepping over the mangled bodies of fallen comrades and through the powder smoke to be picked off by American marksmen shooting from the shelter of a nearby copse.

The noise was deafening; a sustained terror of sound as the redcoats encountered a rain of rifle bullets. Caught in this murderous maelstrom, Thornton's troops were as stubborn as mules, choking on the stench of exploded gunpowder and deafened by the concussive thunder of the cannons but moving steadily forward until with a mighty roar they reached the other side of the bridge and began to fight back. The foul-smelling air was thick with bullets, but all their concentration went into loading and firing.

With a bridgehead established, other British regiments forded the river to stage a concerted assault on the American gun emplacements. To reinforce this attack, mounted Royal Marines trundled wheeled bombarding frames through the fast-flowing water. A horse went down to a blast of American case-shot, screaming and thrashing around, until cut free from the rest of the team.

Ross galloped across the bridge and beckoned to a red-faced Marine officer who was wading ashore. 'If you please, Perkins, prepare the fireworks.' He was talking about the Congreve sky rocket, a thirty-two-pound iron cylinder, packed with powder, attached to a fifteen-foot stick. Fired from a slanting trough, these rockets could fly for two miles and, although difficult to aim accurately, they made a terrifying amount of noise and exploded on impact, ejecting shot like pieces of shrapnel.

'Shock and awe, gentlemen,' said Ross, as the first rocket screamed overhead, 'shock and awe.'

With rockets whizzing through the air, the American batteries began to buckle under the pressure. They were coming under heavy fire from the 44th East Essex Regiment and the 4th King's Own who were gradually outflanking them. Looking around for support, the American gun crews discovered the rest of their army was too far off to be of any use. They were on their own and about to be overrun. In the circumstances, they did what ill-trained soldiers always do. They panicked and fled. Within minutes it became a rout and all that stood in Ross's way were five hundred stubborn flotilla men who engaged in vicious hand-to-hand combat before running out of ammunition. The battle was over.

Rear Admiral Cockburn dusted down his black naval jacket and smiled broadly. 'Splendid, Ross. On to Washington! Glory beckons.' But not even he could know how easy it was going to be. Apart from the odd ill-directed sniper bullet, British troops encountered no resistance that evening as they roamed through the city's broad avenues systematically burning public buildings. The greatest challenge was how to set fire to the sandstone wings of the Capitol building, something they achieved by stacking up all the furniture they could find, tossing in leather-bound volumes from the Library of Congress as kindling, and igniting the bonfire with rocket powder.

Having vandalised America's political seat of power the small British contingent turned west up the wide empty expanse of Pennsylvania Avenue, a rutted road in which the mud had caked into red dust. What they were looking for was the presidential palace. They knew it was a Georgian mansion with whitewashed walls, Greek-style architecture and large gardens.

'It's over there,' a soldier yelled, pointing into the gloom. One of Ross's brigade commanders swung his torch across the portico's decorative masonry and gasped in surprise. There were no guards to be seen. 'Upon my soul, all this pomp and opulence and no one to defend it,' he sneered. 'Where's Jonathan when he's needed? And what about the occupant of this stately pile – what's become of him?'

The officer was referring to the fourth President of the United States James Madison. Having failed to rally his troops at Bladensburg, Madison had gone into hiding, a fugitive in his own country. To the British he was a cartoon character; the slight, unprepossessing figure in black who had had the temerity to declare war on the British Empire. 'Poor Jemmy' was nothing but 'a schoolmaster dressed up for a funeral'.

Ross had learned never to underestimate an enemy. He ordered his fusiliers to search for booby traps in the grounds but none could be found. A relieved British party lit further torches and were about to ransack the palace when the aroma of cooked food reached their nostrils. It was getting late and no one had eaten since dawn. The plundering could wait. Following their noses, the hungry soldiers rushed through empty antechambers to a state dining room where a long table was set for a forty-place dinner, its damask cloth sparkling with silver cutlery and crystal wineglasses. Better yet, decanters of wine and flagons of cider and ale stood invitingly on the sideboard.

Ross doffed his cocked hat and laughed ironically. 'See what we have here, gentlemen, little Jemmy's victory banquet! So confident was he of our defeat that he laid on supper for our conquerors. Sadly, they are not in a position to enjoy it.'

Wearing his two-cornered hat and jet-black uniform jacket with its gold epaulettes, Rear Admiral George Cockburn surveyed the room with an aristocratic scorn. 'Nor do I see any sign of that bird of paradise Madison calls his wife, more is the pity, for I'm told she is a dainty craft, if too readily boarded.'

This quip drew loud guffaws but not from General Ross, who winced at the crude reference to Madison's buxom, vivacious wife Dolley. As an Irish gentleman of impeccable manners, he hated coarse talk, even if the gossip about her affair with former president Thomas Jefferson happened to be true.

'What she *has* done,' Ross added drily, 'is remove the curtains and a picture off yonder wall. But I wonder what she's left in the kitchen that smells so good. Go take a look, Evans.'

A flight of stairs led down to the kitchen where Ross's quartermaster found chickens and joints of beef and ham roasting on spits in front of an open fire. The cooks had left sauces simmering on the stove and a scullery table laden with apple pies, plates of soft gingerbread and cinnamon cakes. There was enough here to feed the ranks as well as the officers.

By the time every scrap of food had been consumed, the British raiding party was pleasantly drunk and in weary good humour. It was time for the toasts at high table. 'The Prince Regent,' Ross proposed, causing diners to lurch unsteadily to their feet. 'Like the sun in its meridian may His Highness spread lustre throughout the world.'

Next it was Cockburn's turn. 'I give you the health of our missing host, little Jemmy, last seen running for his life. What was meant for Jonathan has been gratefully devoured by John Bull.'

As the laughter subsided, a mahogany grandfather clock chimed the midnight hour, reminding Ross of what he had come here to do. 'Any officer seeking a souvenir is free to roam the building, but be back here in twenty minutes to stack up the chairs for another bonfire.'

Beauchamp Urquhart, a fresh-faced lieutenant in the 85th Light Infantry, lit a candle and rushed upstairs. Madison's private dressing room bore all the signs of a hasty departure, drawers pulled out, contents scattered, but what caught the young man's eye was a bundle of papers lying on the rug. They were tied together with a red ribbon and stamped with a presidential seal bearing the motto 'Rebellion to tyrants is obedience to God'.

'Yes, Urquhart, what is it?' Ross looked up from the map he had been studying at the dinner table.

The lieutenant handed over the package. Ross untied the ribbon and read private and political state secrets, including why America had declared war on Britain in 1812. 'Upon my soul,' he muttered. 'This explains a lot, so it does.'

As the minutes ticked by the general's brow became more furrowed. It was a warm night but a shiver ran down his spine. Somewhere in his superstitious Irish soul a small voice was

7

telling him he had opened Pandora's Box and no good would come of it. But he must do his military duty. That always came first.

'Thank you, Urquhart,' he finally said. 'I will take these papers and make sure they are on the next ship going to England. Lord Bathurst needs to see them.'

✶ ✶ ✶

The British Secretary of State for War never got to see the Madison papers. They were lost in a shipwreck and more than fifty years would go by before these confidential letters were discovered on a coral atoll. The man who found them was a British officer who had fought for the Confederacy in the Civil War. How he came to be there and what happened to him subsequently is the substance of this narrative.

THE KNIGHT TEMPLAR

JUNE 18, 1862

They had been on the move since dawn, marching over farmland, across timbered ridges and through pastures where the air was lazy with flies. With the sun blazing down, their sweat-stained uniforms grew stickier with each passing hour, until the unmistakable reek of swamp water mixed with excreta signalled that they had reached their destination and were about to begin army life in Knoxville, Tennessee.

The new recruits came to an uncertain halt between rows of tents in Camp Van Dorn. They were just boys, romantic teenagers, proud to be joining the Second Kentucky Cavalry, and they looked out of place in their new grey jackets and stout leather shoes.

'Well, I'll be darned, fellers, here come the sheep,' a sunburned Confederate soldier called out before spitting into his cooking fire. Nervous young eyes were cast toward the wolves rising to greet them. Morgan's Raiders were a daunting sight to behold: rough, violent men in broad-brimmed hats, straggly beards and worn-out butternut-stained jackets and pants.

'Kind of you young 'uns to bring us these,' said a pock-faced veteran of several months standing as he began to unbutton a conscript's jacket. All over the meadow recruits were being stripped of their clothes and forced to don the filthy rags of their elders. They put up little or no resistance, thinking, no doubt, that it was an initiation rite.

The sentries posted around the camp were too busy clambering into their new grey uniforms to notice the distant glint of metal as the sun caught the polished surface of a pair of field glasses. Hidden behind a flowering dogwood, a tall angular figure in a blue staff officer's uniform lowered his binoculars. His upper lip curled in disdain. What kind of army was this? Where was the discipline? Yet he shouldn't be too critical. They were like soldiers in any war, haunted by thoughts of their own mortality; a loss of life that could just as easily happen between battles, particularly in a camp with filthy latrines and foul drinking water. He had seen it in the Crimea where the death toll from dysentery, typhoid and cholera far exceeded combat casualties. There was an obvious connection between poor sanitation and the transmission of infectious diseases.

The officer refocused his glasses on a wizened, weather-beaten private who was stirring the dying embers of the camp fire. The way he sniffed and wrinkled up his nose made it easy to guess what was uppermost in his mind. Having fought at Shiloh, Caleb Witherspoon of the Lexington Rifles commanded a certain amount of respect in this gathering. 'I reckon you've the most learnin' round here, Noah,' he said, turning to the lean, bespectacled man sitting next to him. 'What in tarnation is the difference between this die-a-rear and dis-ehn-terr-ee?'

Before enlisting, Noah Shelby had been a schoolteacher in Tennessee and he still talked like one. 'Diarrhoea simply gives you the squitters while dysentery causes belly pains and likely kills you,' replied the campfire sage. 'Small wonder on a diet of fried cornmeal, bacon grease and green apples.'

'And that don't mean diddley squat to them that dig those sinks so that the slops go straight into the water supply. It makes me hotter than blue blazes to see such things goin' on.'

'Not a whole lot we can do about that,' said Noah, his voice trailing off as if tired of the topic. 'What have you got there, Lightning? Going to get yerself electrocuted?'

The remark was addressed to a bearded private with droopy eyelids carrying a Morse code receiver under his arm. George 'Lightning' Ellsworth had earned his nickname sitting by the railroad tracks in knee-high water, tapping away on an electrical telegraph during a thunderstorm. Ellsworth's devil-may-care attitude and the fact that he was a Canadian volunteer made him a popular figure in the regiment.

'Got to run a message, boys, any of you seen Stovepipe Atkins today?'

Caleb pointed to a grassy bank on which two men were engaged in a knife-throwing contest.

'Bull's eye,' yelled the tall, cadaverously thin one wearing a top hat as he followed the flight of his twelve-inch hunting knife into the centre of a crudely painted cardboard target.

'Youse just got lucky thar, you uppity banjo strummer,' roared his burly opponent.

'Reckon you're right about that.' Stovepipe gave a honking laugh. It didn't pay to upset a vicious bully like Champ Ferguson.

Champ was feeling bored. 'When are we goin' to see some action?' he complained loudly as he wandered over to the cooking fire. 'While we're training, this here war is bein' lost.'

Caleb spat out some tobacco juice and nodded in silent agreement. The solemnity of the moment was broken by a high-pitched voice. One of the bolder new recruits had come to the camp fire to singe the lice off his shirt and sang while he did so.

> *Ho! Gather your flocks and sound the alarm*
> *For the Partisan rangers have come;*
> *Bold knights of the road, they scour each farm*
> *And scamper at tap of the drum.*
> *How are you, Telegraph?*

Other voices joined in and the sound of the singing reached the blue-coated officer hiding behind the flowering canopy of the dogwood tree. The lyric celebrated the hit-and-run exploits of

11

the Second Kentucky Cavalry and their commanding officer, John Hunt Morgan. The officer had met Morgan in Mobile and they had taken an immediate liking to one another. They were true warriors, men of courage, honour and integrity who shared a common belief in the Southern cause.

With his boyish charm and quiet air of authority it was easy to see how Morgan had become such a cult hero. His daring forays into enemy-held territory to destroy the North's supply and communication lines had led to newspapers nicknaming him 'The Thunderbolt of the Confederacy' and adventurous spirits who could read a recruiting poster had rushed to enlist in Morgan's Raiders.

They are a motley crew and no mistake, the officer thought, as he fixed his field glasses on card players, sock menders and soldiers simply snoozing in the long grass. There was no parade ground drill or any other sign of army order. Informality was the order of the day. Texas Rangers, swarthy laconic men in huge black sombreros, swaggered around with double-barrelled shotguns. A captain with a black ostrich plume in his gold-tasselled hat was tossing horseshoes with scruffy troopers in wide-brimmed hats. He noticed the unkempt hair and bedraggled beards, the harsh sunburned faces and the dirty butternut coloured rags. Morgan had been right about his brigade. They were mostly gullible country boys in need of a good wash who saw themselves as guerrilla fighters, living off the land, looting wherever they went, but doing as little work as possible while in camp. Square-bashing was for toy soldiers, not for them. Their casual behaviour told the officer all he needed to know. Authority would have to be earned, not by rank or reputation but by force of character and bravery on the battlefield. The time had come to meet his new regiment in person.

'When's that mercenary gentleman due?' Caleb asked

contemptuously. 'The one who's gonna teach y'all how to be better soldiers.'

'I reckon he's here already,' Noah replied. His brass pocket telescope was trained on a man on horseback.

'Let me have a look.' Caleb grabbed the telescope and put it to his good eye.

What he saw was an erect, athletic-looking soldier in an English staff coat and a red forage cap riding a grey stallion and leading a big chestnut mare. As the rider came into sharper focus Caleb noticed the stillness reflected in the man's stern face and steady eye. He was self-contained and dangerous.

'He was past forty, strong, tall and muscular,' Noah muttered to himself. 'His countenance was calculated to impress a degree of awe, if not of fear, upon strangers.'

Caleb shut down the telescope and gave his friend a strange look. 'What's that yer saying?'

'Those are Sir Walter Scott's words,' Noah explained. 'It's how he describes the Knight Templar in *Ivanhoe*. Scott's historical novels were required reading in the school I went to.'

They had been talking about their new regimental adjutant for days now. It was common currency. Most of them had never met an Englishman, let alone one who had fought on four continents and carried a personal recommendation from General Robert E Lee. Morgan swore by him, it was said, offering him a commission on the spot.

The lone rider approached the cooking fire, his battered scabbard slapping against his thigh, and reined in his horse. 'Good afternoon, gentlemen,' he said politely, stroking his elegant side-whiskers. There was something unnerving about the intensity of his gaze.

Caleb and Noah stood to attention but Champ Ferguson was not so easily cowed.

'And who might you be?' he asked rudely.

'Colonel George St Leger Grenfell at your service, and the next time you address me, private, I expect you to recognise my rank by saying sir.'

'We'll have to see about that,' said Champ. 'You'd be our new adjutant, I take it.'

'I take it, sir,' Grenfell added helpfully, 'and you take it right.'

'What's an English soldier doin' setting up as a Confederate anyway?'

'That's something you don't need to know and I don't want to talk about.'

'Well, you might want to get ridda that sword of yours,' Champ pointed to the long sabre in Grenfell's scabbard. 'Not worth a hoot and a holler at Shiloh. No use in a ruckus. Save mebbe to skewer meat over a busy fire.'

'You've hit the nail on the head there, Champ,' Caleb chortled.

Grenfell joined in the subdued laughter that greeted this sally, although the smile on his face didn't quite reach his eyes. 'You can't have been using your sabres properly. They're not just for cutting and slashing. The sharp point came in handy when we charged the Russian guns at Balaclava.'

There was an audible gasp. This English cavalry officer had taken part in the charge of the Light Brigade. Now *that* really was something. A soldier in bifocals began to recite Tennyson's poem. 'Was there a man dismay'd?' Noah Shelby declaimed theatrically.

'Of course there was dismay,' Grenfell replied. 'We were shitting ourselves. But you'd do well to remember that we broke through the enemy lines and used those sabres you've just been laughing about to skewer the Cossacks and Russians until the ground was soaked with their blood. We cut their army in two, took their principal battery and routed their cavalry.'

Grenfell enjoyed blowing his own trumpet. He did it

wherever he went. He couldn't help himself. Usually though, he saved his stories of bloody foreign wars for the officer class and waited for them to trickle down to the troops. But with only a few weeks in which to mould these farmhands and cattle herders into a professional fighting force, he didn't have time for such niceties, nor indeed for the exact truth. The nearest he'd actually got to the Crimean War was as a Turkish cavalry officer stationed in Constantinople. But he had described the Light Brigade charge so often he had come to believe he'd been there.

'The Cossacks were *our* cooked meat,' he said pointedly, looking directly at the swaggering ruffian with the receding forehead who had challenged him earlier. Like all bullies, the man had a following and needed taking down a peg or two.

'Why do they call you Champ?' he asked.

'I don't rightly know, *sir*.' The word seemed to have been forced out of him. 'Maybe I was born with it, maybe not. Maybe it's cos I'm a murderous son of a bitch who's killed dozens of them boys in blue.' Champ Ferguson certainly looked the part. He stood with his feet apart like a gunslinger, over six feet tall and barrel-chested with small furtive eyes and a cruel thin-lipped mouth.

'You haven't had time to kill that many,' Grenfell retorted.

'He shot a few prisoners in the back for target practice,' said one of Champ's cronies.

The brawny bushwhacker shook his head. 'That ain't true, Colonel. I've got no feeling agin these Yankee soldiers, except that they oughtn't to have come here. I won't kill 'em unless called upon to do so, but when I catches any of them hounds I've got cause to kill, I sure as damn am going to do it.'

'That's an interesting distinction. Who might these hounds be?'

'Tinker Dave Beattie and his gang!' Champ spat the words out. 'Them that raped my wife and daughter on our farm before this here conflict began. Now they're killin' for the Union and it's my bounden duty to hunt 'em down.'

Grenfell pointed to the Colt revolvers tucked in the bully's belt. 'Those pistols are good enough for close-quarter work but not for anything else. If you're to become mounted infantry, which is General Morgan's wish, you must be able to shoot at long range. What are you like with a rifle?'

'Purty good,' said Champ, laying on the redneck lingo. 'Ah can shoot yer possum's tail off at two hundred yards or more.'

'Good. Pick up that Enfield and measure out two hundred yards from there.' Grenfell pointed to the cardboard target Champ and Stovepipe had used for knife-throwing.

As the distance was paced out, the English colonel unstrapped a lightweight Whitworth rifle from his saddlebag. The sun glinted on its maple stock. 'You take first shot,' he said.

Champ prepared his powder charge, added a 530 gram minie ball, drew the Enfield rifle's loading rod to push the bullet down onto the charge, took careful aim and pulled the trigger. The bullet pierced the target's inner ring, causing Champ's cronies to whoop with delight.

It was Grenfell's turn. He was coolness personified as he measured out his powder charge before fitting a much longer bullet with a pointed nose into his small-bore rifle. He hardly seemed to look at the target before firing. The shot tore through the cardboard bull's eye.

There was a moment's silence before the cheering started. The colonel raised a hand in acknowledgement. 'That, gentlemen, was victory for a superior weapon. The Whitworth fires a .45 calibre conical bullet with a one-in-twenty twist rate. This way the bullet retains its velocity and energy at longer distances. I'll explain more about ballistics in tomorrow's rifle training.'

Grenfell was watching Champ out of the corner of his eye.

He could see the man was scowling. Humiliate him further and he would be a dangerous enemy.

'You shoot very well,' he told his angry adversary. 'Were you by any chance a hunter before the war?'

'No, sir, I was a farmer in Clinton County but there's not a trail I don't know in Kentucky or Tennessee.'

'Well, we're going to need pathfinders to go ahead of the regiment when we make our raids. Do you fancy being one of our guides?'

'I surely do, sir.' Champ Ferguson's face was wreathed in smiles as he went off to spread the good news around the camp.

'It's time I presented my compliments to Colonel Duke. Good day gentlemen,' said Grenfell, swinging himself up into the saddle. He could hear Dixie being whistled as he trotted off.

All in all, he thought, not a bad beginning.

FORTUNE'S FOOL

The sun was starting to rise above the Great Smoky Mountains when a bugle call summoned the brigade to the parade ground to witness the punishment. The miscreant was led forward to hear the charges brought against him. His eyes darted around, looking for a means of escape.

'Hold him fast,' Grenfell told the guard party. 'Private John Shanks, you have been found guilty of attempting to steal army horses and of trying to stab an officer. The punishment is fifty lashes which will be laid on your miserable hide in the hope that they coerce you into a proper performance of your duties as a soldier of the Confederacy.'

Once the charges had been read out, Caleb Witherspoon stepped forward. He had been chosen to carry out the flogging because he was a smallish, older man who lacked the physical strength and stamina to inflict a fatal beating. The intention, after all, was to punish the prisoner, not to kill him.

The victim was stripped to the waist and his hands tied to a post. His whole body was shaking as he waited for the ordeal to begin. In keeping with military protocol, the sergeant major handed Caleb the cat-o'-nine-tails, a whip of nine knotted cords that tore the flesh off a man's back. Caleb took a firm grip on the cat's wooden handle and drew back his arm.

'One,' called out the sergeant major as the blow descended. Each stroke was accompanied by a muffled drumbeat. Shanks writhed in pain but said nothing. Caleb took a deep breath and redoubled his efforts. After half a dozen lashes the blood began to flow but Shanks continued to grit his teeth.

His stoicism was short-lived. As further strokes were laid on his wounded back he began to groan. 'Oh, for God's sake, show some mercy,' he shrieked at his captors.

'Don't call on God, there's a good chap,' Grenfell replied evenly. 'He can't help you now.'

The law of diminishing returns took over. After thirty lashes Caleb could scarcely lift his arm, Shanks was past caring, his back reduced to a bloody pulp, and even the drummer boy seemed to be flagging. Grenfell ordered the sagging unconscious body to be cut down and Shanks's wounds tended by the medical staff.

Once the troops had been dismissed Grenfell made his way to the officers' latrine and was promptly sick. Flogging might be the bedrock of British Army discipline but it was a brutal business, one he hated. Not even a hardened villain like Shanks deserved to be tortured in such a barbaric fashion. But what was the alternative? He had to be disciplined for the good of the regiment.

One of the horses Shanks had tried to steal had been Grenfell's big chestnut Barbary. The mare's loud neighing had wakened her owner in the night and, rushing to the stables, he'd caught Shanks dragging the horse out of her stall. As they wrestled in the hay, the desperate thief pulled out a knife, slashing him across the chest. At a hastily convened court-martial, Morgan's second in command Lieutenant Colonel Basil Duke informed the military court that John T Shanks was a convicted forger released from Austin penitentiary on the understanding he would enlist in the Confederate army. 'If there is any place on God's fair earth where wickedness abounds it is in this army of ours,' Duke said.

After the flogging Duke approached his English adjutant in the officers' mess tent. 'A word in your ear, George,' he murmured in his rich baritone voice. 'The Confederate High Command is about to abolish flogging but plans to retain branding. Perhaps we should have got out the hot irons and stamped T for thief on

Shanks's forehead, but would that have been any better? Neither of these sanctions should be acceptable in law, not even where slaves are concerned.'

Basil Duke was a lawyer who also happened to be Morgan's brother-in-law. Ever since meeting this suave, highly educated officer, Grenfell had wanted to ask him about the legality of slavery. Its Southern defenders argued that slavery was a natural state, enshrined in the Ten Commandments, and an economic necessity, but he had yet to hear whether Duke condoned the practice.

'What worries me is this, sir,' Grenfell told his superior officer. 'If we're ever going to discipline this band of lazy horse thieves we need an effective deterrent, however harsh that might be. Otherwise how the hell are we going to get them to master the new tactics?'

Morgan was planning to turn his cavalry into mounted riflemen. The strategy was simple enough: using horses for mobility but fighting on foot. On approaching the enemy, troopers would rapidly dismount and deploy in a long curving line, charging the enemy in double-quick time or at a half-run. In theory, such a fast-moving battle line would be harder to break, sustain fewer casualties, and preserve horses, but like any military tactic, it would only work if the men practised it time and again.

Grenfell had driven them hard. If there was a horse with a loose shoe or a trooper who didn't know his flank man, it certainly wasn't the adjutant's fault. But brought up in the frontier tradition of rugged self-reliance the men simply hated any form of drilling. Grenfell could bark all he liked but he couldn't make them toe the line.

As the probable instigator of Morgan's plan, Duke held a more optimistic view. 'Don't worry, George, our boys will be up for it, you'll see,' he said.

'How long have we got before the Kentucky raid?'
'Keep this to yourself. We're leaving in a week's time.'
'Oh, my God!'

*

Acting Brigadier General John Hunt Morgan swore softly. The sky was already lightening in the east. His brigade had crossed the Cumberland River into Kentucky the previous evening and begun the long march to Tompkinsville in the hope of catching its Yankee garrison off guard. But what he hadn't anticipated was how his progress would be hindered by tangled underbrush and fallen timber. It was difficult terrain for the bull pups, the men's pet name for the guns they were carrying with them.

Riding behind his commanding officer, Grenfell had guessed that this might happen. His years with the British Army in India had taught him that, in rough country, mountain howitzers were best transported by mules rather than horses. Mules might be difficult to control under fire but had far more pulling power. This was enshrined in the US Army manual on mountain artillery but Morgan obviously hadn't read it. As soldiers go, he was no better than an inspired amateur.

The sun had risen by the time Morgan's outriders returned. They were galloping full tilt and Grenfell could see something was wrong. The chief scout, Tom Quirk, had a blood-soaked handkerchief tied around his head and was swaying in the saddle.

'You look all in, Sergeant,' Morgan said solicitously. 'You'd better go see Doc Williams.'

Quirk shook his head. 'Begging your pardon, General, but it's just a wee scratch. My head was built in County Kerry and toughened by shillelaghs. No need for the quack.'

Morgan helped his Irish scout dismount. 'So how did you get your wound?'

'They'd put out skirmishers and one of them shot me, so he did. But not before we'd seen their battle line. There are about 350 of them under a major's command and they're on top of a hill, dug in behind fences, with open pastureland in front and their flanks protected by forests of oak and hickory. Best if you can get behind them.' Quirk's scouting colleagues Kelion Peddicord and Champ Ferguson nodded in dumb agreement. The 9th Pennsylvania Cavalry would be no pushover.

They had reached a crossroads. 'Where's this leading?' The general pointed to the narrow track intersecting the main road. He unfolded the hand-drawn map he'd bought in a Tennessee store and peered at it. 'Can anyone see where we are on this damned thing?' The chart was rich in topographical features like hills, streams and woods but sadly deficient in road markings.

'This has to be it!' Colonel Duke stabbed the map with a slender finger. 'That spindly red line there, looping around the town. See how it comes out on the other side? It's got to be one of those early hunting trails. Kentucky is full of them.'

Morgan put an arm around his brother-in-law's narrow shoulders. He was very fond of Duke, and with good reason, Grenfell thought, for everything he did was clear-cut and dependable. 'If you're right about this Basil, we can get Captain Gano and his Texas Rangers to sweep around behind Tompkinsville and cut off any possible retreat.'

'Good idea, sir,' said Duke calmly. Although a much better tactician than his charismatic relative, he was content to walk in his shadow.

Once Morgan had given the Texans their orders he turned back to his loyal senior officer, his eyes alight with fervour. 'I know our men are admirable riders,' he said, 'but the ground is against them. A cavalry charge uphill through exposed fields into a thickly wooded area is problematic to say the least; so how about an infantry charge instead? The Yankees won't be expecting that.'

'No they won't, General, you are absolutely right,' Duke agreed. 'Whether we're ready to do this after no more than a fortnight's training is another matter.'

Morgan stroked his imperial beard thoughtfully. 'There's a risk to this, I grant you, but, hell, it's risk-taking that makes life worth living. Where's our English colonel?'

'Here, sir, at your command.' Grenfell had ridden up on his grey.

'What do you think, Grenfell? The enemy camp's on a ridge, open fields in front, woods to the side and back. We outnumber them almost three to one.'

'A good opportunity, I'd say, to see how fast our boys can run.'

'My thinking precisely,' said Morgan. 'You and Duke go with them but stay on horseback in case we have to change our plans.'

'Understood, sir. We'll give those Yankees a good thrashing.'

Grenfell wheeled away. He was feeling less confident than he sounded. The men were confused by the new tactics, uncertain whether they were dismounted cavalry or mounted infantry, and unhappy about losing their horses. They needed leadership but perversely rejected it. With disturbing clarity he could see the outcome. This was likely to be a bloody shambles.

Initially, when the order was given, everything went to plan. Morgan's troopers staged an orderly advance on foot, holding fire until they were close to the Union position. Then on Colonel Duke's command, the mountain howitzers began their bombardment. This was the cue for the infantry to engage the enemy. The Rebel yell went up as they raced across the pastureland, falling over each other in their eagerness. Yankee rifles began to crack and the air was heavy with smoke and the smell of sulphur and saltpetre. The running men were encumbered by their sheathed bayonets and haversacks. Their formation loosened and split. The charge began to falter. Seeing things unfold as he'd predicted, Grenfell considered the alternatives. He could order a withdrawal or set an example, by sharing his courage with his troops. Retreat wasn't an option.

Risking fire from both sides, he spurred his grey between the battle lines, waving his scarlet forage cap in the air. To flaunt oneself in such a fashion was held to be suicidal. Anyone with experience of warfare knew how rifles came to be trained on an officer on horseback, particularly one attempting a solo assault on enemy lines.

Watching this amazing spectacle, Rebel hearts kept pace with the inaudible hoofbeats of Grenfell's pounding stallion and soared when he leaped over the timber and turf barricade, drew his sabre and slashed viciously at the heads of the Pennsylvanian riflemen. Here was a leader who surely deserved to be followed.

The yell went up again as Morgan's infantry, full of hardened and impenitent killers, followed their adjutant's lead, fixing bayonets as they raced full pelt to inflict further damage on the foe. Unnerved by such a ferocious onslaught, the outnumbered Yankee soldiers panicked and fled, leaving their dead and wounded behind them.

'What was that?' a bewildered Morgan asked Duke. 'Is that how the English fight?'

Grenfell would later apologise for his rush of blood. Not that he meant it. His apparently foolhardy behaviour had served an important purpose. In future, 'Old St Lege' would be spoken of with awe and tales of his exploits would enliven many a campfire gathering as Morgan's men roamed through Kentucky.

The storytelling began as soon as alcohol was discovered in Tompkinsville's military store. Sitting under the night stars, sipping whiskey with his new-found friends, Grenfell explained his presence in America's Civil War. 'If England is not at war, I go elsewhere to find one.' It was difficult, he told his admirers, to remember everywhere he'd been. He had fought the French in Algeria, been wounded in the Chinese Opium War, charged the Russian guns in the Crimea, defended Delhi during the Sepoy rebellion and marched through Italy with Garibaldi's Redshirts. And if this impressive list of battle honours grew a little longer with each telling, it was only to be expected. There was the truth about a man, then the half truths that multiplied with frequent repetition, and if a few salient facts got distorted in the process, well, people believed what they wanted to believe.

Before leaving him, his long-suffering wife had called him an attention-seeker and he supposed she was right. He lived through the eyes of others, drawing sustenance from their admiration. Not that people had to like him. He would settle for being recognised. After all, there was no such thing as bad publicity and myths were there to be made.

This was illustrated a week later when Morgan's men arrived in Lebanon where they captured a small Federal supply depot and its guard of two hundred foot soldiers. Reporting on the raid, the pro-Union correspondent of the Louisville *Journal* told a harrowing story of wild and licentious soldiers looting the town and of 'a big degenerate Englishman' called 'George St Leger Grenville' who had chased 'the writer of this story' down the street 'waving his fist and mouthing obscenities'. The fleeing journalist obviously hadn't had time to get his pursuer's name right.

Grenfell pretended to be horrified when he read this report. 'You can imagine my concern to be so traduced in print,' he wrote to his youngest daughter Marie. 'Such scandalous lies, absolute gammon, damn poor show!'

Marie was the only member of his family with whom he communicated. 'I must tell you about Harrodsburg where we received a hero's welcome. We arrived on a Sunday morning to find the churches empty and the entire population out on the streets. Imagine your father in full fig, ramrod-straight in the saddle, accompanied by Morgan's boys, all grimy and grey with dust, a thousand Southern horsemen galloping through the town as the ladies waved handkerchiefs and threw flowers at us. Having circled Harrodsburg we returned to the public park to dismount under the elms. Once the horses were tethered and the handshaking and kissing was over, the picnic commenced. The fat of the land was furnished in rich abundance according to the standards of Kentucky hospitality.'

What he didn't mention, though, was the special hospitality he had received from a secessionist beauty who swore he had ridden out of the pages of *Ivanhoe* to vanquish her. Instead, he talked in flowery fashion about being 'a wild creature of the wayside camp, wood smoke, and the soft earth' who 'needed war to stir him' and found 'the acrid taste of a bitten bullet quite intoxicating'.

Within days he had another chance to bite that bullet. In search of a bigger and better battle, Morgan feinted to attack his home town of Lexington, getting his telegrapher Lightning Ellsworth to transmit false messages to that effect, while taking his brigade south to mount an assault on Cynthiana's military garrison. Even so the word got out and, on approaching the Licking River, Morgan's troopers were greeted with grape and canister. Surprised by this enemy salvo, coming from a twelve-pound howitzer manned, as was later discovered, by a bunch of firemen from Cincinnati, a worried Morgan summoned a council of war.

'Be silent and listen,' he told his chattering officers in a rare show of anger. 'The water may be crimson with our blood, yet there is no need to panic when we outnumber them two to one. If we get our timing right, we'll overwhelm the bastards. I want Companies E and F to ford the riverbank on the left, Quirk's scouts and A Company to enter the stream where it's shallow and wade across, while Grenfell leads C Company in a frontal assault on the bridge into the town. Is that clear?'

The plan was not without merit but Grenfell knew how dangerous a cavalry charge could be, particularly for its commanding officer. Yet he had his image to live up to. Instead of making himself as inconspicuous as possible, he manoeuvred his horse into lead position, donned his distinctive forage cap and drew his sabre from its scabbard while waiting for the signal to attack.

His preparations made, he turned in the saddle to study the eager faces around him. Long-haired and unshaven, most of these cavalrymen were still in their teens. Grenfell thought about the fragility of life and wondered how many of these boys would survive the next few minutes, how many mothers and girlfriends would wait in vain for their sons and lovers to come home. It was already clear that America's Civil War was going to be pure carnage, with great tides of men and metal constantly clashing in combat. The guns were too powerful, the rifles too accurate and defence against them virtually non-existent.

'Steady lads, advance at a trot,' Grenfell said calmly as soon as the command was given. His men kicked their horses forward through the long grass, moving silently but for the rattle of harnesses and the jingling of spurs. Ahead of Company C lay open scrubland and a low embankment that led down to the well-guarded bridge where two lines of blue-coated riflemen were waiting, their muskets glinting in the sun. This was the hard part of any cavalry action, getting the timing right. Waiting for the right moment to charge.

The Rebel cavalry moved from trot to canter as they came within cannon range. Shells whipped around them, smacking into man and beast. White bursts of flame. Bits of casing whistled past Grenfell's head. A shot exploded near his stallion. It was now or never.

'At a gallop, boys,' he yelled, the blood pounding in his ears. Horses screamed, fell and died. The ground erupted and the man next to him lost his face in a welter of gore. A runaway horse was disembowelled by canister shot. Another rider pitched out of his saddle, vomiting blood. Grenfell's heart was hammering in his chest. Their only chance of survival lay in closing fast, reaching the river bank before the riflemen could reload and pick them off.

Fear reared in front of him like a wall, making his deep voice sound thinner than usual. 'Charge! Kill the bastards!' His incoherent cry was taken up by the troopers behind him, screaming out their own challenge. Lashed by rifle fire, flayed by cannon blasts and choking on the smell of gunpowder, they raced on. Time seemed to stand still as Grenfell's cavalrymen waded through a welter of musket smoke and writhing bodies and hit the bridge's wooden planking with thundering hooves, scattering the Union infantry in their wake, before racing up the street towards the enemy howitzer. Realising the hopelessness of their position, the firemen-turned-gunners surrendered, as did most of the Yankee regulars.

But the battle was not yet over. The word came that a Federal company was holding out at the railroad depot. 'It will need another cavalry charge. Perhaps you'll take care of the matter, George.' Morgan made it sound like a walk in the park.

'My pleasure, General, once Meteor has got his breath back.' He rubbed the dirt-caked lather from his grey's back and flanks while thinking that Morgan had a frightful nerve. Two death-defying cavalry charges in one day were a bit much, even for 'Old St Lege'. But that was the trouble with being a hero: people expected you to behave like one. He tried to calculate the odds against a battle-scarred forty-four-year-old soldier managing to survive this war if constantly put in the firing line. They were far from good.

With all eyes on him, he vaulted into the saddle and doffed his cap to C Company. 'Are you ready gentlemen?' he asked, and received a roar of assent from his keen command.

'This time we'll attack in echelon, so go as fast as you like and frighten the hell out of them.'

Eighty cavalrymen emitting bloodcurdling cries galloped towards Cynthiana's railway station firing guns and pistols. Their horses' hooves shook the earth beneath them. And leading the way was this nonchalant English mercenary, dressed in a blue staff coat and forage cap, swinging his sabre. He seemed to be saying, 'shoot me if you can,' but his luck held.

When the action was over, Colonel Duke congratulated Grenfell on his conspicuous gallantry. 'I cannot too highly compliment Col. St Leger Grenfell,' he wrote in despatches, 'for the execution of an order which did perhaps more than anything to gain the day. His example gave new courage to everyone who witnessed it.'

The fact that Grenfell was alive to receive such praise was in itself a minor miracle. His clothing, saddlebag and scabbard were riddled with bullet holes, eleven in all, yet neither he nor Meteor was seriously hurt. It was the hole in his forage cap that aroused most interest. The cap fitted 'so tight upon his head,' Duke wrote, 'that no ball could go through it without blowing his brains out'.

What Duke failed to mention was that the perforation was in the back of the cap! The logic was inescapable. Someone in the brigade was either a very bad shot or had just tried to kill Grenfell. It was a worrying thought for the newly promoted adjutant general as Morgan's men fell in for the long march back to Tennessee.

A crowd of faces hovered near him; any one of whom might

be a back-shooter. Champ Ferguson was the obvious suspect. He had the nerve, the lack of morality and the previous form for the job. But he had no reason to pull the trigger. Unless, of course, he'd been offered money by someone bearing a grudge: that too was a possibility to one who had so often tasted the sourness of aversion. With a shiver of fear, Grenfell realised that the tight seal he had kept on his past was coming apart.

Riding next to him, Duke saw his companion wince. 'Are you in pain, George?' he asked. Grenfell shook his head. It wasn't his physical wounds that bothered him but his mental scars, that swirling blizzard of errors and wrong turnings he'd taken: the family business he had defrauded, the father he had bankrupted, the prison sentences hanging over his head in France and Morocco; a life scoured out by shame in which the follies seemed endless and the list of enemies legion.

There was the Italian vendetta for a start. If anyone wished him off God's green earth it was surely Giuseppe Garibaldi, the republican patriot who had unified Italy. He had fought for him in Argentina and Italy before making a hasty exit when the revolutionary hero's eighteen-year-old bride admitted to being pregnant on their wedding night, naming his friend George Grenfell as the father of her unborn child. How Giuseppina Raimondi could be sure of this when she had slept with several men, including her future husband, still rankled. Yet Garibaldi had taken Giuseppina's word for it, swearing vengeance on the man who had betrayed his trust and besmirched his honour, which was pretty rich coming from a notorious philanderer like him. But that was Italian men for you, emotional and hypocritical. They had had to get on with their Risorgimento without him. But it hadn't ended there. Garibaldi had offered his services to President Lincoln and a redshirted Italian regiment called the Garibaldi Guard was fighting for the Union. For all he knew, Garibaldi might be in America now, with a score to settle.

So many mistakes, the half-forgotten detritus of a misspent life, tipped into view like the contents of an upended wastepaper basket. Grenfell sighed and patted the head of his chestnut mare. Memory was a curse; so much sorrow and regret. What was meant to be would surely find a way. He'd always been fortune's fool.

LOVE AND MARRIAGE

It was a bleak midwinter in Tennessee and Murfreesboro froze nightly in the weather's icy grip. With the mercury plummeting, its citizens wrestled with the dark comedy of wartime shortages, their easygoing laughter stifled in frigid throats as they lamented the absence of candles, matches and cough medicine. Trapped in their homes, short of food and warm clothing, memories had long since faded of that euphoric day when the Confederate flag had been hoisted over the town's courthouse. The war had begun with pageantry, bright uniforms and massed bands. It would be over, people said, in a matter of weeks and young men had rushed off to enlist. How wrong they had been.

By the winter of '62 innocence had evaporated back into the cold, dry air. There would be no easy victory. Yankee soldiers were just as brave as their Southern counterparts and there were many more of them. All kinds of foreigners were fighting for the Union. German, Polish and Italian immigrants were joining up in their droves while Confederate generals cried out for reinforcements that were not forthcoming. Even more alarming was the economic disparity between North and South. The North had the manufacturing industry – the woollen mills, arsenals and iron foundries – and their gunboats were strangling Southern trade by blockading her harbours. The South lived by selling cotton and tobacco and buying what she did not produce, but now she could neither buy nor sell. Unable to get her money crops to their English market, Tennessee was being bled dry by invading armies living off her land.

The citizens of Murfreesboro had learned what it was like to be occupied when columns of blue-coated infantry marched into their town the previous spring. The Yankee general claimed to be upholding law and order but house searches for guns and ammunition had been a flimsy excuse for widespread looting and, for the first time, local people were forced to lock their doors at night. Attitudes hardened under occupation until General Forrest staged a lightning raid to recapture Murfreesboro in July. What couldn't be restored, however, was the town's optimism. Only speculators and profiteers had much cause to cheer with commodity prices sky-high and the Confederate dollar worth only forty cents.

Yet, as the year ended, there were still grounds for hope. With Lancashire's textile mills standing idle for want of Southern cotton, the British government would surely recognise the fledgling Confederacy and, if that happened, the French might follow suit. Meanwhile, the South was developing her own heavy industries, pumping better equipment up the railway arteries to the battle fronts. And there were military successes to boast about. The heady days of secession may be over but the white stars of the Confederate flag still fluttered overhead, particularly in Tennessee where, on December 7th, John Hunt Morgan pulled off an astonishing victory at Hartsville when his Raiders surprised a much larger Federal brigade and took 1800 prisoners.

Within hours, the telegraph wires were humming with the news that, like a Roman general, Morgan would march into Murfreesboro the following morning to celebrate his military triumph. This was the psychological lift the town needed and not even the freezing weather could stop people from turning out to savour it.

Wearing every scrap of protective clothing they could muster, Murfreesboro's patriotic residents lined their icy, windswept streets to cheer the smiling victors and jeer the frostbitten Yankee prisoners, many of whom had lost their overcoats and boots. What was also noticeable was the artillery power. The six cannons now in tow testified to Morgan's status as a powerful warlord and to Colonel Grenfell's surprising skill as a negotiator when sent on a foraging expedition to the Richmond Ordnance Department.

And so the conquering hero rode by, waving his plumed hat and milking the crowd for every last drop of applause, while the Second Kentucky buglers played the de facto anthem of the Confederacy.

Oh, I wish I was in the land of cotton,
Old times there are not forgotten.
Look away, look away, look away Dixie Land!

The silvery notes of this familiar song pierced the frosty air and hundreds of voices responded to the melody. The massed singing caused eyes to water and spines to chill as Murfreesboro's citizens were caught up in the emotion of the moment.

I wish I was in Dixie, Hooray! Hooray!
In Dixie Land I'll take my stand,
To live and die in Dixie.

Morgan's victory march heralded a weekend of wild celebrations in which his cup positively overflowed. On Saturday, he had the rank of brigadier general conferred on him by no less a person than President Jefferson Davis and, on Sunday, he married Murfreesboro's most beautiful girl in a ceremony attended by every member of the Confederate High Command within riding distance.

Despite the obvious hindrance that military service posed to courtship, war acted as a catalyst for marriage. Social conventions were waived by soldiers fearing death on the battlefield and young women dreading the prospect of spinsterhood. But even in this feverish atmosphere there were few more romantic love affairs than that of General Morgan and Miss Mattie Ready. The couple had met earlier that year when Mattie's father invited Morgan to dinner. Months later, with Murfreesboro under occupation, Mattie overheard Federal officers making derogatory remarks about her hero and rebuked them fiercely. 'By the grace of God,' she snapped, 'one day I hope to call myself the wife of John Morgan.' It was, in effect, a marriage proposal and, when he heard what Mattie had said, Morgan took her up on it.

In a time of death and sorrow, John Hunt Morgan was the dashing cavalier whose presence made female hearts flutter and Mattie was only the latest in a long line of ladies to fall in love with his fleshy good looks and celebrity. As a cynical observer, Grenfell spoke out against the marriage. A wife was a hostage to fortune, he told Morgan. She would slow him down; make him more cautious. Besides which, Mattie was too young for him. There was a sixteen-year age gap between them which beauty alone couldn't bridge.

That Grenfell should be offering his commanding officer advice on such a highly personal matter was a reflection of the changing nature of their relationship. Always quick to judge his fellow man, the English adjutant general had lost respect for Morgan, who, in his estimation, was neither shrewd nor particularly intelligent. He had the affection of his men but comradeship was not enough. Even in guerrilla warfare there had to be discipline, yet the easygoing Morgan turned a blind eye to the horse stealing and plundering of private property that were such unwholesome features of his well-publicised raids. Now, with the war at a critical stage, Grenfell had concluded that Morgan's hit-and-run tactics were having little effect on the overall military balance. His thousand-mile rampage across Kentucky had been merely a sideshow.

Whatever Morgan thought about Grenfell's comments it did not prevent him from asking his subordinate to be a groomsman at his wedding nor did it stop the outspoken Englishman from accepting the invitation. So on that Sunday evening in

December, Grenfell stood in front of a bathroom mirror in the Ready household brushing down his dress uniform. To denote his rank as a Confederate colonel he was kitted out in a double-breasted cadet grey tunic with two rows of buttons and cavalry yellow collars and cuffs. He was also obliged to wear light blue trousers with a yellow seam stripe, a tasselled waist sash and a short sabre in its scabbard.

'All present and correct,' he muttered to himself, adjusting his leather sword belt and taking a long hard look at the wearer of this fancy dress. A handsome enough face with bold, aquiline features and a full head of hair stared back at him. But there were flecks of grey in the hair and wrinkles forming around the eyes and mouth. There was no denying it; at forty-four, George St Leger Grenfell had entered middle age with a body that was beginning to creak, particularly at night when a urinary obstruction affected his ability to pass water. He had always believed ageing would be a slow process; now it seemed in a tearing hurry.

All the more reason, he considered, to make hay while the sun shone. Down below in the parlour Mattie's bridesmaids were floating around in their pretty dresses. Surely he could trap one of these young butterflies in his web before the night was out. Dazzle her with stories of derring-do and be rewarded with stolen kisses and maybe even a quick rummage through hooped petticoats, although how this might be achieved at a wedding feast was beyond his powers of imagination.

It was time to join the wedding guests. But his way was blocked by a little girl sitting on the staircase trying to fix a black bow in her glossy chestnut ringlets.

'Excuse me, sir,' she said. 'I wonder if you'd tie this silly bow for me.'

'It will be my pleasure,' replied Grenfell gallantly.

The girl stood up. She carried herself with extraordinary grace for one so young and wasn't in the least self-conscious.

'How old are you?'

'How old do you think I am?'

'Perhaps twelve,' he guessed.

'Actually I am nine. Mother says I'm precocious, whatever that means.'

'It means you're flowering at an early age.'

'Why thank you sir.' The girl curtsied, showing off the green sprigged muslin dress she was wearing. Grenfell thought her enchanting.

'May I know your name?'

'It's Rose but you can call me Rosie. What's yours by the way?'

'George, George St Leger Grenfell, ready to slay dragons upon demand.'

'Now you're teasing me, George. Have you done much killing, Yankee soldiers I mean?'

He was surprised by the intensity in her emerald eyes. 'That's a bloodthirsty thing to say, Rosie.'

'I'm a fierce little Reb,' she replied. 'I hate Yankees. They put me in prison earlier this year. I used to cry myself to sleep from hunger.'

What would a nine-year-old girl be doing in jail? As a practitioner of the art, Grenfell reckoned he could spot a tall story a mile off. She was trying to impress him.

'You must have been very naughty for that to happen,' he said, humouring her.

'No, I hadn't done anything. It was Mamma whom they wanted to lock up.'

A mother and her daughter arrested and left to rot in prison. Was this one of those sensational tales of Yankee soldiers raping women and bayoneting children currently doing the rounds? Delicately bred Southern ladies seemed to expect the worst, almost gloried in it.

'So what's happened to your mother – where is she now?'

37

'Down there.' Rosie pointed through the banisters to a woman surrounded by Confederate officers and the sight of her drove everything else out of his mind. He had seen many handsome women in his time but none more seductive. With raven-black hair parted in the middle and pulled back from a pale olive face in which huge deep-set eyes were offset by a broad brow, a firm mouth and a pointed chin, Rosie's mother positively radiated sensuality. There was a boldness to the way she displayed her hourglass figure in an off-the-shoulder burgundy velvet gown and a cynical edge to the laughter she bestowed on her male admirers.

'Would you like to meet her, George?' the girl asked him.

'I would indeed,' Grenfell replied, trying to keep his voice as neutral as possible.

The downstairs parlour was a blaze of colour. Although candles were in short supply in Murfreesboro, scores of them had been lit to create a romantic glow. The walls were decorated with holly and winter berries, mistletoe peeked through the branched supports of the chandelier and a huge log fire roared in the hearth. Black waiters carrying silver trays dispensed frosted julep cups to the wedding guests who were so busy enjoying each other's company that they hardly seemed to notice what they were drinking. The room hummed with voices, punctuated by light-hearted laughter and the rustle of skirts.

As he weaved his way past giggling teenage girls flirting with Morgan's cavalry officers, Grenfell couldn't help noticing how the elderly matrons anchored along the wall on delicate gold-painted chairs were giving his childish companion sour looks and whispering behind their swishing fans. What could she have done to earn their disapproval? Or was it her mother they were talking about?

A boy forced his way through the crowd and grabbed Rosie's arm. 'You'd better come now,' he said with the urgency of youth. 'The bonfire is lit and the soldiers are about to set off the fireworks.'

Rosie shook her ringlets. 'Not now, Harry, can't you see I'm escorting this gentleman?'

The boy looked so crestfallen Grenfell felt obliged to intervene. 'You don't want to miss the fireworks, Rosie, do you? You run along with Harry and we'll meet up later. That's a promise.'

'Well,' she said, wavering, 'I'd like to see the cascades and rockets.'

'Off you go then and I'll introduce myself to your mother.'

His quarry was standing only a few feet away, encircled by uniforms. Close up, she looked older than he'd imagined. There was the odd grey streak in her hair, faint lines at the corner of her eyes and a slight thickening of the waist but these signs of ageing did not diminish her allure.

She spoke in a low husky whisper in which only the occasional flattening of a vowel betrayed her Southern origin. 'I was fearful at first that she would pine, and said, "My little darling, you must show yourself superior to these Yankees," and she replied quickly, "O Mamma, never fear, I hate them too much. I intend to dance and sing 'Jeff Davis is coming,' just to scare them."'

'What a brave little warrior,' said an admiring captain. 'You must be very proud of her.'

'I am indeed, sir. She never complained although the straw cot in our cell was swarming with bedbugs and there was vermin everywhere. But you don't want to hear about our captivity on a day like today. Nor should you be wasting your time with me when there are so many attractive young women simply dying to make your acquaintance.'

'I am sure I speak for everyone here when I say how delighted we are to have your company.' The compliment came from a slightly built officer with a surprisingly deep voice. Recognising its owner, Grenfell wondered whether Colonel Duke had forgotten he was married to Morgan's sister. Not that he could blame him. The lady in red teased and manipulated men, and the smell of her scent was intoxicating.

Also competing for her attention was Captain Thomas Hines, talking rapidly in a curiously squeaky falsetto voice about his undercover work in Kentucky. 'Intelligence work requires a lot of patience and stealth,' he told her. '*Et calcare diligenter oportet* is my motto.'

Straining to hear what was being said, Grenfell picked a glass of punch off a silver salver he'd been offered by one of Ready's slaves. As he raised the glass to his lips somebody knocked his elbow causing him to spill a few drops. To his horror, he saw they had fallen on the velvet dress.

Without thinking, he dropped to one knee and began to remove the stains with his handkerchief.

'What the devil are you doing there, sir?' Dark eyes with long sooty lashes stared down at him. 'God save me! This is a splendid party and no mistake. A handsome officer on his knees before me and we haven't even been introduced.'

Taking the hint, he rose stiffly and kissed her hand. 'Colonel George St Leger Grenfell, Second Kentucky Cavalry, at your service ma'am.'

She looked back at him, her lips slightly parted. 'Rose O'Neale Greenhow, Confederate spy.'

Here in their midst was the notorious Mrs Greenhow. The military information she'd acquired in Washington was supposed to have helped the Confederacy win the first battle of Manassas. But as Grenfell got over his surprise a question formed in the back of his mind. If she was so outspoken, how could she have been an effective spy?

'I employed every capacity with which God endowed me. The

result was far more successful than my hopes could have flattered me to expect' Mrs Greenhow had answered his unspoken question. Then she smiled. It was a startlingly brilliant smile.

'Men can be such fools,' she added. 'Their inflated egos blind them to a woman's wiles. They will tell you anything if they believe it will help them win your favour. Have I shocked you, Colonel?'

'Not at all, ma'am, not at all,' was all he could think to say.

'Don't call me ma'am, call me Rose, George.'

'You named your daughter after you, although she said I should call her Rosie.'

For the first time this self-confident woman seemed taken aback. 'That's odd,' she murmured, 'I'm the only one who is allowed to call her Rosie. You've obviously made an impression.'

Irritated by the interruption, Captain Hines coughed for attention. With his slender build and shaggy moustache Morgan's intelligence officer looked remarkably like an Airedale terrier. 'Correct me if I'm wrong, Mrs Greenhow, but weren't you a great hostess in Washington before the war?'

His enquiry was greeted with a silvery laugh. 'Well, sir, you might say that. I lived near the White House, hosted dinner parties, did my share of lobbying and was a friend of President Buchanan.'

'Wow!' said a star-struck Hines. 'You're the most famous woman I've ever met.'

'Oh I hardly think so,' she replied. 'In any case, the good ladies of Richmond would use a rather different epithet. They've heard the Washington gossip about my late-night male callers and suspect me of having loose morals. If it wasn't for my late husband's Virginian pedigree I wouldn't be received in their homes.'

'But you risked your life for the Cause. Doesn't that count for anything?' Hines asked indignantly.

Nobody spoke for a moment as Rose's male admirers wondered what she had actually done to acquire vital information about Federal troop movements.

'You were talking about prison, Mrs Greenhow; what was the worst thing about your incarceration?' Colonel Duke wanted to know.

'Being treated like a caged animal in a circus. People were queuing up to see us in captivity and the prison superintendent told me he'd been offered a ten-dollar bribe by a Washington businessman for a closer look at the "indomitable rebel", as I was sometimes called in their papers. The famous photographer Matthew Brady visited our cell to take a picture of me with little Rose. At first I was flattered by all this attention but I soon tired of my notoriety. In truth, I hated prison life – the disgusting food, the filth, the humiliating lack of privacy, the ignorant Northern guards and their Negro helpers – but things could have been worse. It wasn't the Chateau d'If after all ...'

'So you've read *The Count of Monte Cristo*?' Grenfell interrupted her.

'It's my favourite book.'

'Mine too; I had the pleasure of meeting Alexandre Dumas shortly after he wrote the novel.'

'How did that come about?'

'At the time I was the British vice consul in Morocco and was asked to organise a hunting trip for a party of French visitors headed by Dumas. I remember his astonishment when I appeared hatless in the hot sun and wearing a pair of shorts. I explained that Arabs went barelegged and Africans bareheaded and what was good enough for them was good enough for me.'

Rose laughed at the story. 'You do end up in some strange places, George. General Lee told me you'd taken part in the heroic Charge of the Light Brigade. Is that true?'

The truth would not serve his purpose. 'If following that

damned haw-hawing idiot Cardigan into the Valley of Death could possibly be called heroic. Someone should have shot him off his horse!'

'My goodness,' she said admiringly, 'you *have* led an interesting life.'

A clock chimed on the mantelpiece and Rose glanced at her fob watch. 'It's almost time for the wedding and I seem to have lost my daughter. You wouldn't happen to know where she might be?'

Grenfell told her Rosie was watching a fireworks display on the stoop. Rose's brow furrowed. 'The poor girl will be freezing out there and she's not strong, you know. She had such a fever in prison I almost lost her. I must go to her. Perhaps you will accompany me, George.'

He followed her to the door with mixed feelings: pleasure at being selected as her escort and concern because he hadn't thought to ensure that her daughter was properly dressed for the cold weather. He need not have worried. The girl was wearing mittens and an overcoat and was laughing with a group of soldiers who had lit a bonfire in the main street.

Maternal fears assuaged, Rose turned on her heel and went back inside. 'We'll let her be. She is obviously enjoying herself.'

They were alone together for the first time. Grenfell felt his mouth go dry. He knew Rose Greenhow to be an adventuress who ensnared men with her brand of femininity – earthy, courageous and ever so slightly vulnerable – and yet he felt drawn to her like a moth to a flame. His desire was more than physical. He wanted to possess her body and soul.

Once again she read his thoughts. 'You're right, I am a dangerous woman,' she whispered in his ear. 'I believe in the Mosaic Law which exacts an eye for an eye and a tooth for a tooth and I also believe the end can justify the means. You would be best off, George, having nothing to do with me.'

It was a bold statement delivered with unblinking eyes and he loved her for it. He was about to tell her so when, out in the street, the regimental band struck up a tune. 'They're practising for the wedding,' he murmured. 'By the way, what brought you here? Are you a friend of the bride?'

'No, I was invited by the groom. We met yesterday when my travelling companion, Jefferson Davis, presented General Morgan with his gold stars and wreath. Jeff had to leave this morning to visit another army camp, but I chose to remain to see our golden boy take his vows.'

'I am very glad you did. But do you always bring your daughter with you on your travels? Shouldn't she be at school?'

'You ask a lot of questions, George. No, Little Rose is being privately educated. She has her own tutor and, yes, she often accompanies me. Travel broadens the mind, wouldn't you say?'

'I would indeed, ma'am.'

'There you go again, George, being formal with me. My friends call me Rose.'

Instead of bowing, Grenfell gave her a wicked smile. 'Well, *Rose*,' he said, emphasising her name, 'I hope you'll forgive me for asking why an intelligent Washington socialite is such a staunch secessionist when any fool can see we're going to lose this war? The South hasn't the industry or the manpower to sustain a long conflict. She will be brought to her knees in a couple of years.'

'I refuse to recognise that possibility,' she snapped back at him. 'I believe in self-determination. That is why we fought for our independence from the British Empire. Time was when the American flag was the proudest emblem of human freedom on earth but now I think there is no pirate flag that floats upon the sea which is not more honourable, for none covers such infamy.'

'That is a political speech rather than a practical consideration.'

44

Rose's eyes flashed. 'And who are you to speak of such matters? People call you a soldier of fortune but isn't that just a fancy name for a mercenary?'

Now it was Grenfell's turn to get angry. 'Damn it,' he raged, 'I haven't taken a red cent. I believe as strongly as you do in the war but that doesn't blind me to its probable outcome.'

Their raised voices caused wedding guests to turn their heads, although it was almost impossible to catch what was being said in the general hubbub. That was until General Leonidas Polk exercised his considerable vocal chords. 'Will guests please take their places?' he boomed. 'The wedding is about to begin.'

'You are a strange man, George, indeed you are,' Rose whispered. She opened the small silk reticule she was carrying and gave him one of her calling cards. 'I've written my address on there. When you have the opportunity, I trust you will call on us in Richmond.'

The ceremony was to take place in the adjoining parlour where almost a hundred chairs had been set out. As one of Morgan's groomsmen it was Grenfell's duty to show people to their seats. He chose one for Rose that gave her an excellent view of the bridegroom and his best man as they stood self-consciously in front of a makeshift altar.

Lounging against a pillar at the back of the room Grenfell had to admire the way the dark-haired bride glided down the aisle to a stirring rendition of 'The Confederate Flag'. When her father lifted Mattie's bridal veil Grenfell could see how happy she looked and felt a sudden sadness. She had snared the man of her dreams but her joy wouldn't last. Nothing in the world was permanent.

Clad in the vestments of a bishop of the Episcopal Church, General Polk opened his copy of the Book of Common Prayer. 'Dearly beloved,' he intoned, 'we have come together in the presence of God to witness and bless the joining together of this man and this woman in holy matrimony.'

Grenfell remembered the day on which those words had been said over him. He and his French wife had shared a bed and made a home together but they had never really known each other. Hortense had absorbed his unhappiness and reflected it back to him. He hadn't seen her in seven years.

His eyes sought out Rose Greenhow sitting demurely in her aisle seat. He was still holding her calling card. It was an invitation he had every intention of taking up.

OUT OF THE FRYING PAN

The battlefield at Stones River was three miles away from Murfreesboro; close enough for the rumbling of cannon fire to rattle window panes and for the cold northerly wind to carry a whiff of sulphur into the town. News of the conflict came with the cartloads of Confederate casualties needing hospital care. Survivors spoke of a military triumph, a turning point in the war. Yet later, when the battle was over and its dust and debris had become another layer in history, bluecoat soldiers once again occupied Murfreesboro and its bemused citizens wanted to know what had gone wrong. How had the promise of a Southern victory turned into such a shameful defeat?

Drowning their sorrows in a dingy tavern called the Green Dragon, non-combatants held strong views on the subject. One faction of Confederate sympathisers, led by a vociferous veteran who had lost an eye in the Mexican-American War, placed the blame squarely on Braxton Bragg's shoulders. He had been given command of the Army of Tennessee because he was Jeff Davis's buddy. Everyone knew he was an unpleasant fellow who rubbed people up the wrong way, lacked imagination on the battlefield and made a habit of retreating when the going got tough.

Another coterie, too young to have fought with Winfield Scott at Veracruz, maintained Bragg shouldn't be blamed for a political decision that had stripped him of a quarter of his army before the fighting even began. The fault lay with President Davis who had insisted on sending nine thousand troops to reinforce Vicksburg. Peter had been robbed to pay Paul. End of story.

Not so, the one-eyed hero of Veracruz retorted, it was Bragg who stoked the fire. His battle plan was flawed. Having seized the initiative with his dawn attack on the Union right flank, he tossed it away by expecting his advancing troops to execute a right wheel to attack the enemy supply line. Believe me, said the veteran, downing another bourbon and branch, that's a hard manoeuvre on the parade ground, let alone in the heat of battle when your soldiers are stumbling over rocky scrubland. No wonder the assault stalled. But even this know-it-all had to admit he was relying on well-placed rumour. What actually happened at Stones River was still shrouded in mystery.

The first eye-witness accounts came from Mrs Katharine Cooper's female volunteers who ventured out to the battlefield with saddlebags laden with bandages. The talk was of twenty thousand casualties and, whether they fought for North or South, they all needed nursing. As Murfreesboro couldn't cope with the wounded, abandoned farms and outbuildings in the surrounding district were turned into makeshift hospitals and temporary field stations.

These plucky Confederate ladies would never forget their mercy ride. Fields strewn with dead horses and mules, their bloated and decomposing bodies fed on by carrion crows and blowflies. Where the fighting had been worst, farmhouses destroyed, fences flattened and trees mutilated by shot and shell while, on either side of the turnpike, hundreds of bloodless corpses in shallow trenches testified to the slaughter that had taken place.

The first emergency centre the women visited was a former school. Scores of men, some severely wounded, were stretched out in rows on the classroom floor. It was a bitterly cold morning and the building was unheated, yet the patients were only wrapped in thin blankets. Their next destination had been a deserted plantation house. What shocked them here was the casual brutality of the stretcher bearers. The corpses of Confederate soldiers who had died on the operating table had been stacked up behind a curtain like forgotten refuse.

Wherever the ladies went the stench was terrible; sweaty, blood stained bodies, groaning and screaming as surgeons amputated limbs without the benefit of chloroform or morphine. Pressed into action as nurses, the voluntary helpers also became hospital cooks. Drawing on army rations, they conjured up nourishing meals of soup, toast and apple sauce.

Recognising the value of their services, a gentleman from the Christian Commission asked them to continue their work. This was agreed to, on the understanding that they could talk to wounded prisoners. Such encounters, Mrs Cooper promised, would only be of a consoling nature, which turned out to be less true than she had imagined.

Sitting on a camp chair in the corridor of a gangrene hospital was a haggard Confederate officer with a red forage cap perched on top of his bandaged head. 'Pardon me ladies,' he said, doffing his cap to them. 'I wonder whether you can tell me how the battle ended.'

This gallant gesture brought a touch of colour to the cheeks of the prettier of the two nurses. She had scarcely looked at another man since her husband died at Shiloh. 'It would be my pleasure, sir,' she replied coyly. 'May I enquire as to your name?'

'Lieutenant Colonel George St Leger Grenfell and I am at your service, ma'am.'

The young widow began to curtsey before thinking better of it. A bereaved woman shouldn't behave like that. 'I'm Mrs Ann Howard and this is Mrs Katharine Cooper.'

Mrs Cooper's curiosity got the better of her. 'What are you doing in a gangrene hospital?'

'I don't rightly know,' Grenfell said with a dry chuckle. 'I think the stretcher bearers dumped me here by mistake but I couldn't swear to that. I've been in a daze ever since.'

'Where did they find you?' Mrs Cooper was a tall, big-boned, buxom woman married to a Murfreesboro attorney who prided herself on her bluntness.

'In a ditch near McFadden's Ford; the medics think I hit my head on a stone when my horse was shot from under me but I can't remember anything about that.'

'Oh, you poor man, you must be suffering from concussion,' Mrs Howard suggested.

'It's also called shaking of the brain, the symptoms of which are headaches, nausea and mild dizziness,' her companion added. 'Had any of those ailments?'

'I've had all of them, together with a bit of memory loss. The last thing I remember is taking part in Breckinridge's charge and coming under heavy artillery fire. But do either of you know what the outcome was? Nobody here can tell me.'

Mrs Howard shook her head sympathetically. 'I'm sorry to say this, but I think the attack must have failed because once the battle was over General Bragg retreated to Tullahoma.'

'You mean the battle was lost?'

'No, they say it was inconclusive but Bragg decided to withdraw his army.'

'You must be joking!' Grenfell couldn't believe it. His commanding officer had given the Union a victory and handed them most of Tennessee in the process. The man was mad.

'You poor dear, you've gone quite white,' Mrs Howard murmured in her best bedside manner. 'What you need is one of my eggnogs. I'm making some in the kitchen for the amputees.'

'Where did you get the fresh milk and eggs from?'

'From the one farm the Yankee soldiers didn't raid. Do you know the drink?'

'Yes, in England it's served at breakfast time in fashionable homes.'

'We make it for special occasions like Christmas. Not that we've much to celebrate this year.'

'Hard times,' he agreed. 'But we'll try and turn it around. I promise you that. The Confederacy isn't beaten yet.'

His fierce dark eyes softened into a smile and, as he looked at her, Ann Howard felt something stir inside her.

'What's an Englishman doing fighting for the South?' she blurted out. 'It's not your war.'

'Maybe not, but I believe in your cause. People should be free to decide their own destiny.'

She could see Katharine Cooper frowning and pointing to her pendant watch. There was work to be done. But Ann rebelled against it. She wanted to prolong the conversation.

'Where's your home in England?' she asked.

'I don't really have one but I grew up in Cornwall. My father had an estate in Penzance. We were a large family – five boys and five girls – but there was plenty of room for us all at Penalverne.'

'My goodness, you're an aristocrat.'

'I'd hardly say that,' Grenfell laughed, displaying his white teeth. 'We made our money out of tin smelting and banking. What about you? Where do you come from?'

'Originally from Savannah, Georgia, but when I married Johnny we moved to his home town of Murfreesboro and bought a farm nearby.'

'Is your husband in the army?'

'Not any more. Johnny died at Shiloh. He went into battle with a hunting rifle. They couldn't give him anything better.' I'm not going to cry, she told herself, but the tears came anyway.

Katharine put a consoling arm around her shoulders. 'You mustn't go on so. I don't know what Colonel Grenfell will think of us.' She was certain he wasn't thinking of her at all, and was tired of playing gooseberry. 'Come along, Ann, surgery is due to start at any moment.'

A flushed Ann Howard took her leave, promising to return as soon as possible with a glass of eggnog. Watching her depart in a flurry of skirts, Grenfell felt better than he'd done in days. Flirting always put him in good spirits.

Soon he'd be out of this Union hospital. And then what? His cheerfulness departed. Most likely a long train journey north to the prisoner-of-war camp for Confederate officers on Johnson's Island where, as an Englishman, he could expect to be treated harshly. He had to escape. Perhaps he could persuade the pretty widow to help him? But even if she did so, what would he do next? As an aide-de-camp, he was duty bound to report to General Bragg at Tullahoma.

Grenfell's vision blurred. He could feel another headache coming on. Once again in his chequered career, he'd jumped from the frying pan into the fire. How could he have been so stupid? Whatever had possessed him?

No sooner had John Hunt Morgan left on his honeymoon than he'd requested a transfer to Bragg's staff, arguing that he wanted to experience proper military action instead of lightweight skirmishing. Well, he'd certainly had his fill at Stones River, three days of ultimately pointless savagery, in which, as Bragg's message carrier, he'd constantly been caught in the crossfire between the general and his uncooperative field commanders. At times, Bragg seemed to be fighting his subordinates rather than the enemy and they, in turn, had scant respect for an abrasive commanding officer who was far better at planning attacks than executing them.

Sitting in the gangrene hospital corridor, nursing his head, he had to admit that a great deal had changed in the three weeks since he'd first visited the Army of Tennessee's winter headquarters. Such had been his optimism then that the narrow path to Bragg's command post might have been strewn with primroses rather than frozen thistles. Confederate camps were supposed to be laid out on a fixed grid pattern but this hastily erected cantonment was a haphazard collection of canvas tents and huts floating on a sea of caked mud. The general's own living quarters were in a large log cabin with a tumble-down chimney. That the chimney wasn't working properly was apparent as soon as he stepped over the threshold to be confronted by a thick cloud of smoke and soot. Coughing and spluttering and with watering eyes, he had searched the room for the man he'd come to see.

Out of this acrid haze loomed an Old Testament prophet with a tortured face ready to smite the enemies of the Lord; a haggard beetle-browed man with frizzy grey hair, wild eyes and a beard that positively bristled. 'Grenfell, isn't it,' Braxton Bragg growled. 'Saw you last weekend at the Morgan wedding, dancing with that devious Delilah of whom President Davis is so enamoured.'

He could feel his face flushing. Defending Rose's honour was not how he'd planned to start this interview. 'I didn't see you there, sir,' he replied rather lamely.

'No, well, I arrived late, after the feasting was over, and spent my time in the smoking room with those who didn't have partners. Still, enough of that; I hear you want to join my staff rather than ride with Morgan. You've heard I'm sending him north to rip up railroads and burn bridges?'

'Yes, sir, and I fully recognise the importance of guerrilla warfare, but with Rosecrans gathering strength in Nashville it's only a question of time before he attacks you here and that will be a major battle in which I'd like to play a part.'

He had felt fairly happy with this tactful statement until he saw the deep furrows and raised eyebrows. 'Wrong answer,' Bragg barked. The general was displeased.

'What would the right one be?' Grenfell wanted to know, flustered by Bragg's bullying manner.

'That you're like me – you don't trust Kentuckians. They're not good soldiers. They look after one another, no one else, they're very close. When your friend Morgan was given a second brigade the word was that he'd offer you its command, instead of which he appointed General Breckinridge's cousin, a newspaper editor who'd been in the army for less than six months. And do you know why? Let me tell you. They all come from Lexington. They're good ole Kentucky boys!'

Grenfell bit his lip. Bragg was prodding his weak spot. He had been almost incandescent with rage when he'd heard about Willie Breckinridge's brigade command and had told Morgan what he thought of the appointment. Promotions came thick and fast in the Confederate army but Breckinridge's advancement had been nothing short of meteoric. Having enlisted as a private, he was promoted to captain the very next day and made a colonel a few months later.

'You think Morgan let you down because you're twice the soldier little Willie will ever be.'

Once again, Bragg had hit the mark. With his military record, Grenfell had every reason to think he was better qualified for the post. Had he been a Kentuckian, he felt sure it would have been offered to him.

'You can't rely on them, Grenfell. They are slippery customers, indeed they are. They are willing to accept their independence but are neither disposed nor willing to risk their lives or their property in its achievement. When I invaded the state last summer I expected thousands of Kentuckians to flock to my banner. My campaign was predicated on assurances that this would happen.'

There was a frenzied gleam in Bragg's deep-set eyes as he paced up and down his sawn pinewood floor, ranting about the shortcomings of his bluegrass troopers. It was almost as if he'd forgotten that the Confederacy was supposed to defend states' rights rather than attack them.

'I'll tell you what I do think, sir. Rosecrans will move against you as soon as he hears that a quarter of your infantry has been sent to Vicksburg to reinforce Pemberton's army.'

'Stevenson's division left for the Mississippi yesterday. But I don't agree about General William S Roseccrans's intentions. The reports I've received suggest he'll stay where he is in Nashville.'

Bragg slumped onto a chair behind his desk and held his head in his hands. Looking at this hunched figure, Grenfell couldn't help feeling sympathy for someone who was obviously suffering. The question was whether the general's illness was physical or mental.

'My troops are no longer barefooted and ragged. The deficiency in clothing and shoes has been met. They are well fed and healthy, yet they are deserting in their droves. Why do you think that is? I'll tell you why. The Confederate Conscription Act was designed to boost recruitment but what it's done is cause resentment, particularly among Kentuckian conscripts who keep on taking French leave. We're trying one of these deserters tomorrow and already I've had General high-and-mighty Breckinridge, former vice president of our now divided land, warning me that passing a death sentence on this soldier is tantamount to murder. What do you think of that, Grenfell?'

He would have to choose his words carefully. 'I think military law has to be upheld.'

'Precisely so, although in making a plea for clemency, Breckinridge claims there are extenuating circumstances. Apparently, Corporal Asa Lewis is a farm boy who ran away to help his starving mother and sisters, after which he intended to return to camp. My view is he shouldn't have left in the first place. Besides which, Lewis has done this before. He is a multiple offender who deserves to be court-martialled. Bleeding-heart Breckinridge won't like my decision but I'm his superior officer and he'll just have to accept it. By God, he will!'

'You will be doing no more, sir, than enforcing the discipline without which an army cannot operate.'

'My thoughts entirely. We seem to be of one mind. Look

here, Grenfell, I need a new aide-de-camp to act as my assistant, take messages and see they are carried out. When can you start?'

And so it was, a fortnight later, on a frosty New Year's Eve, that Grenfell came to be carrying battle orders to one of Bragg's corps commanders. His gut instinct had proved correct. Hearing of Bragg's troop depletions, Rosecrans had decided to advance and the formidably strong Army of the Cumberland was encamped on the Nashville Turnpike, ready for battle the following morning. But Bragg had a surprise in store. Although outnumbered, he intended to beat the Union general to the punch by staging a dawn attack.

Grenfell watched as General William Hardee lit the oil lamp in his tent before reading his orders. His men called him 'Old Reliable' and it was easy to see why. His neatly trimmed beard and waspish expression were softened by shrewd, intelligent eyes and, when he talked, there was something calm and reassuring about his manner. 'Tell Bragg I'm fixin' to do what he's askin' for,' he said in a soft drawl. 'Let's hit them before they hit us.'

As Hardee issued his staff instructions, Grenfell got the tingling sensation he knew so well, the heady cocktail of fear and excitement that came before a battle. General Lee claimed war needed to be terrible or people would grow too fond of it. Well, he was totally infatuated. He embraced war like a lover. It stirred him as nothing else did. The harder the conflict, the more glorious it became. Yet here at Stones River he was to be denied the thrill of combat. As Bragg's aide-de-camp, it was his job to act as a message-taker, a glorified go-between for a commander who preferred to stay in his tent.

'Would you mind if I accompanied the attack?' he asked Hardee. 'General Bragg expects me to report on its progress.'

There was a glint of amusement in the Georgian's eyes as he let this white lie go unchallenged. 'Fine by me,' was his laconic response. 'Be here by six o'clock.'

In volunteering for an early morning start, Grenfell hadn't counted on spending the better part of the night on horseback carrying last-minute orders to Bragg's frontline officers, and it was with bleary eyes and saddle sores that he rode past the darkly silhouetted corn cribs and cotton gins out onto the open farmland where a ghostly army was assembling.

Emerging eerily out of the mist was a solid wall of butternut and grey: thousands of infantrymen from McCown and Cleburne's divisions drawn up in a long double line, rubbing chilled hands together as they waited for their whiskey ration. Once they had had their tots, and without so much as a spoken command, the foot soldiers picked up their rifles and came to attention. They were mostly unpaid and self-equipped, a homogeneous army of white, Anglo-Saxon Protestants fighting for self-determination.

The colours were lifted, the Stars and Bars of the Confederacy and the Hardee battle flag with its blue field and full moon. The silk barely flapped in the still air. It was time for the blessing. General Leonidas Polk, the fighting bishop, showed the men the cross and absolved them from guilt. They were doing the Lord's work, taking part in a righteous crusade.

With enemy campfires' little more than half a mile away on the Franklin Turnpike, the silence was almost tangible. Grenfell had muffled Barbary's hooves in burlap sacking and when the big chestnut mare threatened to whinny he backed her up with expert horsemanship. All eyes turned to the wiry little man on the white horse. General Hardee waved his felt hat in the air. 'Go fast but be real quiet!' he warned his troops. 'Drive these damned Yankees off our land.'

Another voice took over. 'Are you ready?' questioned divisional commander Major General John McCown, whose long drooping moustache and goatee beard strengthened a pinched face and rapidly receding hairline. 'Ready!' the men growled, anxious to get on with it. Battalions from North Carolina, Georgia, Alabama and Tennessee lined up on the left, dismounted cavalrymen from Texas took the centre with the 1st and 2nd Arkansas Rifles on the right, ready to storm across the frosted fields. The weather had come to their aid with sufficient moisture in the air to reduce visibility to a hundred yards. These water droplets were Bragg's secret weapon.

The attack was to be led by 'Reckless' Rains. Handsome, fearless and only twenty-nine, Rains was an iconic figure in the Army of Tennessee. Stepping forward, he pointed to the enemy's cooking fires. 'Fix your bayonets, boys, and let's catch those Yankees having breakfast,' Rains said. 'When I give the order scream as loud as you can and show them your steel. They'll panic, I promise you!'

Grenfell looked at his watch. It was twenty past six. He tightened the reins on his chestnut mare and set her off at a steady trot. The thick fog deadened the sound of pounding feet as the Rebel infantry raced across the flat icy ground toward the enemy encampment. The loudest noise came from fluttering birds, disturbed by the advancing troops.

They had almost reached the breakfast fires before Rains gave the command. 'Now!' he roared, and the Rebel yell went up. It was a weird, ululating cry like the howl of a wild beast, guaranteed to frighten all but the stoutest hearts.

The sight of so many shrieking Southern fiends in rat-grey uniforms swarming out of the fog caused some startled Union pickets to turn and flee but others held their ground. A hail of bullets splintered a clump of cedars behind the onrushing Rebels, bringing down a shower of needle-like leaves and torn twigs. 'Fire!' a Yankee voice shouted and a better-directed volley slashed into the attackers. Above the crackle of gunfire and the screams of anger and pain, Rains could be heard exhorting his troops. 'Forward my brave boys, forward!' he yelled. Those were his last words. A cartridge tore through his double-breasted tunic and thudded into his chest.

Seeing Rains fall, Grenfell didn't hesitate. He spurred Barbary forward. His blood was up and he wanted vengeance. A blue-coated colonel with an eye patch was bawling orders to his men. Grenfell drew his Remington from its holster and shot from the saddle. Through a pall of gun smoke he saw the officer's head jerk back as bullets entered his neck. The colonel staggered backwards before crumpling to the turf. But instead of weakening morale, the death of their commanding officer seemed to strengthen Union resolve. In the oaks and poplars ahead, steel ramrods rattled and scraped in rifle barrels as marksmen reloaded for another round of fire.

Left on the edge of the woods, Grenfell weighed up his chances. He could either turn tail or continue with the attack and trust to luck. He had never backed down before and didn't intend to start now. With sabre in one hand and pistol in the other, he rode towards the trees. 'Tally ho!' he shouted at the top of his voice, caught up in the excitement of the moment. Hearing the solitary horseman's strange cry, hundreds of whooping, long-haired Southerners followed his lead, diving into the thicket, hell-bent on hand-to-hand combat.

A frenzied mass of sweating, screaming antagonists wrestled for supremacy in a couple of acres of blood-soaked brushwood. In such a whirlwind of lead and iron there was only one rule: kill or be killed. Bayonet parried bayonet, swords hacked, knives flashed and rifles exploded at close quarters. Bullets pinged off trees and soldiers were hit by ricochets.

Unaware he was yelling like a maniac, Grenfell sliced at a soldier's face with his sabre and stamped on the fallen man with his horse's hooves. He was a savage at heart.

Barbary emerged from this smoke-filled inferno into a

forest clearing where, to his surprise, Grenfell was challenged to a mounted duel by a major from an Illinois regiment. One thrust and a couple of parries were all the chivalrous major managed before a quick slash of the Englishman's sabre left him gasping for air. The wounded man tried to say something, but the words wouldn't come, just blood and spittle, as he slowly slid out of the saddle, only for one of his feet to be trapped in a stirrup iron.

The sight of the major's horse dragging its dead rider off into the distance persuaded the remaining Union pickets to make a bolt for safety. Fleeing out of the trees they came under attack from 'Old Punch', the Eufaula Light Artillery's fourteen-pound cannon. The Alabamian gunners flayed the retreating bluecoats with a hail of canister that turned the rocky scrubland into a slaughter pen.

The Rebel horde swept on. The 34th Illinois and the 29th Indiana had hardly finished breakfast when the dismounted Texas Cavalry slammed into them. One brigade after another collapsed under the sheer weight of the Confederate attack, losing thousands of men in the process.

So far, Bragg's battle plan had worked perfectly. A well-timed dawn offensive had taken the Union army by surprise causing its right flank to crumble, but his next move was the difficult one. He wanted McCown's division to wheel right and sweep up the Yankee supply line. This enveloping strategy looked good on paper but, as Grenfell knew, such manoeuvres rarely worked in practice. To expect a bunch of hot-headed farm boys to change direction under enemy fire was asking a lot, particularly when the terrain was against them. Bragg hadn't taken the stony outcroppings and woodland into account. Nor had he considered how easily discipline could disappear.

Wherever Grenfell looked, excited groups of young soldiers were disobeying orders by chasing rapidly scattering Federal forces through the wheat fields. He could see the bloodlust in their eyes; the primal instinct that defeated reason. Suddenly he stiffened, sensing danger. Were enemy sharpshooters training their telescopic sights on him at this moment? It certainly felt like it. He knew war was a game of chance. It did not determine who was right, only who was left.

The crackle of distant gunfire ended his introspection. Judging by the clouds of black smoke drifting overhead, the main battle was raging two miles away to the east. It was time to report back to Bragg. His path lay across broken ground. Fields of cotton and corn tested Barbary's prowess as a hunter but the big mare relished the challenge. Soaring over a split-rail fence, Grenfell almost collided with an infantry brigade. The men of the 5th Arkansas were all lean weather-beaten veterans. Their boots were falling to pieces and their trousers held up by string, and they too had succumbed to the temptation of chasing a beaten enemy.

'There was a whole Yankee skirmish line in them woods back there,' a lieutenant explained, 'and we Dixie boys gave them a good whooping, but we don't rightly know our way back now. I've lost my goddam binoculaters.'

Grenfell struggled to keep a straight face. 'You don't need binoculars. All you've got to do is follow the sun.' The early morning fog had lifted and a weak light was struggling to break through the grey clouds overhead. 'Follow me,' he suggested, turning his horse towards the Wilkinson Pike.

The road's corduroyed surface was decidedly the worse for wear. Its splintered wooden planks were smoking with shell fragments, burning wagons and wrecked artillery pieces. But what gave this sorry scene a truly macabre quality were the dead soldiers and horses lying in pools of blood in the surrounding fields. There was so much limestone in the soil the blood couldn't seep through.

Bragg had set up his headquarters near the intersection of

the Nashville and Wilkinson pikes and his command post was swarming with staff officers. Grenfell gave the reins of his horse to an orderly before entering the tent. 'Where's the general?' he enquired.

'Don't ask,' replied an ashen-faced major. 'Bragg's in an absolutely foul mood.'

There was however one friendly face under canvas. 'Hi there, George, I hear you've brought some of my Arkansans back to me. You sure are the Good Shepherd.' Brigadier General St John Richardson Liddell was, by his own admission, a curious cove. As well as being the only plantation owner in Louisiana to emancipate his slaves, he was a fearless critic of the Confederate leadership from President Davis downwards.

'All this gold braid and they don't know what to do next.' Liddell spoke with a Cajun drawl. 'Little Phil is holding them up good and proper. You see, size doesn't matter on the battlefield. Napoleon surely taught us that!' Little Phil was the diminutive Union general Philip Sheridan who, alone among his colleagues, had anticipated a dawn attack and positioned himself accordingly. His skilful rearguard action had allowed Rosecrans to rally his shattered troops and form a new defensive line along the Nashville Pike, although he had been greatly aided by the piecemeal nature of the Rebel assaults on his position.

'Our attack has lost momentum,' Liddell observed. 'Some units are out of ammunition and most of them are totally exhausted. We need reinforcements badly.'

'You know what I think, George,' he added rhetorically. 'John Barleycorn is in charge of things. Our eagles have kissed John a little too often. They can't see straight.'

Grenfell smiled thinly. Confederate generals could be distinguished by the eagles imprinted on the brass buttons of their uniforms and several of those under Bragg's command were rumoured to have a love of the bottle. 'We call it Dutch courage in the British army,' he told his friend.

'What's the origin of that phrase?' asked Liddell, taking an academic interest.

'I'm not sure anyone knows. It may go back to the seventeenth century when British troops were fighting in the Low Countries and liked a few drops of Dutch gin before battle.'

'A few drops you say? More like whole whiskey jugs, where Frank Cheatham is concerned.'

Grenfell liked the hard-drinking Tennessean major general Benjamin F Cheatham, rating him a functioning alcoholic, rather like the Union's star performer Ulysses Grant who was a belligerent drunk in off-duty moments. Generals were only human and had different ways of letting off steam.

'What do you make of our commander-in-chief who is, to my certain knowledge, stone cold sober?' he asked disingenuously.

'Sober as a judge,' agreed Liddell lighting a long cigar, 'which leaves only two possibilities: General Bragg is either stark mad or utterly incompetent. He has lost the confidence of his officers. Hardee can't abide him and Breckinridge openly rejects his orders. Mark my words George; we're going to lose this battle because of our leadership.'

Suddenly the tent flap was pulled open and Braxton Bragg entered, doing up his flies. He looked a sick man and his shoulders were drooping as if weighed down by an invisible burden. 'Where the hell have you been?' he growled. 'You're supposed to be my eyes and ears, Grenfell, yet this is the first I've seen of you today. What have you been doing, man?'

'I've been doing my duty,' Grenfell replied evenly. 'I joined the dawn attack and was with Brigadier General Rains when he fell. After that I helped Rains' brigade drive the Union troops back. The first stage of your plan worked perfectly …'

'No it didn't, that fool McCown disobeyed orders and I've

a good mind to have him court-martialled,' Bragg snarled. 'Instead of chasing after the enemy he was supposed to wheel to the right.'

'With respect, sir, it's a difficult manoeuvre and McCown's men are pretty undisciplined.'

'For God's sake, that's why we have generals!'

Suddenly Grenfell had had enough. He regretted joining the Army of Tennessee and being harnessed to this paranoid old porcupine. Bragg was, in essence, a desk soldier commanding from the rear, who believed he could motivate people by belittling their efforts.

'Your generals have done you proud,' he said, bridling at Bragg's negativity. 'Cleburne has smashed into Sheridan's flank while Polk ...'

'Don't talk to me about Polk! Bishop Polk is a pompous priest who thinks he knows best! He may have buckled a sword over his gown but holy orders are the only ones he takes! I ask him to mount a coordinated attack on the centre and what does he do? The bishop commits one brigade at a time and allows Rosecrans to hunker down on the Nashville Pike and in that damned cedar thicket. If he'd followed my instructions, we would have routed the entire Federal army by now.

'And General Cheatham's no better. His division was supposed to hit Sheridan's front but his assault was sluggish and half-hearted. Do you know why? I'll tell you. Because Cheatham is a hopeless alcoholic, that's why. He was so drunk this morning he actually fell off his horse. What sort of example does *that* set?'

Grenfell was saved from having to answer such a loaded question by the appearance of an aide. Major William Clare had brought a message from Major General John Breckinridge. Bragg's brows beetled together in an angry frown as he read the dispatch. Breckinridge was his bête noire.

'Clear the tent,' he barked. 'No, not you Grenfell, you stay behind.'

Once his staff officers had filed out, Bragg took Breckinridge's message and tore it into little pieces. 'You see what I'm up against!' he ranted. 'That lily-livered Kentuckian constantly undermines my authority. He wants me to fail! I hold Breckinridge's division in reserve but when I ask him to reinforce Polk he refuses to do so because he reckons he is about to come under heavy attack. So I order him to confront the enemy and he has the nerve to ask for reinforcements. I mean how many men does he need? He already has *seven* thousand and they haven't done anything all morning!'

Grenfell couldn't believe it. Rosecrans was hardly likely to have sent a substantial force across the Stones River to attack the Confederate right flank when he was fighting for his life on the Nashville Pike. It didn't ring true. But nothing made much sense. What, for example, was the logic behind Bragg's decision to station Breckinridge's division east of the river when his brigades could and should have been adding their considerable weight to his enveloping manoeuvre? It was almost as if the man was trying to fight two different battles at the same time.

'May I make a suggestion, sir?' he asked.

'I hope it's a good one.' Bragg slumped on his camp bed, tugging at his ear lobes.

'Clare's horse is spent, why not send me instead, urge Breckinridge to check his intelligence, and ask him to advance at least two brigades to the river, ready to go to Polk's assistance?'

Bragg peered at him. 'That's the first sensible thing I've heard all day. Jump to it! Time is precious. I need our political general to stir himself.'

Grenfell mounted Barbary and made for the ford where

Federal troops were supposed to be massing. It was a calculated risk. He followed the bends in the river until he found a shallow crossing place where hardened mud had been scuffed up by trampling boots. There had been a Northern incursion but judging by the way the footprints criss-crossed, it had come and gone away again.

He knew what had happened. Bragg and Rosecrans had had the same idea: they had both planned to attack their opponent's right flank but Bragg had got in first with his dawn raid, forcing Rosecrans to recall the infantry he'd sent east of the river. Why hadn't anyone else realised this?

Breckinridge was camped on Wayne's Hill, a high ridge which gave his artillery command of the surrounding countryside. He found the general carrying out an inventory amidst the upturned shafts of wagons and gun limbers in the baggage area. Grenfell coughed politely. Breckinridge swung around. 'What can I do for you, Colonel?' he asked with an easy grace.

'Fresh orders from General Bragg, sir, if I may be so bold.'

Breckinridge said nothing but held out a manicured hand to receive them.

Grenfell shook his head. 'I'm sorry, sir, but General Bragg didn't have time to write anything down. He hopes you might accept oral instructions.'

Breckinridge's large, round eyes widened further. 'Then we have a problem here, Colonel. I would want you to understand that, in little more than an hour, I have received three sets of orders from General Bragg instructing me to advance my division west of the river to support Polk, to fight the Federal forces east of the river and to defend my present position. What does he want me to do now?'

The question was asked with a smile but in the manner of a man accustomed to being the centre of attention. No wonder Bragg loathed him.

'May I ask you something, sir?'

'Ask away,' Breckinridge replied with an airy wave.

'Have you checked the intelligence you received about enemy movements on your side of the river?'

The general brushed an imaginary crumb off his uniform before replying. He was, Grenfell thought, a truly charismatic man, handsome, charming and self-confident. 'No, I haven't. Our cavalry spotted a substantial Federal force crossing the stream early this morning and, as intelligence gathering is the cavalry's chief role, I never doubted the accuracy of what I was told. Put it another way, why keep a dog and do your own barking?'

To answer one question with another was political sophistry and Grenfell wondered how best to respond. 'I'm sorry, General Breckinridge, but you've been misled,' he said. 'Yes, Union infantry crossed the river but they were called back to defend Rosecrans's position on the Nashville Turnpike.'

'And what makes you so sure of this?' An angry note had crept into the general's voice.

'I followed the path they took and saw where they turned round. I am surprised your cavalry scouts didn't spot that.'

The general considered this carefully. 'If you are right,' he said, with a tell-tale quivering of the jawline, 'we have been very remiss and precious time has been wasted in waiting to fight an imaginary enemy.'

Encouraged by this response, Grenfell offered to accompany Breckinridge's outriders in reconnoitring the area around his camp.

'And what would Bragg have me do in the meanwhile?'

'I think he'd want you to use your discretion but Polk could do with a couple of your brigades.'

'And he shall have them. Tell me, Colonel, what's your name? You sound English.'

The conversation had taken a new twist. 'I am English and my name is George St Leger Grenfell, late of Her Majesty's Army in India.'

'Well, Colonel Grenfell, before you go off in search of enemies, I'd like you to tell me what Bragg is up to. Is he trying to destroy me?'

Grenfell's mouth fell open. Paranoia was obviously a contagious disease in the Army of Tennessee. 'No, sir, not to my knowledge,' he stammered.

'Then you can't have been at the staff dinner where he described me as being "an utterly worthless old woman". To insult me publicly in such a fashion is not to be borne. When this battle is over I intend to challenge him to a duel and I think he knows that. As the man is a coward, he would like nothing better than for me to die in combat. Second book of Samuel, Chapter 11, Verse 15!'

Brought up in a devout Christian household, Grenfell knew his Bible. 'You mean King David putting Bathsheba's husband Uriah in the forefront of the hottest battle.'

'You think I am exaggerating, don't you?' Breckinridge said bitterly. 'But there is so much bad blood between us. It began, I suppose, during Bragg's Kentucky campaign when he blamed me for the lack of volunteers in my state. He doesn't like my family connections either. I'm related to half a dozen Confederate commanders. But what really sticks in his craw is my popularity, whereas he's despised, particularly after poor Corporal Lewis was executed for desertion. I pleaded for clemency but Bragg wouldn't hear of it, forcing me and my fellow Kentuckians to witness the execution. Bragg may be my commanding officer but I warn you Grenfell, the man's a monster!'

There was a stunned silence as Grenfell considered how best to reply. He couldn't tell Breckinridge the truth, namely, that

Bragg would like to skewer his elegant body on a spit. Besides which, the two generals needed each other if the South was to win a vital victory.

'I've only known General Bragg for a few weeks,' he said eventually, 'and as his aide-de-camp you wouldn't expect me to comment on his character. What I do know is that he's trying to win this battle, and he needs your help.'

Breckinridge clapped his hands in approval. 'You, sir, could be a politician,' he said, grinning broadly. 'Forget about the scouting – I'll get that done. Tell Bragg that two of my brigades are on their way to the front. Not that it will do anything to improve his mood!'

Breckinridge was right about that. Bragg talked about having the general horse-whipped. 'Politicians don't make real soldiers,' he shouted. 'They can't be trusted. Men like Breckinridge were born under a treacherous star. I want you to go to the front to make sure his men actually turn up.'

The Union battle line was drawn up on a sharp salient, north-east of the Nashville Pike. Within this salient, Confederate assaults were concentrating on a timbered four-acre knoll known as the Round Forest which looked out onto open fields of cotton and winter wheat. Brigades of bluecoat riflemen with scores of artillery pieces had been defending this cedar thicket since mid-morning and repeated attacks had failed to dislodge them.

Wondering why this small enemy position mattered so much, Grenfell rode along the turnpike with the discordant screech of shot and shell swelling in his ears. On either side of the road, fields had become open-air hospitals, full of wounded men waiting for surgeons to operate on their torn and shattered flesh. A canister round exploded in front of Barbary and pieces of casing whipped past horse and rider. As the smoke lifted, he could see puffs of artillery fire coming from a clump of cedars and hundreds of butternut soldiers running away from the guns through already trampled fields.

Dismounting in front of the burnt-out ruins of a brick house he joined the group of foreign observers who followed the Army of Tennessee. He thought, with irrational savagery, that they were like vultures hovering around the kill, although far more brightly coloured in their gold braid uniforms. One of them was a French cavalryman. '*Mon Dieu, ils on subi au moins cinq cents blesses,*' the officer said, lowering his field glasses. '*Cet évêque damné est a blâmer.*' The attackers had incurred at least five hundred casualties and, in the Frenchman's opinion, that 'damned bishop was to blame'.

Instead of waiting for all of Breckinridge's men to reach him, Polk had ordered Adams's Louisiana infantry to charge the enemy stronghold on their own. Showing the utmost gallantry, they had marched towards the guns with heavy losses, until they could take no more. When Breckinridge's other brigade reported for duty, it too was ordered to make a frontal assault on the Round Forest and was quickly shot to pieces.

Grenfell shook his head in disbelief. It was utter folly. Hundreds of men had been sacrificed in futile attacks on a defensive position that was growing stronger by the minute as the already crowded thicket was further reinforced.

Finally, as the winter sky began to darken, Breckinridge arrived with the rest of his troops and was appalled to see the carnage. Like the French officer, he blamed Polk for what had happened and refused to talk to the corps commander whom, he said, was more of a butcher than a bishop. Instead, he singled out Grenfell. 'Ah, there you are, Colonel. If the British fought like this you'd lose all your wars. The best way to get these Yankees out of the forest is to outflank them. Don't you agree?'

'Absolutely, sir,' Grenfell replied, relieved to find someone thinking clearly. 'What do you have in mind?'

Breckinridge unfolded a map of the area. 'Perhaps the best approach would be to get Colonel Palmer's brigade to slip into the woods here, near McFadden Lane, move up to the cotton field west of the Nashville Pike, and attack the Federal back door while they are busy dealing with Brigadier General Preston's frontal assault. What do you think?'

'Perhaps I could accompany Colonel Palmer?'

Breckinridge shook his head. 'Not this time, my friend. I have enough problems with Bragg without putting his special staff in the firing line. You and I must sit this out.'

'As you wish, sir,' Grenfell shrugged his shoulders. Breckinridge was right of course. Why, he wondered, did he get such a thrill out fighting? War was at best a necessary evil, a duty to be performed. To love war was to scorn the values for which people fight. But what war gave him, as nothing else did, was moral clarity. Gone were the grey areas. In war you knew who your friends were. You trusted your comrades with your life. War was also a fresh start, an opportunity to reinvent oneself. Before the war, Ulysses Grant had been selling firewood on street corners in St Louis. If Grant could change his stars, anyone could.

Cheers of encouragement greeted General Preston's brigade as they began their charge in double-quick time. 'Fire!' a Federal officer shouted from the cedar thicket and hundreds of rifles slashed flame into the gathering dusk. Bullets whipped over the corn stalks before finding their mark in human flesh. The grey line faltered. Grenfell watched men flung backwards like rag dolls, haloed in their own blood. A flag was dropped, snatched up again and lost in the billowing gun smoke. Men screamed, fell and died. The survivors regrouped and fired a volley of their own, only to be raked by a deadly hail of grapeshot, canister and shell.

Out of this bedlam came a new command. Preston's

remaining troops turned sideways and ran for cover in the woods. Tied down by artillery fire, Palmer's encircling brigade took shelter in a cane brake and stayed there. Like all the other attacks on the Round Forest, Breckinridge's offensive had failed. The enemy position was too well defended.

The general sat impassively on his horse surveying the battlefield. 'My men have given this place a name,' he told the French cavalry colonel. 'They call it Hell's Half-Acre.' What Grenfell couldn't understand was why Bragg and his commanders had become so fixated on storming this cedar thicket. There were more profitable ways of attacking the Union left.

The setting sun signalled an end to the day's hostilities and Grenfell reluctantly returned to the command post where he found his general dictating a wire report for Richmond. 'God has granted us a happy New Year,' Bragg was boasting. 'We attacked Rosecrans's army near Murfreesboro and gained a great victory. We drove him from all of his positions, except the extreme left, and after ten hours' fighting occupied almost the whole field.' Bragg seemed to think a defeated Union army would withdraw under cover of darkness.

Grenfell retired to his tent with a heavy heart. He was serving a military leader who couldn't adjust to the ebb and flow of battle. When his initial attack stalled, Bragg's only answer had been to commit his reserves to a suicidal frontal offensive which was like putting steak into a meat grinder. It had been a criminal waste of men. And what might tomorrow bring? The Federal commander had managed to protect his supply line and would almost certainly reinforce his position by morning. Bragg was living in cuckoo land if he believed the battle was over.

It was a clear night, with a cold crust of stars illuminating the sky. Lifting the tent flap, the depressed Englishman hoped to hear a welcoming bark. He had adopted a starving mongrel bitch he'd found scavenging for food in the army camp. Tonight, Belle would share his unappetising supper of salted beef and hardtack which he intended to wash down with a tumbler of Applejack. He had developed a taste for apple brandy and a full bottle was waiting on his bedside table.

When Grenfell lit his oil lamp a bad day got even worse. On the ground beneath the canvas awning were shards of glass and puddles of amber liquid. The lamp's fitful gleam also revealed Belle, curled up on his sleeping bag as if asleep. But the dog was inert and her fur stiff and rigid. In the grip of an unfamiliar feeling, he dropped to his knees and cradled Belle's lifeless body in his arms. It was years since he had last cried but he did so now. He had loved his scruffy little dog.

With spade in hand, he took her outside and began to dig a grave in the hard, unyielding earth. How had she come to die? There had to be a connection between the spilt brandy and the dead animal. But why should apple brandy kill a dog? It didn't make any sense, unless, of course, the drink had been poisoned.

Paranoia took over. Someone was trying to kill him. Denied images rose before his eyes: the bullet hole in the back of his forage cap at Cynthiana, the feeling he'd had earlier of being caught in the crosshairs of a telescopic rifle sight.

His spade bit into the frozen soil. The sound it made seemed unnaturally loud in the thickening silence. As he lowered Belle into the ground he thought he saw something move behind him, a shadow flitting across his peripheral vision. An ice-cold wave crashed over him and he shuddered beneath its impact. His mind was playing tricks. Click – a gun's trigger being cocked. Now that was real enough.

He threw himself sideways as a bullet whistled past his ear. Whipping out his own revolver he fired into the darkness. There was movement off to his left. A running figure silhouetted against the full moon. He fired again and missed. The camp woke up. Sentries rushed towards him, shouting warnings, fearing a surprise attack.

Grenfell stood up and raised his hands in the air. A candle lantern shone in his eyes as he identified himself. He had been shot at, he said, but he didn't know by whom. Anyway, whoever it was had gone now, and he was off to bed.

Tossing and turning in his sleeping bag that night, he reckoned there had to be better ways of seeing in the New Year.

*

Braxton Bragg was woken the next morning by a smiling orderly carrying a cup of rye coffee and wishing him a Happy New Year. But that was as good as it got. Outside, in the cold morning air, he received a nasty shock. The same blue lines of infantry were there to greet him. The sight of the Union army seemed to paralyse Bragg. When his corps commanders asked for fresh battle plans he had none to give them. Instead, he sank into a kind of torpor and the only orders Grenfell could get out of him were for the retrieval of dead bodies and the movement of wounded into field hospitals.

By Friday morning Bragg had perked up sufficiently to change his headquarters to a riverside farmhouse and to take a close interest in the positioning of his batteries. He wanted his guns placed on high ground and was horrified to learn that the hill he'd chosen on the east side of the river was already occupied by the enemy. Believing that Van Cleve's field howitzers, twelve-pound Napoleons and Parrott rifles could pour down a devastating fire on his army, Bragg decided to storm the Federal-held ridge and sent a courier to General Breckinridge demanding his immediate presence.

It was a cold, gloomy day. Wrapped in his woollen frockcoat,

Bragg paced up and down the river bank until Breckinridge arrived. They met under a large sycamore where, without ceremony, Bragg began to bark out orders. Frustration was etched on Breckinridge's face as he listened to the plan of attack. Once Bragg finished, he exploded angrily. 'Your plan won't work. You are asking for the impossible.' Picking a stick off the ground, Breckinridge illustrated his objections in the river bank's soft mud. His men would have to advance over exposed ground, subject to heavy enemy fire, and, if they reached the Yankee artillery, all they could do was to push Van Cleve's batteries back onto even higher ground which had to be self-defeating.

Observing this exchange of views from a discreet distance, Grenfell knew trouble was brewing. Bragg would never allow a hated subordinate to lecture him on tactics.

'You're not much of a soldier, are you Breckinridge?' sneered the wild-eyed commanding officer. 'Your Kentucky soldiers have got off lightly so far. Now it's time for them to show their mettle.'

'That's not at issue,' Breckinridge persisted. 'I've seen the Federal gun emplacements from the top of Wayne's Hill and I am telling you again they cannot be taken by direct assault.'

Bragg's mind was made up. 'My information is different. You are to begin your assault at four o'clock and that's an order!' Faced with such intransigence Breckinridge offered a mocking salute before turning on his heel and riding off to make the necessary arrangements.

'Follow him, Grenfell,' Bragg demanded. 'Make sure he does as I say.'

The unwilling messenger arrived at the Wayne's Hill camp in time to hear the cries of outrage as Breckinridge told his senior officers about their mission. General Roger Hanson, commander of the Fourth Brigade, offered a 'practical solution'. He would go down to headquarters and shoot Bragg.

'No, Roger, we must exercise proper restraint,' said a tight-lipped Breckinridge.

Once his angry officers had stomped off to prepare their troops, he turned to Grenfell and shook his head despairingly. 'When I was doing my rounds yesterday, I overheard a couple of privates in Palmer's 45th Tennessee bemoaning the quality of our leadership. "Those danged fools," and I'm quoting now, "don't never seem to learn anything. They keep throwin' us in thar piecemeal just like at the Hornet's Nest." That's what ordinary soldiers think and you know what? They are absolutely right. It's Shiloh all over again.'

The two men looked at one another. Breckinridge broke the silence by asking a political question. 'What does Bragg think I'm going to do?'

'He expects you to reject his order. Bragg is looking for a scapegoat in case he loses this battle. Turn the mission down and he'll tell Jeff Davis you sabotaged his victory and, who knows, the president may believe him.'

Breckinridge smiled wearily. 'My sentiments exactly and, for that reason alone, we must do our duty and fight the best we can, but it goes against the grain. If I am among the fallen, perhaps you will do justice to my memory, Grenfell, by telling people I believed this attack to be unwise.'

'I am sorry, sir, but you'll have to get someone else to do that. I mean to accompany you this afternoon. Make sure you come to no harm.'

The general hid his emotions with a brittle laugh. 'I am honoured to have your company,' he murmured, 'and to hell with Bragg!'

'That sounds like a good battle cry.'

The last light was filtering through the clouds and icy rain was falling when the doomed assault began. Breckinridge had arranged his division at the edge of the wood in two long rows.

The front line was made up of Hanson's Kentucky Brigade and the Second Brigade, commanded by a Bragg appointee General Gideon Pillow. Preston and Gibson's brigades were placed three hundred yards in the rear with Breckinridge and his staff officers behind the centre of the second line.

A cannon shot acted as the starting gun. The grey and butternut troops surged through the brushwood with fixed bayonets. Many of the marchers hadn't any boots and the prickly shrubs and sassafras roots tore at their bare feet. Yet they kept perfect order as they swept out onto the open, undulating plain, their regimental flags flying in the driving sleet. The Rebel yell echoed eerily as they rushed forward, an advancing wave that quickly engulfed enemy skirmishers.

'This is going well,' Breckinridge yelled. He spoke too soon. White puffs of smoke and spitting orange flame erupted from the Union artillery concealed in the wooded limestone bluffs across the river. Cannons pumped their percussive explosions through the cold wet air. Shot and shell screamed overhead. Smoke poured off the hillside where Van Cleve's howitzers were placed. An iron ball thumped into the dirt, parting the hurrying ranks. The Northern gunners had found their range.

Shredded by shrapnel, Breckinridge's front line wouldn't give up. Wounded men staggered and fell into the craters created by earlier shells. Blue-coated infantry rose from behind the rocks near the river and let fly with a murderous volley. Hanson's Kentuckians shuddered like a wounded beast but didn't stop, forcing the Federal soldiers to turn and flee.

A jubilant Breckinridge galloped over the scrubland in pursuit of his troops. 'Perhaps we can do this after all!' he shouted into the wind. 'The Orphan Brigade has done us proud. They are a credit to Kentucky.' But joy quickly turned to sorrow. Someone had spotted General Hanson lying against a rail fence. He was white-faced and breathing shallowly. A shell fragment had entered his leg, slicing open the femoral artery.

'No, no, not you,' Breckinridge moaned. He vaulted off his horse and knelt beside his injured friend. 'Call an ambulance wagon. General Hanson needs a tourniquet!'

He cushioned Hanson's head in his bent arm and whispered. 'How are you, Roger?'

'Dying, I think,' his friend murmured. 'You should have let me shoot Bragg.' The wagon arrived and Hanson was lifted into it. No one believed he'd survive the journey to the field hospital.

Once the ambulance had gone, Breckinridge wanted to know the whereabouts of his remaining frontline general and was told General Pillow had been spotted in the woods, being sick. Breckinridge's anger soared uncontrollably. 'What's that sycophantic son of a bitch doing there?' he roared. 'His troops are all over the place. They've got to get back into line.'

Grenfell didn't stop to think. 'Leave it to me, General,' he said, spurring Barbary towards the limestone bluff where the fighting was fiercest. With sleet driving into his face, he galloped down to the river bank. It was the same old story, he thought. The Southern boys were fighting like demons but without discipline. They had turned the Yankee line and were splashing across the creek in hot pursuit. As the triumphant greys crested the mound above McFadden's Ford, they were greeted with a deafening salvo. Grenfell could feel the earth tremble beneath his horse's hooves as a pitiless hail of iron hissed around his ears. Rebel soldiers were snatched backward, their blood splattering Barbary. Those who could still stand turned away from the blinding flashes and exploding shells, stumbling over the bodies of their fallen comrades in the soggy river bottom, trying to retrace their steps.

'To me,' Grenfell bellowed. 'Fight as you go, damn it!' But it was too late. Panic had set in. Breckinridge's remaining troops thrashed their way through the crimson water, desperate to escape the deadly fire raining down on them. One frightened man screamed as he was hit in the calf and another collapsed onto the muddy bank clutching his lower back.

The Confederate retreat was turning into a rout. Grenfell felt both shame and anger. He had failed once again.

This was his last thought before an enemy shell smacked into his beloved horse sending him spinning through the air into a world of complete darkness.

PLAYING POSSUM

A cool hand was soothing his brow. Grenfell opened his eyes and saw Ann Howard's anxious face peering down at him. 'Are you all right?' she asked.

'Much better for seeing you again,' he said.

'I've brought you the eggnog I promised. Sorry it's taken so long.'

The patient swallowed it in a single gulp and smacked his lips appreciatively. 'Who would have thought it,' he said, 'eggnog in a gangrene hospital?'

She began to laugh at the absurdity of the situation. The laugh lit up her face, and he saw what nice eyes she had – a deep blue-green that matched the ultramarine of her cotton dress.

'Can we hope to see you and the other ladies again?'

'Oh yes, I intend to look in on you again tomorrow.' She shook her honey-blonde hair and blushed slightly. 'What's going to happen to you when you get out of here, George? Will you be paroled?'

'I'm afraid not. Those days are over. I will be sent up north to a Confederate officers' prison.'

'And what will that be like, do you know?'

It was time for the stiff upper lip of an English soldier. 'I'll get by somehow, if I have to.'

'How do you mean?' His damsel was showing signs of distress.

'Once I've worked out how to get past these armed guards, I intend to escape. I don't suppose you'd be able to help me, Ann?' It was a contemptible thing to say to a grieving widow. He was exploiting her generous nature, taking advantage of her obvious interest in him. Only a cad would behave in such a way.

'Do you think you can play possum?' The question came out of the blue. 'There are dead bodies lying in the hospital's backyard. Do you think you could join them tomorrow morning, say at eight o'clock?'

'If it helps me get out of here, of course I can,' he replied, rising gingerly to his feet.

She studied him carefully. Whatever she was thinking made her blush. 'There is one problem,' she admitted. 'The corpses are wrapped in blankets but they are naked underneath. You'll have to take your clothes off.'

'Oh, that's all right,' he said, grinning broadly. 'I'll be glad to be rid of them.' He'd been wearing his calico shirt and threadbare wool trousers so long they were attracting lice. 'But what's your plan?'

A new Ann Howard emerged, a shrewd woman who could whip up an escape strategy as easily as she could make eggnog. 'Shortly after you join the corpses, I will arrive with a horse-drawn wagon, carrying sacks of potatoes for the kitchen. Once we've unloaded the sacks, the yard should be empty and you can climb into the back of the wagon and hide under a tarpaulin.'

While enjoying their new conspiratorial relationship, Grenfell felt an unexpected urge to do the right thing for once. 'You're taking an awful risk for me, Ann. What if you're caught aiding my escape? No, I can't let you do this. There's got to be another way of getting out of here.'

'But I'm not doing it for you, George. It's for the Confederate cause.' Her eyes gleamed with an intense ardour. 'We are fighting to preserve our way of life. We are fighting to repel invasion and, as we are badly outnumbered, we need every last soldier we can get.'

He had taken part in many wars but this one was different and it was the Southern female that made it so. Her fervent belief in a just conflict took his breath away. He imagined it was something to do with being a woman in what was still a frontier society. She knew what she wanted and stuck to it, dogmatically at times.

'You must let me help you,' Ann insisted. He wanted to hug her but she beat him to it, slipping into his outstretched arms and lifting her face to his. He wondered whether it was possible to kiss chastely. The sensation of skin on skin removed all possibility of choice. When their lips met, he decided innocence was never lost, but it could be given away.

When they finally pulled apart, she gave him a shy smile. 'I really like you,' she said.

'And why would that be?' he replied, making a weak joke of it.

'I've been trying to figure that out. I guess you have an unsettling effect on me.' There was a heaving bosom within her boned bodice.

'Now, kind sir, I must bid you good day.' Ann curtseyed and turned away. 'Until tomorrow at eight,' she added in a whisper.

The memory of that kiss still lingered in his mind when he woke next morning. He lit an oil lamp and forced his frozen fingers to prise open his pocket watch. It was shortly after seven o'clock. He would be joining the dead soon. Ann's escape plan seemed a lot less inviting in the cold light of dawn.

As the ranking Confederate officer he'd been given a small windowless attic which was both a blessing and a curse. He had a freedom of movement denied to other prisoners in their guarded dormitory, but to reach the hospital's backyard he needed to negotiate three flights of stairs and a long corridor without anyone seeing him. And he was expected to do so stark naked. Better get on with it, he thought, stripping off shirt and pants and stuffing them under his lumpy mattress.

There had been a heavy snowfall in the night followed by a hard frost. He could hear clumps of ice sliding across the roof above his head. His body began to shiver uncontrollably. Grabbing a thin cotton blanket off the bed he draped it around him like a Roman toga and tried to stop his teeth from chattering. Cautiously he opened the attic door.

There was a draught outside but very little light. He crept forward in the darkness wondering how the Romans ever ruled the world in such a cumbersome garment as a toga. His outstretched hand located a banister rail. Like any old house, this one made noises. The wooden stairs creaked whenever his bare feet came into contact with their well-worn centres. At each tiptoeing step he expected to be challenged but nothing happened. The guards must be asleep.

A shaft of grey light on a flagstone floor confirmed he had reached the bottom and was standing in what had once been an entrance hall. He turned left and blindly felt his way along an oak-panelled corridor towards the emergency operating rooms where he gagged on gangrene's sickly sweet smell.

He had almost reached the back entrance when two guards appeared carrying an oil lamp and bottles of sour-mash. 'Where yeh goin' now, Jethro?' the taller man slurred, lurching dangerously. 'To the shithouse, if yeh must know,' the other said, kicking open a door and stumbling inside. Flattened against the wall in his flimsy toga, Grenfell sighed with relief. In their drunken state they hadn't spotted him.

On opening the back door he was met by the full force of a Tennessee blizzard, against which his toga offered scant protection. He crouched in the doorway, unwilling to venture out onto the snow-covered cobbles. Ice stung his exposed face and he could see no further than a few feet in any direction. He would have to move. Forcing himself into the yard he tripped over a body. The dead soldier had lost his blanket. His mouth was open and his eyes stared into the unknown. Startled by this spectre, Grenfell offered up a silent prayer, as much for himself as for the man lying by his feet. How long could he survive in this freezing weather? It was time to find out. He dropped to the ground and became a cadaver, gibbering in the cold, his numb ears straining to hear a vehicle rattling into the yard.

He had almost given up hope when a welcome whinnying noise was followed by the steady clip-clopping of hooves on cobbles. It sounded as if something heavy was being dragged across the courtyard. A muffled voice gave directions. Goodbyes were said and a driver whistled and clicked his tongue to get his horses moving again.

'Right, George, now!' a woman's voice commanded.

He leapt to his feet. Through the falling snowflakes, he could see Ann staring at him from the box seat of an open wagon. 'Get in the back and cover yourself with that sheet,' she whispered urgently. Grenfell hurled himself into the cart and drew the tarpaulin over his head.

It was the beginning of a long and painful journey to freedom, bouncing up and down in semi-darkness, as the wagon jolted over ruts and ridges before finally coming to a stop.

'I think it's safe now,' Ann said softly. 'You'll find some of my husband's clothes under that gunnysack. Try them on. We won't look.'

The shirt and pants were a surprisingly good fit and once he'd unwound his filthy head bandage, she introduced him to her driver, an old black man called Lucius whose thick white eyebrows frowned at him disapprovingly. 'Jes' so you knows it, Master Grenfell, ah is a house nigger an' ah cares for this fambly and ah ain' goin' to stand by an' see this little lady come to no harm, no sir.'

'Your sentiments do you credit, Lucius,' Grenfell replied. 'I think I should get off here and be no further burden to Mrs Howard.'

'That's ridiculous,' Ann snapped. 'You need a horse and

there's one waiting for you back at the farm. And there's food too. You look as if you could do with a good meal and a decent sleep. You'll stay the night and that's final.'

He stayed for three weeks and it could have been longer.

CITY UNDER SIEGE

The three-star general swivelled around in his Windsor chair and gazed at the grandfather clock in the far corner of his cluttered office. The clock ticked away remorselessly, as if allocating the time its owner could spare for his visitor. 'Bring a chair over, why don't you, and sit down.'

'Oh, certainly,' agreed a flustered George Grenfell, searching the room for an available seat.

'There's one over there you can use. Just move those maps out of the way, would you.'

Grenfell put the maps on a side table, noticing they were stamped 'Top Secret.' A memory came back to him of his school days in Cornwall, waiting to be caned in the headmaster's study with *Caesar's Wars* tucked inside his pants.

Facing him across a different kind of desk in Richmond, Virginia, was a far greater figure of authority. Adjutant General Samuel Cooper was the senior ranking officer in the Confederate Army. Yet he was far from awe-inspiring. The man was old, well into his sixties, with tired bespectacled eyes, receding white hair and a face as pockmarked as a nutmeg grater. Although he was Chief of the General Staff, he didn't even wear a uniform, preferring to transact business in a frockcoat.

'Grenfell, isn't it?' he enquired mildly, using a forefinger to settle his head in his cravat. 'What do you want to see me about?'

'As Adjutant General I believe you handle military commissions. Major General Joseph Wheeler appointed me inspector of cavalry for the Army of Tennessee two months ago but I've had no confirmation of my appointment and no payment for the job I've been doing.'

'English, aren't you?' Cooper asked, still tugging at the inside of his collar.

'Yes, but please don't get the idea, sir, that I am a mercenary. I have been fighting for the Confederacy for ten months now without rank or pay.'

'Forgive my curiosity, but how have you got by without money?'

'I brought a quantity of gold with me from England which is now all but gone. Daily rises in the cost of living have outstripped my resources and made me beg for what I think I am entitled to.'

Instead of responding to this mild rebuke Cooper began to sift through the papers on his desk. 'Here we are,' he said proudly, untying the red tape around a bundle of documents. 'Your military personnel file is in here. I had it brought up from the vaults specially.'

Grenfell couldn't help but be impressed. He was sitting in the official archive of the Confederate war machine. What had once been a humble mechanics' institute, a seat of learning for workers in the nearby iron foundry, was now the Department of War, keeping records on a million soldiers and the problems associated with maintaining them in the field. Yet at the heart of this undertaking was an insignificant cipher of a man who had never fought a battle or commanded even a platoon of soldiers. General Cooper was the perfect bureaucrat, content to move pieces of paper backwards and forwards.

'Oh my word, this is highly irregular.' The administrator shook his head as he studied the file.

Now what have I done? Grenfell wondered. He must have found my name on that inaccurate 'killed in action' list issued after Stones River and wonders whether I'm an imposter.

With mothers and wives desperate for information about their loved ones, and no adequate system of notification, newspapers published rolls of the dead and wounded after every major battle. Unfortunately, soldiers listed as 'slightly wounded' were often in their graves while the officially 'dead' sometimes turned out to be hale and hearty. George St Leger Grenfell belonged in the latter category.

But Cooper's complaint was of a different order. 'There is no record in your file of the date of your appointment to Wheeler's staff,' he said sorrowfully. 'It seems General Bragg failed to notify this office. The paperwork simply isn't here and without it my hands are tied. I am sure you are sensible of the need to adhere to the proper chain of command.'

If he had had such a chain, he would have cheerfully wrapped it around Cooper's stiff neck. For all his eminence, the general was a dyed-in-the-wool functionary who slavishly followed rules and regulations. Such men were the bane of Grenfell's military life.

The object of his flaring hatred picked up a hand bell and rang it. 'Let us see whether Jones can throw any light on this matter. He handles my daily dispatches.'

A small, mousy man slid into the room with a worried look on his face. At the sight of his clerk, Cooper sprang into life. 'Lieutenant Colonel Grenfell, let me introduce you to our famous writer, John Beauchamp Jones. Have you read his popular novel about Daniel Boone and frontier life in Kentucky? No? Well, I recommend it to you most heartily.'

'Honoured, sir,' said the clerk, shaking hands with Grenfell. 'Your fame precedes you. We don't often meet a man who has fought all over the world as you have.'

To bring these pleasantries to an end Cooper coughed loudly. Understanding the code, Jones handed his boss a couple of letters written on manila paper. 'I'm sorry, these dispatches arrived a few days ago and should have been filed but we've been rushed off our feet with all those passport applications.'

Cooper dismissed staffing problems and his assistant with

a tired wave of the hand before perusing the letters. His mood lightened as he read. 'This puts a different perspective on things,' he said. 'Indeed it does. Wheeler says you have proven yourself to be an outstanding inspector general of cavalry and General Bragg adds a most flattering endorsement, stating that you are a meritorious and efficient officer and the soul of gallantry on the battlefield. I will forward these documents to the Secretary of War and to President Davis and I think you may expect a satisfactory outcome.'

As he took his leave Grenfell reflected on life's little ironies. He had hated being Bragg's errand boy and had betrayed his trust, yet his commanding officer had praised him to the skies. He was not, he had to confess, a particularly good judge of men. His contempt for pen-pushers had blinded him to Cooper's basic decency. The general might be pedantic but he was performing a thankless task and it was not his fault that the Confederacy was running out of money and manpower.

'May I have a word in private, sir?' John Beauchamp Jones had followed him down the staircase. 'I would ask your forgiveness for the clerical oversight,' he murmured. 'We are trying to limit the number of people who have access to sensitive information for security reasons and have been overwhelmed by the extra work.'

'Why have you needed to do that?' he asked, wondering whether Jones might be paranoid.

'Because the New York *Herald* prints such accurate lists of our military forces,' the clerk replied, dropping his voice to a whisper as a thin-faced man in an ill-fitting suit slipped past them on the stairs. 'There are Federal spies working in this office.' Grenfell thanked Jones for this confidential insight and promised to read one of his books.

As he crossed into Capitol Square he was splashed with mud by a wagon carrying wounded soldiers to the huge hospital on

Chimborazo Hill. A steady procession of oxcarts, buggies and carriages were making a similar journey. It was a doleful sight. The South was haemorrhaging its lifeblood away. This was not the future Thomas Jefferson had envisaged when he designed the elegant Roman temple that was now the Virginia State Capitol. Such a classical building was supposed to mediate between the authority of the ruling class and ordinary people's desire for a safe and secure existence – if safety was possible in a city under constant siege.

It was a hot humid day in early April and a crowd was gathering in Capitol Square. Its well-trodden grass was often used for military drills, political speeches and public meetings but Grenfell doubted whether today's rally fitted within these parameters. Hundreds of hollow-eyed women in ragged clothes, some with children, were waiting for something to happen.

His interest piqued, Grenfell sat down and watched their numbers grow. A pale, emaciated girl, who looked as if she was about to faint, joined him on his wooden bench. She raised a skeletal hand to fan her sweating brow and noticed the expression on his face. Hastily pulling down her sleeve, she said with a short laugh, 'That's right, this is all that's left of me! I'm starving. My kids are eating rats and squirrels! When there are enough of us here, we are going to the bakery to steal loaves of bread. The government can surely spare us that after taking all our men.'

'Isn't there any food you can buy?' he asked.

'Not that we can afford. A loaf costs a dollar and a pound of butter eight times that!'

It wasn't long before this assembly of thin, desperate women turned into a mob and the mob acquired a leader. Mrs Jackson, the girl told him, was the widow of a butcher in the Old Market; she was the one brandishing a meat cleaver. With the butcher's wife at the helm, the procession set off. His young companion rose unsteadily to her feet to join the long line moving towards the square's western gate. 'Goodbye,' she said, 'I'm going to get something wholesome to eat.'

'And I devoutly hope you find it,' he shouted after her, before tagging along behind, curious to see what would happen.

The mob proceeded down Ninth Street, past the War Department he had so recently visited, and crossed into Main Street. By now, there were more than a thousand protestors, all of them chanting 'Bread!' but otherwise keeping good order. That was until the Governor of Virginia had the Riot Act read, thereby provoking the very thing he was seeking to avoid. The angry women smashed store windows and stole anything they could get their hands on – food, groceries, clothes and whiskey bottles – before halting outside the Exchange Hotel where uneasy soldiers waited with primed rifles.

The women fell back sullenly but did not disperse. There was a stir in the crowd and President Davis climbed onto a beer dray to address them. This was the first time Grenfell had seen the Confederate leader in the flesh. He was a tall, thin man, strong-jawed and obviously blind in one eye, but what distinguished him most was his oratory. He had a musical, well-modulated voice and spoke in a calm and deliberate manner. He understood the ladies predicament. They had had to endure a terrible winter when food was scarce and drastically overpriced. They had mouths to feed. If they returned home now, he would do his best to ensure that food was provided at a more reasonable price.

'In the meanwhile,' Davis delved into his pockets, 'you tell me you are hungry and have no money. Here, this is all I have.' With a sudden gesture he threw Confederate dollar bills into the crowd and watched women fighting for them. When the squabbling was over, and he had the crowd's attention again, he looked at his watch and told them they had five minutes to disperse before he ordered the militia to fire upon them. Stick had followed carrot. The women melted away into the side streets, taking their looted goods with them.

Grenfell entered the Exchange Hotel and ordered a double whiskey at the bar. My first morning in Richmond, he told himself, and I've seen something as remarkable in its way as the revolutionary barricades in Paris. Yet was this bloodless riot really so extraordinary? Hens and other female birds fight to protect their young so why not women when driven to the point of desperation?

His thoughts turned, as they often did, to Rose Greenhow. How was she faring in this starving and potentially dangerous city? Here was an opportunity to find out. He asked the bartender for directions to a house on East Grace Street.

Richmond was built on seven hills like Rome, the garrulous tapster told him, and the one he wanted was where the tobacco merchants lived. Church Hill had the weight of history behind it. It was named after the church in which Patrick Henry delivered his famous 'Give me liberty or give me death' speech to the Second Virginia Convention. To get there, he should travel east on Broad Street until he reached the Twenty-Fourth Street intersection. It would be a lovely walk at this time of year. Spring had finally arrived and the gardens were bursting with colour.

What the barman neglected to mention was the other side of the urban story. Richmond may be full of fine houses shaded by magnolia and flowering dogwood trees but the streets were filthy. Grenfell had expected macadam pavements like those in London, not rutted dirt tracks that heavy rainfall and horse traffic had turned into quagmires, swallowing boots in a thick squelchy mud.

Climbing up Church Hill's steep slope at the end of a three-mile hike, he felt his age catching up with him. Leaning against a gas streetlight to get his breath back, he took a closer look at a neighbourhood that reflected the profits of a plantation economy. In East Grace Street alone, he counted six different architectural styles – classical Greek Revival, Italianate, Queen Anne, Second Empire, Federal and Colonial Revival – seeking to outdo each other in three-storey grandeur.

It came as a pleasant surprise to discover that Rose's house was a comparatively modest clapboard affair with honeysuckle growing around its small front stoop. He wiped the mud off his sky-blue pants and rang the wired doorbell. Waiting to catch sight of her, his heart jumped into his throat.

The door was opened by a young girl in a white muslin pinafore dress. She took one look at the caller, gasped in surprise, and hurled herself into his arms.

'We thought you were dead,' the child cried, fighting back tears. 'I buried you in the back garden.'

He didn't know what to say. 'I hope you gave me full military honours, Rosie.'

'I did my best. I made a wooden cross and carved your name on it – George the Dragon Slayer.'

'What made you think of that?'

'You promised to slay dragons for me when last we met. Not that there are any dragons, are there? But there are plenty of Yankees that need to be fought. Would you like to visit your grave?'

'Absolutely, but perhaps I'd better pay my respects to your mother first.'

'Sure, I'll take you to her.' Rosie grabbed Grenfell's hand and led him into a white-painted entrance hall with rooms going off on either side of a central staircase. She made for one on the right shouting, 'Guess who's come to see you, Mamma.'

He could hear the soft hum of female voices as he walked down the passage. Rose Greenhow was framed in the doorway, wearing a black velvet and lace dress with a tight buttoned bodice and a full, bell-shaped skirt. He had imagined how she

93

would look: those deep-set eyes and striking features framed by silky black hair tied into a low chignon at the nape of her neck. What he hadn't pictured was the incredulity stamped on her face.

She held out her hands to him. 'Lazarus has risen,' she murmured huskily. 'You were listed among the dead in the *Examiner*. That was three months ago. We'd given up hope.'

Grenfell bent to kiss her trembling fingers. 'I am sorry to have given you even a moment's grief, Rose, but, as you see, I am well and in one piece.'

'Thank God,' she said. 'But do come in. There's someone I'd like you to meet.'

He was shown into a comfortable parlour furnished with sofas and a rocking chair. Heavy curtain swags framed the small-paned sash windows and American primitive paintings added colour to the whitewashed walls. But what took his eye was the large statesmanlike portrait of Jefferson Davis hanging above the mantelpiece.

A polite cough drew his attention to a woman standing almost behind him. She was the paradigm of a Southern lady; fashionably turned out in a purple day dress with gored skirt.

'Oh dear, I am forgetting my manners.' Rose sounded agitated. 'This gentleman is Colonel George St Leger Grenfell, an English officer who charged with the Light Brigade at Balaclava. And this is my dear friend, Mrs Mary Chesnut, who is a confidante of our beloved president.'

Grenfell bowed stiffly. 'Delighted to make your acquaintance, ma'am,' he said with a flourish.

'The pleasure is all mine, I assure you.' For a middle-aged woman, Mrs Chesnut spoke with a light, girlish voice. She had dark eyes and an ironic smile.

'You've arrived at just the right moment, Colonel Grenfell,' she added. 'Rose and I were discussing the merits of Jane

Austen's book *Pride and Prejudice* and we could use an English perspective. Why do Jane and Elizabeth Bennet stand by and watch their foolish mother spoil their silly youngest sister? In America that would never happen. The superior minds in the family would bring boy-crazy Lydia into line.'

She was testing him. 'You're quite right, ma'am, there is a cultural difference here. In England, a parent's word is final but in a new democracy like America children can say what they think.'

Rose clapped her hands in delight. 'Well said, George.'

Mrs Chesnut would not allow herself to be bested. 'That's all very well, Colonel Grenfell, but when you were a boy in England I do not see you submitting easily to parental authority.'

'Ah, but I did. Although I wanted to join the army, my father made me work in his bank in Paris and I did his bidding.' And bankrupted him into the bargain, he thought bleakly.

'We should celebrate George's resurrection,' said Rose, aware of a developing battle of wills in her drawing room. 'I believe I still have a bottle of Thomas Jefferson's favourite wine. Have you ever drunk Madeira, Mary?'

'Not since my days in Charleston. The boarding school I went to stored the wine in a specially heated cellar. As I recall, Madeira has high levels of acidity and sugar and a caramel flavour but you can't get it now. The Yankee naval blockade has seen to that.'

'I managed to secrete a bottle in my luggage when I left Washington. Now where did I put it? Is it still in the trunk?'

'No Mamma, it's in the small pantry. Shall I get it for you?' Rosie spoke up, eager to please.

While the little girl hunted for the precious bottle of wine, the ladies sat down on an antimacassar covered sofa and Grenfell lowered himself into the rocking chair. The small talk took a familiar turn. 'We had hoped your government would support our freedom struggle, if only out of self-interest. Do you not miss our cotton?'

Grenfell contemplated the question. Even intelligent Americans were insular in their attitude. 'Of course Britain wants to trade with America but she is very conscious of the North's rapidly developing economy. She is standing by, watching your Kilkenny cat fight, waiting to see who comes out on top. She can afford to do this because of the Indian cotton she is importing.'

'What can we do, George, to change this policy?' Rose wanted to know.

'General Lee must cross the Potomac and achieve a shattering victory in the North. Nothing less will do.'

'Let us hope that happens soon,' Rose replied. 'On to Washington must be our motto.'

'I believe you can't go there while the war continues. Wasn't it a condition of your parole, Rose?'

'I do not feel bound by any Yankee document, Mary. Not after how they treated me.'

'It must have been truly terrible, my dear. All that time exposed to view in prison with those leering sentinels watching you. No woman would like the mysteries of her toilette laid bare to the public eye. I don't know how you put up with it.'

'But you still have friends in Washington, don't you?' Grenfell interjected.

'No friends, only mortal enemies. Instead of loving the old flag of the Stars and Stripes, I see in it only the symbol of murder, plunder, oppression and shame.'

Rosie came back with a hand-blown bottle and a corkscrew and was rewarded with a small glass of wine herself – for medicinal purposes, her mother said. She was taking her first tentative sip when there was a loud knocking on the door.

'That must be Madame Bonheur. Let her in, my darling.'

'Do I have to, Mamma; can't the beastly French lesson wait?

'It's no use pulling a face, young lady. It is important that you should be proficient in French.'

Rosie said nothing, but downed the rest of her Madeira in a single gulp before running off to open the door for her French tutor.

'Did you learn French as a girl, Mary?' Rose asked.

'Indeed I did. My father sent me to Madame Talvande's School for Young Ladies in Charleston where I exceeded Madame's expectations in the conjugation of French verbs and the art of repartee.'

That explains a lot, Grenfell thought, as he smiled politely at Rose's vain friend.

'You were luckier than I was,' Rose said wistfully. 'Then again, how few girls receive a proper education? They are taught drawing and watercolour painting, encouraged to play the piano and sing at parties, chiefly for the benefit of gentlemen. As women are allowed none of the aspirations for which an enlarged education is considered requisite, that education is denied them so that they may remain docile and subservient.'

'You are so right, my dear. Even with wealthy, progressive parents and a vigorous nature the best a woman can hope for is to be free upon sufferance. My father-in-law was one of the wealthiest planters in the South with more than four hundred slaves but I was never happy at Mulberry, preferring the pleasures of the urban salons. That I could enjoy such a life was due to my husband James's political career and, I suppose, to God seeing fit to leave me childless.'

Rose's eyes dropped. 'Whereas I had eight children and lost five of them. As women, we learn to live with tragedy. Grief is the price we pay for love.'

Grenfell was shocked. He had thought of Rose as having had only one child and her maternal brooding worried him.

'Have you read Harriet Martineau's book *Society in America*?' he asked.

'Of course we have,' Mrs Chesnut replied scornfully. 'Your British writer thought the condition of American women only differed from that of slaves in that they were treated with more indulgence.'

'I have mixed feelings about that book,' said Rose, cheering up. 'I liked Martineau's observation that the principles of the Declaration of Independence bore no relation to half the human race. On the other hand, she talks of slavery being "a reign of terror" and I can't abide abolitionism.'

'You said earlier that your in-laws possessed a large slave plantation, Mrs Chesnut. Does that influence your opinion on the issue?' Grenfell asked tongue-in-cheek.

'Why should you suppose it would?'

She was prevaricating, he thought. 'I imagine you might see the advantages of a system that created your husband's wealth.'

'It has always seemed natural to my father-in-law. Old Colonel Chesnut is like the emperor of Austria. His métier is to be an autocrat, a prince of slaveholders. His forefathers paid good money for their slaves. They are his by divine right, he thinks.'

'But what do *you* think of the institution of slavery?'

'You are very persistent, Colonel Grenfell. If you must know, I hate slavery. It sickens my soul. I am mighty sorry to part company with you on this issue, Rose, but I hold slavery to be a monstrous institution. Seeing old patriarchs living in one house with their wives and black concubines and the mulattoes that exactly resemble the white children – surely that can't be right.'

'But you didn't grow up on a plantation, did you, Mary? Slavery was part of my upbringing. My father owned slaves, as did his father before him. Every family of distinction in the South owned slaves. Condemn slavery and you condemn the

South. Lincoln claims this is a war to end slavery. Do you believe that to be the case, George?'

He took a deep breath before answering. 'I share Charles Dickens's opinion that the Northern onslaught upon slavery is no more than a piece of specious humbug designed to conceal its desire for economic control of the Southern states.'

'On that we can all agree,' said Rose with feeling. 'I think people's hatred for the Yankees has deepened since that human beanpole signed the Emancipation Proclamation.'

Mrs Chesnut nodded her head in agreement. 'As you can see, Colonel, we talk of nothing but the war, as we watch our world, the only world we care for, kicked to pieces.'

'I witnessed a bread riot on my way here,' Grenfell remarked.

'I'm not surprised,' said Mrs Chesnut. 'Galloping inflation is destroying our society. And the newspapers don't help by attacking ladies for lolling back in their landaus while poor soldiers' wives are on the sidewalks. There is no room for class hatred in a city where even gently nurtured women are forced to wear ill-fitting shoes, such as Negro cobblers make. We are all down on our uppers.'

Rose shook her head. 'That may be the situation, Mary, but I think we have to admit that Richmond possesses a unique social structure. In the rural South class is based on slave and land ownership, but here in our capital city class is determined by birth and what is called "good breeding". That is why the snobbish ladies of Richmond shun me.'

There was no humbug about Rose Greenhow, no pretence, and Grenfell admired her for it. Ever since their first meeting he had wondered about his infatuation for her. There was, of course, a strong physical attraction but it was more than that. No, her glory lay in a rare combination of beauty, bravery and blinding honesty. But there was something else too, a steely, unswerving determination to get her own way, and it was this that worried him. Once she had achieved her goal, would she be satisfied or move on to something new? Rose was an enigma, a *femme fatale* who embraced motherhood, a complex and mercurial woman whom he could never control or fully understand. His relationship with her was almost certainly doomed to failure.

'It is undoubtedly true,' Mrs Chesnut was saying, 'that our great ladies disapprove of a strong-willed, independent woman, Rose. Instead of praising your heroic work in Washington, they question how you attained your information. But you have friends in Richmond, most notably President Davis who doesn't care a jot for such idle gossip. Why, he even found this house for you to live in.'

'And we are grateful for our home, although I think we must soon share it.'

The conversation turned to how Richmond was coping with the rising tide of wounded soldiers flooding into the city. They were coming by train, wrapped in bloody bandages with missing limbs, requiring instant medical attention. The big Chimborazo and Winder hospitals were taking the bulk of these patients while the rest were being placed in care homes set up in churches and private residences. Amputations were having to be carried out without anaesthetic and severed arms and legs were piling up all over the place, as were the coffins waiting for burial at Oakwood Cemetery. Beds, blankets, bandages, medicines and trained nurses were all in short supply.

'I am a poor caregiver,' Mrs Chesnut admitted. 'I visit patients, dress their wounds, arrange their pillows and read their letters, but I am far too squeamish to assist with amputations.'

Rose was working in a private home where twenty-five patients were being treated. The odours were sickening, she said, and some of the volunteer helpers weren't up to the job. 'They try too hard. A zealous young woman approached one of my patients and asked if she could bathe his face. "Yes, miss," the soldier replied wearily. "It's been washed a dozen times already today, but do go ahead."'

Mrs Chesnut also had a hospital story to tell. 'Did you hear what Phoebe Pember did? She's the chief matron of Hospital No 2 at Chimborazo. Well, to protect the hospital's whiskey barrel from a bunch of thirsty ruffians, she pulled a pistol out of her pocket and took a shot at them. They beat a hasty retreat, I can tell you.'

Grenfell was beginning to warm to Rose's friend. At least she had a sense of humour.

Mrs Chesnut looked at her fob watch. 'Oh, my goodness, is that the time. I must be off to the Wayside Hospital, if only to apologise for my last visit when I swooned at the sight of blood. Hopefully I can get there without having to witness another funeral procession. I am sick of hearing the Dead March from *Saul*. Such a mournful dirge! Make sure it isn't played over you, Colonel Grenfell.'

'I'll do my best,' he promised, kissing her outstretched hand.

'Let me see you to your carriage.' Rose led her out of the parlour.

No sooner had they left the room than Rosie rushed in, her cheeks flushed, as if she had been running uphill rather than grappling with the intricacies of French grammar.

'I heard the door closing,' the girl whispered. 'Has she gone? Good. I don't like her. She's too proud of herself.'

'That's a terrible thing to say, little Rose.' Her mother had re-entered the room. 'Mrs Chesnut has been a good friend to us. What will Colonel Grenfell think of such an outspoken girl?'

That he knows who she takes after, was what he wanted to say but didn't.

'You don't mind, do you, George?' Rosie pouted and fluttered her eyelashes.

'What I'm wondering is what you've done with Madame Bonheur.'

'Oh, her. She's preparing my next lesson which is English poetry. We're studying the Romantic poets Keats and Shelley. She's given me a ten-minute break while she sorts herself out. I want to show George my treasures, Mamma. Please say yes, you won't have to scold me again. I'll be as good as gold, word of honour.'

Rosie took Grenfell into a homely kitchen with whitewashed walls in which a large, sturdy table was the primary work surface. It was centrally placed with storage furniture, a sink and a cooking stove around the perimeter of the room. 'We've just had this stove installed,' she enthused. 'It's the very latest thing. Can you believe it, George, one scuttle of anthracite coal will keep it running for a whole day? We can bake bread and pies in the oven and cook a turkey in the tin roaster at the front.'

'You seem to know a lot about this, Rosie. Do you help with the cooking?'

'When Mamma lets me. This is the best room in the house. It's like an old smock. It's comfortable and warm. We make soup and biscuits with all these utensils.' She pointed to the well-stocked cupboards and the open shelves on which copper pots and pans vied for space alongside pastry cutters, jelly and pie moulds and biscuit tins.

The girl picked up one of these tins and placed it on the kitchen table. 'This is where I keep my favourite things. I'll show you my calotype first,' she said proudly, taking a faded photograph out of the container. 'This is my father, Robert Greenhow. The picture was taken in the early fifties when he was in San Francisco. It's a bit blurry I know.'

Compared to other photographic processes, a calotype lacked clarity due to its semi-transparent paper negative. Its advocates claimed that this not only reduced the exposure time of the image but softened the appearance of the human face.

Grenfell could see no sign of that in the stiff features staring back at him.

'I never met my father,' Rosie said with a sob. 'He died when I was only a few months old.'

'A sad loss,' he murmured.

'Tell me George, how can you miss what you've never had?'

It was a grown-up question for which he had no answer. 'So what have we got here?' he asked cheerfully, poking his hand in the tin and bringing out a yellowing piece of paper.

'Oh that, it's the Cuban purchase note.' Rosie explained that the letter had been written to her mother by former president James Buchanan when he was minister to the court of St James. In it Buchanan described how, in 1854, the United States government had offered to buy Cuba from the Spanish for $130 million while secretly planning to seize the island if their monetary offer was rejected. If it served no other purpose, this indiscreet letter revealed Rose Greenhow's political influence in antebellum Washington.

'I would like you to look at these,' Rosie said, fishing some scraps of paper out of the box. Each piece of notepaper contained a resolution. On one fragment a childish hand had scribbled 'I must eat less', on another 'I must learn six new French words every day' and on a third 'I must be kind to the peg-legged man who delivers the coal'.

'I make bushels of good resolutions every week,' she explained.

'But do you keep them?' he asked.

'No, I'm afraid not. I long to be a better person but I don't seem to have the time for it and the coalman is an irritating old man who doesn't blow his nose properly.'

She hadn't finished yet. Next he was handed a piece of rag paper that someone had signed. 'That's Dolley Madison's autograph,' she said proudly. 'Mamma says I'm her great-grandniece. Dolley is one of my heroines like Joan of Arc.'

'What have they got in common? I'm pretty sure Dolley Madison wasn't burned at the stake.'

'No silly, they were both patriots. Dolley rescued Washington's portrait from the beastly British.' Rosie's hand flew to her mouth. 'I'm so sorry, George, the British aren't beastly. At least you're not.'

To cover her confusion, she gave him a recent newspaper cutting from the *Daily Enquirer*. The story was about how Rose Greenhow's daughter had uncovered a Union spy. The man had disguised himself in a Confederate uniform and was having dinner in the American Hotel on Richmond's Main Street when she spotted him.

'Unfortunately he got away. He took to his heels before I could summon help.'

'How did you know he was a Yankee?' he asked her.

'I'd seen him before. He'd come to stare at us in our Washington prison. In any case, I can spot an enemy agent a mile off.'

Rosie pointed through the kitchen window to one of the finest mansions on Church Hill. 'I'm sure Crazy Bet is one. She lives in that big house there.'

'How did she get that name?'

'I guess because she dresses like an old witch and talks to herself all the time. But she's putting on an act. There's nothing the matter with her. Mamma says her real name is Elizabeth Van Lew and she's very rich. Men visit her at night and stay in that third-floor attic. I've seen them come and go.'

Her interest in the neighbour's espionage waned as Rosie took a leather-bound book off one of the kitchen shelves. It was a copy of James Fenimore Cooper's best-selling novel *The Last of the Mohicans*.

'This is my favourite book. I've read it three times,' she said proudly.

'I've also read it. Which is your favourite character?' he asked.

'Oh, La Longue Carabine of course.' She was referring to Hawkeye, the frontier scout with the long rifle, who protects Colonel Munro's daughters from the Hurons with the help of the Mohicans, Chingachook and his son Uncas.

'It's an exciting story. I particularly like the fact that Hawkeye and Chingachgook are blood brothers.'

She gave Grenfell her sweetest smile. 'Will you be my blood brother, George?'

'If you wish it,' he replied, somewhat startled by the question.

'I mean the full ritual in which we exchange blood through cuttings.'

'Why me?' he asked.

'One should only enter into a blood relationship with someone who is of real worth because more than blood is exchanged: each person receives part of the other's spirit.'

Rosie opened a drawer in the table and took out a sharp knife. 'I have read that one of the safest places to make a cut is the outside of the upper arm, well away from veins and arteries.'

She had begun to roll up the right sleeve of her dress when Grenfell stopped her. 'There's no need for that. We can prick our thumbs and make them bleed.' He took the knife from her and drew blood with it; blood that intermingled when the pierced fingers rubbed up against each other.

Once the knife and the biscuit tin had been stored safely away the new blood brother and sister returned to the drawing room to find Rose darning one of her daughter's dresses.

'Madame Bonheur is ready for you in the playroom, my love,' she said. 'Run along now.'

'Will you still be here when I've finished my lesson?' Rosie asked her secret sibling.

'I'm afraid not. I've got an appointment in town. But I will be back to see you very soon.'

'Make sure you are. Ah well, to Keats I go! "Season of mists and mellow fruitfulness ..." Drat! I can't remember what comes next.'

'"Close bosom friend of the maturing sun."' He recited the line without thinking.

Rosie threw her arms around him and gave him a big hug. 'Bosom friends, George,' she cried.

'Always,' he replied as she trotted off to join her French tutor.

There was an awkward silence after the young girl disappeared. Rose put down her needle and thread and beckoned for him to join her on the settee. Alone at last with the woman he had come to see, Grenfell hardly knew what to say. He apologised for arriving out of the blue. He'd been training General Wheeler's cavalry in Tennessee when told to report to Adjutant General Cooper's office at the Department of War.

'That slowcoach,' she said witheringly. 'What did he want with you?'

Grenfell explained the mix-up over his promotion and how it had been resolved. The good news was that he would be staying on in Richmond because Wheeler wanted him to turn Camp Lee into a national training centre for Confederate cavalry.

'Do they need to be trained?' she asked. 'I thought our cavalry was better than the Yankees.'

'And so they were, at the start of the war. Every Confederate trooper owned his own horse and brought it with him into service. Our boys knew how to ride. But things have changed since then. Enemy artillery fire for one. We must rethink our tactics.'

'That sounds rather prosaic. I thought a cavalry officer was a chivalrous figure, all glitter and romance.'

'I did too, Rose. As a boy, I read about knights with plumed helmets and shining armour, rescuing fair damsels. But that was just make-believe. It's the grim realities of war I have to deal with now.'

He glanced at the clock on the mantelpiece and winced. 'Oh dear, I'm supposed to be discussing cavalry plans with General Robert E Lee at the New Fairgrounds at five o'clock but I'm never going to get there on time, not on foot. "My kingdom for a horse!"'

'There's a livery in the next street, George. I know the stableman. He'll take care of you.'

She gave him a quizzical look. 'How strange you should quote from Shakespeare's *Richard III*. Would you like to see the play with me?'

He could hardly believe his luck. 'Of course I would,' he replied, 'if it's at all possible.'

'I'm getting tickets for the opening night on April 11 in Grover's Theatre.'

'I suppose that's one of Richmond's theatres?'

'No, it's actually in Washington.'

He stared at her in open astonishment. 'If you're caught, they'll throw you back into prison. And with you gone, what'll become of little Rose?'

'An old friend of mine will look after Rosie for a few days. There's a Confederate agent up there I must see. Will you come with me?'

He laughed aloud, enjoying the absurdity of the invitation. 'Of course I will. It will be a great adventure. But you will need to disguise yourself.'

'I'll wear a blonde wig and the kind of low-cut evening gown Mary Lincoln has popularised in Washington. I'll fit right in. How about you? What will you wear?'

Grenfell thought for a moment. 'I'll dress as a Wall Street banker having a naughty night out.'

'And what does that outfit look like?' Rose chuckled.

'I was thinking of a dark frockcoat, embroidered waistcoat and grey striped pants.'

But how were they going to cross Union lines in their finery? Had she thought of that?

Rose gave him a terse answer. 'In a balloon, George.'

A STRANGE JOURNEY

The reluctant passenger peered at the earth below him and felt giddy. He was suspended in space and, at any moment, he might be tipped out of this large picnic basket and fall a long way to his death. If man had been meant to fly, he would have been given wings.

Rose was saying something. Her voice sounded distant and distorted. 'Isn't this feeling of weightlessness wonderful? It's like floating on air.'

They were indeed floating beneath a huge multi-coloured silk balloon whose nonporous bag contained thousands of cubic feet of hydrogen. Don't worry, he had been told, a balloon basket is a very stable platform. The centre of gravity is in that great swelling sphere above your head. Yet these assurances were of little comfort to someone with an inherent fear of heights.

Grenfell cursed his inner frailty. He had envisioned a slow, careful seduction of the beautiful woman by his side but how could he appear masterful when his body was shaking. Rose may be in her element but he was not. He was not meant to be up here. Like Icarus, he had flown too high and would come crashing down. Even in the gathering gloom he could see that his knuckles had turned white from grasping the edge of the basket too tightly.

The sympathetic Confederate signals officer had also noticed this. 'Would I be right in thinking you are feeling insecure, Colonel Grenfell?' Porter Alexander ventured. 'You are not alone, sir, by no means. When I was a cadet at West Point, I had a serious fall over a cliff and after that I suffered from vertigo. Inside of me was this blind terror that if I got too close to the edge, then something would take over and I would just step off into space. You can imagine how I felt when General Lee ordered me to be a balloonist. The first time I went up I was in a blue funk until I realised how much protection the basket afforded me.'

Grenfell gazed at Alexander with respect, mixed with fear. 'I'm sure it does,' he lied, not wanting to reveal his weakness. 'I've got an upset stomach, that's all.'

Rose rubbed up against him. 'Oh dear, my dashing hero is flesh and blood after all.'

He could feel himself responding to her touch. Rose had taken his measure. She knew he was seeking carnal knowledge and seemed quite relaxed about it. So here he was; a weak-kneed aeronaut with lecherous intentions, having a panic attack in a swaying basket while listening to the object of his desire discussing wind speed and velocity with their travelling companion.

She had talked of balloons ever since their chaotic early morning meeting at the train terminal. A further trainload of casualties had just arrived at Richmond station. Railway officials were dashing around trying to direct stretcher-bearing medical orderlies to the hospital wagons while wounded soldiers, in wheelchairs or on crutches, jostled for room on the main platform. The train from which they were disembarking was scheduled to travel north again to Lee's military camp at Fredericksburg.

Even as Grenfell barged his way towards their carriage, Rose insisted on talking about ballooning. Her enthusiasm for the subject knew no bounds. 'Almost anything is possible in a balloon, George. If there is a mountain, I can pass over it; a river, I can cross it; I can fly high in the air, sometimes close to the earth. Ballooning will lead to aerial warfare and could be a great aid to spying.'

To deflect her discourse, he had suggested that her days of

espionage might be over. Spies had to remain anonymous to be effective and almost everyone had heard of the notorious woman whom Abe Lincoln had had to lock up because she knew more about his cabinet meetings than he did himself. Her response to his clumsy flattery took him by surprise. She had undertaken this assignment, she said, because of its inherent news value. Their balloon flight would make a great story for the Richmond press. It would add fresh lustre to the legend of the patriotic Southern belle who outwitted the Northern war machine and bolster the morale of those who fought so valiantly for the Stars and Bars.

'This is a serious mission,' she added, as the train moved off. 'We have to see whether our reconnaissance balloons can be used to drop spies behind enemy lines. I think you'll like our balloonist. Colonel Alexander is not only a signals officer; he's head of our spy network and he's had considerable success in gathering information about troop movements. But most of his agents are just enthusiastic amateurs, like I was when I was sending messages from Washington. What we need now are properly trained operatives and we must find ways of getting them into the North. That's what we're testing out today.'

It was, in Grenfell's estimation, a harebrained notion, but the more she talked, the better he understood her. Rose could hear ancestral voices calling out to her. Her forefathers had fought for their freedom against savage Indian tribes and British and French invaders. She was proud of the revolutionary blood in her veins and of the plantation culture it had given rise to. 'Now it's my turn to fight for what I believe in.'

She told him about the tragedy that had scarred her childhood. After a heavy day's drinking in a tavern near their Maryland plantation, her father had been found dead by the side of the road. John O'Neale had been in the company of his favourite slave Jacob who was later hanged for his murder.

111

'I know what you're thinking, George. You are thinking my father was a drunk and that his black slave was found guilty by an all-white jury. Both of these things are true but the fact remains that Jacob crushed his skull with a stone. Not that I blame him for that, any more than I blame Eve for eating from the tree of knowledge. The serpent is to blame, the snake-like Northern abolitionists who have been putting ideas into the black man's head ever since Britain abandoned the slave trade.'

Rose paused to see what effect her words were having on him. 'Where do you stand on slavery?' she challenged him. 'You say you believe in our cause but do you believe in slavery?'

He had known she would get round to this sooner or later. 'Put like that, Rose, the answer has to be no. I've seen forms of slavery all over the world, wrapped up in different guises. In India, it's called the caste system, in China it's the Manchu household people. Here it's a whole way of life which is easier to understand but still morally repugnant. When the war began, like many of my countrymen, my sympathies lay with the North. But that was soon replaced by an admiration for the gallantry and determination of the Confederacy, together with revulsion at the bullying conduct of Northerners who seem hell-bent on destroying the livelihood of the Southern states in order to free their slaves. Ultimately, I believe in self-determination, Rose, that's why I'm on your side.'

It was a stumbling statement but it had the desired effect. 'What's at stake here is control,' she explained. 'Ever since Jefferson's day plantation owners have dominated American politics as surely as they have dominated the American economy. To the North, slavery is a symbol of Southern domination while to us it's a question of our identity.' She rested a hand on his arm as she spoke and he felt a physical connection. The spectre of intimacy quivered between them.

As the train rattled over the rusting, single-track line Rose peered out of the grimy carriage window at the ravaged Virginian countryside and sighed deeply. 'And I looked, and beheld a pale horse: and his name that sat on him was Death, and Hell followed with him.' He could see what she meant. Massive armies had collided here during the past two years, stripping the forests, burning the homesteads, trampling the fields, leaving trenches and rifle pits gaping like open wounds in the ground. 'These are locust years and no mistake,' he replied, also drawing on the Book of Revelation.

When the train stopped at a track pan to replenish its water supply she gave him another slice of her family history: how difficult it had been for a widow with five young daughters to run a failing plantation on her own and how the O'Neales had fallen heavily into debt. Eventually, her mother reduced the number of mouths she had to feed by sending two of her children, Ellen and Rose, to live with a married sister in Washington.

Aunt Maria ran Hill's Boarding House near the Capitol. Her boarders were mainly congressmen and judges and, even at the tender age of fourteen, Rose was encouraged to eat her evening meal with the guests and to join them afterwards in the drawing-room. Her aunt realised men liked the company of a pretty young girl, particularly one who was bright and flirtatious. Exposed to a steady stream of political talk, Rose learned how things were done in Washington; the importance of backroom manoeuvring and of knowing the right people. She also discovered how to use her sex appeal. It didn't matter how distinguished a politician might be, he could still be beguiled by a tiny waist, a fluttering eyelash and a heaving bosom.

Rose spoke of erotic beauty as if it was a commodity to be traded on the open market. 'A woman should take advantage of what God gave her, George. Men cannot be overpowered or outthought but they can be manipulated. Not that I'd want you to think I'm a completely heartless and conniving female. I loved my husband Robert dearly and I adored Senator John C Calhoun who was for many years my friend and mentor. He taught me that freedom of speech was my birthright, signed and sealed by the blood of my forebears.'

The legendary politician from South Carolina, who served as vice president under John Quincy Adams and Andrew Jackson and secretary of state under President Tyler, was one of Hill's regular boarders. Calhoun was a tall, austere man who rarely smiled but that hadn't put Rose off. She treated him like a father, talking and corresponding with him. 'I used to sit in the visitors' gallery when he spoke in the Senate,' she explained. 'He was a superb orator with a wonderful silvery voice and his speeches made perfect sense to me.'

Calhoun eloquently expressed what Rose and many Southerners held to be true: that liberty and equality, the core values on which the nation was founded, related only to white folk. He argued that slavery was essential to the Southern economy and opposed any political attempt to protect Northern manufacturers by taxing imported goods on which the South relied. In his eyes, such tariffs were unconstitutional. Yet, for all his misgivings, Calhoun was an optimist who believed in the eventual triumph of civilisation over barbarism.

'But do you know what, George? A decade ago, when Calhoun was dying of consumption and I was nursing him, he lost confidence in the future. I remember him telling me the day would come when the Southern states were no longer comfortable remaining in the Union and would seek to go their own way. I'm glad he didn't live to see this though!'

The train had reached the outskirts of Fredericksburg and was passing through a squalid camp where thousands of homeless civilians were living under canvas or in temporary log cabins. Beside the track, an emaciated workforce of black and white refugees armed only with shovels were trying to dig drainage channels in the unyielding earth.

'These people aren't going to last long out here,' said Rose sadly. 'Look, they haven't even got proper sanitation. It's a toss-up whether disease or starvation finishes them off first.'

A piercing whistle sounded and with a screech of brakes and a fierce clanking of pistons, the steam locomotive jolted to a halt. They had reached their destination. Beyond the railway station lay the town of Fredericksburg, now under military occupation and sweltering in the late afternoon sun.

Waiting on the platform was their contact, Colonel Porter Alexander, an earnest young man with keen eyes and a heavily bearded face, who bent low to kiss Rose's hand.

'Let me take those.' Alexander pointed to the carpetbags Grenfell was carrying.

'Thank you kindly, but I can manage,' he replied stiffly, his manhood under threat.

Rose made the introductions, but as soon as she had done so Alexander set off at a brisk pace along the platform. 'I've brought a buggy to take us to our military camp at Hamilton's Crossing. There is no time to lose. The breeze is getting up. It's a south-westerly, thank goodness, perfect for our purposes. The balloon is being inflated as we speak. We'll leave just before dark.'

'How are things up here?' Rose asked politely.

'Not good at all. Another big battle is looming and there's a lot of sickness around. General Lee is indisposed and has had to leave his house-tent. Hooker's army is only a couple of miles away across the Rappahannock River. The Yankees staged a huge military parade for our benefit. I guess it was designed to frighten us.'

General Lee's winter camp was in a forest clearing. There were tents everywhere, apart from a small area that had been reserved as a launching pad for an enormous balloon made of bolts of different coloured dressmaking silk. 'Where did you get the material from?' Rose asked. 'I've heard that patriotic Southern ladies donated their summer dresses to form a patchwork.'

Alexander laughed. 'No, the truth is far more prosaic. The balloon is a chemist's creation.' Dr Cheves had bought up all the silk he could find in Savannah and Charleston, sewed the pieces together and varnished them with molten rubber to make the silk gas tight.

'You're looking at a very strong envelope containing thirty thousand cubic feet of hydrogen,' Alexander added. 'Welcome to *Gazelle Two!*'

'What happened to the first *Gazelle*?' Grenfell wanted to know.

'It was captured a few months ago while being carried back to base on a tug boat. What we cannot do, I'm afraid, is take one of these machines with us on our flight.' He pointed to the portable generator that had just finished pumping gas into the balloon.

'Now for the gondola,' he said. 'It must be securely attached to the ground, to make sure the balloon doesn't take off on its own. The ropes are being checked now.' The signals corps completed their safety examination of the basket and gave Alexander the thumbs up.

An aide approached holding a curious contraption. It consisted of four hemispherical cups, mounted on horizontal arms, soldered at equal angles to each other on a vertical shaft. The cups were whirring away like miniature windmills. Alexander took the instrument from his orderly. 'This is my anemometer,' he said proudly. 'It measures wind speed. What we've got is a six-mile-an-hour tailwind. I think we should get going.'

The young colonel went first with the luggage. Grenfell scrambled in after him so that he might have the pleasure of lifting Rose into the gondola's three-foot-high wicker basket. 'You are too kind,' she said huskily, obviously enjoying the physical contact.

Alexander gave the order to cut the ropes. The balloon instantly leaped into the air. Grenfell's heart lurched. 'How high will this go?' he asked nervously.

'That depends on the amount of gas in the balloon and the weight you are carrying. I'm aiming for a thousand feet. If we want to come down from that height, I'll pull a rope and let some of the gas out of the bag. If we need to climb higher, I'll have to throw something overboard. No, not you, Colonel; those bags of sand near your feet are the ballast.'

This was the first time Grenfell had ever looked down on the world. Viewed from above, everything seemed neat and tidy. 'How do you navigate a course?' he asked, seeking reassurance.

'You can decide when to start in a balloon and usually when to stop. The rest is down to nature. How fast you go and what course you follow depends on the wind. But that is also true of a sailing ship. Indeed, there are many similarities between a balloon and a ship at sea.'

Grenfell shook his head. 'I don't accept your analogy. A balloon is not like a ship in the ocean, whatever you may say. Air is much less dense than water, in which, moreover, a ship is only half-submerged. The captain of a ship can steer a better course than you can up here. It seems to me that we are at the mercy of the prevailing winds and air currents.'

Alexander beamed at him. 'I warrant you'll have a better opinion of balloon travel once this trip is over. Now, a word of warning. We should be over Aquia Creek in a few minutes' time. There is a big Federal camp there and they've got artillery so we can expect to be shot at.'

Grenfell drew in his breath. In his lectures on cavalry tactics he often talked about the need for more than one battle plan.

Yet, up here in the clouds, there didn't seem to be any plan at all and could only suppose that inviting Yankee gunners to shoot at the balloon's gas-enhanced rubber bag was not part of one.

'Are we already off course?' he asked with feigned calmness.

'No, not at all. We must cross the Potomac somewhere and there are Federal camps all along the coastline. We're taking the most direct route. Running the gauntlet, you might say.'

The breeze began to pick up. Grenfell wrapped himself in his thick wool overcoat. 'This balloon is a big target. What are our chances of escaping unscathed?'

Alexander gave him a condescending smile. 'Pretty good, I'd say. It will soon be dark and the Yankees aren't expecting us. We will have flown by before their artillery is ready to fire. As for the infantry, last I heard they were still using muskets that haven't the range to hit us but, as a further precaution, I'm going to take *Gazelle* higher.'

Grenfell helped Alexander throw bags of sand overboard and watched as the balloon rose gracefully to an altitude of fifteen hundred feet. His young companion could scarcely conceal his excitement. 'Look, there's the Potomac River up ahead, and down below us is the landing on which Hooker's Twelfth Corps are camped. I wonder if they've seen us.'

At this height soldiers seemed no more than ants, but judging by the way they were scurrying around in confusion it looked as if they had spotted the balloon. Flashes of gunfire and a trail of fuse-smoke confirmed the impression. But no bullet or shell came anywhere near them.

'There, you see, nothing to worry about.'

Scores of seagulls settled on *Gazelle*'s silken surface as it flew over the coastline. In his heart of hearts Grenfell knew the balloon's specially prepared cloth couldn't be damaged by a bunch of gulls, but the sight of these wretched birds scratching away with their sharp claws was still a cause for concern. He had entered a psychological drama, he thought, a waking nightmare, which lacked any solid foundation.

'I don't like the look of those thick cumulus clouds,' he said. 'I think we're in for a downpour.'

'That's odd. It was supposed to be a fine evening.' A note of uncertainty had crept into Alexander's voice.

'But you don't have accurate forecasts, do you?' The pettiness of his motive dismayed him.

'And you do, I suppose.'

'Yes, there are daily weather bulletins in *The Times* newspaper.'

A bright flash of forked lightning illuminated the night sky, thunder rumbled in the distance and gusting rain and sleet heralded the gathering storm.

Alexander bent down and extracted a black umbrella from a pocket in the gondola. 'Sorry, you're going to need this,' he said. His face seemed unnaturally pale in the fading light.

'Do you know why this is happening?' Alexander's words were snatched away from him as the wind strengthened ominously.

'I think so,' Grenfell replied. 'Sometimes on a hot day you get a breeze moving from cooler water towards the hotter land mass and when this collides with a prevailing wind moving in the opposite direction it forces the air upwards creating rain bearing clouds that can trigger a thunderstorm.'

'How do you know so much about the weather, George?' Rose was struggling to keep hold of the umbrella in what was quickly becoming a gale force wind.

'I was once on a voyage with Admiral Robert FitzRoy who was the first man to accurately predict the weather. He taught me a lot about meteorology. For instance, I know that heavy rainfall generates a downdraft, so hold on tight!'

Caught in a spiralling movement of cold air, the balloon

began to plummet downwards. Alexander threw more ballast overboard to check their descent. 'We should be rising soon,' he shouted above the crashing rain.

'But we're not,' Grenfell yelled back in alarm.

Rose lost her battle with the umbrella and watched helplessly as it soared off into the night. Her bonnet soon followed, torn away by the wind, and her long hair wound about her neck.

'Do you want us to throw our luggage overboard?' she shouted. "Is it time for that?'

Alexander shook his head. He could hardly make himself heard above the shrieking wind. 'Not yet,' Grenfell lip-read, 'we're still at a thousand feet.'

Although a thick vapour hung over the surface of the river, they could hear the crashing of the waves. *Gazelle* was spinning like a top, seized in a whirling vortex that drenched the balloon's passengers in flying spray. Hailstones fell from the towering thunderclouds and a lightning flash revealed the broad expanse of water below them, choppy breakers whipped into whitecaps.

Alexander was panicking now. He jettisoned the last of the sandbags and all the passenger luggage. However, despite his feverish efforts, the balloon continued to spin and fall. Lightning flashed overhead and, briefly, night became day. They were heading for a giant whirlpool; a funnel of hissing swirling water rotating in clockwise eddies that looked big enough to swallow them up.

'It is too late,' Rose cried out, 'too late for everything.'

Grenfell expected to see fear in her eyes but found calm acceptance. We're not going to die, he wanted to tell her, but the words wouldn't come.

With a loud crack the heavens opened. The balloon jolted violently and they landed in an undignified heap in the bottom of the wicker basket. As Grenfell struggled to regain his feet he felt the balloon begin to rise again and saw to his horror that they were being propelled upwards on a huge rotating pillar of water rising out of the seething river. A roaring, hissing waterspout had taken hold of them. They had exchanged one watery grave for another.

The balloon lurched abruptly, causing him to lose balance and fall on top of Rose. 'Forgive my clumsiness,' he yelled, as if he could do anything about it.

'Decorum doesn't exist here George,' she mouthed, trying to keep her composure.

It was only then that it dawned on him that a miracle had occurred. The balloon had detached itself from the spout and was floating free. He pulled Rose to her feet and, shivering in their drenched clothes, they hugged one another.

Her voice registered disbelief. 'What the hell was that?' she asked.

'That's what they call a waterspout,' Grenfell explained. 'I saw one in the South China Sea twenty years ago. It's a freak of nature. A spout can rise two thousand feet before disintegrating. The Roman naturalist Pliny likened it to a monstrous beast with sinews formed out of thick water vapour.'

'Well, he was right about that,' Alexander conceded. 'I've heard about boats being destroyed by waterspouts in the Potomac. We've had a lucky escape.'

'Now that that's over, can we get back to business?' Rose snapped, impatiently dismissing their near-death experience. 'Have you any idea where we are?'

Alexander looked pained. 'Well, the plan was to land at Piscataway in Prince George's County, Maryland, but I guess we've drifted well to the south of that in the storm. Not to worry though. We've got the rest of the tidal basin to cross and the offshore wind will bring us back on course.'

'Let's hope so,' Grenfell shook himself like a wet dog, wondering how the signals officer could possibly be so confident.

After what seemed like an eternity on a cold night, Alexander announced that they were flying over Indian Head. 'We'll reach our destination in about an hour.'

'Well done, Porter,' Rose said admiringly. Grenfell felt a twinge of irrational jealousy.

'What were you thinking about back there when we almost lost our lives?' he whispered to her.

It was too dark to see her eyes but he felt them boring into him. 'I thought that if I was to die I couldn't have chosen better company,' she murmured.

Alexander let some gas out of the bag by pulling on a rope and, as the balloon began its descent, a light flickered ahead of them. Gradually, it became more solid and, as they got nearer, they could see the flame was coming from a burning torch that was being waved backwards and forwards to guide them to a safe landing place.

'That's our man down there. Prepare for landing!' Alexander started to pull ropes like a church bell-ringer causing *Gazelle* to tilt over at an angle of forty-five degrees. This, the pilot told them, was to help the basket lose speed and come to a halt when they reached ground level.

'Landings can be quite bumpy,' he warned.

The basket hit the dirt road with a bone-shattering thump and skipped forward before coming to rest on its side with its passengers lying on top of each other in their capsized wicker cage.

'I've heard of people kissing the earth on returning to their native country but not like this,' Grenfell grunted, spitting mud out of his mouth.

'And as a well-bred Maryland girl, this wasn't how I'd envisaged our relationship developing, George,' gasped a winded Rose, wriggling beneath him.

Strong hands sought to disentangle them. 'Have you out of there in a jiffy, ma'am.'

Once they had been helped to their feet, the bedraggled travellers were introduced to their helper. Elbert Grandison Emack hardly lived up to his fine-sounding name. He had a weather-beaten old face and was dressed like a farmer in a sack coat and a soft felt hat.

'Don't I know you?'

'Yes, Mrs Greenhow, we were neighbours in Washington many years ago. I lived in K Street and owned the retail store on Capitol Hill.'

'Of course, Hodges and Emack, wasn't it? I remember the wonderful slogan outside your store, "We supply your needs from beans to bread and pots to pudding cloths." I used to shop there. But wasn't it burned down?'

'That it was. We upped sticks and moved to Locust Grove in Beltsville, where I started a truck farming business.'

'Lucky for us he did,' Alexander intervened. 'Farming offers a perfect cover for our kind of work. It's made him the best damned courier in the state. Isn't that so Elbert? Why, only last week he sold his early-season greens in a Washington street market and bought a wagonload of manure in which we could hide a whole pile of parcels and correspondence. No Yankee soldier was going to examine such a fragrant cargo.'

'Aw, shucks, Porter, it weren't nothin' to speak of,' the wizened vegetable grower said modestly. 'I've got the horse and cart with me down the road. I'll go fetch 'em.'

While he was doing that, Alexander deflated the balloon and rolled the silk up so it would fit into the wicker basket. When Emack returned, they hauled the basket into the back of the wagon and invited Rose and Grenfell to sit on its tailboard for the short ride to the village of Piscataway.

'I don't know about you, but even my bruises are getting bruised,' Rose whispered to her English companion as the cart went over another pothole. 'I'll be mighty glad when this is over.'

'Wherever we're going, I hope they've got a fire.' Grenfell shivered. A breeze was blowing and his wet clothes had dried on him.

'Poor George, I think I can promise you that. We're going to a Confederate safe house.'

'It's an inn called Harbin House, named after one of our most important agents,' Alexander said over his shoulder. 'Elbert and I will leave you with him while we see to this balloon.'

Their host was warming himself in front of a roaring log fire when they arrived. Thomas Harbin was a small man of stocky build in a single-breasted knee-length frock coat and baggy woollen trousers who had a surprisingly loud voice and bright eyes that were never still.

'A real pleasure to meet you, Mrs Greenhow. You are a heroine, ma'am, a true Southern lady.' Harbin could turn on the charm.

His low bow was met by Rose's curtsey. Her dress brushed against the sawdust-strewn floor. 'I thank you, sir, for your generous words.'

As the pleasantries continued Grenfell's eyes wandered across the candlelit room. It was certainly cosy enough with a low-beamed ceiling, lattice windows, wooden panelled walls, an inglenook fireplace and a large centrally placed wooden table already set for dinner.

The chiming of a standing clock caused Harbin to break off his conversation. 'Good heavens! It's one o'clock in the morning and we haven't offered you anything to eat yet.'

The compact spy rang a hand bell. 'Mrs Steuart has stayed up to cook for us,' he explained.

Grenfell was glad to hear it. Their last meal had been the sandwiches he'd bought from a platform vendor in Richmond and his tummy had begun to rumble. He wondered idly what the cook might look like, imagining a little old lady in a pinafore offering them chops and cherry pudding.

He couldn't have been more wrong. Clad in a vermilion day dress, Mrs Steuart turned out to be tall and slim with perfect cheekbones and the kind of creamy skin and soft eyes that would make any red-blooded man think of hot nights and cool sheets.

'Would you like to begin with Maryland oysters? They're really good,' Harbin enthused. 'But maybe not to an English gentleman's taste.'

'Why should you think that?' Grenfell asked, anxious to sample Mrs Steuart's molluscs.

'We were taught that the first English settlers thought oysters a very common food indeed.'

'We'd love to have some oysters, Mrs Steuart,' said Rose, settling the matter.

Their exotic-looking cook nodded politely and left the room to fix the food.

'Drusilla is Creole,' Harbin explained. 'She's the daughter of a Georgian plantation owner and a Jamaican slave. We call her Mrs Steuart although she's not actually married to Major General George Steuart. She started living with him after his wife died.'

'I've heard of Steuart', Grenfell said. 'Isn't he the cove who wanted Maryland to secede from the Union and, when it didn't, he joined the Confederacy at the ripe old age of seventy-one?'

'That's the man,' Harbin replied. 'They said he was too old for active service but Steuart wouldn't hear of it. Told our High Command he had fought the English at Bladensburg when Robert E Lee was still in short pants and he was damned well going to have a crack at the Yankees.'

The inn door swung open and a cold wind blew in. Standing under the lintel was a willowy young dandy with wavy brown hair and a very disarming smile. He was sporting a flamboyant silk waistcoat, riding breeches and a pair of tall leather boots.

'Hello everyone,' he said. 'The name's Walter Bowie. I've

ridden seventeen miles to get here; passed a couple of patrols without being stopped.'

'Meet Walter.' He's Maryland's answer to Wild Dick,' Harbin told them.

The blank looks that greeted this remark made him realise that further explanation was needed. 'Wild Dick was a female impersonator who worked the Mississippi riverboats a few years back. When the need arises, Walter can also turn himself into a fine filly – begging your pardon, Mrs Greenhow.'

'You must be Captain Bowie,' said Rose, 'who escaped from Washington's Old Capitol Prison the night before his execution.'

The young man bowed. 'That's right. I was about to be shot as a spy. The guards were bribed to leave my cell window open and I shinned down a rainspout and got away on a horse.'

'Tell them about your visit to Bald Eagle.' Harbin pulled out a chair for his friend.

Bowie sat down and began his story. 'I was crossing the lower Potomac with plans I'd stolen of Washington's fortifications when I got myself captured again. One of the guards tried to handcuff me, but as he struggled with the bracelets I snatched his gun, shot him and escaped in the confusion. After a bit of a chase, I decided to lie low at Bald Eagle, a plantation belonging to one of my kinsmen, Colonel Waring, but my pursuers followed me there and threatened to burn the house down. I was about to make a dash for it when one of Waring's daughters took me into the kitchen, blacked my face and hands with boot polish, gave me a slave dress to wear, a bandana for my head and an empty milk pail to carry, and out I sashayed through the Union lines, a slave fetching water from the well.'

'He didn't have a droopy moustache then or he'd never have passed muster,' Harbin chuckled. 'What about the other time you pulled the same trick?'

'You mean when I was cornered in the Newman house? On

that occasion, I wore a wrapper dress with a sunbonnet and carried a basket of eggs and a live chicken through a squadron of soldiers. One of them propositioned me but I told him my name was Chastity and I aimed to live up to it.'

'Quite right too,' said Rose, trying to keep a straight face.

As the laughter subsided Mrs Steuart returned with a large bowl of oysters and a jug of beer. 'Jus a word,' she trilled in patois. 'A beg yuh to come and eat now.'

Once his guests were seated at the dinner table, Harbin asked the cook whether she'd heard from her husband. 'No sir,' she replied. 'Mi warned the chupid mon about fighting at his age but he paid no heed. Now he gone and got himself locked up after that battle at Manassas, maybe for good.'

'I'm sure it won't be that bad, Drusilla,' the kind-hearted Harbin assured her. 'You'll see him again real soon, mark my words.'

Mrs Steuart gave him a wan smile. 'Mi step out yah and baste the turkey.'

Harbin swallowed an oyster and smacked his lips in appreciation. 'While I'm thinking of it, I should give you your theatre tickets for tomorrow and tell you a suite has been reserved at the Willard Hotel in the names of Mr and Mrs George St Leger. Here's some greenbacks to pay for your accommodation and other necessities.'

The Confederate agent handed over the tickets and a thick wad of United States bank notes. 'There's two hundred dollars there,' he said. 'That should be enough.'

'Absolutely,' said Grenfell pocketing the notes. 'That's capital.'

Rose gave him a knowing look and hid her mouth behind a table napkin.

'Forgive me for mentioning it, but you don't seem to have any luggage.'

Grenfell explained that they had had to throw their

carpetbags overboard when Alexander's balloon was in danger of falling into the Potomac.

'So what are you going to wear at the theatre? Buying new clothes in Washington could be a risky business.'

Rose nodded in agreement. 'It would indeed, but don't worry Mr Harbin, I made contingency plans before coming here. I can assure you that George and I will be properly attired.'

Grenfell stared at her in admiration. He was still marvelling at her foresight when Captain Bowie asked him whether he did intelligence work.

'No, not clever enough for that,' he replied, shucking his last oyster. 'I'm just a cavalry inspector with General Wheeler.'

'George is being too modest,' said Rose. 'He's a war hero and those are Robert E Lee's words.'

'I wouldn't doubt that for a moment ma'am, but, unless I miss my mark, your escort is an Englishman. What's he doing fighting on our side when his country refuses to recognise us?'

'I regard it as an honour to serve in the Confederate Army.'

Bowie raised an eyebrow. 'Whatever you may think, I am not a mercenary,' Grenfell added defensively. He was sick and tired of being questioned about his allegiance.

The young dandy found this amusing. 'No one fighting for us could possibly be doing it for the money when our currency devalues daily.'

Before anything more could be said, Mrs Steuart reappeared with a wooden platter. The sight of her succulent, beautifully browned turkey drew a round of applause from the four diners. Colouring slightly, she curtsied and retired.

Harbin did the carving and handed round the plates. The room was cosy in the candlelight, and full of cheerful talk and laughter. As they ate, Harbin described his work as an agent in Maryland. Before the war he had been the postmaster in Charles

County and had set up a spy ring that involved local landowners and a slave-holding doctor called Mudd. Since then, he had visited every part of the state disguised as a travelling salesman. 'Thomas Wilson peddles snake oil and insurrection,' he said with a shallow laugh.

For all his apparent boldness and bonhomie, Bowie also preferred to work alone. The state of Maryland, he said, was full of liars and rogues ready to betray a loose-tongued spy to the authorities. His activities centred mainly on a tiny hamlet called Surrattsville where his principal agents were another local postmaster, John Surratt Junior, and his inn-keeping mother, Mary Surratt.

'I hear Mary is planning to move into the boarding house she owns in Washington. Her eyes and ears will be sharper there, I warrant,' said Harbin, winking to his colleague.

'That beats all!' Bowie smote his brow in mock disgust. 'I'd almost forgotten what brought me here in the first place. I was in Washington two days ago – yes, that's right, dressed as a washerwoman – and one of my sources told me Union cryptographers have finally cracked our Vigenère cipher. They know we've been using "Manchester Bluff" as keywords. I hope you'll pass that on to your agent, Mrs Greenhow.'

Although fascinated by talk of codes and ciphers, Grenfell could feel his eyes closing. He looked at the clock on the wall and saw it was almost three in the morning.

Rose, too, was struggling to keep awake. 'It's been a long and eventful day, gentlemen,' she said. 'Now, if you'll excuse me, I'd like to lie down for a few hours before the stagecoach arrives.'

'We have a bedroom ready for you, Mrs Greenhow,' said Harbin. 'It's upstairs, next to mine. Let me show you to it.'

'What about George? Where's he going to sleep?' she queried.

For once Harbin looked slightly agitated. 'I'm dreadfully sorry, Colonel Grenfell, but I couldn't get you a room here.

Perhaps you can doze in front of the fire. There are plenty of logs in the hearth.'

'I'll be taking my leave too,' said Bowie. 'It's a long ride back to Upper Marlboro.'

The room emptied and Grenfell was left alone, huddled in his overcoat, sitting as close to the fire as he could get. He had hoped to spend these precious hours in bed with Rose but it was not to be. Perhaps he'd have better luck in a Willard Hotel four-poster.

His hands roamed over her eager body, discovering the softness of her skin and the silkiness of her loosened hair. He slipped the nightdress off her shoulders…

'Wake up George! It's gone nine o'clock and the stagecoach is already here.'

He opened his eyes and saw Rose smiling down at him. 'Judging by the look on your face,' she said mischievously, 'you were having a marvellous dream. I wonder what that was about.'

'Who knows,' he grunted, rubbing the sleep out of his eyes.

'There's a wash bowl and a pitcher of water in my room if you want to freshen up before breakfast. It's being served in the bar.'

'Don't we have to be on our way?'

'Not yet, the stagecoach driver is having a meal while his horses rest up. It's a five-hour journey into Washington.'

'Are you eating, Rose?'

'Goodness me, no.' She wrinkled up her nose at the idea. 'I can't stomach beef steak and boiled ham at the best of times, let alone after last night's turkey.'

Her fellow passengers were less abstemious and more than an hour went by before they were ready to move. Nine people clambered into the Concord coach's narrow interior alongside the sacks of mail. In an age when propriety required a lady to maintain a dignified deportment, Rose found herself interlocking knees with the bald businessman sitting opposite, while Grenfell lurched into her whenever the carriage wheels encountered a fresh obstacle in the dirt track.

'Not exactly comfortable, is it?' Rose murmured. 'My spine is jarred every time we hit a bump.'

The only shock absorption came from the thick leather belts beneath the carriage. It was, in effect, a cradle on wheels. Grenfell might have told her that if he hadn't been choking on the dust blown through the coach's open windows.

'I was led to believe that the Concord was a luxury vehicle. Surely it should have glass windows,' Rose complained.

'Glass would probably shatter on this rough terrain,' he wheezed.

The stagecoach came to a juddering halt. They had reached a road block and a blue-coated cavalry officer opened the carriage door and asked for identification. Now we're in trouble, Grenfell thought, as he searched for the leather wallet in which his English passport was pasted.

'Your name is George St Leger Grenfell,' the man said sneeringly, 'and what might you be doing in these parts?'

'I'm an arms salesman,' he said, improvising wildly. 'My company makes repeating rifles.'

'And who is this lady beside you?' the soldier asked.

'This is my French wife, Hortense, and, as you can see, she is travelling on my passport.'

'All right. I just hope your rifles work better than the ones we've got.'

The Union officer moved on to look at other passports. Rose squeezed his hand. 'Well done, George,' she whispered in his ear. This was the first of three military inspections. Because of its strategic location, Maryland was full of Union troops on the lookout for Confederate spies and sympathisers, but, much to their relief, the bogus couple passed muster at each stop.

It was early afternoon when the stagecoach finally rattled across the wooden Navy Yard Bridge and entered Washington. America's capital had become a military encampment. There were soldiers everywhere. Howitzers, sandbags and cement barrels surrounded almost every classical building and the place stank to high heaven. To make matters worse, swarms of mosquitoes flew through the open windows of the coach. Rose lashed out at the tiny bloodsuckers with her gloved fist. 'This is George Washington's fault,' she said grimly. 'Our first president chose to build the capital on top of a swamp. He wanted to be close to his Mount Vernon home and didn't care how humid and unhealthy it got in spring and summer.'

Grenfell thought Washington's most striking feature was the number of black faces in its crowded streets. Lincoln's Emancipation Proclamation had made it a gathering place for freed slaves, many of whom worked as labourers in the city.

'Bet you've never seen so many free niggers before,' said the bald man with the over-active kneecap. 'I'm a pro-slavery Democrat from New York City,' he told Grenfell. 'As an industrialist I object to the new Federal Draft Law which forces white workers to fight in this here nigger war.' 'Hear, hear,' said a ferret-faced, pale-skinned man in a dark suit. Emancipation may have ended slavery in the North but it had done little to eradicate racial prejudice.

The coach pulled up outside Willard's, a large six-storey building on the corner of E Street and 14th Street. The capital's pre-eminent hotel was a meeting place for Washington's power brokers. 'Lots of senators and congressmen have rooms here,' Rose told him, 'and fall prey to all the place-seekers and petitioners in the city.'

On entering the lobby, he saw what she meant. A heaving mass of humanity in top hats, derbies, kepis and forage caps were talking loudly and spitting tobacco juice onto the badly stained hotel carpet. Littered with dirt, scraps of paper and cigar stumps, the reception area looked more like a railway station than a celebrated hostelry offering its guests 'the last word in luxury'. Holding on to Rose, Grenfell pushed his way through the glad-handing crowd and gave his name to the concierge at the front desk.

'Delighted to have you staying with us, Mr St Leger,' the young man gushed. 'We have put you and your wife into our Presidential Suite. The Lincoln family used it before his inauguration. I'm sure you'll be comfortable there.' He rang a small bell. 'One of our porters will take up your luggage.'

Grenfell was about to explain that they didn't have any bags when he caught sight of Rose waving to a young woman who was sitting on a high-backed sofa guarding a round-topped leather trunk. 'Hold on a minute,' he said. 'I think our luggage may have arrived. If you'll just …'

The girl waved back and rose to her feet. With a cry of delight Rose rushed over to embrace her. Grenfell picked up their room key and followed her across the lobby. She had tears in her eyes as she turned towards him. 'George, I'd like you to meet one of my dearest friends, Lizzie Fitzgerald. Lizzie was my maid in Washington when I was under house arrest. She did so much for me.'

'We did get up to some strange shenanigans and no mistake,' Lizzie said laughingly. She spoke with a soft Irish voice and had an open, friendly face and an easy smile.

'Do you remember Pinkerton's agent, the one with the smooth tongue who tried to make love to you in the hope that you would betray me?' Rose asked.

'I certainly do. Conor Ryan thought he'd kissed the Blarney Stone but I led him a merry dance. He took me for sentimental walks and gave me all kinds of inducements, but it didn't avail him none.'

'Did he leave you alone after I was imprisoned?'

'No, I'm afraid not. When you were arrested, the Union soldiers kicked me out of the house and he was waiting for me in the street. He dragged me to a nearby inn where he had a

134

room, saying he was going to finish what he'd started, and would have done so if it hadn't been for this gentleman here who was working behind the bar.'

A thick-set individual in an ill-fitting brown suit appeared at her side. Grenfell noticed the cauliflower ears, the pugilist's thick brow and how well balanced the man was on his feet.

'Let me introduce Pat Flannery, former All Ireland bare-knuckle champion and saviour of my virtue,' Lizzie announced proudly. 'He beat Ryan to a pulp, so he did.'

'We are very grateful to you, Mr Flannery,' said Rose. 'I hope we can rely on your discretion, sir?'

'You certainly can, Mrs Greenhow. Mum's the word, as the English say.' The mildness of Flannery's manner was out of keeping with his formidable frame.

'Have you always lived here, Flannery?' Grenfell asked.

'No sir, I was born in Cork. If it hadn't been for the famine I'd not have left the Emerald Isle but then I'd never have met Lizzie, so it seems that things work out for the best.'

'Done any fighting in America?'

'Oh, bless you, yes. Plantation owners used to hire me to take on their black slaves down in Mississippi and then I had a big prize fight in Kent County, Maryland against the American champion John C Heenan which lasted six hours until he battered me senseless. I gave up after that and invested the money I'd made in a Washington pub. That's where Lizzie came into my life.'

Lizzie's pale face lit up and her blue eyes sparkled. Typical Irish colouring, Grenfell thought, as he watched her smoothing down her green calico dress. 'Pat's here to do the fetching and carrying,' she said, as if her beau's presence had to be justified. 'Your Saratoga trunk is too heavy for me to lift, Mrs Greenhow. I've packed a lot into it. There are evening gowns, cosmetics and perfumes, a blonde wig and two of your late husband's suits for

Colonel St Leger to try on. That's all we could find in the dark.'

'I'm surprised you found that much.' Rose patted her hand. 'How did you get into my house?'

Lizzie giggled. She obviously loved intrigue. 'Pat and I broke in at the dead of night. Here we were, a couple of bad eggs, lurking in a fashionable street, four blocks from the White House, and we could see the neighbours' lace curtains twitching. There were soldiers in the vicinity so we dared not light a lamp. The moths had got at one of your dresses which I've tried to repair as best I could. I'm a seamstress now so I hope you don't mind.'

'Of course I don't mind.' Rose stifled a yawn. 'Forgive me, my dear, it's been a long journey and I'm rather tired. Perhaps Mr Flannery will carry the trunk upstairs for me.'

'And I'd like to come too,' Lizzie said. 'Perhaps you'll let me lay out your clothes and help you with your toilette. It will be like old times.'

With that agreed, Flannery picked up the trunk and the four of them took Willard's big steam elevator and hissed up a couple of floors to Parlour No 6. This palatial corner suite consisted of two bedrooms, a marble bathroom, a lounge with armchairs, and a large dining area with a varnished hardwood floor.

'This must cost a pretty penny,' Grenfell murmured in Rose's ear. 'Why didn't Harbin find you something cheaper and more discreet?'

'The rooms were booked on Porter Alexander's instructions. He called it misdirection. Where would you least expect to find a well-known Confederate spy in Washington? He thought the answer would be here in the Presidential Suite. And whether he's right or wrong, I certainly intend to take advantage of his generosity by having a hot bath.'

Flannery undid the trunk's leather handles and took out its compartment trays for Lizzie's inspection. The Irish girl picked out an oilskin sponge bag and carried it into the bathroom, turning on the tub's hot water tap as she did so. Returning to the trunk, she selected a black lace negligee for Rose to wear after she'd got undressed.

It was time for the men to leave. 'Something tells me we're not wanted here, Flannery. Shall we go and get a drink downstairs? I noticed a bar on the ground floor.'

The Round Robin & Scotch Bar was a sight to behold. It was full of good-natured drunks, purple of nose and moist with perspiration, eyes luminous with whiskey or rum, trying to sell goldmine shares and railroad bonds, and posses of newspaper journalists seeking interviews with state governors and two-star generals. The noise was deafening as everyone talked at the same time.

Flannery elbowed his way to the bar and whistled loudly for service. Exchanging nods with people he didn't know, Grenfell followed him to the counter.

'Bedlam, isn't it?' said a silver-haired old man who was drinking on his own. 'This is truly the temple of Mammon, Washington's hub, where you encounter pompous politicians, office seekers, wire pullers, confidence tricksters and jaded writers looking for inspiration.'

'And which category do you fit into?' Grenfell asked a trifle rudely.

'Oh, I belong to the last category. I am a struggling wordsmith currently earning my keep by writing an article on our great capital city for the *Atlantic Monthly*.'

Grenfell noticed his companion's high forehead and sharp observant eyes. 'Forgive me for saying this, but you don't belong here.'

The old man laughed. 'On the contrary, it contributes greatly towards a man's moral and intellectual health to be brought into habits of companionship with individuals unlike himself and, judging by your accent, I fancy you might be one of those.'

'I'm what you Americans call a merchant of death, an English arms salesman. The name is St Leger, Colonel George St Leger, at your service.'

'Then we are indeed very different. My name is Nathaniel Hawthorne and I live in Concord, Massachusetts, home to such distinguished authors and transcendentalist philosophers as Ralph Waldo Emerson and Henry David Thoreau.'

The light of recognition dawned in Grenfell's eyes. 'You are too modest, sir. You are a famous novelist. Your *Scarlet Letter* is a modern classic.'

'You are very kind, Colonel St Leger. What did you make of my book?'

'Well, for a start, I found it easy to read.'

'Easy reading can be damn hard writing!'

'As I turned the pages I came to sympathise with your fallen woman Hester Prynne who is so harshly treated by the Puritans. I saw your novel as an indictment of a censorious, cheerless religion.'

'Quite right, Colonel. Perhaps we are more alike than I thought. Hester's public shaming allows me to explore New England's lingering taboos. Time may fly over us but it leaves its shadow behind.'

'You speak with great feeling, Mr Hawthorne. Are there shadows in your life?'

'You are too perceptive to be a salesman. One of my ancestors, John Hathorne, was a presiding magistrate in the Salem witch trials. I added a "w" to my surname to distance myself from him.'

Hawthorne had disowned his ancestor. The thought ricocheted around inside Grenfell's brain, reminding him of how he'd been disowned by the father he bankrupted. George Bevil Grenfell had been forced to sell the family home and seek lowly employment in an iron works in Wales. The prodigal son had tried to bury the past by making a career as a soldier of fortune. But by then his father was dead and past caring. Besides, personal bravery wasn't enough. It didn't begin to make up for his character flaws: the casual amorality, rootless drifting and rank bad judgement.

'I read a very unsettling short story of yours, Mr Hawthorne, which made a big impression on me. It described an intermediate space between sleeping and waking.'

'Oh, you mean *The Haunted Mind*. I wrote that long ago.'

'I was particularly struck by what you had to say about an individual's responsibility for his actions and how he tries to hide away from them.'

'In the depths of every heart there is a tomb and a dungeon,' Hawthorne recited from his own book, 'though the lights, the music, and the revelry above may cause us to forget their existence.'

Hawthorne broke off when he saw a fresh glass of whiskey standing in front of him on the bar. Flannery's patience had finally paid off.

'Let me introduce my friend, Mr Hawthorne. Pat Flannery was once a famous bare-knuckled champion and is now an eminent Washington publican who appreciates the good things in life.'

'That's bunkum,' said the self-effacing pugilist. 'I'm not important, never was.'

Hawthorne smiled and shook his head. 'Every individual has a place to fill in the world, and is important, in some respect, whether he chooses to be so or not. You've only to look down the bar to see a man who thinks he is mighty important. The Natick Cobbler is holding court again.'

A group of journalists with notebooks had gathered around a squat clean-shaven man whose elegant three-piece suit failed to conceal a substantial paunch. The forceful way he dealt with the newsmen's questions, punching the smoke-filled air when he spoke, testified to his powerful rhetoric.

'He doesn't look much like a cobbler to me,' Grenfell said.

'That's what we called him in Massachusetts. You'd never think it to look at him now but he started off as an indentured farm labourer. He was born Jeremiah Jones Colbath but changed his name back in '33, migrated to Natick and became a cobbler. After that, there was no stopping him. The shoemaker got into politics.'

'I know him,' said Flannery. 'That's Senator Henry Wilson. He sometimes drinks in my pub.'

'Yes, he likes the odd drink and yet he claims to support the temperance movement. Wilson believes in having things both ways. He's a happily married man and a philanderer on the side. He was once a pacifist, yet now, as chairman of the Senate Committee on Military Affairs, he runs the war machine. But what I can't stomach about the man is his rabble-rousing abolitionism.'

'Coming from Concord I would have thought you would be anti-slavery and regard John Brown as a national martyr.'

'Not a bit of it.' Hawthorne gulped down his whiskey. 'Nobody was ever more justly hanged than John Brown and I sincerely hope his soul doesn't go marching on, although I fear it might do. Unlike Senator Wilson and his crowd, I do not find this a noble war. My chief feeling is one of infinite weariness. I want the end to come, and the curtain to drop.'

'Do many people think like you?' Grenfell wanted to know.

'No, not many. This is a popular war to end slavery but in my eyes it's a questionable conflict. I cannot share the wartime pieties. Battlefields seem empty of meaning. A bullet offers a pretty little orifice through which the tired spirit might seize the opportunity to be exhaled! What do you think, my Irish friend, is emancipation worth so many dead bodies?'

Flannery took his time before answering. 'Irish Americans are afraid of the flood of liberated slaves marching into the

North to oust them from their jobs by accepting lower wages. Principles are fine but they don't put food on the table.'

Hawthorne nodded in agreement. 'That's true. There's always an economic argument.'

The sound of a throat being cleared was followed by a booming voice. 'Forgive me for interrupting you, but I thought you might like to take a look at these.' A stranger had sidled up carrying a portfolio of plans, drawings and financial calculations. He was smartly dressed and of grave demeanour but what caught the eye was the quantity of hair on display above the jutting heights of his collar. He had cultivated enormous side whiskers that connected to a huge bushy beard and moustache. 'You look like the kind of gentlemen who would appreciate a good business proposition,' he rumbled. Above the bristling splendour of his facial hair, his eyes were unnaturally bright, as if he had seen a vision and simply had to share it.

'I have here a prospectus for the Union Pacific Company which is constructing a railroad to run from the Missouri River to the Pacific. When it's built the United States will have the largest market in the world. Settlements will spring up like strings of pearls along the track. Corn, wheat and cattle will replace open prairies and the buffalo. The railroad is a sure-fire winner and I can offer you thousand-dollar shares in its construction. Buy thirty of these and you will own a mile of railroad in Kansas or Utah and, according to my projections, the value of your holding will treble in the next twenty years. It's the opportunity of a lifetime!'

The bewhiskered seller of dreams tried to hand Hawthorne a prospectus. 'Sorry,' the writer said. 'You've come to the wrong person. I couldn't afford to buy ten yards of track, let alone a mile. Why don't you go and talk to that man over there? He's backing your railroad.' He pointed to Senator Wilson who was still giving interviews at the bar.

Once he had gone, Hawthorne began to laugh. 'That, my friends, was a typical Washington swindler. Our bearded prophet is stock watering.'

Flannery shook his head. 'Can you explain that to a simple Irishman?'

'Sure I can. He and others like him buy large quantities of stock to inflate its value and then sell the stock on at an unrealistically high price. He learned the trick from our farmers who let their cattle get real thirsty and then fill up with water just before they hit the scales to be sold by weight.'

'Faith, it's a wicked world we live in.'

'Talking of which, I must leave you now,' said Hawthorne. 'I've got an appointment on Capitol Hill to see Senator Howard of Michigan about a bill he's sponsoring to hold fraudulent government contractors to account.'

Grenfell was thinking about beards. They had been banned in the British Army until the Crimean War when freezing winter temperatures and a lack of shaving soap led to a softening of the rules. Since then, fighting men had grown luxuriant whiskers to assert their masculinity and the fashion had spread to London where 'dundrearies' and 'Piccadilly weepers' were in vogue. But, for all their popularity, British beards couldn't hold a candle to those of their hairy American cousins. It was as if the safety razor had never been invented.

'Before you go, Mr Hawthorne, I wonder whether you could satisfy my curiosity on a particular matter?'

'Of course, pleased to be of service in any way I can.'

'Can you explain why American men are so hirsute?'

Hawthorne eyes twinkled. 'That's a complicated question,' the writer said, self-consciously fingering his own droopy salt-and-pepper moustache. 'Firstly, I think it's because we are a young nation. We have to do things bigger and better than anyone else. Then there's the frontier spirit. Rugged men heading out into untamed territory, living with nature, unable to shave and growing large beards – they're modern heroes and heroes tend to be imitated. And, believe it or not, there is also a medical reason. Some doctors argue that beards filter out germs before they can get into the nose or throat.'

'Well, that takes the biscuit,' Grenfell chuckled.

'Yes, it does sound rather far-fetched,' Hawthorne agreed. 'Then there's the contrary view that shaving can be dangerous.'

'You mean cutting your own throat by mistake?'

'No, it's the risk of infection. Whatever else you do, you must keep your razor scrupulously clean. My good friend Henry David Thoreau lost his brother to a shaving accident. The poor man nicked himself with a dirty razor and died of lockjaw. And on that thoroughly depressing note, I must take my leave. It has been a pleasure talking to you gentlemen, and I don't often say that. If you're ever in Concord look me up at the Wayside.'

Hands were shaken and Hawthorne departed to collect more information for his magazine article. When he had gone Grenfell turned to his Irish companion. 'Another drink, Pat, before we go back upstairs? I want to hear all about your fight with Heenan.'

An hour later, and rather the worse for wear, they returned to Parlour No 6 where, to their surprise, the ladies were having afternoon tea. Rose was wearing a pink-and-black ribbed day dress with a white lace collar and looked particularly beautiful. Her long black hair was held by combs at the side and tied to the nape of her neck with a knot.

'Where did you get the food from?' Grenfell asked her.

'I reminded the manager that we were staying in the Presidential Suite and requested the same consideration Willard's had shown Abe Lincoln and his family.'

'I hope you remembered to put your wig on when you met the manager.'

'Of course I did. I'm not a complete fool.'

Grenfell cursed under his breath. What a stupid thing to say to a woman who didn't like to have her competence questioned.

'We met a writer in the hotel bar,' he said brightly. 'Have you heard of Nathaniel Hawthorne?'

'Naturally,' she retorted icily. 'He wrote *Tanglewood Tales* and *The Marble Faun*. A bit of a recluse, they say.'

'Well, we didn't find him so. He was a most amiable conversationalist, save when he talked about the abolitionist senator from Massachusetts, Henry Wilson, who was also in the bar.'

He noticed how Rose's shoulders stiffened. 'And did you talk to Senator Wilson?' she asked.

'No, we didn't have the chance. He was too busy answering reporters' questions. He seemed a rather unpleasant, self-absorbed individual.'

Rose didn't say anything but Lizzie Fitzgerald did. 'Actually he's quite a nice man when you get to know him. He used to come to Mrs Greenhow's dinner parties before the war and he didn't abandon her when he took high office.'

'How do you mean?' Grenfell could sense Rose's discomfort but was curious to hear what Lizzie had to say.

'Once he became chairman of the Military Affairs Committee he didn't have time for parties but he used to call in now and again for a late-night drink with Mrs Greenhow. And he wasn't the only one. There was that senator from Oregon who had eight children. What was his name? Oh yes, Joe Lane. He too was on the Military Affairs Committee, wasn't he, ma'am?'

Instead of answering, Rose asked her garrulous maid to pass the scones. But Lizzie failed to take the hint. 'Mrs Greenhow was such a good hostess. She'd give them a glass of fine whiskey, let them light their Cuban cigars and listen to what they had to say. Senator Wilson told me she was the most persuasive woman he had ever met.'

I bet, Grenfell thought grimly. She was more than a match for any preening power broker who ventured into the honeyed realms of her attraction. She knew exactly when to flatter, when to listen, and how to share scraps of gossip to elicit more information.

Rose was speaking now. 'You haven't eaten all day, George. Perhaps you and Mr Flannery would like to finish the sandwiches. They are really rather good.'

'I'm dreadfully sorry, Mrs Greenhow, but I must return to my pub. It gets busy about this time, what with the soldiers and all.'

'If it's all the same to you, Pat, I'd like to stay on to help Mrs Greenhow get ready for the theatre,' Lizzie said.

'Fine by me, lass, I'll see you later.' Flannery bowed awkwardly to Rose before shaking hands with Grenfell. 'It's been a pleasure, sir, and good luck tonight! You're taking a big risk.'

Lizzie wiped her mouth on a linen serviette and stood up to receive a kiss from her departing beau. 'I'll move these tea things out of the way, Mrs Greenhow, and then I'll press your clothes. I brought a flat iron in the trunk.'

'You think of everything, Lizzie. I don't know how I've managed without you.'

In the fifteen months since her employment had been rudely terminated, the outspoken Irish lady's maid might have forgotten some of the rules of service but not the basic duties. She could also appreciate that Rose and her English friend wanted to be alone together.

'I'll do the ironing in the main bedroom,' she said.

Rose watched her bustle off before turning to Grenfell. 'There's something I need you to understand. One of my gentleman callers, a military man called Keyes, was so ill-mannered as to talk about me behind my back. He told a fellow officer that a beautiful woman was like contraband of war, captured wherever found. Those were his words and I abominate them. Like so many men, he saw an attractive shape in a skirt as booty, the spoils of war. I tell you George, I will not be conquered!'

Her outburst left him speechless. No woman had ever spoken to him quite so fiercely. 'I realise that,' he said eventually, in a cold voice he didn't want to acknowledge as his own. She was laying down the rules of engagement before they had even kissed.

Yet, on reflection, how else should she behave? Rose was a determined female in open rebellion against the stereotyping of her sex. Instead of espousing Victorian ideals of purity and submission, of a woman without a will of her own, she had sacrificed herself in the interests of the Confederacy. As an Englishman he could not hope to understand, let alone share, her passionate devotion to the Southern cause but he could admire her fierce independence, her stubborn refusal to surrender without a fight. At that moment he felt it was her mental strength rather than her physical loveliness which had pierced his heart. She lived inside him like a bright lamp that could never be extinguished.

'I hear what you say, Rose, and respect you for it. But there is a question I would like to ask.'

'Go ahead.' She canted her head to one side and gazed at him quizzically.

'How did you ever get to be a spy?'

'I guess it was because of my social position and the hold I seemed to have on men, particularly top political and military officials. I was the merry widow who happened to be a good friend of President Buchanan. I had access to the White House, and all of Washington's political salons. And, of course, I gave a lot of dinner parties. I was still quite handsome and a good conversationalist who knew how to elicit information from tight-lipped politicians.'

What she had done to obtain these secrets was best left unsaid. There were rumours of love affairs. He preferred not to think about them. Men pursued her; she chased them back.

'Did you volunteer to spy for the South?'

'No, I was asked to help the Confederacy by Captain Thomas Jordan, who was resigning his commission in the United States Army to fight for his native Virginia. He wanted me to organise an espionage ring in the capital.'

'Did you enjoy the experience?'

'Yes, I suppose so. The role appealed to my patriotism as well as my vanity. I turned my large house into a meeting place for secessionists, assembled a host of accomplices, organised letter drops around the city, and learned how to use a simple substitution cipher so that I could send coded reports to Jordan. Those were heady days.'

'And successful too, by all accounts. Didn't Jefferson Davis credit you with supplying the information that led to the Confederate victory at Manassas?'

'He did indeed. What I'd wheedled out of one of my late-night callers was the date on which the Union commander, General McDowell, was going to launch his attack in the summer of '61.'

'So how did you get the message out of Washington?'

'I encoded the news on a slip of paper, placed it in a tiny purse I'd made out of one my black mourning dresses and hid the purse in the tresses of a young girl's hair. Bettie Duval disguised herself as a farm worker and carried the message through Union lines on a wooden milk cart. None of the soldiers thought to stop her.'

'Bravo, Rose,' said Grenfell. 'I don't know how you got away with it though.'

'There were so many Southern sympathisers in Washington it was hard to tell friend from foe. But I wasn't cut out to be a spy. I didn't know what I was doing. No trained spy would keep copies of their reports but I did and they were used against me. It was so silly!'

'I think you're being a bit hard on yourself.'

'No, I'm not! To tell the truth, I was puffed up with my own importance. As the good book says, pride comes before a fall. It certainly did in my case.'

'How do you mean?'

'Instead of leaving Washington as I should have done, I asked my scouts to gather more intelligence about Union troop movements and fortifications and stitched their reports into the lining and cuffs of one of my travelling gowns. In truth, I spent too long at my sewing machine. The Assistant Secretary of War called in Allan Pinkerton, the railroad detective, to investigate me and burly men with revolvers began to skulk outside my house. Pinkerton arrested me himself, ransacked my home and subjected me to the indignity of a body search. Other members of my spy ring were caught and brought to my home. 398 West 16th Street became a prison camp and, eventually, Rosie and I were carted off to a military prison on Capitol Hill. An appalling experience for my little girl and it was my fault. Sheer hubris on my part. I see that now.'

Rose burst into tears. Grenfell wanted to comfort her but something stopped him. He desired this clever, alluring woman but didn't entirely trust her. If she cared so much for her daughter, and little Rose was an enchanting child, why charge off on a madcap spying mission she could have left to someone else? Nasty, suspicious thoughts crowded into his mind.

'It's time we dressed for the theatre,' she said dabbing her eyes with a handkerchief. 'Our carriage will be here within the hour.' She lifted her skirts and disappeared off into the main bedroom.

It was time to find out whether he could get into her late husband's clothes. Lizzie had laid out a choice of garments in the second bedroom, all that remained of Robert Greenhow's wardrobe. The dress coat with velvet collar and cuffs simply wouldn't do. The style had gone out of fashion. The black tailcoat and dress trousers with the ribbon braid seemed more promising, as did the plain-fronted starched white shirt with eyelets. Bless the girl; she had supplied gold cuff links and studs, along with a white bow tie and the kind of collapsible top hat that could be fitted under a theatre seat. Black silk stockings and patent-leather boots completed the transformation. Not that he relished the idea of walking in a dead man's shoes.

He returned to the living area and slumped on a cane-backed rocking chair to wait for Rose. The gentle motion of the chair caused his eyes to close and he was dozing off when the swishing of a skirt alerted him to her presence. That it was indeed her wasn't immediately apparent. The vision before him had long blonde hair with banana curls and was wearing a daring off-the-shoulder blue silk dress that revealed not only the fullness of her breasts but the tiny cinched waist of a young girl. Everything about her was different. Her eyes looked larger, her cheekbones higher and her lips plumper.

'You're a different woman,' Grenfell gasped. 'How did you manage that?'

Rose giggled playfully. 'You cannot expect me to share all my secrets but, as you are my husband for the night, I am duty bound to give you an answer. The metamorphosis, as you might call it, was greatly aided by the cosmetics Lizzie brought with her. Beyond that, we had to improvise. The wine bottle on the sideboard now lacks a cork. We burned it and used the residue as an eyeliner. Also, the sandwiches we didn't eat have lost their filling. Lola Montez's book, *The Arts of Beauty* recommends applying rare beef to the cheeks to improve the freshness and brilliancy of a lady's complexion.'

He made a sweeping bow. 'I compliment you on your

ingenuity, Mrs St Leger. I am extremely lucky to have such a beautiful wife.'

He meant it too. She was incredibly lovely, he thought, as she swept towards him. Suddenly she stopped and the colour drained from her face.

'What's the matter?' he asked.

'You're wearing his cuff links,' she stammered. 'I bought them for Robert in San Francisco, just after the Great Fire. They're eighteen-carat gold and ... Please forgive me, I'm being very silly.'

She started to weep again. This time he didn't hesitate. He took her in his arms. 'Seeing me in your husband's finery must be terrible for you. I'll change into the clothes I came in.'

'No, stay as you are, I think you look very handsome.' Rose put her head on his shoulder and left it there for a few precious seconds. He could feel her heart pounding and waves of hot lust surged through his body. Recognising this, she pulled away from him and pretended to adjust her wig. 'Shall we go?' she asked coyly.

They didn't have far to travel. Grover's Theatre was only a few blocks away and they were soon sitting on plush velvet seats in the orchestra stalls taking in their surroundings. Built on four levels with boxes, a dress circle and a family balcony, the playhouse's blue walls glimmered in the gaslight below a domed ceiling on which cherubs sported with allegorical figures representing Comedy, History and Tragedy while, in the ground-floor aisles, half-circular niches contained the busts of famous actors such as Keen and Macready.

The orchestra began to play medieval English music featuring viols, fiddles and a plaintive flute. The sound drifted over the packed auditorium and the lights dimmed in preparation for the first act of *The Tragedy of Richard III*.

Grenfell noticed the seat next to Rose was still empty. 'What's happened to your agent?' he whispered. 'Have you come all this way for nothing?'

'Don't worry,' she murmured in reply. 'He'll be here soon.'

The curtain rose and a deformed figure limped into the limelight. 'Now is the winter of our discontent made glorious summer by this son of York,' he snarled, emphasising the pun.

Hailed as 'a star of the first magnitude' and 'the most promising actor of his age', John Wilkes Booth was making his eagerly awaited Washington debut in what was his favourite Shakespeare role. In playing the murderous hunchback Richard, Duke of Gloucester, he was following not only in his father's footsteps but in those of his equally famous elder brother, Edwin Booth, with whom he competed in the most blatant form of sibling rivalry.

Grenfell, who had seen Edwin play Richard III in London, found John Wilkes' performance very different. With a keen eye for the box office he had turned the usurping king into a loathsome but athletic monster who murdered for murder's sake. With a huge hump strapped to his back and a withered leg trailing behind him, the actor somehow managed to leap and caper about the stage while his powerful voice soared to the rafters in what was an undeniably thrilling rendition of Shakespeare's tragedy. Judging by the frequent bursts of applause, his audience fully appreciated his vocal and physical dexterity. Yet as an enthusiastic if infrequent theatregoer Grenfell was less impressed. He expected more of a production than artificial, declamatory acting and couldn't help wondering how John Wilkes' melodramatic villain could have wooed Lady Anne or deceived the dukes of Clarence and Buckingham. Shakespeare had made Richard's character black enough but young Booth employed even darker daubs.

The main interval came at the end of Act Three and Grenfell was glad of a break. Perhaps now they'd meet Rose's mysterious agent. They went into the lobby and climbed the stairs to a gaming saloon where theatre patrons could enjoy a drink, providing they didn't mind being poked in the ribs by a billiard cue. Grenfell put a five-dollar bill on the bar and ordered Rose the house speciality, a Brandy Julep, with an Irish whiskey for himself.

His partner feigned horror at what he was drinking. 'Do you really like to imbibe a burning fluid that reddens the eye, coarsens the features and ages the body beyond its years?' she asked playfully.

'Ah yes, but this is an Irish whiskey, a golden ambrosia that loosens the tongue, gladdens the heart and brings conviviality to billiard-playing navvies during their hard-won moments of relaxation.'

'I stand corrected sir, but what do you make of the play? Do you like our new star?'

'Booth is full of fire, I grant you that, but I would prefer less hump and more humanity.'

Rose looked disappointed. 'There is a cultural difference at work here in that we Americans like our actors to be larger than life.'

'But do they have to be so pretentious? John Wilkes is tearing a passion to tatters.'

'I see you know your *Hamlet*.'

'Where's the poetry in this production? Tell me that.'

Grenfell didn't wait for an answer. A group of blue-coated soldiers were eying Rose up and down. 'I don't like the way they are looking at you,' he whispered.

She dismissed his fears with an airy wave of the hand. 'They're men aren't they? There's only one thing on their mind.'

'You might say the same about me, Rose.'

'Yes, George, but with far more justification,' she replied, fluttering her false eyelashes. This happy thought was quickly dispelled. Approaching them with a broad smile on his handsome face was a tall, two-star Union general. 'How nice to see you again,' he drawled, fixing Rose with his piercing blue eyes. 'Your beauty leaves me speechless.'

'That is clearly not the case, General Hooker, but what is a hard-drinking officer doing with a glass of sarsaparilla?' She pointed to the reddish soft drink in his hand.

'Clever of you to notice, ma'am, that I am currently teetotal. I swore to steer clear of alcohol until I'd given Lee a good whipping.'

'And will that be soon, General?' she asked in all innocence.

This couldn't be happening, Grenfell thought. Rose was asking the commander of the Army of the Potomac to reveal his battle plans. Surely they would be arrested at any moment.

'Soon enough I guess, but that's not for you to worry your pretty little head about.' Fighting Joe Hooker's reputation as a lady's man was obviously not misplaced. He clicked his heels like a Prussian officer and left them to their drinks.

'Whew! That was a close call,' Grenfell muttered. 'You took a bit of a chance in asking him about his spring offensive.'

Rose smiled. 'It seemed the right thing to do. He knew me but couldn't remember who I was, so I took his mind off the subject by asking him questions. Attack is sometimes the best form of defence, as you military men say.'

'Had you ever met before?'

'Oh yes, he visited me when I was in prison here.'

'Didn't you think he'd recognise you?'

'No, I was confident in my disguise. In any case, who would expect to find a Confederate spy in a Washington theatre?'

'Where's that agent of yours?' he grumbled. 'He must have got lost.'

'No, he's here all right. I've already seen him,' she said enigmatically, 'and so have you.'

He could hear a hand bell ringing in the lobby below. It was time to return to their seats. Grenfell did so with some reluctance.

At last, the play reached its climax with the battle of Bosworth. The scene opened with the contesting parties fighting their way diagonally across the stage. Booth entered at the back, bursting through the Lancastrian lines, slashing right and left with his broadsword, until aglow with hatred and passion he reached the footlights to deliver his final speech. 'I think there be six Richmonds in the field!' he roared. 'Five have I slain today, instead of him. A horse! A horse! My kingdom for a horse!'

At that moment, Henry, Earl of Richmond appeared and the two men began to fight viciously, hammering each other with their weapons, until Henry brought his sword smashing down on Richard's unprotected head and blood spurted everywhere. But the wounded villain refused to lie down. Flinging the blood from his eyes with his left hand, he continued with the combat until Richmond's soldiers encircled him and delivered the coup de grâce. After that, it only remained for Henry to be crowned before the stage lights finally faded.

The applause was deafening as the actors took their curtain call. John Wilkes Booth entered last, still hunchbacked and staggering slightly, his face masked in blood, bowing deeply to the audience. He had to repeat this several times before the clapping died down and the lights came up.

'Was that realistic enough for you?' Rose wanted to know.

'I can't believe all that blood was a stage effect. I think it was genuine.'

She gave him that strange smile of hers. 'Perhaps we'll find out when we go backstage in a few minutes time. In the meanwhile, how about buying me a drink upstairs?'

The raw whiskey interacted with an empty stomach to make him feel quite lightheaded. Could it be that Rose's elusive spy was connected with the Washington theatre company, an actor even?

Rose looked at her bracelet watch. 'I think we should go now,' she said. 'A word of warning, George, don't be put off by the crowd of young women outside the stage door. They are there to catch a glimpse of John Wilkes Booth.'

'Is he worth looking at? With all that makeup on I couldn't tell.'

'Most women think he's beautiful and want to possess him. They tore the clothes off his back in Boston.'

Grenfell shook his head. Why should actors be idealised? On second thoughts, it was a simple enough proposition: public performance brought fame and hero worship.

A wind had got up and Rose had to hold onto her bonnet as they made their way to the back entrance. A gaggle of excited young girls was milling around the stage door in hooded cloaks and capes hoping to set eyes on the famous actor. Many of them held autograph books or bunches of flowers. Pushing his way through the animated throng, Grenfell gave his name to the burly stage door keeper. 'Right, sir, you and your wife can go right in,' the man said. 'You're expected.'

Hearing this, Booth's female admirers surged forward and a pretty young woman thrust an envelope into Grenfell's hand. 'Perhaps you'd be so kind, sir, as to give this letter to Mr Wilkes Booth when you see him.'

'But I don't think I am going to see him,' he replied.

'Well, take it anyway, just in case you run into him, and be sure to tell him Emily sent it.'

The door closed behind them, cutting off the clamour in the street. They were in a dark, dingy corridor in which stage scenery was being stored. 'We're going to the dressing room at the end of the passage,' Rose explained. 'It's on your left, just before the green room.'

'You seem to know your way around, Rose. Have you been here before?'

'No, I was told what to look out for and warned about theatre etiquette. The rules state that a lady is not allowed to enter an actor's dressing room unless she is married to that actor or accompanied by her own husband. I'm here as Mrs St Leger, pure and simple.'

'Nothing is simple about you, Rose.'

A semi-naked actress came charging out of a door and collided with him. She muttered something under her breath and skipped away, rubbing cream into her face. This voyeuristic glimpse of backstage flesh left Grenfell feeling uneasy. He was entering a strange, almost subterranean world.

They reached a door labelled 'Dressing Room No 1' and Rose knocked for entry. 'Are you in there, Johnny?' she yelled.

'My goodness, you've actually made it,' a voice replied. 'Come into my parlour.'

The room was awash with flowers. Roses in urns, tulips in vases, lilies in jugs; almost every surface was covered apart from the console table on which a large mirror reflected the frightening profile of the demon king who was sitting in front of the glass, still in costume, with a white bib around his neck. Leaning over him, a portly man in evening dress was stitching the actor's badly gashed eyebrow with a needle.

'Come in, my dears. You catch me at a disadvantage. Behold, the pattern of my butcheries,' he declaimed harshly. 'This is what happens when physical actors seek to thrill their public.'

'It's so nice to see you again, St Leger, and of course your charming wife.' This last was delivered in an altogether softer and more mellifluous tone. Richard III had been replaced by the real John Wilkes Booth, still lathered with greasepaint and encased in a prosthetic hump and hooked false nose.

The physician tied off the last stitch and proclaimed himself satisfied with his work. 'Perhaps you will send your bill to the National Hotel, Dr Hall. I am uncommonly grateful that you came at such short notice.'

'I was in the audience, sir, when I noticed your obvious distress and volunteered my services.'

'Oh, I had no idea where you came from. I fainted as soon as I got off stage and had to be carried down here. But as the Bard says, all's well that ends well.'

Booth watched the doctor depart before shouting, 'Where are you, Albert? Stop slouching in the dark over there! I need you now!'

There was the sound of a curtain being drawn and a pale-faced young man with a skin rash minced forward. 'Your word is my command, O mighty liege. What is your bidding?'

'I would have you venture upstairs to the green room and assure James McCollom that all is well. The poor man is quite distraught.'

'And well he might be,' trilled Albert. 'Impairing my king's beauty is a treasonable offence.'

Booth pointed to the door. 'Stand not upon your going but get thee gone and don't come back for a while.'

'Master I obey. Exit stage left.'

'Albert is my dresser and we play these silly games,' Booth explained apologetically. 'Now he's gone perhaps you'll be so kind as to lock the door, St Leger. We don't want to be interrupted, do we?'

There it was, Grenfell thought, confirmation that John Wilkes Booth was a Confederate agent and that secrets were about to be shared. Not that Rose seemed anxious to begin. 'What went wrong in your sword fight, Johnny?' she wanted to know.

'It was my fault really. I thought the combat scene would have greater impact if Richard and Henry turned it into a personal duel. Unfortunately, the actor who plays Henry is a bit stiff. So I kept on at him in rehearsals, urging him to loosen up and fight as if he meant it. This made McCollom so nervous he forgot the moves we'd choreographed for tonight's performance. I was expecting to parry a thrust, instead of which he brought his broadsword crashing down on my forehead, cutting one of my eyebrows to the bone. There was blood everywhere and I almost fainted but, of course, the show must go on. We finished the play and took our curtain calls before I collapsed. When I regained consciousness everyone was running around looking for vinegar paper and raw steak to reduce the swelling. McCollom came to my dressing room in a terrible state but I told him to forget it. If I'd lost an eye it would have been different. Anyway, we achieved a truly spectacular stage effect, don't you think?'

'And how are you feeling now?' Rose asked gently.

'My head aches a bit, nothing to worry about though. Will you excuse me while I get out of my costume? Take a seat over there. Move those bloody flowers.' Booth pointed to a threadbare chaise longue festooned with iris blooms and medieval costumes before disappearing behind a folding screen.

Whether it was the incessant hissing of the gas-jets on the dressing table or the dizziness that came from too much alcohol and too little food Grenfell couldn't say, but he felt weak and disorientated as he sat on the couch waiting for the actor's grand re-entry. He didn't feel comfortable in this world of make-believe. 'How did you come to recruit a famous actor?' he murmured to Rose.

'I didn't do it, Thomas Harbin did,' she replied in an undertone.

'I heard that!' Booth said from behind the screen. 'How is Harbin? I haven't seen him in ages.'

'Well enough, Johnny. He sends his regards.'

Booth broke into song. 'The despot's heel is on thy shore,

Maryland! His torch is at thy temple door, Maryland!'

'It's our battle hymn,' she whispered in Grenfell's ear. 'Like me, Johnny was born in Maryland.'

The song had nine verses and Booth knew them by heart. After a final chorus of 'Maryland, my Maryland' he reappeared from behind the screen. Dressed in dark clothes and devoid of makeup, the actor turned out to be of medium height with a slender, athletic build but it was his face that was memorable. Jet-black hair, dark eyes and an olive skin set off classical features and a ready smile. It was easy to see why the ladies loved him.

'There's a bottle of champagne in the bucket over there. Be a good chap and do the honours, St Leger.'

Grenfell did as he was told, popping the cork while Booth fished tulip glasses out of the sink and cleaned them on a towel. Once the wine was poured and handed out, their host lowered himself into the dressing-table chair and stretched out his shapely legs.

'Health and long life,' he said, toasting his guests. 'This is Great Western Champagne made from American grapes native to New York. It's probably the best thing to come out of the North!'

As they sipped their wine Grenfell tried to make small talk. 'Where did you find that hideous nose that looked so realistic on the stage?'

Booth laughed good-humouredly. 'Actually I found it in a junk shop.'

'Do you always try to look like the parts you play?'

'Absolutely. Actors have been wearing false noses since Shakespeare was treading the boards and to play the murderous usurper I needed a hooked nose. You see, as an actor, I work from the outside in. I believe you are more likely to inhabit a role if you get the appearance right. My brother Edwin adopts the opposite approach. He is an interior actor who finds the parts in himself.'

'I saw your brother play Richard III at the Haymarket Theatre in London two or three years ago.'

Booth's eyes glittered. 'What did you think of his performance?'

Grenfell could feel tension in the air. 'Well,' he replied, 'the Haymarket usually houses comedies and the play I saw was little better than a burlesque. It was under-rehearsed and badly costumed. The tin armour was so heavy and clumsy that one actor who knelt in homage couldn't get up again while another couldn't move at all. *The Times* theatre critic went so far as to call it "a tragic production".'

Rose laughed but Booth didn't join in. 'What of my dear brother? How did *he* perform?'

'Well enough, sir, in the circumstances. I would say he gave a restrained and thoughtful performance, better suited perhaps to the melancholic Dane than the hyperactive hunchback.'

His reference to Hamlet did the trick. 'You're quite right, St Leger. "To be or not to be" is Edwin's favourite speech. My brother is of such a temperament he would turn a violent villain into an introspective man. My style is more like that of my father, Junius Brutus Booth, who played Richard with fire and dash. I throw myself into a part. When I was Romeo, the passion of my embrace lifted Juliet out of her shoes and my Othello almost squashed the life out of Desdemona when I fell upon her with breastplate and scimitar.'

Now everyone was laughing. The actor was into his stride. 'I need hardly say this after tonight's mishap, but we suffer for our art. Many is the time I've slept smothered in oysters to heal the bruises acquired during stage combat.'

'I must try that remedy,' said Grenfell, thinking of the real battles he'd fought in. 'Can't you use your acting technique to fake a sword fight?'

'You can try but it never looks real unless you throw yourself into it.'

Could two actors be more different, he wondered, and still be brothers? Booth seemed to hear the unspoken question. 'I remember my relief when Edwin sailed for England in 1860. At last I was free, no longer saddled with my family's reputation, and could strike out on my own. My first starring tour took me to St Louis, Chicago and Baltimore where they had posters printed with the words, "I Am Myself Alone!"'

There was an awkward silence in the room. 'I guess I've always been the odd one out,' Booth added. 'Edwin is staunchly pro-Union. My eldest brother Junius Brutus Junior – we call him June for short – pleaded with me to stay neutral but I couldn't do that. If you ask why, I would say that Abraham Lincoln's election was a declaration of war on Southern rights and institutions. This country was formed by white men, not blacks, and African slavery is the source of our wealth and power. I've lived in a slave society all my life, and have seen less harsh treatment from master to servant than from father to son in the North.'

Booth raised his glass in an imaginary salute but whether it was to the land of cotton or to his own eloquence was not clear. 'This is my profound conviction. There is nothing else in this world that matters half as much to me.'

'Bravo, Johnny,' said Rose, responding to his heartfelt words. 'You speak for all of us.'

Not quite all, Grenfell wanted to say. As a schoolboy he had been forced to read one of Plato's Socratic dialogues in which the Greek philosopher argued that oratory was a kind of mystical sorcery that should be approached with scepticism and mistrust. And after all, when stripped of their emotional appeal, what did Booth's fine words add up to? His defence of the plantation South was implacable in its cold righteousness.

Yet in other respects, he had to admit, the actor seemed a warm, likeable human being.

'Guess who is coming to see me in *The Marble Heart* on Monday?' Booth asked rhetorically. 'Well, I'll tell you: Abe Lincoln's youngest son, Tad. The ten-year-old wants to meet me and, whatever I may think of his tyrannical father, I won't let his sins be visited on the son. So, I am going to invite Tad into my dressing room; give him some of these damned flowers to take away with him. I don't suppose you'd like a bunch of roses would you, Granny Greenhow?'

The leering way he said this made Grenfell bristle. 'Why do you call her that?' he snapped.

'Oh it's an old joke, St Leger, no need to get upset about it. As you've probably gathered, I am a lover of the female form, particularly when it comes in a delightful shape so, naturally, I made a pass at Rose, but she repelled my advances, saying she was almost old enough to be my grandmother, which is the most transparent lie I've ever heard; ergo, Granny Greenhow.'

Grenfell's smile was a sickly one. He felt foolish.

'There's more to it than that. Tell him the whole story.' There was an angry edge to Rose's voice.

Booth reacted as if he had been stung and sat up straight in his chair. 'I'm sorry to tell you this, old man, but the truth is I tried to take advantage of her when she was comforting me. I was having one of my panic attacks.'

'Johnny was put into a Quaker boarding school in Cockeysville when he was young,' Rose explained, taking up the story. 'One day when he was playing in the nearby woods he met a gypsy who insisted on reading his palm. Tell him what she saw there.'

'She said I had the worst palm she'd ever seen. The lines were all criss-crossed. I was born under an unlucky star and would die young with everyone's hand raised against me. She advised me to escape my destiny by becoming a missionary or a priest.'

Grenfell stared at Booth, trying to see inside this driven and complex man. 'You're not telling me everything, are you?' he said.

The actor nodded slowly. 'No, I'm not. It's best that way.'

There was a loud knocking on the dressing-room door. 'My sovereign lord, bestow yourself with speed and admit me to your chamber.' Albert had returned with his half lines of Shakespeare.

'Go to the bar upstairs,' Booth yelled back at him, 'and buy yourself a large Old Crow whiskey with the money I gave you yesterday. Take ten minutes to drink it and return with the food.'

'I go, my dread lord, to do my duty with all swift dispatch.'

This talk of duty reminded Grenfell of Emily's letter which he took out of his tailcoat pocket and handed to the actor. 'A pretty girl at the stage door asked me to deliver this. She said her name was Emily.'

Booth took the envelope without looking at it. 'Emily, Lucy, Jane, Lizzie, they are all the same, star-struck girls who imagine they're in love with me.'

He opened a drawer in his console table and extracted a bunch of letters. 'These came today,' he said. 'I haven't bothered to open them because I know what they say.'

'What's the matter, Johnny,' said Rose teasingly, 'lost your liking for young girls?'

'No, you know that's not true. But I want to be admired for my acting ability rather than for any masculine charm I might possess.'

He added Emily's billet-doux to the bundle and dropped it into a trash can. 'You know what this female adulation does for me? It makes me feel like a piece of meat.'

Rose smiled faintly. 'Now you know what women feel like when men won't leave them alone.'

'There's something in here you might actually like.' The

actor rummaged through the open console drawer and brought out a box of Cuban cigars. 'Take one, St Leger. How about you, Rose?'

She declined the offer. 'Fighting Joe Hooker was in your audience tonight. Did you know that?'

'I'm not surprised. He's pursuing my leading lady, Alice Gray. The eager general is concerned about her moral welfare and has invited her to one of his parties for "fallen doves".'

'So he treats actresses as whores.'

'They are, aren't they?' Grenfell had boyhood memories of going to the Strand playhouse to watch actresses undressing in the theatre's green room.

'You're out of date, old chap. Actresses no longer perform behind the curtain, only General Hooker doesn't seem to realise this.' Booth rubbed his hands together in what was a nervous mannerism. 'I guess you want to hear about his military strategy.'

Rose pursed her lips. 'Whatever gave you that idea, Johnny?' she said ironically. 'No, we risked life and limb getting here purely for the pleasure of being at your opening night.'

The look of amusement vanished from Booth's face. 'Here's what I've learned. Hooker plans to keep Lee pinned down at Fredericksburg while taking the bulk of his army across the Rappahannock River on a flanking march to strike the Confederate rear. He's coming at Lee from all angles with a force of about 150,000 men.'

'And do you know when Hooker will begin his advance?'

'Yes, Fighting Joe plans to cross the Rappahannock the day I next play Richard III.' Booth opened a small diary. 'That's a fortnight on Monday. April 27th to be precise.'

Rose's eyes darkened with distress. Lee's barefoot army was about to be squeezed like a nut in a cracker. It was almost as if she could hear the cannons booming and see the Virginia hills painted blue with Yankees. 'What a complete nightmare,' she said, 'but at least we're forewarned. Thank you, Johnny. What you've done will not be forgotten.'

John Wilkes looked suitably modest. 'No more than my duty, Rose.' He moved to unlock the dressing room door.

'There is something you need to know,' she said urgently. 'Federal cryptographers have cracked our Vigenère code. Use the Rosicrucian instead.'

'You mean the Pigpen cipher! And talking of greedy hogs, here's Albert right on cue.'

The star's dresser had arrived in the doorway carrying a bowl of oysters and a plate of thinly cut sandwiches. Booth took the food from his assistant and bade him goodnight.

'Do try these oysters,' he urged. 'They are fresh from the Rappahannock River and have the sweetest, smoothest flavour.'

Grenfell glanced at Rose. Given what he had in mind, this was the perfect hors d'oeuvre. Oysters were an established aphrodisiac. Casanova, the great eighteenth-century lover, was supposed to have eaten fifty oysters for breakfast to improve his sexual stamina.

Another bottle of champagne was opened and toasts drunk to Jefferson Davis, Robert E Lee and Alice Gray who had kept her ears open after joining 'Hooker's division'. Then John Wilkes pulled out a map to show them the underground route chosen for their escape.

'You leave tomorrow lunchtime,' the actor said, 'if all goes well, you should be in Fredericksburg by Monday.'

*

It was one o'clock in the morning before they got back to Willard's and Grenfell was straining at the leash. They had kissed in the carriage and he had felt the urgency of her embrace. As soon as the door to their suite closed behind them, he pinned her against the wall forcing his tongue between her lips. A wave of longing swept through him, making him groan aloud. His hunger knew no bounds.

'No, George, not now,' Rose said breathlessly. 'This isn't how it's meant to be.'

She slipped away into the darkness leaving him to deal with his frustration. There was nothing he could do but retire to his room. Lighting a candle he flopped on the counterpane to wait for her.

Time dragged by until he heard a light tapping noise. He jumped off the bed and rushed to the door. Rose was standing there. She moved into the small circle of light beside his bed and turned to face him. She was wearing a black negligee which hung open at the front to reveal a delicate lace chemise. She underlined this act of self-display by extending her arms to him.

'Do with me as you wish, my darling,' she whispered. 'We have so little time and I want to give you pleasure.'

AN EXCHANGE OF LETTERS

Culpeper Courthouse, April 10, 1863
Dearest Rose,
This is the third letter I have written to you. The love I bear you and, I suppose, my own self-esteem will not permit me to believe you received my previous missives and failed to answer them. No, I assume the fault lies with the Confederate postal service. The late or non-delivery of mail is a constant complaint. I must apologise for running out of stamps and can only hope that the enclosed sentiments are worth the ten cents you must pay to read them.

Let me begin with a piece of news. I have just taken part in what was probably the largest cavalry conflict in the entire war. Yesterday's battle at Brandy Station involved more than eighteen thousand horsemen and, you will be delighted to hear, the boys in butternut prevailed in the end. But it was a close-run thing.

As you know, the information we obtained in Washington helped Lee and Jackson win a great victory at Chancellorsville but did little to change the strategic situation in Virginia. With Middle Tennessee lost to the Confederacy and Vicksburg under siege in the West, General Lee decided to take the war onto Northern soil and ordered Jeb Stuart's Cavalry Division to screen the army's march into the Shenandoah Valley by patrolling the southern bank of the Rappahannock River. With the Army of the Potomac gathering in force on the river's northern bank, Stuart moved his cavalry into bivouac at Brandy Station, a minor stopping point on the Orange and Alexandria Railroad, from which he could guard the two conceivable crossings of the river at Beverly Ford and Kelly's Ford.

Not to put too fine a point on it, we were taken completely by surprise when General Pleasanton staged a two-pronged attack, sending his troopers across both fords at dawn. I was having an early morning shave when the dull rumbling of the first cannon shot reached my ears, almost causing me to cut my throat. Rushing out of my tent I beheld an alarming sight. Thousands of Yankee cavalry were swarming towards us supported by artillery batteries pounding away with shot and shell from Fleetwood Heights, a hill overlooking the railway station.

There was no time for inquests into what had gone wrong. It was a case of every man for himself, saddling up in double-quick time and devil take the hindmost. There had been no rain for weeks and the roads were bone dry. Blinded by the thick cloud of dust thrown up by our horses' hooves we couldn't see where we were going and my stallion stumbled over some obstacle and went down. Imagine my shame! Stuart's new cavalry inspector unhorsed and rolling around in the dust before we'd even engaged the enemy. Picking myself up, I remounted and charged after my comrades, finding them in hand-to-hand conflict with the bluecoat troopers. Here was a chance to regain my honour. As you are fond of remarking, I am a tall man and sitting above your opponent on horseback is a definite advantage when fighting with sabres, particularly when height is allied to speed. Every slash you make is aided by gravity and this allowed me to dispose of several adversaries.

When last we talked, you showed a lively interest in military strategy which I will try to satisfy in this account. What we needed to do, of course, was regain the Fleetwood Heights. To achieve this feat our cavalry would have to charge uphill, which reminded me of the battle of Balaclava where Scarlett's Heavy Brigade was set a similar task. I told my men about this precedent, omitting to mention that charging uphill against an entrenched enemy was generally regarded to be the height of folly, and up we went with gleaming sabres held aloft and the Rebel yell on each man's lips as the Union artillery opened a terrible fire upon us from the crest of the hill. Shells burst all round us, tearing through the turf, seriously wounding the riders either side of me. And still we pressed on through the cacophony of whizzing shot and exploding shrapnel that stunned our senses.

Cavalry charges are overrated, Rose. They rarely achieve their objective but this one did. The sheer weight of our attack proved irresistible and the cool bravery and rigid determination shown by our troopers forced the enemy to give way. After hours of fighting, the Yankees were driven from the hill, leaving three canons behind them.

But that was only the start of it. The thunder of their guns continued to roar throughout the afternoon while thousands of horsemen clashed in close-quarter combat all over the plain. This was followed by an attempted counter-attack on the hill involving two bluecoat cavalry brigades. When this was repulsed with heavy losses, the rest of the Yankee horsemen finally withdrew from the field, disappearing into a wood, and were seen no more. The battle was over.

It had been hot work throughout and credit must go to General Stuart who was always to be found where the battle raged the fiercest, dashing hither and thither, without any consideration for personal safety. You will be pleased to hear that I am in good shape to fight another day with no more than the bruises I picked up when my horse rolled on me in the dust.

Sometimes I think I lead a charmed life. I am not what you might call a 'good' man, nor am I cut out to do great things in this world, so why am I spared when so many die around me? All I know is this: if I continue to escape with my whole skin, I shall count myself blessed for each day brings me closer to your affection.

I have reason to believe that this is one piece of mail that will reach its recipient intact and unopened. General Stuart is sending a courier to Richmond with dispatches for Jefferson Davis and he has promised to deliver this letter to you by hand. With such a guarantee of privacy, I intend to risk your blushes, my darling, by speaking of the passion that has changed my life.

Let me begin with our first kiss in Washington. The feel of your soft, warm lips sent shivers down my spine. It was as if I had never kissed a woman before. I was seized by an unimaginable tenderness, a desire to touch your satin skin and taste your rich, musky sweetness. Yet even those moments of heightened pleasure were tinged with irrational fear. Can love last and at what cost to those who indulge in it?

I have been thinking a great deal about the nature of sexual attraction recently. Sex often intrudes into our thoughts and yet it is not considered to be a fitting subject for discussion, even in a love letter. The purity culture would have us believe that sex exists solely for male gratification and the reproduction of the species. It is something women are supposed to endure rather than enjoy. What is almost as insulting is the modern notion that female virtue depends on wearing corsets. If current language is to be our guide, a 'loose woman' is one who is without a corset. The terms 'strait-laced' and 'pulling yourself together' stem from lacing corsets and a lady is an 'upright person' because of the whalebone stays that hold her in position.

So, where does George St Leger Grenfell, soldier and arch sinner, stand on sex? If sex is merely the machine that moves the dreadful wheels of lust or the erotic burr under the saddle that brings a good man to his knees in search of a pelvic spasm, then it is to be renounced. But if sex means that unselfish passion for another human being, that pure romantic love which is still new and strange to me, then I am four-square in favour of it and look forward to sharing my future with a woman of spirit who loves without restriction, a woman who flouts convention and challenges the tired cliché that her place is in the home, a woman who is ahead of her time, a woman who is a man's equal. In short, Rose, I want to be with you and you alone.

Those April days we spent together in Richmond were the happiest I have known. I was never a good husband or an attentive father but I feel I've been allowed another shot at domesticity with you and little Rose. I am reminded of Rosie's delight when I gave her a belated tenth birthday present. She couldn't believe her eyes when I laid out my gifts on your kitchen table. 'George,' she said, 'who are these for?' 'They are for you, courtesy of a Potomac blockade runner,' I replied. How she shrieked when she opened the parcels and found a billowy blue dress, a day coat, a straw hat and, of course, a corset, which made her feel very grown up. You said something about her being too young to start corseting *but, like a good mother, you gave in to her protestations.*

Well, that's about it for now, my darling. I am sitting outside Culpeper Courthouse watching Lee's troops begin the long march north. General Ewell's Second Corps has already left, followed by General Longstreet's First Corps. Some of these good-humoured but ragged butternut soldiers will fall by the wayside, victims of the summer heat and the inadequacy of their footwear. The rest, however, will press on. We all know it's a case of do or die for the Confederacy. A crushing victory on Northern soil is the only way to change the military balance in our favour.

Pray for me as I will pray for you.

Devotedly,

George

*

2309 East Grace Street, Richmond, June 13, 1863

My dearest George,

I supposed from your unbroken silence that you hadn't received any of my letters and had almost given up hope of hearing from you. Patience is said to be a virtue and I have had to practise it to the utmost capacity of my endurance. This morning was as gloomy as my thoughts. Then things improved dramatically. The rain stopped, the sun came out, and the gallant captain arrived on my doorstep with your letter. Words cannot describe my joy on opening it and reading the assurances it contains. I could hear your voice framing the sentences.

The last six weeks have been a misery without you. I have not felt so alone and bereft since I learned of the death of my dear husband nine years ago. You and Robert could not be more different. At heart, he was a scholar, a veritable bookworm, while you are a warrior, a man of action. He made me feel warm and comfortable while you take my breath away.

Let me congratulate you on your appointment as Job Stuart's cavalry inspector and on forcing the enemy to leave the field at Brandy Station. I must tell you, however, that the Richmond newspapers do not count this as a victory and are far from satisfied with General Stuart's conduct. According to the local press, he should never have been caught unaware by the Union attack.

Attitudes are changing in the South. The romantic ideals we cherished about courage and chivalry have been eroded by the bestiality of warfare. Those belles that rushed their beaux off to battle now want them back again. Terror and cynicism are the order of the day. And suspicion too. Women fear the enemy within, fancying one another to be Union spies. False hairpieces are searched for secret papers. Bustles are suspect.

I fear I must bear some responsibility for this paranoia. Stories about my espionage activities in Washington have furthered the belief that the Yankees have placed female spies here in Richmond. Indeed, if little Rose is to be believed, our neighbour is one such spy. She is convinced that the spinster lady who inhabits the large mansion opposite us is a Union sympathiser. Elizabeth Van Lew makes no secret of her opposition to slavery and her house would make an excellent hiding place for escaped Union prisoners. To catch her at it, my daughter spends long hours watching the Van Lew mansion through a small telescope. Talking of my darling girl, she plagues me for news of George. In her sweet childish innocence, I think she is infatuated with you.

I cannot forget our first meeting and the way you looked at me with those cool, appraising eyes of yours. You *were so tall and dashing, a charming cavalier who aroused mixed emotions in me – pleasure in our mutual attraction but embarrassment too. I felt you could see right through me. But what turned liking into something much deeper was the discovery that your confident exterior was merely a protective covering for a complex and sensitive man.*

What pleases me most about our relationship is how quickly we lapse into an easy informality. Not that that has always been the case. Do you remember the dreadful row we had over the scented letter that slipped out of your uniform when I was about to press it for you? The green-eyed monster lurks in all of us and I admit to feeling incensed when I read Mrs Howard's detailed description of the war wound on your left buttock. How, I asked, had she come to see such an intimate part of your anatomy? Well, you said, I was lying in a pile of corpses with only a cotton blanket to cover my nakedness, and you told me about the courageous way she had rescued you from that dreadful prison hospital in Tennessee. And as this happened before we properly knew each other, I felt ashamed of my behaviour. Love is not a rational emotion.

As you rightly remark, American society will chastise a woman for stepping outside accepted social boundaries. While refusing to bow to such pressure, I do feel some moral constraints. Yes, I would like to marry again but, unfortunately, that cannot be to you while you have a wife.

You need have no concerns about my reputation. It is far too late to worry about that. I am now, and will always remain, a social outcast. The good book says, 'As you sow, so shall you reap.' Even as a newlywed, I was determined to rise to the top of Washington society. I understood that who you know is more important than what you know.

A succession of presidents invited my husband and me to dine at the White House and I, in turn, entertained them back, even after being widowed. President Buchanan's regular visits to my house on 16th Street certainly set tongues wagging. Rose Greenhow was a scandalous lady long before she became a spy.

One thing alarmed me about your letter, my darling, and that was the gloomy way in which you described Lee's invasion of the North. I have not forgotten what you said when we first met at the Murfreesboro wedding. You prophesied that the South would lose the war because it possessed neither the industry nor the manpower to sustain a long conflict. Well, the war is two years old and we have won many battles, so I cannot share your pessimism.

Do not forget me and believe me always to be,
Your loving Rose

*

Dover, Wednesday, July 1, 1863
My dearest Rose,

I received your wonderful letter shortly before setting out on what must be the most arduous cavalry raid I have ever taken part in. We left Culpeper a week ago, forded the Potomac and made our way through Maryland up into Pennsylvania. Between skirmishes with the boys in blue, we have ridden at least twenty-five miles a day and I have the saddle sores to prove it. We are almost too tired to sleep at night and our poor horses are worn out. But still we press on with the intention of linking up with the main army somewhere north of here.

It hasn't stopped raining since we crossed into Union

territory. I spent last night in a wedge tent listening to it drumming on waterproof canvas. We have a captured Yankee wagon train to thank for our creature comforts. The woollen blankets that cover my cot and the writing paper on which I am composing this letter were taken from their supply wagons. Forgive my rushed handwriting. We will be mounting up again at dawn and there is so much to say.

My overriding feeling is of being in the wrong place. A major battle is brewing and we are separated from Lee's army when he needs us most. Even Jeb Stuart seems to have recognised this. Last night he dispatched couriers to break through the Union lines and locate our main force. Two days ago, when I raised my concerns at an officers' meeting, he laughed in my face and called me 'an old woman'. Now he's no longer so dismissive. He's seen how much harder the bluecoats fight when they are defending their own soil instead of attacking ours and General Lee is badly outnumbered. To make matters worse, he is a sick man. His surgeon thinks he has a heart complaint. By riding off with three brigades of cavalry Stuart has deprived Lee of his eyes and ears.

As you have never met James Ewell Brown Stuart I will attempt to describe him to you. He is quite a showman. With his immense auburn beard, yellow sash, red-lined cape, plumed hat and golden spurs he draws attention to himself. He is, for sure, an excellent horseman and a courageous leader but the praise showered upon him for his cavalry raids has turned his head so that he cannot accept criticism. To be advised by a previously sycophantic newspaper like the Richmond Enquirer that he should 'see more and be seen less' after Brandy Station came as a total shock to him, and I am inclined to think *that our mad gallop around the Union army is little more than a publicity stunt arising from his hurt vanity.*

Stuart claims to be acting on orders, albeit by exploiting their vagueness. General Lee asked him to locate the Army of the Potomac and, depending on the strength and disposition of the enemy, cross the river into Maryland on the strict understanding that he linked up with General Ewell's Second Corps before the end of the month – which we have failed to do.

It seems a long time since eight thousand troopers set out from Culpeper in straw hats on a scorching midsummer's day. I travelled with Colonel Chambliss's brigade. Of all the officers, Chambliss is the friendliest towards me. Sad to relate, my appointment as cavalry inspector has not gone down well with Stuart and his senior staff.

On descending through Glasscock's Gap we discovered a long blue snake crawling through the valley below. General Hancock's Second Corps was waiting to do battle. After some desultory fighting, Stuart broke off the engagement and decided to cross the Potomac. We were preparing to do this on the morning of June 27 when we learned that the twenty-thousand-strong Federal Sixth Corps was waiting for us at Edwards Ferry.

Casting around for an alternative crossing point, Stuart was told the Potomac was only half a mile wide at Rowser's Ford. Unfortunately, when we got there, we found the river deeper than anticipated and too full of rocks for a safe crossing. I could see Stuart's nimble brain working out a solution to this problem. Once he'd done so, he turned to me with a nasty glint in his eye and growled, 'Well, Grenfell, you're our inspector, how are we going to keep our caissons of ammunition dry? What do you recommend we should do?' He was trying to humiliate me in front of the men.

'Unpack the ammunition boxes and give each trooper a shell or powder bag to carry over with him,' I replied. If you'd seen his face, Rose, you would have laughed – such disappointment. 'Quite right, Grenfell, they obviously taught you something in the British Army,' Stuart said begrudgingly, and ordered the boxes to be opened. The main difficulty was dragging the wheeled vehicles and cannons across when the horses' ears were barely visible above the swollen water. By sheer determination, the entire command was safely on Maryland soil by three o'clock in the morning and with dry ammunition. A remarkable feat, all things considered.

No sooner had we completed our labours than shots rang out. One shell whizzed past my forage cap while another lodged in my horse's pommel. 'They are shooting at you, Grenfell.' Stuart sounded aggrieved not to be the main target. 'You're very unpopular with the enemy, aren't you?' 'That would seem to be the case, sir,' I replied coolly. At that moment, the battle-scarred face of Brigadier General Wade Hampton loomed out of the darkness. 'My scouts tell me the 39th New York Infantry Regiment is stationed down here. They call themselves Garibaldi's Guard and a bigger bunch of cut-throats you're never likely to meet.' That gave me a start and no mistake!

You know my guilty secret and have forgiven my sinful weakness. Not that that seemed likely during our last night together when you sought an explanation for my deep dread of Italians. When I told you about my brief dalliance with Garibaldi's young wife, you flew at me with clenched fists, pummelling my chest and face, calling me a scoundrel. I tried to restrain your anger and you know

what happened next. Ours is a passionate relationship,
my darling

The bugle is sounding outside my tent. If I do without breakfast, which only consists of hardtack and chicory coffee, I should manage to finish this letter. Now where was I? Ah yes, on the banks of the Potomac where we rested after our night's toil. The sun was quite high in the sky before we moved on towards Rockville. The progress of the main column was delayed by the need to tear down telegraph and railway lines, and it was past noon before we reached the town.

Rockville's parishioners were known to have divided loyalties. Doors were hastily closed and curtains drawn as we rode into town past the immaculate clapboard houses on Washington Street. A Sunday service was in progress at the Christ Episcopal Church, which was a recognised hiding place for escaped slaves. We marched into the chapel and waited for the last hymn to finish before arresting the priest and several of his parishioners who were taken to a holding pen in the town square.

At the nearby Rockville Academy, a seminary for young ladies, we received an altogether warmer welcome. A host of attractive girls in bright frocks rushed out to greet us and, what with their giggling and the troopers wolf-whistling, things rapidly got out of hand. As the oldest man there, I thought it incumbent on me to say something. 'Do not be afraid, ladies, we mean you no harm. You may have heard stories about soldiers molesting the fairer sex but I can assure you this will not occur. We Southerners are gentlemen.' That's what I said, as if I came from South Carolina rather than Cornwall, and do you know what Rose, some of those little minxes looked quite crestfallen, as if they had been looking forward to a good ravishing!

At that moment a courier rode up with a message from General Stuart. I was to take my troopers onto the Rockville pike and intercept a large wagon train carrying supplies to the Union army. What a race that turned out to be. The wagon drivers lashing their mules mercilessly, their buckboards hitting rocks, going up in the air, crashing down on one another, and us whooping and hollering as we gave chase. In the end, we captured 125 wagons. Stuart was euphoric on our return. 'Wait until our Chief Quartermaster sees these beauties,' he chortled, opening up cases of new rifles and ammunition. 'As for the perishables, the ham and the salt beef, we'll put them to good use. Well done, George!' For once, I seemed to be in favour but it was not to last.

Looking back on it, I can see that capturing the wagon train was a mistake. These mule-drawn wagons slowed us down when it was imperative that we should link up with our main column as soon as possible. Had Stuart been unencumbered we might have been back with Lee by now. But I am getting ahead of myself.

Having concluded affairs in Rockville on the 28th we rode on to the small Quaker town of Brookeville, arriving in the early evening, where, to our surprise, we were greeted by a bevy of smiling girls carrying baskets of cakes, bread and meat and pitchers of iced water. I was fascinated to see the market town that was the capital of the United States for one day! The day in question being August 26, 1814 when President James Madison took refuge in Brookeville after we, the British, had burned his White House.

Stuart's decision to bivouac here went down well with our younger cavalrymen who desired better acquaintance with the Quaker girls while I was happy to spend time in

180

Madison House, a federal-style brick residence in which visitors are shown the bedroom in which the president slept. What I found more interesting was the living room's false stone wall, behind which escaped slaves had hidden. I sensed fear in this dark and dank place. For some reason, it made me think of my uncle Pascoe Grenfell MP, who was a staunch supporter of William Wilberforce's campaign to abolish slavery in the British colonies. Poor Pascoe would turn in his grave if he knew his nephew was fighting for the slave-owning Confederacy.

Next morning there was a further delay due to Stuart's decision to parole four hundred Yankee prisoners which required a lot of paperwork. Judging this to be ill-advised, I raised the matter at an officers' meeting. 'Begging your pardon, General,' said I, 'perhaps you are unaware of the fact that the Federal authorities refuse to acknowledge parole terms and return officers and men immediately to duty. Let these boys go and we'll have to fight them again.' Stuart stroked his bushy red beard, always a dangerous sign, before fixing me with an icy stare. 'I don't need an English mercenary telling me how to fight my war, Grenfell. I was brought up to be a chivalrous Southern gentleman and will keep my code of honour, whatever the Yankees may do.'

As you know, I hate to be called a mercenary and, in my stupid anger, I suggested that common sense was more important than chivalry and that our priority should be to link up with Lee. That was when he laughed in my face and called me an old woman who had no stomach for the fight. 'We are riding into the history books,' he claimed, 'and have no place for frightened foreigners in our ranks. Stand down sir, and await further orders!' I am still waiting.

Having crossed into an exceedingly wet Pennsylvania, I took no part in yesterday's inconclusive street battle in Hanover which cost us more than two hundred casualties. Now I am sitting in a dripping tent in Dover waiting to mount up and travel with our baggage train, while wondering whether we are getting any nearer to our own army. I don't think Stuart has the slightest idea where Lee is. I must admit to having handled things badly but my instinct tells me that Lee is in deep trouble. Yet that red-headed glory hunter refuses to see it. The cavalry should not be a detached unit.

There goes the call. I must love you and leave you. Give little Rose a kiss for me.

God bless you, my darling.

George

*

Williamsport, Tuesday, July 7, 1863

My dearest Rose,

I can imagine your despair on reading of our defeat at Gettysburg. Lee's invasion of the North was always a gamble but it could have paid off. If Stuart's cavalry had been scouting the army's advance instead of indulging in a pointless joyride for the benefit of the Southern press, Lee might well have found a better tactical position from which to engage the Army of the Potomac. As it was, Stuart left Lee blind and he stumbled into a fight on ground not of his making and without his three crack cavalry brigades who missed the first two days of the battle. If a British cavalry officer had behaved as Stuart did, he would have been court-martialled.

By now you will have read my last letter, written

from Dover on the morning of July 1, and know that my premonitions were fully justified. The fighting had already begun in Gettysburg and yet we knew nothing of the battle until a courier reached Stuart just after midnight. You can imagine the urgency with which we broke camp and began to march due south. We covered thirty-four miles that day and on reaching Gettysburg in the early evening our weary column was relieved to discover that the battle wasn't over. Immediately upon arrival, Stuart was summoned to Robert E Lee's command post where, according to eyewitnesses, he was severely reprimanded and told to support General Ewell's Second Corps.

On the morning of July 3 Stuart led more than five thousand troopers out of the town of Gettysburg, heading northeast on the York Road. We rode for three miles, much further than was necessary to cover the left flank of the army, before heading south. I have since learned that Lee hoped to turn the tide of battle by a timed assault on two fronts. While Pickett's infantrymen hurled themselves at the Union front line, we would ride around the enemy and attack their rear. If this was the strategy it failed dismally. Our departure from Gettysburg was impossible to hide. Union lookouts positioned on hilltops near the town could not fail to notice the clouds of dust created by so many horses and any last vestige of surprise was lost when Stuart insisted on firing his guns to tell Lee he had taken position on Cress Ridge, ready to lead a cavalry charge. The stupidity of his action became obvious when Union artillery shelled our position and cavalry brigades led by Brigadier General Custer and Colonel McIntosh blocked our way forward. We also discovered to our cost that Custer's troopers were armed with Spencer repeating rifles which greatly enhanced their firepower.

Stuart decided on a direct cavalry charge led by the First Virginia Cavalry to which I had been reassigned. The charge began at one o'clock when our old friend and fellow balloonist Colonel Porter Alexander opened an artillery barrage on Cemetery Ridge. The ensuing action was one of the most disappointing of my career. We had superior numbers but they had better weaponry and, as became apparent, a more effective leader in George Armstrong Custer.

Imagine the scene, Rose. We are charging towards dismounted Union cavalrymen who are firing at us from behind cows and sheep when Custer leads a counterattack. Hundreds of horsemen collide in a pasture. We fight at point-blank range. I hear a cry of 'Come on, you wolverines!' and see a Union general with flowing blond hair on a large bay horse. I draw my pistol and shoot the horse. Down goes Custer, only to remount. I lose sight of him in a melee of yelling, swearing men slashing at one another with their sabres.

This furious affair ended in a stalemate. We retired to our ridge and by nightfall the battle of Gettysburg was over. Pickett's charge had been a disaster and the Union had its first major victory. Next morning, as exhausted armies stared at one another in stunned silence, I was summoned to see Lee. He acknowledged my 'valiant service' to the cause and asked me to be his messenger. He held about four thousand prisoners and wanted to exchange them for captured Southerners. I eagerly accepted the mission and, under a flag of truce, rode across the desolate battlefield to General Meade's headquarters. I am far from squeamish but the sight of so many blackened and bloated bodies festering in the sun turned my stomach. The stench of the unburied dead was so overpowering that it came as a relief to encounter the cleaner air of the enemy camp.

Meade saw me in his tent. The victor of Gettysburg was a tall, careworn man with sunken eyes, hooked nose and an almost bald head. He declared himself to be greatly intrigued by my accent. 'I didn't know we were fighting the English,' he said. 'Nor are you,' I replied. 'You are dealing with a man of the world.' Meade began to laugh, a strange braying noise, and we got on famously thereafter. He was not, however, prepared to grant my request for prisoner exchange, reasoning perhaps that the guarding and feeding of Union prisoners would slow down Lee's retreat. I thanked him for his courtesy and returned to my own camp. On my way back I saw many harrowing sights: militiamen hooking their bayonets through the belts of dead soldiers to drag their bodies into shallow graves; surgeons operating outdoors on long tables literally awash with blood. I will say no more about the terrible aftermath of war.

We are now at Williamsport waiting for the Potomac to stop flooding so we can rebuild the pontoon bridge that the Federals destroyed. Even the weather is against us. No sooner had we left Gettysburg than the heavens opened, turning the roads to mud, and it didn't stop raining for two days. Protecting a seventeen-mile-long wagon train has been well-nigh impossible in such conditions and we have come under frequent hit and-run attacks from Federal cavalry detachments. Now, with our backs against the swollen river, we are sitting ducks.

These are desperate times, Rose, but they have convinced me of one thing: when this wretched war is over I want to settle down with you. To that end, I have written to my wife in Paris begging her for a divorce. Stay strong, my darling, and don't get too depressed by the bad news from the north.

God be with you always,
Your loving George

*

Hayward's Lodging House, Bermuda
Monday, August 10, 1863
My dearest George,

Love is what happens when you are making other plans. I am a woman at war with herself. I want nothing more than to spend the rest of my life with you but, as you know, I also have the keenest sense of duty and feel that my loyalty to the South must take precedence over my selfish desires.

Several months ago, Jefferson Davis approached me with a scheme he'd hatched to win European support for the Confederacy. He wanted me to be his emissary. Davis thought that sending a woman on such a diplomatic mission would go down well with the upper classes in Britain and France, particularly since my barbarous imprisonment in Washington had evoked so much sympathy abroad. While seeing the strength of his argument, I felt Lee's military successes would make a much stronger case for the Confederacy and we agreed to await the outcome of his invasion. But after defeat at Gettysburg and the fall of Vicksburg the following day, our beleaguered president felt obliged to revive the issue and, with a heavy heart, I have agreed to be his overseas ambassador.

Little Rose and I left Richmond a month ago and travelled to Charleston, finding that beautiful city under bombardment from heavy artillery. This has been a dreadful year for the South, a year of heartache and despair, in which we have been sorely pressed. Finding it impossible to get out of port, I remained in Charleston for more than a fortnight in an uncharacteristic state of gloomy introspection, until word came that passage had been arranged for us on the blockade runner *Phantom* that would leave Wilmington in two days' time. Built in England, it is one of the fastest steamships afloat. Captain Porter managed to escape the ever-tightening net of the Union blockade by slipping out at night on the rising tide. Three ships gave chase but *Phantom* was too quick for them. Sailing at sixteen knots an hour she soon lost her pursuers.

Once we reached the Gulf Stream currents our small ship began to dance upon the choppy waves and I spent most of my time lying on a mattress retching into a bucket. No sooner had I stopped being sick than Captain Porter informed me that a Federal cruiser was chasing us. But all was well. We outran the cruiser and, last Saturday evening, reached the Port of St George in Bermuda where we took up lodgings while awaiting onward transportation.

Time hangs heavily. The narrow bounds of this island oppress me, and I am impatient to be gone. I am told we must wait for a British brig called the *Harriet Pinckney* which will carry us across the Atlantic and put us ashore in the port of Falmouth on the south coast of Cornwall. So I am to see where you grew up. I will write again when we reach Cornwall and tell you what I think of your home.

Please believe me, George, when I say I love you. Leaving you is the hardest thing I have ever had to do and can only hope that my sacrifice will be rewarded when I present my credentials to the Court of St James. You will always be in my thoughts. Try to understand my motives and forgive me.

Ever yours,

Rose

THE WITCH OF THE NORTH

The witch had arrived. He'd been told to watch out for her. From the land of limitless snow a bitterly cold northern wind had arisen to blow a blizzard into the frozen heart of the already windy city. The icy blast searched beneath layers of clothing for cringing flesh and the dancing, swirling ice crystals bit sharply into his already chapped face.

If ever there was a time to feel depressed it was surely now as he stumbled blindly through the dismal back alleys of the shantytown that had grown up alongside Chicago's railroad tracks. He had been miserable for so long; yet tonight, battling into the teeth of a gale, he felt a strange sense of exhilaration. Each step was a test of strength, stark and primitive. The more the storm howled, the more he revelled in its fury. Long before towns were built, man's lot on earth had been to struggle like a wild beast through cold and heat, blood and fire, simply to survive.

But it wasn't just about survival. In his short time in Chicago he had lived more intensely, his waking hours more charged with expectancy, than at any time since Rose's departure fifteen months ago. The letter she wrote in Bermuda left him feeling dry and empty, and the absence of any further mail convinced him he had been rejected. Dark days had followed, devoid of plan or purpose, robbed of any emotion. Slowly though, he'd been jolted out of his apathetic torpor by the realisation that he had nothing more to lose and could take any risk he liked.

The challenge he had accepted was a daunting one, born of a desperate desire to prolong the civil war. Tomorrow night, as Chicago prepared to go to the polls in the November 1864 presidential election, he and a small group of Southern sympathisers were due to execute a spectacular jailbreak to release 5500 Confederate soldiers from a hellish prison called Camp Douglas. Well, that had been the intention anyway. But the military authorities had got wind of the plot and the net was closing around him and his co-conspirators. He had to leave Chicago as soon as possible. First though, there was a knife wound to be bandaged and belongings to be retrieved from his downtown hotel.

With the ear flaps of his red plaid hunting cap buttoned under his chin, shoulders hunched inside his wool-lined greatcoat and gloved hands deep in his pockets, Grenfell gritted his teeth as the wind continued to buffet him. Up ahead, between the one-storey hovels that lined the snow-covered dirt track, a warm glow penetrated the whiteout. As he got closer, he saw the beam was coming from a lamplighter and the cage of fire he'd created revealed the presence of two woebegone horses pulling a passenger wagon along rails laid in the road.

He jumped onto the streetcar's step, opened the rear door, and showered its passengers with snow. The tram seated as many as twenty travellers on facing wooden benches. But because of the weather and the time of night, it was only half full. Grenfell slumped down beside an Irish labourer who was drinking something out of a stoneware bottle. Sitting opposite him was a prim lady with a handkerchief held to her nose. She was wedged between a restless bearded gentleman in a bowler hat and a group of Republican Party workers returning from a day's canvassing in the Chicago slums.

'If our findings are right it should be a landslide,' enthused a tall, spare man with a campaign cockade pinned to his waterproof poncho. 'That's if people vote early and often.'

His squat colleague shook the snow off his umbrella and guffawed loudly. This was obviously a Chicagoan in-joke.

'Do you intend to vote sir?' The question was directed at

Grenfell by one of the canvassers, an earnest youth with a face covered in pimples.

'I'm not eligible, I'm an Englishman,' Grenfell replied truthfully.

'Supposing you had a vote, who would you go for, Lincoln or McClellan?' the pockmarked stripling persisted.

'Oh, Lincoln of course,' said Grenfell, recognising discretion to be the better part of valour.

'That's right, sir. Don't change horses in mid-stream,' the youth said, repeating what was obviously a campaign slogan.

Grenfell's shoulder was being tapped. The streetcar conductor was standing over him. 'Five cents please,' the man demanded. Numb fingers located a nickel in his greatcoat pocket. 'Here you are,' he murmured, slipping the coin into the collection tin.

But the conductor hadn't finished. He didn't often have the pleasure of addressing an Englishman and he wanted him to recognise that the self-important British Empire depended on the wheat and cereals grown in the great state of Illinois. On the receiving end of a moral shower bath, Grenfell found himself marvelling at the insularity of the average American.

Tiring of tattle about exported breadstuffs, he cast around for a change of subject. Outside the snowstorm had turned to sleet and was pounding the streetcar's roof with tiny shards of ice. Ah, the weather, he thought. 'She's evil tonight, isn't she?'

This stopped the conductor in his tracks. 'Who's evil?' he asked.

'Why, the Witch of the North,' Grenfell replied. 'Isn't that what you call this wind?'

'No, we call her Hawkins or the Hawk Wind, but one thing's for sure, she blows no one any good.'

Having delivered this dire warning, the conductor swung around to seek his fare from the well-dressed woman on the opposite bench. Swaddled as she was in shawl and mantle, she somehow managed to find a small coin in her black silk reticule. Grenfell wondered what could persuade a refined lady to venture into Chicago's slums on a wild night like this: an act of Christian charity perhaps, feeding the poor or visiting a sick relative. What was her untold story?

What, for that matter, was *his* story? If anyone was travelling under false colours it was George St Leger Grenfell. His papers proclaimed him to be an entrepreneur, currently in America on a hunting trip. But the deer hunter had set his sights on a different target.

He had arrived yesterday by train, having crossed the prairies in a great cloud of steam. Looking through the window, as the locomotive slowed to a sedate fifteen miles an hour for the final stage of its journey, he had noticed wide streets full of tall stone buildings and, on approaching the quayside, a forest of masts and the massive grain elevators that had literally hoisted the city to fortune. Chicago was America's fastest growing city and, so long as a hungry Europe needed to be fed, she would continue to increase in size and wealth.

What no one mentioned though was a stinking, disease-ridden internment camp built on eighty acres of land that had once belonged to Chicago's favourite son Senator Stephen Douglas. Thousands of Confederate prisoners of war had already perished in Camp Douglas. Every day a wagon left the compound with a cargo of pine coffins. Grenfell had learned these grisly facts from an old friend, Captain Thomas Henry Hines, whom he'd known as a fellow officer in Morgan's Raiders. Hines had escaped to Canada where, with the help of a group called the Sons of Liberty, he had raised a militia for the express purpose of storming the northern prison camps.

He'd run into Hines six months ago on the steps of the War Department in Richmond. Things were going from bad to worse for the Confederacy. Under its new commander General Ulysses

Grant, the Army of the Potomac was threatening Richmond while General Sherman was marching on Atlanta with little to stop his advance. Over drinks in a hotel bar, Hines had outlined his audacious mission and asked Grenfell to join him. He had agreed immediately, partly on humanitarian grounds but also because of the danger involved.

Arms had been purchased with money raised by Copperhead sympathisers, Northern Democrats who wanted peace with the South, and legends created for the conspirators. Grenfell's role was that of the disillusioned mercenary. To establish his cover story, he resigned his commission in the Confederate army and became a gentleman of leisure with a passion for hunting and fishing. He even went to Washington and sought an interview with the Union Secretary of War Edwin Stanton. And it had paid off. On the understanding that he would give no further aid to the Confederacy, Stanton allowed him to travel where he pleased in the North, and he had spent several weeks shooting deer and pheasants in the Carlyle Lake area of Central Illinois before moving on to Chicago where he checked into the Richmond House Hotel under his own name.

Everything had gone well until a few hours ago when an unexpected visitor knocked on his bedroom door. Standing in the corridor was a bedraggled figure in a scruffy overcoat and muffler, stamping snow-encrusted boots on the hotel carpet. 'Pleased to see you again, Colonel, mighty pleased,' the vagrant said.

Grenfell had no idea who the man was. 'Have we met before?' he asked.

'Oh, bless you, of course we have. I thought you'd remember me. The name is John T Shanks, Morgan's Brigade. You had me flogged for trying to steal your horse and drawing a knife on you,' the man added helpfully. 'I still carry the marks on my back, if you'd like to see them?'

Grenfell's hand tightened on the derringer he kept in his jacket pocket. 'So you've a score to settle. Is that what you're doing here?'

'Dear me, sir, you've got the wrong end of the stick. That flogging was the best thing that ever happened to this poor sinner; sorted me out good and proper. Each stroke of the lash was a reminder of how far I'd sunk into the pit of depravity and, when I could take no more, I heard the voice of the Lord calling out to me. He raised me up from despair to hope and salvation.'

The repentant wrongdoer reached out and grabbed Grenfell's arm. 'I mean you no harm. Quite the contrary,' he whispered urgently. 'I have news from the camp.'

Grenfell hesitated at the open door. Was Shanks truly a reformed character or the scoundrel he had once known? There was only one way to find out. 'You'd better come in and close the door behind you,' he said gruffly. 'Here, let me take your coat, it's absolutely sodden.'

Shanks peeled off his grimy coat and muffler to reveal a coarse flannel suit and yellow neckerchief. 'I'm sorry about the rags but they were the best I could steal when I broke out of Camp Douglas. I got them off a washing line in Cottage Grove Avenue, may the Lord forgive me!'

'You were in Camp Douglas? How did you manage to escape?'

'Along with other prisoners I dug a tunnel in a rat-infested latrine the Union guards never visited. What with the squealing rats and the interminable darkness it was awful down there, I can tell you, but eventually we burrowed out near the gate and ran for it. I got away, the others didn't.'

'Perhaps you'll take a whiskey, Shanks. You look as if you could use one.'

'Thank you kindly, Colonel.' Grenfell heard the Texan twang in Shanks' voice. It hadn't been there before.

'You can stop calling me Colonel. I'm plain Mr these days.'

'You'll forgive me for saying so, Mr Grenfell, but I think you're a very brave man who is about to strike a great blow for the South.'

He could feel his breath shortening, his heartbeat racing. 'What makes you think that?'

Shanks seemed to be gaining in confidence. 'The word is you're planning an armed attack on the camp on election night and, if that's really the case, I've been asked to tell you that the prisoners are right behind you. That's why I'm here tonight, to pass this on, and to say that I'd like to take part in the action, if you'll have me. That's the honest truth, as God is my witness.'

'You'll have your whiskey now.' Grenfell took a bottle of barrel-aged rye bourbon off his bedside table, pulled out the cork with his teeth and poured a tot into a tooth mug. 'Here, drink that.'

As he watched his gaunt visitor gulping down the fiery spirit, questions began to form in his mind. Would anyone break out of a hellhole like Camp Douglas and risk recapture to pass on a vague message of support? How had Shanks known he was staying in Richmond House? Would a man dressed like him walk up to the front desk in one of the city's smartest hotels and be shown the guest register? No, it was far more likely that he was a Union spy, a paid informer whose cheap clothes had been acquired from a local slop-shop to support the role he was playing.

Grenfell tried to conceal his thoughts. 'You're looking better already,' he said evenly. 'But I'm afraid you're wrong Shanks. Whatever you may have heard, I'm not involved in any prison raid. I'm a non-combatant, here on a hunting trip. Now, if you don't mind, I've another guest calling on me. It's a bit delicate, a lady friend of mine, don't want to embarrass her. So let's shake hands and say goodbye.'

'Well in that case I'll be off.' Shanks donned his grubby

overcoat and made for the bedroom door before turning to face him. 'Don't worry sir, old John T won't peach on you. There is no more chance of that than of catching a weasel asleep. And should you want to get in touch, you can find me at 81 West Randolph in Hairtrigger Block.'

As he watched Shanks shuffle away, alarm bells rang in Grenfell's head. If this crude approach proved anything it was that the military authorities knew about the prison raid and were preparing to round up its perpetrators. He needed to warn his friends before it was too late.

Wrapping up well against the weather, he transferred the loaded pistol to his greatcoat pocket before locking the bedroom door and taking the back stairs. Shanks or one of his accomplices might be watching the front entrance on South Water Street. On reaching the ground floor he turned away from the brightly lit reception area and marched down a dark corridor, through a set of swing doors, into the hotel kitchen. Swerving to avoid two tray-bearing waiters he incurred the wrath of a Chinese cook by knocking a wok of noodles off the stove.

Out in Michigan Avenue the cold hit him like a physical blow. He stopped to catch his breath, and saw that Chicago's main street was deserted. It was hardly surprising. No one in their right mind would venture out on a night like this unless it was absolutely necessary. The wind had been howling for hours and snow was falling.

The address he had been given was for a livery stable, about three miles away in one of the city's slum areas, a district overrun with crime, drug addiction and poverty, in which the thump of a drunkard's blow or the scream of a tortured prostitute hardly attracted attention. The instructions for getting there were simple enough, yet he didn't relish the prospect of making this journey on foot in a gale-force wind. But what choice had he? There wasn't a carriage in sight.

He set off quickly, sliding and slithering over a sidewalk rutted with snow and ice, until he lost balance and fell, hitting the ground with a crack. Winded by the fall, he sat in the snow counting his bruises, before the biting cold forced him into renewed action. There was almost no feeling in his body as he tried to rise, muscles moving by memory rather than will as he pushed on into the teeth of the wind, wishing he'd brought a pair of long johns with him to Chicago.

Up ahead, through the raging blizzard, he could see what had to be Wells Street, an unpaved road running parallel to the new railway track, lined by squalid frame houses, derelict shops and rubbish piles. This was where the poor had been dumped after their previous rented dwellings had been demolished by ruthless construction companies hell-bent on making a quick profit. Such a social upheaval had done nothing for the health and happiness of the city's working class but had added a few words to the English language. Here was living proof of how powerless people could be 'railroaded' into living 'on the wrong side of the tracks'.

No one lived willingly on Wells Street and few tried to walk along it. Wooden plank sidewalks had been raised several feet high to protect pedestrians from the worst of the muck and mire but, in the absence of any street lighting, woe betide anyone who lost their footing and fell into the fetid swamp below. Blindly scrambling across the last of these rotten timber bridges, Grenfell began to talk aloud. As an old campaigner, he was acutely aware of how silence could turn fear into a deadly terror.

'That's it,' he said, stepping off the final ramp. 'That wasn't so bad.'

'Glad you think so,' a voice came out of nowhere, low, nasal and sinister. 'Lost your way, have you?' hissed another voice behind him. 'Give us your wallet or your dead meat,' the first voice added threateningly, elongating his vowels.

Grenfell froze and peered into the darkness. Two shadows emerged from the driving snow. They were armed with knives. He whipped his pistol out of his greatcoat pocket and pointed it at the advancing forms. 'This here's a .41 calibre, two-shot derringer and I know how to use it. I hope you boys can run fast.' His chuckle was lacking in humour.

There was a momentary pause while the muggers calculated the odds before launching themselves at him. He shot one of his attackers between the eyes before he was slammed against a brick wall. A blade sliced through his clothes and into his ribcage. Somehow, he managed to break free and fire again at point blank range.

Standing over the dead bodies, badly shaken and dripping blood into the snow, he thought how crazy it all was. Two small-time gangsters had sacrificed their lives trying to steal a few dollars. He had killed many men in battle but never like this before.

He shook himself angrily, breaking the introspective mood into which he had fallen. Other lives were at risk here. He must press on. He felt the warm blood seeping through his torn shirt, running down his forearm and pooling on the ground below. It was only a flesh wound but it hurt like blazes. He would have to get it patched up.

They had told him the stable was between a clothing store and a gin shop at the corner of Wells and West Polk Street. A dim gaslight revealed his destination. O'Brien's Livery Stable Boarding and Shoeing, the signboard said. There was a faint glow coming from inside the barn. One of the big double doors was slightly ajar and a greenish-white light spilled through the opening; enough to illuminate a yellow notice pinned on the doorpost, declaring in bold letters, 'Diphtheria Here!'

Grenfell recoiled in horror. There had been outbreaks of diphtheria in some of Richmond's livery stables so why not here in Chicago? He'd seen several such notices posted on housing around the city. He took a closer look at the notification and sighed with relief. It was crudely printed, not at all like an official document. The warning was simply a ruse to frighten people away from the stable in which Hines and his Irish political friend Charles Walsh were keeping not only their mounts but a small arsenal of weapons.

He opened the door sufficiently to slip inside. The light he had seen came from an oil lantern hanging from a rusty nail driven into one of the thick wooden beams that supported the barn's ceiling joists. Ahead of him lay a dirt aisle between two rows of box stalls. The overpowering smell of manure and compressed hay convinced him they were fully occupied. The horses were here but where was everyone else? The place seemed deserted.

'Hello! Is anybody around?' he called out. The only answer was a whickering noise from the nearest stall. He felt suddenly dizzy and had to steady himself by putting his hand against the door. He was losing too much blood. Fortunately there was a water trough in the stable and a pile of rub rags on a nearby work surface. Stripping off, he cleaned the knife wound and tied the longest of the rags around his chest. He was about to pull on his shirt when he felt the cold steel of a rifle barrel up against his neck. He froze, knowing any movement might be fatal.

'What do you want, mister?' It was a boy's voice, not yet fully broken, and there was fear in it.

Grenfell could sense the muscles in the youth's arm tensing. 'Don't pull the trigger son, and I might tell you.'

'Turn round and keep your hands where I can see them,' the boy ordered.

'Complete Victory,' he said.

The boy relaxed and lowered his rifle. 'Thank God, you know the code. The name is Billy Pettigrew and I'm here on my own with a dozen horses and a shitload of guns.'

This worried Grenfell. 'Where are the others?' he asked. 'Where are Mr Hunter and Mr Wade?' These were the aliases adopted by Hines and Walsh.

'I don't rightly know what's happened to those gentlemen. I was told to wait here for them but they haven't shown up. Plenty of other people have been lurking around though. That's why I put up the health warning to get rid of them.'

Grenfell couldn't help grinning. 'Then let me congratulate you, Mr Pettigrew. You are a clever young man.'

Billy Pettigrew, a sixteen-year-old Rebel from Pine Bluff, Arkansas, positively swelled with pride. 'Will you be taking part in the raid, sir?' he asked.

Grenfell avoided the question. 'So people have been skulking around here, have they?'

'Yes, I spotted three of them this morning, watching the stables from across the road.'

'Was one of them a hollow-cheeked, dark-haired man with a muffler around his neck?'

Billy scratched his chin. 'That sounds about right but I'm not absolutely certain.'

'Why are you here on your own? Where's the owner of this place?' Grenfell asked.

'Mr O'Brien you mean? Oh, he's drunk as usual and sleeping it off in there.' The boy pointed to an unlit office at the back of the barn.

Grenfell shook his head in disgust. Months of careful planning and all for nothing because of lax security and operational incompetence. How best to batten down the hatches? Hines had adopted a cell structure so that he and he alone knew the composition of the raid party. It had seemed a sensible precaution at the time but it left the other conspirators fumbling in the dark.

'When Mr Hunter arrives, perhaps you'd give him a message

from me. Tell him the cat's got kittens.' He hated these silly codes. 'Have you got that?'

'Yes, sir, but who do I say you are?'

'Say I'm the guy from the Richmond War Department and, once you've passed that on, I suggest you get the hell out of here. Find yourself a new job.'

*

How long would it be before he was arrested? Had the others been rounded up, he wondered, as the streetcar lurched to a stop.

'Do you know Jesus?' The words came from the remaining passenger left on the car, the energetic bearded gentleman sitting opposite. His whole face burned with missionary zeal.

'No, I can't say I do,' Grenfell replied cautiously.

'Well, I used to be like you, in spiritual darkness and despair, until I found God. You really should get to know Him.' The man stuck out his hand. 'The name is Dwight L Moody, revivalist in a sinful city, although I'm often called Crazy Moody because of the familiarity I display to strangers.'

'Yes, you have a unique approach.'

'I guess you're a military man. You've got the bearing of a soldier and, if you'll forgive me, the eyes of a killer. I refused to fight in the war. In that respect I am much like the Quakers. But I've visited plenty of battlefields as chaplain to the Nineteenth Illinois. I was at Shiloh and Stones River, such bloodbaths! Have you seen much action? I suspect you have.'

Grenfell nodded. 'I did some soldiering in the Crimean War and the Indian Mutiny.'

Moody whistled with surprise. 'Phew, you've got around a bit. Do you enjoy fighting?'

'Not like I once did,' he answered truthfully.

'The only war we should be fighting is against poverty and ignorance. I've been living in Chicago for six years now, setting up Sunday schools and branches of the Young Men's Christian Association, but there is so much more to be done. The West Side slums are getting worse and the number of homeless children is growing, street urchins taught to burgle and pick pockets by the Fagins who operate in the ghettos. What's needed is a message of hope and it has to be taken to the doorstep and, yes, carried onto the city's streetcars. Can you open your heart to the Lord?'

'I wish I could, Mr Moody, I really wish I could, but it seems as if all feeling has been sucked out of me. I'm dead to the world.'

The stocky evangelist stroked his beard. 'I can't accept that. There is love in you. I can sense it. You have done bad things and known sadness and remorse, but one day you'll be happy. I promise you that. This is my stop! God be with you, brother.'

Grenfell watched Moody disappear into the snowstorm as the streetcar started off on the final stage of its journey. Moody was a man of simple faith, seeking to make the world a better place, and they called him crazy!

There is love in you. The words struck him like a blow to the solar plexus. He had kept his emotions bottled up since Rose left. Until he met her, he had never cared for anyone properly. Not his wife, his children or his family. Rose had brought joy into his life and taken it away again. It was as if his heart had been ripped out and replaced with a mechanical muscle that pumped blood efficiently but without any trace of feeling.

She had promised to write but what had become of her letters? All he knew was what he'd read in the press – her ambassadorial audiences with Queen Victoria and the Emperor Napoleon III, the gowns she had worn, the words she had spoken.

The streetcar reached its terminus at the Ellsworth Armoury on the corner of Randolph and State Street. The snow had stopped but an icy wind carried the breath of winter from the frozen prairies. The other thing that struck him was the noise: iron-shod hoofs and wheeled vehicles grating on the cobbles, whips cracking on horseflesh and drivers cursing as they crossed the intersection.

Hundreds of soldiers marched past in their new dark-blue uniforms, followed by a brass band and a crowd of well-wishers. He reckoned these recruits were on their way to the Illinois Central depot where a troop train must be waiting to take them to the front. As he walked towards his hotel he could hear loud cheering and the raucous whistle of a locomotive.

He tried to relax, to think positively about his next move. Shanks's visit and the fact that the conspirators' meeting place was under surveillance meant it was only a matter of time before the military authorities pounced on him. He should leave Chicago immediately. But the last train had already gone. He would have to wait until morning. He looked over his shoulder to see whether anyone was following him. What he saw instead were drops of blood in the snow. His wound had opened up again. Once in his bedroom he'd clean the cut and bandage it properly. After that, he would find a way of passing the time.

*

The banker shuffled the cards with practised hands, cut them and put the pack into a spring-loaded metal dealing box, face up. He was plump as a pouter pigeon with spectacles, wiry silver hair and a nicotine-stained moustache, and there was about him a confidence born of years in similar saloons. He didn't say much but his Southern drawl suggested recent residence on the Mississippi riverboats.

A patched-up Grenfell was sitting at a rectangular green felt table on which squares had been painted to represent the thirteen square-cornered cards in the suit of spades. The layout was for a game of faro in which players gambled on the value of the cards to be drawn from the deck rather than on their suit. In the opening round Grenfell placed a five-dollar bet on the 'high card' bar. This signalled his belief that the second card drawn by the dealer would be higher than the first.

The betting was done with tokens known as checks purchased from the banker's cash box. To ensure fair play and protect the bank in a game that often became violent, a lookout stood behind the dealer's chair. This sinister figure was dressed in black with a Colt revolver in a low-slung holster tied to his thigh. Grenfell guessed his gunfighter's rig was purely for show.

Once bets had been placed on the layout, the dealer threw away the so-called 'soda card' which everyone had seen when the deck was placed in the box and revealed the one below it. This was known as the 'losing' card. It was the jack of diamonds. Grenfell hadn't lost yet but, with a jack to beat, the odds were against his high card bet. The dealer flipped over the 'winning' card and Grenfell got lucky. It was the king of spades. Five more checks were added to his pile. The tall, sour-faced man sitting next to him grunted in dismay as the dealer removed his check from the baize.

As the betting began again he weighed up his fellow players. On his left, sucking a briar pipe and rocking back and forth in his seat, was a skeleton of a man in a heavy winter coat and a slouch hat, whose unsteady hand betrayed anxiety and indecision. To his right was the heavy-browed individual who had lost a ten-dollar bet in the opening round. His cracked lips were set in a self-pitying scowl; the look of a born loser. Beyond him sat a big red-faced youth picking away at his teeth with a matchstick. His head was cocked forward and to one side, like a barnyard fowl, as he tried to work out his next bet. He was an amateur. So too were the remaining players, a couple of office clerks in stiff collars and ties. There was nothing to worry about here, Grenfell concluded, no seasoned gambler or skilful cheat – apart from the dealer who looked at him with cold, calculating eyes.

He left his five-dollar check on the high card bar and placed exploratory single-dollar bets on the seven and queen of spades, neither of which turned up in the ensuing flop. This time the losing card was the three of hearts and the winning one the nine of clubs. Grenfell was handed five more checks. Before the third round he quadrupled his stake on the high card bar and placed a copper token on top of his checks, thereby reversing the bet. By 'coppering' it, he was gambling on the winning card being of a lower value than the losing one. And once again he was right.

'How do you do that, mister?' asked the surly card player, his brows knitting together threateningly. 'That's three times in a row you've guessed right.'

'Luck is what I'd call it,' Grenfell replied evenly.

The dealer turned around and muttered something to the man in black who repositioned himself behind Grenfell's chair. It was time to back off a bit. He made only small and inconsequential bets on the next few turns, losing more than he won. Twice the losing and winning cards were of the same denomination and the dealer called 'splits' which gave him half of any bet placed on that card. Statistically, splits only occurred three times in two shuffles, but Grenfell could remember the bank dealing matching cards six times already which aroused his suspicions.

The gaunt figure in the overcoat had come to a similar conclusion. 'There is something mighty strange about that dealing box of yours,' he said in a staccato voice.

'Are you accusing the bank of cheating?' growled the black-suited gunman, poking his Colt into the thin player's ribs.

'Keep your shirt on,' said his potential victim, hastily backing down. 'I meant no harm. I was merely remarking on the unusual number of splits we've had on this table.'

'Yeah, well, that's cards for you.' The gunman grinned evilly, displaying a mouth of yellow, decaying teeth. He obviously enjoyed frightening people. Twirling his revolver around his trigger finger, he returned it to its holster and the game went on.

Grenfell knew this was a rigged table. The only question was how the dealer was cheating. Either he was using a stacked deck with many paired cards or the cards themselves had been specially sanded or shaven so that he could manipulate them during the shuffle.

Gambling in the hotel's saloon had seemed a better way of passing the hours than tossing around in his bed waiting for morning to come, but Grenfell was having second thoughts. He had the uneasy feeling he was about to be arrested. And if the soldiers arrived before morning, wouldn't he be better off in a bedroom that offered him access to a skylight and an outside fire escape? He would finish the game and retire for the night.

The game went on with more and more checks on the baize. He pulled off another high card bet to bolster his pile of chips. What he was waiting for though was the final round when there were only three cards left in the deck. There was big money to be won on predicting how they would fall. Call the turn right and the bank paid out four to one. He had memorised all of the earlier falls and knew which cards remained. The challenge lay in placing the two of spades, eight of hearts and king of clubs in the correct order. The odds against doing so were five to one.

Counting his checks, he discovered he had fifty dollars and, after a momentary indecision, he went all in on an eight, king, two drop. The dealer blinked and tugged his moustache nervously. There was nothing he could do to adjust the cards to his advantage. He placed the losing card on the table. It was the eight of hearts. The winning card followed. The king of clubs! If Grenfell had counted right, the final card had to be the two of spades.

'Yes,' he cried in delight, as the hock card was laid on the baize. He had won two hundred dollars.

'No payout,' barked the lookout. 'That guy switched his bets.'

'I most certainly didn't,' Grenfell said indignantly, taking a firm grip on the pistol he'd placed on his knee beneath the table.

'Yeah, I saw you, mister. Leave the money on the table and get out of here!'

'And if I don't?'

'I'll have to chastise you.'

The gunfighter's hand was a blur as he reached for his revolver. But he wasn't quick enough. Grenfell shot the weapon out of his hand.

A hush fell on the saloon, broken only by the whimpering of the lookout whose trigger finger was covered in blood. 'And now, gentlemen, I'll take my winnings and bid you goodnight,' Grenfell said coolly, pointing his smoking pistol at a frightened dealer.

'I do hope you'll stay and have a drink on the house,' said a relaxed Irish voice, 'if only to show there's no ill feeling.'

The talking was being done by a slight man in his mid-twenties dressed as a riverboat gambler. He was wearing a black broadcloth coat and trousers, a frilled and ruffled white shirt and a pair of high-heeled boots. 'The name is Michael Cassius McDonald and I own this disreputable joint.'

Grenfell pocketed his pistol, debating what to do next, before shaking the proffered hand. 'Mine's George Grenfell, and I'm sorry for what just happened here.'

'Don't be. Benny had it coming to him. Thinks he's a hot shot. Here, Benny, go and get cleaned up.' McDonald tossed his sobbing lookout a dollar coin before turning his back on him.

'If brains were dynamite, Benny wouldn't have enough to blow his nose,' he said loudly, before lowering his tone to an urgent whisper. 'I've something to tell you. Trust me; I'm on your side.'

Was it a trap? Grenfell's mind was racing.

McDonald beckoned to a blonde barmaid in a low-cut

polka-dot dress. 'Maudie, honey, I'd really appreciate it if you'd bring a bottle of our best whiskey and a couple of glasses to my office tout de suite.'

McDonald took him into a small room behind the bar. It was sparsely furnished with a desk and two chairs placed either side of a cast-iron grate in which a log fire blazed. 'Come and get warm,' he said. 'Fierce weather we've been having.'

Maudie entered with the whiskey and was rewarded with a playful smack on her rump as she deposited the tray on the desk. 'She's one in a hundred, that girl,' said the saloon keeper after she left, pouring out a generous tot for his guest. 'But I'll not act the maggot. You need to know someone's been asking questions about you, Colonel.'

Grenfell felt his mouth go dry. 'Who would that be?'

'A man called Maurice Langhorne. Does that name mean anything to you?'

It certainly did. Langhorne had joined Thomas Hines in Canada claiming to be an escaped prisoner of war. He had been privy to all the planning for the Camp Douglas raid and had travelled to Chicago to take part in it.

'Yes, I know him,' Grenfell replied cautiously. 'What of it?'

'Well, he says you're a colonel in the Confederate army who is about to lead a Copperhead attack on our prisoner-of-war camp.'

The skin tightened across his scalp. He stared at McDonald, anger burning inside him. 'Why would he tell you that?'

'Because he wants me to spy on you while you are staying here.' McDonald's eyes were twinkling. 'Now before you reach for that pistol of yours, let me explain why Langhorne thought he could trust me. He knew I was a recruiter for the Union army.'

McDonald poured out more whiskey. 'You know what they say about Democrats in this city? They stand for Rum, Romanism and Rebellion. Well, I sell a lot of rum, I'm a practising Catholic and I've always been a wild Irish rebel. So when the war came I wanted to find a way of supporting the Confederacy without actually fighting for it. It was clear from the start that the South couldn't compete either in wealth or numbers, especially when new bluecoat recruits were being offered a signing-on bonus of three hundred dollars by the government. You can imagine how well this bribery went down. And that gave me an idea, a way of helping the South while feathering my own nest. I organised a bounty-jumping scheme. Through running floating faro games and a soup kitchen for down-and-outs in Chicago, I had got to know thousands of desperate, destitute men who were only too happy to collect their three-hundred-dollar bonuses, give half the money to me, then desert as soon as possible and return to Chicago to re-enlist again under an assumed name while I paid local officials backhanders to look the other way. I am telling you this because I trust you and want to be your friend.'

Grenfell couldn't help smiling. He was in the presence of a Napoleon of crime. 'Most ingenious, I grant you. What a wonderful scam, recycling the same soldiers! You get rich, army recruiters achieve their enlistment targets and the needy receive welfare payments. Everybody's happy, particularly you.'

'Call me Mike,' the diminutive emperor requested.

'Right, Mike, tell me exactly what Langhorne said.'

'He sidled up to me yesterday evening and asked for a private word. I sat him down where you are now. He said he had escaped from Camp Morton in Indiana but my guess is he's a deserter. Anyway, according to Langhorne, he made his way to Canada where he won the confidence of Captain Hines and his fellow conspirators and learned that they were planning not only to attack Camp Douglas but to set fire to Chicago and other Northern cities. He was absolutely appalled to learn of such wanton terrorism. Therefore, although he was betraying his friends and the South, his conscience would not let him rest until he had washed his hands of this horrible crime. That's what he told me and a more treacherous self-serving hypocrite I've yet to meet'

'How did my name come up in your conversation?'

'Oh, he said an English colonel called Grenfell was staying in the Richmond House Hotel. What makes you think he'll visit my saloon, says I. You'll see him alright, replies our boyo, for he's an inveterate gambler and a reckless villain and we need to know his movements. With Chicago about to go up in flames, he calls on my loyalty to the flag, and says he'll drop by again to find out what I've discovered. So, you've probably got until lunchtime to make yourself scarce.'

'I'll be alright,' Grenfell told him, 'but thanks anyway.'

McDonald didn't look convinced. 'I've made a few enquiries and my sources tell me that they've doubled the garrison at Camp Douglas. They know you're coming. The commander of Chicago's military post Colonel Sweet takes Langhorne seriously but obviously hopes to collect further evidence before arresting you.' The sworn testimony of John T Shanks for example, Grenfell thought grimly. He was surrounded by traitors. But what could you expect when you recruit criminals into your army? Shanks should have been left to rot in his Austin prison cell.

'There's a freight train leaving the north-western terminal on Wells Street at seven o'clock tomorrow morning. I think you should be on it. In the meanwhile, do have some more whiskey.'

Grenfell hesitated. Was McDonald really interested in his welfare or simply setting him up? 'You seem to know a lot about trains,' he said defensively.

'God bless you, I grew up on the railroad. Here I was, the fourteen-year-old son of a poor Irish immigrant suffering from a double dose of original sin, when the Great Western Railway Company opened a line where we lived in Niagara Falls. I became a candy butcher.'

'What in heaven's name is a candy butcher?'

'He's a hustler who travels on trains selling candies and newspapers to passengers. It's a job that requires a keen wit and a quick eye, both of which I possess. I've sold gum drops to people with no teeth and peppermints to old ladies as a cold cure. But that was only the start of it. I invented the prize package swindle, a con game that was later practised by candy butchers on every major rail line in the country. Would you like to hear how it worked?'

Grenfell grinned. There was something likeable about this disarmingly frank if boastful Irishman.

'I guaranteed travellers a cash prize in every box of candy they purchased. That much was true and I'd prove it to them by selecting, apparently at random, boxes stuffed with five-dollar bills. But this was just sleight-of-hand. The boxes the punters purchased only had a penny inside them.'

'Wasn't that a wee bit dishonest?' Grenfell asked, wiping the smile off his face.

'It depends how you look at it. All I was doing was encouraging people's greed,' he said proudly. 'There's a sucker born every minute and you should never give a sucker an even break.'

'Does that principle extend to your faro tables?'

'Aw, sure it does. The game is played with a unique deck of cards and a dealing box with hidden compartments to skim money from the players. Yet you managed to beat the system and had enough gumption to defend your winnings. I admire intelligence and courage in a man.'

'And where did you learn to be a card sharp? Was that on the trains too?'

'That's right. Wealthy passengers taught me to play poker and, as a keen student of human nature, I made enough money to exchange my rags for fancy clothes and fat cigars. Then I took myself off to New Orleans to complete my education.'

'And learned the odd word of French into the bargain,' Grenfell added.

'That too, but what really struck me was the lack of police interest in the city's glaring vices and I wondered whether this laissez-faire attitude might be repeated in a frontier town like Chicago.'

'And can it?'

'Yes. I drifted back, you might say, at the outbreak of war. A lot of Mississippi riverboat traders fled north to avoid conscription. That's why Chicago is full of Southern sympathisers and is such an easy-going place. I'm into card games, dicing, illegal boxing and after-hours liquor. The one thing I won't touch is prostitution. That's against my principles.'

'Do you have any trouble with the police?'

As if on cue, Maudie knocked on the door to say a Daughter of Charity was seeking a dollar donation for the family of a dead police officer. McDonald handed the barmaid a five-dollar bill. 'Tell the sister to bury four more!'

'Funny, isn't it,' he stated. 'You can't respect those whom you can buy.'

'Making money isn't hard,' Grenfell said bitterly, 'but doing something worthwhile definitely is.'

'Is soldiering for the Confederacy worthwhile? You wouldn't be Irish now, would you?'

'Why do you ask?'

'Because the Irish champion lost causes, that's why.'

'Yet it was an Irish hero, Major General Patrick Cleburne, who advocated the abolition of slavery in the South and the recruitment of blacks to fight for the Confederacy: two policies that could have changed the course of the war.'

'Well, it's too late now; fire and the sword lie in waiting, that's the word, what with Sherman about to torch Atlanta and Grant moving against Richmond. All that's left is the carnival of death.

Your best and bravest lie under the sod and your last hope of foreign support disappeared with that pretty lady.'

'Which pretty lady?' Grenfell asked in a voice stiff with tension.

'Why, that ravishing Irish beauty Rose Greenhow, whom Jeff Davis sent to Europe to seek recognition for the South. Now there was someone I admired.'

'Did you ever meet her?'

'No, I never did, more's the pity. But I tried to keep in touch with her.' McDonald went to the desk and pulled out a scrapbook in which he had pasted pictures and newspaper cuttings.

'This is the portrait Matthew Brady took of Mrs Greenhow with her little daughter when they were imprisoned in Washington and this is an account of her arrival in Richmond after Lincoln released her.' McDonald also showed him newspaper accounts of Rose's meeting with Napoleon III at a masked ball and of the party the British prime minister had thrown for her in Piccadilly. 'Palmerston couldn't take his eyes off her, lecherous old sod,' he enthused. 'What a woman she was.'

Grenfell felt an icy hand clutching at his heart. 'Why are you using the past tense? She's still alive, isn't she?'

'Haven't you heard the news? She drowned when the blockade runner bringing her back to America was caught in a storm off the North Carolina coast.'

Realisation broke over him like a wave, leaving him gasping for breath. She couldn't be dead; she couldn't have stopped being. In the silence that followed he heard a glass shattering. It was the one he had been holding. Bending to retrieve the broken pieces, his legs suddenly gave way and he sank to his knees on the polished wooden floor.

'What's the matter, old chap?' McDonald helped Grenfell to his feet. 'Did you know Mrs Greenhow?'

'I hoped to marry her,' he mumbled. 'How did you hear of her death?'

McDonald handed him the scrapbook. It was open at a cutting from the *Wilmington Sentinel* dated October 1,1864. His hand was shaking so badly he could barely read what was written there.

THE FUNERAL OF MRS ROSE GREENHOW

The death by drowning of Mrs Rose Greenhow, near Wilmington, North Carolina, last week, has been already noticed. She leaves one child, an interesting little daughter, who is in a convent school at Paris, where her mother left her upon her return to this country. Hundreds of ladies lined the wharf at Wilmington upon the approach of the steamer bearing Mrs Greenhow's remains. The Soldiers' Aid Society took charge of the funeral which took place from the chapel of Hospital No 4. A letter to the Sentinel, *describing it says: 'It was a solemn and imposing spectacle, the profusion of wax lights around the corpse, the quality of choice flowers, in crosses, garlands, and bouquets, scattered over it, the silent mourners, sable-robed at the head and foot; the tide of visitors, women and children, with streaming eyes, and soldiers, with bent heads and hushed steps, standing by, paying the last tribute of respect to the departed heroine. On the bier, draped with a magnificent Confederate flag, lay the body, so unchanged as to look like a calm sleeper, while above all rose the tall ebony crucifix – emblem of the faith she embraced in happier hours, and which we humbly trust, was the consolation in passing through the dark waters of the river of death. She lay there until two o'clock of Sunday afternoon, when the body was removed to the Catholic Church of St Thomas. Here the funeral oration was delivered by the Rev Dr Corcoran, which was a touching tribute to the heroism and patriotic devotion of the deceased, as well as a solemn warning, on the uncertainty of all human projects and ambition, even though of the most laudable character.'*

He had thought he was over her, yet now it felt as if he had lost her once again. The assurances they had given each other made the blood swirl in his veins. But it was too late for that. She had gone and her death merely added to the mystery of her life. Had Rose returned to America to see him or merely to report to President Davis? He would never know the truth.

'You're as white as a sheet, George,' McDonald told him. 'Here, have another whiskey.'

Instead of dulling his senses, the whiskey sharpened them. He could hear her talking to him, feel the touch of her hand. Rose had been the love of his life and he would never know such closeness again. Death idealised her.

'Take the bottle,' came McDonald's voice. 'It's on the house. I guess you want to be alone.'

Grenfell rose unsteadily to his feet and grasped the saloon owner's hand. 'I owe you a debt and won't forget it.'

'Just stay safe, George, and visit me again when this wretched war is over. By then I should be running Chicago.'

'See that you do, Mike,' was all he could think of saying.

'Oh, I almost forgot your winnings!' McDonald threw him a wad of greenbacks. 'You see, there *is* honour among thieves.'

*

A loud ticking noise was coming from somewhere in the darkened bedroom. Was there a clock on the wall? The question worried him as he woke from his drunken stupor. He wanted time to stand still. But the terrible thing about losing someone you love is that everything goes on as before. The world keeps on turning, the seconds' tick away. He screwed up his eyes and tried to recall what Rose had written in her last letter but the exact words escaped him. She had talked of love and longing. Had she embarked on her fatal voyage on his account? It didn't seem likely.

Lying fully dressed on a cold bed, grasping an empty whiskey bottle, he found some solace in the thought that she had followed her own star. Had he imagined that she would sit still and wait for him to come home from the war? No, she was not that kind of woman. Rose had chosen to fight and die for her beliefs. Out of respect for her memory, he would travel to Wilmington to visit her grave and then go to Paris to rescue her daughter from the clutches of the French nuns.

He was so tired. Mustn't sleep though. It wasn't safe to sleep. The bottle fell from his hand and rolled across the floor.

He was awoken by loud knocking on his door. 'Who's there?' he mumbled.

'An urgent telegram,' replied a muffled voice. That couldn't be right. No one would deliver a telegram in the middle of the night. He was raising the skylight above his bed when the door was ripped off its hinges with a resounding crash and a dozen soldiers burst into his room.

'This is an outrage, gentlemen, breaking into a guest's bedroom and treating him like a common criminal,' he blustered.

'You *are* a criminal, Colonel Grenfell,' a Federal captain replied, 'and I'm placing you under arrest.' His hands were cuffed behind his back. With a splitting head and a broken heart went the sickening certainty that his luck had finally run out.

CRIME AND PUNISHMENT

He listened impassively as the sentence was read out. The military tribunal had found him guilty of treason and he was to be hanged by his neck until he was dead. The verdict made no sense whatsoever to the prisoner. To commit treason you either had to betray your country or murder someone to whom you owed allegiance. He was an Englishman and he'd murdered no one. It was monstrously unfair. Of the seven suspects put on trial only he had received a death sentence and for a crime he never even got to commit.

Grenfell was like a man in a dream: he felt numb and made no resistance as he was handcuffed and marched off to McLean Barracks. Here he was shackled to a sixty-pound ball and chain and thrust into a dank cell where the only ray of light came from a narrow iron grating. He could hear soldiers exercising in the yard outside. Was that where he would be executed?

Might as well explore my temporary accommodation, he thought ironically, advancing with hands outstretched until he touched the dripping outer wall and slid down its slimy surface to the straw-strewn floor. Gradually his eyes grew accustomed to the lack of light and his nose to the stench wafting from the latrines above his head.

His military training had stopped him from showing emotion in the courtroom but, left to rot in this dungeon, he broke down and cried; pent-up tears of frustration splashing on the flagstones where he lay. Pulling himself together, he got to his feet and dragged his ball and chain around the cell. On and on he hobbled, like a wild beast circling its cage, until tiredness and the bleeding of his chafed ankles forced him to stop. For want of something better to do, he ate the food his jailer had left:

a small portion of salt pork and doughy bread. But whatever he did, the thought was still there, gnawing away at him, that he had been the architect of his own misfortune.

He should never have tried to hoodwink Secretary of War Stanton in that fateful interview in Washington. He had played a dangerous game and been destroyed by it. It was one thing to pose as a disillusioned foreign soldier seeking safe passage in the North, quite another to offer information about the size of Lee and Beauregard's armies. His estimates had been utterly bogus of course – he had deliberately exaggerated their numerical strength – but the fact that he'd made them at all proved he was an unprincipled mercenary ready to sell his soul to the highest bidder. He could see disgust etched on the faces of his military judges when the stenographic record of his interview with Secretary Stanton was read out, and the prosecution capitalised on this.

The case against him had been based almost entirely on the tainted evidence of two turncoats, Shanks and Langhorne, who claimed he not only intended to free Confederate prisoners of war but to put the whole of Chicago to the torch. What made matters worse was the timing of the trial. The prosecution summing up began four days after the assassination of Abraham Lincoln and the dead president's ghost seemed to hang over the court crying out for vengeance.

'As to this man Grenfell, I confess I have no sympathy with him,' the Judge Advocate Colonel Burnett had said contemptuously. 'No sympathy for the foreigner who lands in our country when this nation is engaged in the struggle for human rights and human liberty; and who takes part in the quarrel against us, and arrays himself on the side of those who are trying to establish tyranny and slavery. I have no sympathy for the man whose sword is unsheathed for hire and not for principle; for whom slavery and despotism have more charm than freedom and liberty.'

It was powerful oratory and Burnett's words went down well with a military tribunal that would neither allow the accused to speak in their own defence nor countenance their lawyers' objections to the biased nature of the proceedings. As he listened to the judge advocate blackguarding him, Grenfell realised he was being tried by a kangaroo court. Yet even when the courtroom was cleared and the judges began to deliberate, he never expected to receive a death sentence. How could they possibly kill him for what was no more than an attempted crime?

He was still grappling with this as he paced out his prison cell. Fifteen hobbled strides in one direction, twelve in the other, and the bitter knowledge of what was to come.

Days turned into weeks and no one visited him, not even his Scottish lawyer who had fought so valiantly in the courtroom. Perhaps Robert Hervey had written him off too. In desperation, he asked his jailer for pen and paper and, sitting cross-legged on the floor in the dim early evening light, he composed a letter to the British Legation in Washington, asking whether he had 'anything to hope for from the protection of the British Government'. He said little about the unfairness of his trial, choosing instead to emphasise his nationality which should have ruled out any treason charge. The minister Sir Frederick Bruce might wish to use this as a mitigating argument.

To mark the passage of time he took to scoring the stone wall with a piece of chalk he'd found in his cell. Each day warranted a separate mark. But the nights were worse, when his fitful slumber was interrupted by the barracks clock striking the hour. There were so many hours in a crowded, active life, but to a condemned captive, lying on an uncomfortable stone bench, they brought nothing but misery. The boom of every iron bell carried the same deep, hollow sound of death. Four o'clock in the morning, wide-eyed and staring, stalked by sleep but with a mind determined to stay awake, searching for answers to random questions. Since his sentencing, how many people had died who imagined they would enjoy a long life? Everyone was condemned to die. What, in any case, had he got to live for? His family hated him, his estranged wife and children managed without him and Rose was dead. What should he regret leaving behind? Not this dungeon with its foul air, backache and ladlesful of watery soup.

One night, worn out and weary, he curled up on his bench and closed his eyes. He slept so soundly he was oblivious to the clanking of the jailer's keys or the rusty grating of the locks. It was only when a rough hand shook his shoulder that he became aware of his surroundings. 'Wake up, Grenfell,' said the prison guard, 'your attorney has come to see you.'

Looking down at him with obvious concern was a round, unlined face in which a long hooked nose was the dominant feature. It belonged to a man in his mid-forties, broadly built but of somewhat lesser height than Grenfell. Robert Hervey wore a dark sack-cloth suit with a starched white shirt and winged collar. 'How have you been, George?' he asked in a curious hybrid accent that combined the gravelly melodies of a Glaswegian tongue with North American vowel shifts. Born in Scotland, Hervey had studied law in Canada before moving south of the border to become a founding member of the Chicago Bar Association. 'Tell me what ails you.'

'I've known better times,' Grenfell muttered, heaving himself to his feet. The lawyer's urge to sympathise with his plight made him feel uncomfortable. He was also painfully aware of how he must seem to his visitor; hair greasy, beard unkempt, clothes filthy and torn and reeking to high heaven.

Hervey's aquiline features split into a sickly smile as he struggled to ignore the smell. 'There have been interesting developments in your case. The British Foreign Secretary Lord John Russell is deeply concerned about the state of civil liberties in the United States and has written to Secretary of State William Seward airing his complaints. Now that has to be good news.'

'I suppose so.' Grenfell's response was perfunctory.

'Aye, well, it emboldened me to seek an audience with Sir Frederick Bruce in Washington. I impressed on him my conviction that you should not have been found guilty of a capital crime in a case resting almost entirely on evidence supplied by untrustworthy witnesses, particularly when, almost certainly, those worthless wretches were perjuring themselves for pecuniary reward. I also pointed out that it is a well-established principle of military law that anyone convicted of forgery is disqualified from giving evidence, and that the prosecutor was conscious of the fact that Shanks and Langhorne had both committed this crime.'

Grenfell stroked his matted beard and gave his attorney a long, hard look. 'When I caught Shanks stealing my horse at Knoxville I wish I'd broken his scrawny neck rather than had him flogged.'

'That's as may be,' Hervey said hurriedly. 'At least Langhorne told the court that you were the best soldier he'd ever known. Sir Frederick was struck by this character assessment, coming as it did from a hostile witness, and plans to raise your case when next at the White House. However, I am bound to tell you he isn't too optimistic. There's been such a strange mood in America since Lincoln's assassination; the Northern states are fired up with an anger that amounts to a bloodlust, and it's led to the most arbitrary use of power. The military can arrest anyone they please, bring them to trial or detain them without trial. Due process has gone out of the window.'

Damn you, John Wilkes Booth, Grenfell murmured under his breath. The actor had torn an already divided country further apart by killing Lincoln. If only Booth had stuck to playing villains on the stage instead of becoming one in real life. Still, he thought sourly, Johnny must have enjoyed his death scene, going down in a blaze of glory in a burning bullet-strewn barn.

'But the pinch of the game has yet to come,' Hervey was telling him. 'It is up to the new president to confirm the sentence of the military commission and, judging from Washington tattle, Andrew Johnson is sorely perplexed by the position in which he finds himself. Sir Frederick may be able to persuade him to exercise a pocket veto which could secure your freedom. On the other hand, Johnson believes treason to be an odious crime deserving of the severest punishment and, given his abhorrence, he is hardly likely to grant you a full pardon. In the circumstances, Bruce favours a less confrontational approach. He wants to argue for executive clemency on the grounds that an English subject cannot be held to have committed a treasonable crime against the American government. And for aught I know, he could be right in his assessment. These are difficult times and the British minister understands the politics better than I do.'

He gazed at his attorney through bloodshot eyes. 'Is this your advice then?'

'Aye, I think an appeal for clemency stands the best chance of success. It lets you live to fight another day.'

What did Hervey mean by this euphemism? His chief concern appeared to be to mitigate the verdict of the military commission, and to substitute the punishment of hard labour for life. Not much there to look forward to, said an inward voice, but at least I can stop counting the hours. But was permanent fettered captivity actually preferable to death? How could he answer that?

'I'll take my leave now.' The attorney didn't wait for a response. His twitching nose and paleness of complexion indicated the onset of nausea and the strongest possible desire to get out of the clammy cell with its all-pervading stench of soiled clothing.

And that was the last Grenfell saw of Hervey. The weeks went by and the lawyer didn't return. Bruce's appeal for clemency had obviously failed. There was to be no reprieve. Yet even when hope had vanished, the prisoner could not resign himself to his fate, dreading the walk to the gallows that each passing hour surely hastened.

Then, one day in June, he heard voices in the corridor. A key turned in the lock and the door flew open. He forced his cracked lips into a smile, before realising with a sickly lurch that his visitor was not Hervey but a wiry dark-haired man in a smart blue military uniform. It was John T Shanks.

'You fucking bastard,' Grenfell roared. 'You've a nerve coming here.' Forgetting the heavy iron ball chained to his leg, he leapt towards his nemesis only to fall flat on the floor.

'We've got a dangerous one here and no mistake, Master Jailer. Better manacle him, and leave us alone for a few minutes. I've got things to say to this wild beast.'

The dazed, half-starved prisoner was in no position to put up a fight. Shackled hand and foot he was entirely at Shanks' mercy. But he still had his dignity. 'Come to gloat, have you, Shanks?'

'Captain Shanks, if you don't mind, newly appointed officer of the Fifth US Volunteer Infantry of Galvanised Yankees.'

'And what pray are Galvanised Yankees? Traitors like you, bribed into service by the Union?'

Shanks answered this taunt by drawing his Colt revolver out of its holster. Like a cat stalking its prey, he circled his helpless victim, before coming closer and sticking the gun in Grenfell's face. 'Galvanised Yankees are former Confederate prisoners of war who've seen the error of their ways, sworn allegiance to the United States and joined the army,' he snarled. 'It was Colonel Sweet's idea that I should spy on you and I was happy to oblige. Now, my fine friend, the only question is whether to put a bullet through your brain and claim self-defence, or leave you to the hangman. What shall it be, I wonder?'

It was difficult to talk with a loaded revolver pressed against his mouth, but Grenfell gave it a try. 'Why do you hate me so much?'

'I don't hate you.' Shanks sneered at him through narrow, shifty eyes. 'I just don't like the fact that you exist. You want to know why? Because you had me flogged in front of Morgan's whole brigade: fifty lashes, wasn't it? Not that I was counting. After I was cut down from the whipping post the medics rubbed salt into my mangled flesh. Now salt may be nature's disinfectant but it leaves scars on the back that never heal properly. The Egyptians held the quaint belief that the victim gained virtue from the whip; scourging the flesh to set the soul free, that sort of thing. Well, that's not the effect it had on John T Shanks, no sir. Every time I took my shirt off and looked in the mirror, I saw your handiwork and vowed to have vengeance on you.'

'Were you the one who put a hole in my forage cap at Cynthiana?' Grenfell could hear his heart pounding. He had to stay calm.

'That's right. When you led your gallant cavalry charge on the Union-held railway station, I took a pot shot at you from an upstairs window in the town hall. I'd have got you too, if you hadn't moved your head at the wrong moment.'

'What about Stones River? Did you poison my dog?'

'Yeah, right again. Took a job as one of Bragg's scouts to finish you off, only this time I thought I'd be clever and lace your brandy with arsenic. It never occurred to me your mongrel would drink it. Imagine my surprise when you emerged from your tent that night carrying the dead mutt and began to dig a grave. Right, I thought, he can join the dog in it, only you heard me cock the trigger and got out of harm's way. I'll say this for you; you're a hard man to kill.'

'Well, now's your chance!' Grenfell swallowed the barrel of Shanks' gun and waited for oblivion.

Shanks thought about it for a moment before withdrawing his revolver. 'Nah, I'll let them string you up and read about your death in the papers. By then, I'll be in Indian country.'

'Doing what?'

'Restoring law and order to the Montana trail. Red Cloud and Crazy Horse are on the warpath again, attacking wagon trains, and the settlers need army support. So it's Captain Shanks and his regiment to the rescue.'

The prisoner shook his head in disgust. To think that this black-hearted villain had actually profited from his betrayal was more than he could stomach. 'If the Sioux don't get you, I will, and that's a promise,' he hissed.

Shanks laughed aloud. 'How are you going to do that? They're planning to hang you before the month is out. You might as well face it, Grenfell, you're finished.'

He watched in impotent rage as his tormentor flipped a coin to the jailer before swaggering down the prison passage into the interior of the barracks. A whistling turnkey locked the cell door and he was alone once more. Sinking onto the stone bench, he cast bloodshot eyes upon the paving stones beneath his shackled feet and felt a surprising sensation; not quite a Damascene conversion but certainly a reawakening of the soul. Out of frustration and hated came a sudden insufferable longing for life, for the bridges yet to be crossed. If only he could get out of here.

Tortured by these thoughts, he began to lurch around his claustrophobic cell, dragging his ball and chain behind him. There was penance to be done. He must express contrition for his sins. Drill for the debauched, a vision of hell even a medieval moralist might approve of. As one painful step followed another, he could hear the echo of the voices that accused him, see all the negatives of his life, the fecklessness, self-pity and anger, laid out like so many dead rats on the flagstones. What he would give to turn back the clock. But the old George, the schoolboy George with his big ambitions, was gone and wouldn't return.

'For the kingdom of heaven is as a man travelling into a far country, who called his own servants, and delivered unto them his goods.'

A young boy, barely into my teens, is sitting on a hard, wooden pew in the family chapel with his four brothers and five sisters.

'And unto one he gave five talents, to another two, and to another one; to every man according to his several abilities; and straightway took his journey.'

His father George Bevil Grenfell is reading the lesson. Matthew Chapter 25 is his favourite text. The boy calls it the banker's creed.

'Then he that had received the five talents went and traded with the same, and made them other five talents.'

The Grenfells live on the Penalverne estate near Penzance. There are rigid social rules for the children of the landed gentry, especially those who make their money out of trade. They are expected to adopt an honourable profession. The oldest son, Pascoe, will inherit the estate and join the family bank. The second son, Owen, should follow his uncle, another Pascoe, into politics, which leaves George, the third in line, free to join the army. Unfortunately, his father doesn't see it that way.

'But he that had received one went and dug in the earth, and hid his lord's money.'

The weight of patriarchal privilege lies heavily upon this family. Young George's eyes wander to a portrait of the founder of the Grenfell fortune. Pascoe Grenfell mined and smelted tin and copper in the eighteenth century but wanted to be painted as a Roman senator surrounded by weeping cherubs. His portrait hangs above a wall mosaic in which vines and foliage entwine with frisking lambs and angels carrying precious metals up to heaven.

'*After a long time the lord of those servants cometh, and reckoneth with them.*'

My father's eyes are cast down upon the Bible while mine are fixed on the stained-glass window in which Celtic saints in armour fight a horde of flying demons.

'*And so he that had received five talents came and brought other five talents, saying, Lord, thou deliverest unto me five talents: behold, I have gained beside them five talents more.*'

Parables are supposed to illustrate a moral lesson and, according to George Senior, St Matthew is emphasising the importance of not squandering your spiritual and intellectual gifts. But St Matthew was a tax collector and his 'talents' were material riches and property: things very dear to the Grenfell heart.

'*His lord said unto him, well done, thou good and faithful servant: thou hast been faithful over a few things, I will make thee ruler over many things; enter thou into the joy of thy lord.*'

I am sick of the sanctities of the ruling class. We live off profits generated by Cornish miners, many of whom won't live to see forty. They die young from rock falls, flooding, explosions, and the diseases they inherit from working in hot, damp and dusty conditions.

'*Thou wicked and slothful servant, thou knewest that I reap where I sowed not, and gather where I have strawed: thou oughtest therefore to have put my money to the exchangers, and then at my coming I should have received mine own with usury.*'

There you are! That's the tax collector talking and the banker repeats his mercenary words as if they were articles of faith. If my father must read St Matthew Chapter 25, let it be the earlier verses about the foolish virgins who didn't trim their lamps.

I am up on the hillside with Mary Bolitho. She shrieks and her tight golden ringlets come loose and blow in the wind as I hold her over the edge of a high granite cliff until she agrees to do my bidding. Later, in her father's barley field, she lets me fondle her firm breasts. I am only sixteen, and have taken no precautions, yet she trusts me. God knows why!

'*Here endeth the lesson. Praise be to God.*'

My lesson was learned in Paris where my father insisted on setting me up with an investment bank. G.S Grenfell Browne & Co was a private partnership designed to capitalise on the global railroad boom. I didn't mind living in one of the world's most beautiful cities but found the job mind-numbingly boring. To shake things up a bit, I gambled on stocks that offered the highest potential return. Casino banking, as I liked to call it, saw me invest in fledgling railway companies with smart prospectuses that promptly crashed and burned. To regain the money I'd squandered, I put most of the firm's remaining assets into coalmining in Belgium. But my luck was out. A Belgian mining disaster destroyed the value of my shares. In my first year of trading I ran up debts of several million francs for which, as a partner in the firm, my father was fully liable. Then, in desperation, I forged a commercial document and was caught out.

On October 26,1836 – the date is engraved on my heart – the *London Gazette* announced the winding up of Grenfell family businesses in Paris and London. Through my ill-judged speculations I had forced my father into bankruptcy. In the weeks that followed, I lived in a state of denial, blaming him for trying to fit a square peg into a round hole. The family expected me to show remorse but I wouldn't oblige them. Tears involved recognition of guilt and I wasn't ready for that yet. What I couldn't evade however was my day of reckoning. A lawyer's letter reached me in London requesting my presence in Penzance to discuss the 'serious liquidity problems' arising from the 'performance' of G.S Grenfell Browne & Co. The meeting was to take place in the Clarence Street offices of Borlase, Milton and Borlase.

'Come in Mr Grenfell and be seated,' says Walter Borlase, a bald, unprepossessing man who speaks in a low-pitched, apologetic tone, almost as if the destruction of our family's fortune is somehow his fault. My father and my eldest brother Pascoe are already at the conference table. The lawyer wastes no time in giving us the bad news. 'Mr Grenfell Senior, having accepted responsibility for your son's debts, I'm afraid you will have to sell the family estate to meet your financial obligations.' Pascoe groans aloud. His inheritance is gone. My older brother is normally a languid creature but today he is agitated, anger coming off him like knives.

'How long have I got, Walter? Are our creditors prepared to wait?' asks my father in that calm, measured way of his. George Bevil Grenfell seldom shows any emotion, yet I know he cares deeply for his children and is ambitious for them, which makes my behaviour all the more reprehensible. I have repaid his love by ruining him. For the first time, as we sit opposite one another in the lawyer's office, I allow myself to feel shame.

I clear my throat. 'There's something I want to say, Papa, if you will allow it.'

'Go ahead George, speak up son.' He is ready to welcome my repentance.

'I never wanted to be an investment banker but that does not excuse my betrayal of your trust. I cannot expect you to forgive me but I want to make amends in any way possible.'

'It's a bit late for that, isn't it?' Pascoe butts in angrily. 'Whatever made you think you could get away with embezzlement and fraud anyway?'

'I was trying to do what it says in the Bible.' My tone is surly. I never liked Pascoe.

'That's absolute nonsense,' my brother shouts. 'We are commanded to *honour* our fathers and mothers, not destroy them!'

'I know that,' I say defensively. 'But let me remind you of Matthew 25, verse 16. Papa gave me five talents and I traded with the same and tried to make another five talents.'

There is a stunned silence at the table. My father nods sadly and opens his mouth to speak but Pascoe beats him to it. 'I don't know how you can have the effrontery to quote Papa's favourite Bible reading. In any case, you lost the talents you were given and more besides, and you know what happened to the unprofitable servant, don't you? He was cast into outer darkness. And that's where you are going. No one in the family will speak to you from this day forth. Furthermore, because of your criminal activities, it has become necessary for Mr Bolitho to draw up a document in which Papa formally disowns you.'

I left for London on the next stagecoach, never to see my father again. I moved abroad and married an Anglo-French girl but quickly realised I was unsuited to Hortense's highly managed domesticity. Yet, despite our frequent bickering, she made a good home and bore me three daughters. But I couldn't settle down. I fought in the French wars in Morocco before accepting a post in the British Consulate in Tangier. After that I became a privateer off the Barbary Coast. Eventually, the risks I ran and the scrapes I got into proved too much for my long-suffering wife. 'You are utterly irresponsible and will come to a bad end,' she prophesied, before moving back to Paris.

How right she was, Grenfell thought, as he dragged himself across his cell. 'I am truly sorry,' he croaked. But there was no one to hear his words. His repentance had come too late. Silence seemed to stretch away from him. All the being and the doing disappeared as he shrank into a narrow core of darkness, invisible to the world. His fettered body ached and bled but what was physical pain compared to the mental torment of waiting to be executed?

Months went by. Yet nothing happened. Then shortly after

dawn on an August morning, Grenfell woke from a fitful sleep to hear a loud hammering outside his cell window. They were building a scaffold in the exercise yard. His time had surely come. There were heavy marching steps in the corridor outside, the sound of rusting bolts being pulled back, and the door was flung open. Two armed soldiers entered with torches. He wanted to scream.

'Rise and shine,' one of them said brusquely. 'It's time to get these chains off you.'

The prisoner did not hear what had been said to him. The moment he had long expected had finally arrive. They were taking him to the gallows. 'Be upright, true and brave,' he mumbled to himself. 'Better a knight than a slave.'

'What's that you're saying, buddy? Don't worry, we're not going to harm you.'

Having been shackled for so long Grenfell could barely stand up, let alone walk, and the guards had to support him. He was vaguely aware of ascending a flight of steps and passing through a door into blinding light.

'Is this it?' he asked, blinking in the sunshine. 'Are you going to hang me now?'

'Where did you get that idea from?' The soldier laughed. 'No, we want to tidy you up a bit.'

They took him into a bathhouse, stripped him out of his filthy rags, and scrubbed his body with horse brushes. After this came vigorous towelling, healing ointments for his sores, and the provision of clean prison clothes. Then to complete the transformation, they put him in a barber's chair to have his shaggy hair and beard trimmed.

Once the soldiers were satisfied, they led him across the parade ground to the guardroom where he was greeted by a young officer. 'I'm pleased to make your acquaintance, Colonel Grenfell. The name is Captain William Mahon and I will be escorting you on the first stage of your journey.'

'Where are you taking me?' the prisoner asked.

'I'll answer that, laddie.' Grenfell swung round to behold a smiling Robert Hervey. 'It's good news, George,' his attorney gushed. 'Sir Frederick Bruce has persuaded President Johnson to commute your sentence to life imprisonment with hard labour.'

He wasn't going to die after all!

'You're being sent to the Dry Tortugas,' his lawyer added.

EXTRACTS FROM COLONEL GRENFELL'S PRISON DIARY

SEPTEMBER 28, 1865

A-a-ll ha-a-ands! Up anchor a-ho-oy!' In response to the bosun's hoarse command sails are loosened, yards braced, and willing hands heave up the anchor that ties us to the American mainland. The last of the evening light is fading as our three-masted clipper slips its moorings and glides past the Battery out into the Atlantic Ocean.

We are sailing with the tide to avoid the currents that plague the southern end of Manhattan Island. At least that's what I'm told by a friendly rating in the ship's kitchen where we are being fed on salt beef, canned carrots and hardtack.

Along with a dozen other convicts, I am chained to a bench. We are an insignificant part of the merchant ship's cargo. In addition to the two hundred tons of tea, spices and timber carried in her cavernous hold, the *John Rice* provides accommodation in her rat-infested steerage for a less precious consignment of 'lifers' who are to be transported to a prison fortress off the coast of Florida.

The ship's cook shakes his ponytail. 'Make no mistake,' he says, 'the Dry Tortugas is a terrible place.' I can well believe it.

OCTOBER 1, 1865

The *John Rice* treats her convict cargo in a most peculiar fashion. We are shackled at night and yet free to move around the ship by day. At sunrise, we lose our iron fetters, wash in a bucket of cold water, and are fed on salted meat. At six bells in the forenoon watch we report to the upper deck where we can stretch our limbs. We walk fore and aft under escort, covering the entire length of the vessel, watching ordinary seamen swabbing and holystoning the wet lower decks and painting exposed parts of the ship as she swoops and plunges through the Atlantic swell. These hardy men of the American merchant marine are prisoners too. Herded together like animals, with only fourteen inches of room in which to sling their hammocks, they are fed a wholly inadequate diet and exposed to numerous perils at sea. In return, they are paid a pittance for their labour.

Were I in their shoes I'd be planning mutiny. But then I've always had a rebellious streak. I act on the spur of the moment, often in an ill-considered way. This character flaw has cost me dear. It has led to my reclassification among the dregs of humanity.

I am the only educated prisoner on the ship and, as such, I have been given access to the sailors' reading room where there is a plentiful supply of paper. I have decided to keep a record of this voyage. It will help pass the time.

OCTOBER 2, 1865

I dreamed last night of John T Shanks; his narrow, rat-like face leering at me as I lay in chains, mocking me, glorying in my imminent execution. Well, I have cheated the hangman, and where there is life there is hope. And anger too: a cold, all-consuming rage that will help me bear captivity patiently before, finally, seeking my revenge on that scoundrel.

OCTOBER 3, 1865

I have been asking the ship's crew about our ultimate destination. The Dry Tortugas are a group of small islands of coral rock and sand at the western end of the Florida Keys discovered by the exotically named Ponce de Leon. The explorer called these reefs Tortugas because of the thousands of huge green sea turtles that dig their nests and lay their eggs in its sandy surface. The prefix 'dry' was added to indicate an absence of fresh water anywhere on the islands. Given this major drawback, as well as the swarms of man-eating sharks and the number of shipwrecks in the surrounding waters, it is hardly surprising that sailors view the Dry Tortugas in an ominous light. The inaccessible solitude of these islands is an appropriate metaphor for a stranded soul, wallowing in desolation and self-pity.

It would seem that every change in my life is for the worse. Yet, as I write this, I am painfully aware of how melodramatic and lacking in contrition this sounds. I have brought evil on myself and it is up to me to change my stars. No one else can do it.

OCTOBER 4, 1865

I wake to hear a shrill howling in the rigging. We are off the coast of South Carolina in that narrow strip of cold water that separates the Gulf Stream from the shore. The sea is rising and the *John Rice* lurches mightily on the mounting waves. All is confusion in steerage. Our coffin-shaped cabin is full of spare sails and coils of rope that bang around in the dark. The filthy mattresses on which we sleep slide from under us, leaving us chained to metal rings in the wall, bombarded by fallen hawsers and a chest of cutlasses. Even the rats have had enough, scampering through the bilge water in search of a drier domain.

Hearing our cries, a petty officer removes our shackles and covers our nakedness with oilskin jackets and loose duck trousers before marching us onto the foredeck. It is dawn now and judging by the anxious glances cast to windward, a tropical storm is brewing. We crowd on as much canvas as the yards will take, but the crew is fighting a losing battle with the elements. I watch in awe as huge, menacing waves roll towards us. The sound is deafening as the heavy head sea crashes against the ship's bows with the force of a sledgehammer. Fifty feet of spray flies over the deck, drenching us through. We are running higher and higher then plunging madly, as every wave buries the forward half of the vessel. The wind whistles through the rigging and stinging horizontal rain lashes against my oilskin. The topsail halyards have been let go and the great sails fill out, billowing against the masts with a noise like thunder. Down below, orders are given and executed by sailors 'singing out' at the ropes. The sails are stiff and wet, the ropes slippery to handle, the crew virtually blinded by the violence of the storm.

All hands are called for, including ours. There is no time to find my sea legs as sickness overtakes me. It is in this desperate state that I am ordered to reef the topsails. 'Tumble up there and take in sail,' yells the chief mate. 'Go on, you puking ninny! If anyone is going to die today it had best be you!'

Out on the bridge, the commodore hears these sarcastic words, points to me and shakes his head. 'Not you, Grenfell,' the mate snarls, 'three men next to you.' I watch in fascinated horror as my fellow prisoners climb up the swaying rigging.

It is pure lunacy. None of them has ever been aloft, let alone grappled with a splitting sail in a force ten wind. By now, the main topsail is shaking so violently the masthead must have broken if regular sailors had not rushed up to cut away the sheet. The ship's crew cheer wildly but my eyes are on a fellow convict who is standing uncertainly on a footrope beneath the lee yardarm. Without any warning the rope gives way and he falls silently into the sea, disappearing instantly from sight.

Once again, the commodore shakes his head. Putting out a boat in this weather would be madness. 'Ah well,' says the mate defensively, 'that's one less mouth to feed.' I might have been the one to fall from that yardarm. Why did the commodore spare me? I may never know.

OCTOBER 5, 1865

As an active soldier, I have had little time for the reflective arts, thinking there was no excitement in the use of ink or paints. Now I know differently. Writing is an exercise in self-discovery. Even the simplest narrative explores the inner workings of the author's mind and how he interacts with the world around him. Today I am thinking about the relationship between cause and effect. To what extent does a man control his destiny? Is there such a thing as historical inevitability? Was the American Civil War inevitable and, if so, what made it so?

The Greek poet Homer claims the Trojan War was the direct result of the abduction of Helen of Sparta by Paris, prince of Troy, and infers that the Greek ships would not have sailed to rescue her if she had been any less beautiful. I don't know whether the Trojan War actually happened but, even if it's a myth, the question is still a valid one. Can the random fashioning of a woman's face change the course of history? Is fortune really predicated on such tiny turns as these?

Let me bring this argument closer to home. Had my head ruled my heart, would I have joined the Camp Douglas conspiracy? I think not. It was a foolish undertaking from the start but, on losing the woman I loved, I stopped caring about the risks I ran. That much I know to be true.

OCTOBER 6, 1865

It is said a ship is like a lady's watch, always out of repair, and how true that is. No sooner had we left port in New York than the standing rigging had to be overhauled and canvas added to each line or spar to protect it from friction. Sailors tackle these tasks as if their lives depend on it, which is no more than the truth. The fight to stay alive is a never-ending one at sea.

This voyage will soon be over and a fresh ordeal will begin. What bothers me most is the limitless nature of my punishment.

I am condemned to do hard labour on a godforsaken coral reef for the remaining days of my life. I say these words to myself but somehow cannot believe them.

In my search for solace I turn to the ocean. Water is infinitely wide and incalculably deep; it extends indefinitely and flows endlessly. It gives and takes life and seeks no reward. I have heard the seductive voice of the sea since I was a small boy living on the Cornish coast and I have to believe that, just as the tide turns, so will my fortune.

OCTOBER 7, 1865

Few soldiers can have spent more time at sea than I have and fewer still can have been worse sailors. The merest swell is often sufficient to make me feel queasy. It is therefore with a profound sense of relief that I now report that our ship is encountering calmer waters as we voyage down the Florida Keys.

These coral reefs remain a great mystery to marine biologists. They were built by colonies of small coral animals whose cup-shaped skeletons accumulated over time and yet the Florida Keys rise from deeper water than the sunlight-craving corals could possibly have survived in. An explanation for this conundrum can be found in one of my favourite books, Charles Darwin's account of his voyage on HMS *Beagle*. He suggests that the inexplicably deep reefs were formed when the sea floor was nearer to the surface. I am much taken with this idea.

I feel such an affinity with the scientist. He too was constantly seasick.

OCTOBER 8, 1865

Our clipper will soon reach its destination. We have been marshalled onto the foredeck and our skin burns under the scorching rays of the sun. The lookout spots the first of the Tortugas, an acre of coral covered in thick brushwood, mango and prickly pear. Other islands with blinding white beaches and stands of mangrove duly follow. I see where the whitish-blue waters of the Gulf of Mexico meet the deep blue water of the Gulf Stream. The anchor watch calls out a draught of five fathoms. The shallows teem with tropical fish. Sponges, octopuses and sea urchins thrive here. Schools of dolphin and flying fish stage an aerial ballet for our benefit.

The *John Rice* steadies on her course, with the wind three points on the starboard quarter. Out of the dancing heat haze, a weird-looking vessel looms up in front of us. Although her outline is blurred by the thickening air, a turreted battleship is bearing down on us. Is this one of the ironclads that fought in the Civil War? No, by God, it's a mirage. What I am looking at is an immense fortification, a three-tiered, six-sided castle with ochre-coloured brick walls that seems to be resting on the surface of the sea.

'Welcome to Fort Jefferson,' says the first mate ironically. I have seen many strange sights in my lifetime but none to equal this floating fortress. Why build such an imposing structure on a coral atoll? It beggars belief. Everything must have been brought from the mainland: all the skilled artisans, labourers and slaves, all the timber and cement, every last brick and nail. And to what end? This fort with its massively thick walls and mounted gun emplacements can hardly have been finished before developments in warfare such as the rifled cannon rendered it obsolete.

The *John Rice* drops anchor in deeper water and we are rowed ashore in shallow-draught boats. The closer we get, the more amazing the fort looks. Its turrets and tooth-like battlements belong to the days of chivalry and, to enhance the fantasy, there is also a substantial moat that can only be crossed when a drawbridge is lowered from the sally port. As we are escorted over this drawbridge I am shocked to see dorsal fins cutting through the water. One of the guards notices my alarm. 'You like our little display, do you?' he chortles. 'We call these ten-foot sharks the provost marshals. No one is going to jump into the moat with our sentinels on patrol.'

The sheer size of the fortress is staggering. Its walls are eight-feet-thick and stand fifty feet high with embrasures for hundreds of heavy guns. The place positively bristles with warlike intent. Yet inside its perimeter walls is a large parade ground of fine Bermuda grass planted with cottonwoods, evergreen mangoes, cocoa palms and gum trees.

Black soldiers march our shipload of offenders past the lumber shed and out onto the parade ground where a white sergeant major gives us a guided tour. Once again my jaw drops. The officers live in a handsome three-storey brick block, about three hundred feet long, festooned with jasmine and cypress vines and shaded by mangrove trees. We are also shown the soldiers' barracks which are almost as fine. That is when I realise the fort is unfinished. 'What you are eyeballing,' barks the sergeant major, 'are the future hospital and naval store while that cottage over there will be the commandant's new headquarters. Your home, however, will be in the cells above the sally port.'

As I look at my new home, I see signs of decay. This partially built brick behemoth is already falling apart. The casemate walls are crumbling and coated with slime, there are large cracks in the cistern that is supposed to filter the rainwater, and buckets of sea water give off a sour, stagnant smell. The Dry Tortugas are determined to remain dry.

The only thing that seems at home here is the insect life. The island's tropical climate is a perfect breeding ground for mosquitoes, cockroaches and scorpions. God knows what our cells are like.

We line up to be deloused and supplied with our prison uniforms. No one born into a cosy world of economic and social certainties should have to queue up with naked, evil-smelling convicts in a prison compound. Yet my first encounter with Fort Jefferson's penal system was to have a surprisingly satisfactory outcome, one I could hardly have anticipated. But I am getting ahead of myself.

The fort's physician, a small, sickly-looking man with a squint, wants to make sure we are not carrying any contagious or degenerative diseases, although the attention he pays to our tattoos, scars and other deformities convinces me that this is his way of classifying new convicts. As I wait my turn to be poked and prodded like a dumb animal in a cattle market, I feel my life has reached its lowest ebb. Yet, in the event, I don't need to mortify myself. My scars speak for me.

During a long military career, I have taken part in a dozen military campaigns and have the wounds to prove it: the punctured left shoulder blade caused by an arrow from a Chinese crossbow; the gashed chest from an Algerian spear; the puckered back from repeated stabbings during the Sepoy Mutiny; the sabre-slashed right arm while fighting with Garibaldi in Italy; not to mention the bullet holes and powder burns I picked up in serving the Confederacy. In truth, my body bears witness to almost every kind of weapon system known to man.

The physician is about to put his stethoscope to my chest when he notices all these mementoes. 'Oh my God, what have we got here?' he gasps. 'This fellow carries the whole history of warfare on his hide.'

Since Roman times, opening your tunic to reveal your scars has often been a way to assert authority. Indeed, when disrobed, a man's wounds can do more than that. I learned this lesson in the boudoir. When eager females wanted to explore my body with their fingers, I'd make no complaint when they encountered a cut or lesion in my flesh, apart from a manly wince or a barely perceptible intake of breath. Scars did capital service with the ladies but I hadn't expected them to have a similar effect on a prison quack.

'Here is a superior specimen,' says the doctor, treating the prison guards as if they were a medical lecture class. 'He cares nothing about personal injury. What matters is not winning or losing but the fight itself, the willingness to trade blows, to shed blood. You see gentlemen, bruises and scars add to a man's prestige and that of his lineage. Alexander the Great gloried in his war wounds.'

The post surgeon runs his hands over my chest before looking me in the eye. 'Tell me, of all your many wounds which is the most painful?'

'The minie ball lodged in my bum, sir.'

He spots another scar on my abdomen. 'What's it like to be run through with a sword?'

'At first, you feel nothing. Then a hideous, tearing agony until the blade is withdrawn, the blood wells up on your shirt and you know you are still alive.'

'Is there anything you're afraid of?'

'Yes, a soft-nose bullet lodged in the pelvis,' I say without flinching. 'It shatters the bone and spreads its splinters through your intestines, guaranteeing a dreadful death.'

'Any pain down here?' The post surgeon searches my testicles for a lump or swelling.

'No, sir,' I reply, wishing he'd keep his hands to himself.

'How long have you been confined in prison?'

'Eleven months in all.'

The doctor nods before turning to the guards. 'I am going to excuse this man from hard labour, at least until his health improves. Find him a decent cell and treat him well.'

The soldiers give me solitary lodgings in an unfinished gunroom on the second tier of the fort and, instead of joining my fellow convicts in breaking rocks, I am taken to the prison library where the chaplain provides me with pen and paper so that I can resume this diary. Apart from the lack of freedom, I find my situation quite tolerable.

NOVEMBER 6, 1865

I'd been here less than a month when soldiers of the 82nd United States Coloured Infantry came banging on my cell door. Their commanding officer had received orders that I should be transferred to 'the dungeon'.

My life of leisure is over. I am marched down a flight of stairs and thrust into a dark, airless ground-floor gunroom. I know I have company. The rank smell of unclean bodies and a persistent hacking cough tells me that. As my eyes grow accustomed to the dim shafts of light emanating from slits in the wall, four figures materialise out of the shadows. They are sitting on a narrow wooden bench.

'You must be Grenfell,' a soft, musical voice says.

'Guilty as charged,' I reply with forced humour.

'Welcome, brother, you are now a political prisoner. Allow me to introduce myself.' A tall, thin man rises from the bench. 'The name is Samuel Mudd, the Maryland doctor who had the misfortune to treat a patient who had just killed President Lincoln.'

I am shaking hands with the infamous Dr Mudd who set John Wilkes Booth's broken leg. An intelligent man, I think, with his blue eyes and domed forehead, probably in his early thirties.

'Now meet your cellmates,' the good doctor continues. 'We're very unpopular in Fort Jefferson. Given half a chance, those darkies in uniforms would string us up. This here is Samuel Arnold, a farmhand from Baltimore, once a classmate of Booth, joined his plot to kidnap Lincoln but was wrongly convicted of trying to kill the president. Say hello, Sam.'

An intense-looking man grabs my hand and mutters something. 'Sorry,' I say, 'I couldn't make that out.'

'I said we're kindred spirits. We were both involved in plots to free Confederate prisoners. Leastways I heard of a Colonel Grenfell who was given the death penalty after the Chicago conspiracy. What happened to you?'

'I was granted a last-minute reprieve and sent here instead. Glad to meet you.'

'Moving along the rogue's gallery,' says Dr Mudd, 'this handsome lad is Michael O'Laughlen, a feed salesman from Baltimore, who also took part in Booth's madcap scheme to abduct Lincoln.'

A small, delicate man in his mid-twenties stands up to greet me. 'I think that's less than fair, Sam. I was prepared to snatch the president but when Booth talked about capturing Lincoln at Ford's Theatre I reckoned he was plumb crazy and backed off.'

'I've met John Wilkes Booth,' I say. 'He was playing *Richard III* at Grover's Theatre in '63 and we went backstage after the performance.'

'What did you make of him?' Dr Mudd enquires. There is barely concealed venom in his tone.

'I couldn't decide whether he was a genuine Confederate agent or an actor playing at being a spy, but his loyalty to the South was plain enough.'

'Pity he couldn't have shown it in a more positive way,' says Dr Mudd dismissively. 'But I guess actors always perform to the gallery.'

'So you think he simply went off script and turned a kidnapping into a murder?'

'That's about the shape of it.' My guide's hands clench and his eyelids flutter with suppressed emotion. He turns to the last man on the bench. 'And this is Edmund Spangler, the stagehand who held Booth's horse when he went inside the theatre to shoot

Lincoln. Ned doesn't have much to say for himself.'

I hold out my hand but Spangler ignores it. With his low receding forehead, ridged brow and swollen red face he looks feebleminded. Not that stupidity will stop him from being violent.

'Make yourself at home.'

The irony in the doctor's comment is not lost on me as I look around the small, damp cell into which we are squeezed. I see four plank beds on the stone floor. 'Where am I supposed to sleep?'

'Good question,' Dr Mudd replies. 'I recommend this bench. We don't need it at night. There's a pile of blankets in the corner. Take one.' He points to some filthy rags that must be swarming with dust mites and lice.

I am about to express my horror when a bugle blows and our cell door is yanked open. Three black soldiers bustle in, two carrying iron shackles while the third covers them with his rifle. 'I forgot to mention this, my friend,' Dr Mudd whispers. 'You will be working on our chain gang.'

Heavy leg irons and fetters are fastened to our ankles to prevent any thought of escape, although I have no idea how we might accomplish such a feat with so many guards, a shark-infested moat and a huge stretch of water between the Tortugas and the mainland.

NOVEMBER 12, 1865

Clad in grey flannel overalls and hobbled by leg irons, we 'politicals' go to work shadowed by Negro guards. We are not permitted to talk to our fellow prisoners who are a mixture of army deserters, rapists and robbers. We are allotted pointless tasks.

Along with Spangler I have been detailed to clean the second floor brickwork. The bricks we are refurbishing are light red in colour and were laid in the ante-bellum years when supplies came from the Southern states. The darker red bricks elsewhere in the fort are of more recent origin and were shipped from Connecticut. While hardly demanding, scrubbing mildewed bricks is a tedious occupation. Spangler and I compete to see who can do the least work. He usually wins.

NOVEMBER 13, 1865

A new commanding officer has arrived which has led to a restoration of privileges. All prisoners can send and receive letters and are permitted an hour's recreation time each day.

I have taken the precaution of secreting my diary inside the library's copy of *The Count of Monte Cristo*. An appropriate hiding place and a safe one too, since it's the original French version of the book and I am the only person here who understands the language. The librarian sees what I am doing but as he is the prison chaplain and a good-natured fellow he turns a blind eye.

I ask for the name of our new commandant and he tells me it is Brigadier General Bennett Hill. 'Not the Colonel Hill who first informed Colonel Sweet of the Chicago Conspiracy?' say I, recalling testimony at my military trial. 'The very same,' replies the vicar. How small the world is!

NOVEMBER 15, 1865

I am not a malicious person yet I attract animosity like a horse attracts flies. Today, as I stumble towards the library, I am stopped by the officer of the day, a small pompous lieutenant called William Van Reed. I have noticed him before, strutting around the compound.

'How the mighty have fallen,' he sneers, compensating for his lack of inches by putting his weight on his toes. 'It's Colonel Grenfell, the English mercenary who killed my brother at Stones River. You piece of shit! Look at you now, a convict in chains. Where's your precious honour now?'

His contemptuous words cut me to the quick. 'At least I have more honour than you,' I lash back. 'Only a coward would insult a defenceless prisoner.'

I see the colour rising in his pale face. Fortunately for me, a captain crosses the parade ground and calls for a salute. While the angry pipsqueak is observing military protocol I slink away. There will be repercussions.

NOVEMBER 16, 1865

I have heard nothing about yesterday's altercation with the lieutenant. Perhaps General Hill does not approve of his officers goading prisoners and plans to treat us better than his predecessor did. So far, there has been no improvement in our diet, which consists of chunks of salt pork and beef, supplemented by a few root vegetables, mouldy bread, and a mincemeat stew of dubious provenance, washed down with dirty water taken from the rain barrels. Nor has anything been done to rid our dungeon of the mosquitoes, bedbugs and roaches.

NOVEMBER 18, 1865

We have just had a violent tropical storm: two days of high winds, driving rain and rough seas. Under such a deluge our cell leaks horribly with almost a foot of water on the stone floor. We bale out as best we can, using pieces of flint to dig trenches to divert the rainwater under the door. This communal effort seems to loosen tongues in our cell.

I start things off. 'This hurricane is a force of nature. It reminds me of Henry Burnett in full spate.'

Sam Arnold seizes on my remark. 'Don't tell me *you* were prosecuted by him too?'

'Absolutely,' I reply. 'He lied, cheated and introduced tainted witnesses who should never have been allowed inside a court of law. And I was his prime target, not because I was guiltier than anyone else but because I was a foreign soldier who could be portrayed as an unscrupulous, amoral mercenary. Colonel Henry Lawrence Burnett was a holy terror.'

My cellmates growl in agreement and Michael O'Laughlin speaks up. 'After Lincoln's death there was no way we could get a fair trial, and Burnett certainly didn't intend to give us one. The facts he set before his fellow judges were extorted, perverted or invented. We had no idea Booth meant to kill the president, there wasn't a scrap of evidence to say we did, and yet the tribunal convicted us of conspiring in his assassination. I hope Burnett rots in hell!'

'And so say all of us.' Sam Arnold nods vigorously. 'The worst we did was getting mixed up in a ridiculous scheme to abduct Lincoln and take him to Richmond where he would be held in exchange for Confederate prisoners-of-war. As kidnapper-in-chief, John Wilkes Booth planned to ambush Lincoln on his way to Campbell Hospital but, as luck would have it, the president cancelled his visit at the last moment. After this failure, I backed out and sent Booth a letter explaining why. Unfortunately, Booth kept my note and it was found in his trunk after the assassination. You can imagine the selective use Burnett made of it during my trial. He read out what I said about being "in favour of the enterprise" but neglected to mention that I had withdrawn from the plot and was urging Booth to do likewise. "Do not act rashly or in haste," I wrote, but Burnett chose to ignore these words, and I was found guilty of conspiring to murder the president, long after I'd cut my ties with his assassin. That bastard Burnett chewed me up good and proper!'

Another hard luck story, I think, with more to follow. What about Ned Spangler, the star-struck stagehand at Ford's Theatre who got six years hard labour for holding the actor's horse while he went inside to give his final performance? If anyone got a raw deal it was Spangler. But it's not him who speaks next.

'Like Sam, I was condemned for what I said rather than did.' Dr Mudd's gentle voice is barely audible. 'Imagine being woken at four o'clock in the morning by loud banging on your front door – two men are standing outside in the dark, one of whom is a limping John Wilkes Booth.'

'So you knew Booth?' I feel compelled to ask.

'I'd met him once before. He was looking for a horse to buy and I helped him find one. Anyway, to get back to my story, Booth's companion tells me the actor has fallen off his horse and is badly in need of treatment. I help Booth inside, cut off his boot and discover he's broken his left fibula. I dress the leg and agree that the two men can stay for the rest of the night. Next morning, I go into Bryantown on business and learn that Lincoln has been assassinated in Ford's Theatre and that the principal suspect is a man who injured his leg jumping from the president's box onto the stage. Unwittingly, I have harboured a murderer.'

Mudd's blue eyes are fixed on mine. 'I do not know what to do or say and when a military investigator comes to my farm two days later, I panic. I tell him I'd never seen Booth or his companion before. Later, under further questioning, I admit to lying but, by then, the damage is done. Burnett produces a string of witnesses in my trial who claim to have seen me with Booth on numerous occasions. My attorney, General Thomas Ewing, argues that my only prior encounter with the actor was in November 1864 but to no avail. The country doctor who did his medical duty for someone he barely knew is portrayed as a monster, an arch conspirator.'

Listening to this softly delivered tirade, I remember the Confederate agent I'd met in Maryland after my balloon trip with

Rose. Thomas Harbin claimed to have set up a spy ring in Charles County that included a slave-holding doctor called Mudd.

'You said you had a farm. Was medicine a second string to your bow?' I ask breezily, conscious of sounding like an interrogator.

'That's right,' says Dr Mudd. 'I was primarily a tobacco farmer, not a doctor.'

'Did you have slaves?'

'Sure. I had eight slaves until Maryland voted to abolish slavery last year.'

'How did you vote on the issue?'

'I voted against abolition, as did almost everyone in Charles County, but the anti-slavery lobby won. This left me virtually destitute, unable to market my crop.'

Angry enough to turn your farm into a safe house for the Confederacy, I think to myself. Booth and his associate didn't end up on your doorstep by accident.

NOVEMBER 21, 1865

I have been reading about prison reform and how the ideas of the eighteenth-century English philanthropist John Howard are gradually penetrating the American penal system. Howard believed most criminals could be rehabilitated and that prisons had a humane duty to reform offenders as well as punish them.

The nearest For Jefferson gets to such liberal thinking is in the provision of a prison library. What distinguishes our bibliotheca from any other is its location in a disused powder magazine. Entry is through a tunnel which leads into a large brick room with oak-shelved walls and a high arched ceiling. It is cool inside with a distinctive smell; a combination, I imagine, of the mustiness of old books and the acrid, sour odour of spent gunpowder. The room would be dark but for an oil lamp suspended from the ceiling that can be adjusted by means of chains and a brass ball. Beneath the lamp is a centrally placed table and balloon-backed chairs. On the table's baize-covered top is an enormous volume bound in leather and stamped in gold. The Reverend William Matchett, our chaplain and librarian, believes in keeping Cruden's *Concordance of the Bible* on permanent display. If he had his way the library would be stacked with religious tracts instead of novels and non-fiction.

I am alone in the library when the chaplain arrives after his morning service. 'You've taken quite a fancy to *The Count of Monte Cristo*, Grenfell,' he says knowingly. Reverend Matchett has a keen sense of humour. 'Do you have a special affinity for Edmond Dantès?'

'Not particularly,' I reply, 'but I got to know Alexandre Dumas during a big game hunt in Africa.'

'Well there's a surprise,' says the dog-collared librarian. 'And what was Dumas like in the flesh?'

'As I recall, he was a fat, large-hearted man who never stopped talking, especially about himself.'

Reverend Matchett laughs loudly before pointing to a bookshelf above his head. I can see that some of the books are badly damaged. 'Those are real bullet holes,' he tells me. 'There was an actual gunfight here when some prisoners tried to escape.'

'Has anyone managed to get off this island?' I ask in an offhand sort of way. 'I was told it was impossible.'

'I believe some slaves working on the building of this fort got away in a boat once. There's a newspaper cutting about it. Shall I dig it out for you?'

I express mild interest in the story but my heart is pounding. If slaves can escape, so can I.

NOVEMBER 22, 1865

Reverend Matchett kept his word. The newspaper cutting was waiting for me in the prison library when I arrived this morning. The story of the slaves' bid for freedom appeared in the *Chicago Tribune* on July 16, 1847, and a copy of the article had been pasted into an album about the building of the fort.

DARING ESCAPE THWARTED

We announce the recapture of the seven enslaved workers who made a daring escape from Garden Key in the Dry Tortugas where they had been employed in the construction of what promises to be the largest coastal fort ever built. Early on July 10, under the cover of darkness, the seven slaves named Jerry, Jack, John, George, Ephraim, Howard and Robert removed the schooners Union, Virginia *and* Active *and the lighthouse keeper's small boat from their island moorings and sailed them into the Loggerhead Channel. There they disabled and abandoned all the vessels apart from the* Union, *on which they continued to sail in the general direction of the Bahamas.*

Two days later they were spotted in a rowing boat near Key Vacas, some 120 miles east of the Dry Tortugas. The alarm was sounded and several ships pursued them. The slaves came ashore on Long Key and raced across the island before throwing themselves into the sea in sheer desperation. The chase ended when a sloop's boat rescued the exhausted men from the water.

The slaves were carried to Key West where they were thoroughly searched before being returned to their owners. The ringleaders of the group, Jerry and Jack, were found to have dozens of George III guinea coins dated 1813 in their trouser pockets. They claimed to have found these coins while digging the foundations for Fort Jefferson. They also talked of human bones and a wooden shipping chest holding a bundle of old papers.

Fort Jefferson's Commanding Officer Lieutenant Isaac H. Wright dismissed the slaves' story as fanciful although he was at a loss to explain how they came by the English money. His second in command, post surgeon Dr Daniel Whitehurst, refused to condemn the men for seeking their freedom. When asked about the guineas in their possession he said, 'The gold came from Africa and so did they.' Dr Whitehurst is an active supporter of the American Colonization Society which seeks to repatriate all Negroes to their ancestral continent.

I can hardly contain my excitement on reading this account. If the slaves were telling the truth there must be buried treasure on Garden Key that predated the building of the fort. But how had it got there? The obvious answer is a shipwreck. The Dry Tortugas are notorious for their treacherous reefs and the first permanent structures on Garden Key were a lighthouse and a lighthouse keeper's residence.

I imagine a tropical storm boiling up, stirring the waves to frenzy. A bullion ship runs aground on a reef near Garden Key and begins to sink. A few sailors manage to reach the shore, bringing a ship's chest with them, only to die of thirst because there is no fresh water on the island. This would account for the human bones and the chest with its golden coins. The most likely explanation for the George III guineas is that the shipwrecked vessel was a British one, carrying specie to pay her troops in America.

To test this theory, I need detailed information about early nineteenth-century shipwrecks and coinage. But how to get it without giving the game away? The chaplain is my best hope.

On returning from morning prayers he finds me seated at the library table with Buckle's *History of Civilisation* open in front of me. 'I have been reading about the fate of the Spanish plate fleet of 1622,' I say, 'the one that got caught in a hurricane near the Florida Keys. At least four of these Spanish galleons sank off the Tortugas with their cargo of silver bars and gold coins, and later attempts to salvage the ships led to further accidents and loss of life. I am thinking of writing a short monograph for *Harper's Weekly* about this strange sequence of maritime disasters and, to improve my knowledge, I wonder whether you might be able to borrow any books on Florida shipwrecks and gold coinage.'

The chaplain beams with pleasure. Here is a prisoner who wants to improve himself. Rehabilitation beckons. 'Of course, I'll help,' he tells me. 'There's a public library in Key West. I'll get in touch with them.'

DECEMBER 7, 1865

The books have finally arrived on a supply ship from Key West. One is entitled *Shipwrecks of Florida* while the other two are grim-looking tomes on numismatics, *Lettres du Baron Marchant sur la numismatique et l'histoire* and *The History of Gold Coinage* by Mungo Campbell.

I opt for Mungo's lengthy volume in the hope that it covers not only Spanish doubloons and Louis d'or but English currency, and I am rewarded with a chapter on the guinea. What Mungo has to say about the final minting of this coin captures my attention: 'The last issue was known as the military guinea. Eighty-thousand guineas were struck to pay the Duke of Wellington's army in the Pyrenees and British soldiers stationed in North America. Each of these guineas had the year, 1813, stamped between its edge and the crowned shield and garter inscription.'

I now have a precise timing for my imagined shipwreck. The military guineas found by the slaves must have been carried to Florida by a British bullion ship in either 1813 or 1814. It couldn't have been earlier because the coins didn't exist then and it couldn't be later because British troops left America in 1814. I open *Shipwrecks of Florida* and my body tingles with excitement when I read that more than two thousand vessels have been lost off the coast of Florida, many of them British. In listing these maritime disasters, the book divides the Floridian coastline into sections, the third of which is the Lower Keys. I scan the early nineteenth-century entries:

WRECKS IN THE DRY TORTUGAS

Maria – ship, Captain Rundle, from Jamaica bound for Halifax; wrecked on the Dry Tortugas in 1806. All hands lost.

Ceres – brig from New Orleans, Captain Twain; ran ashore on Dry Tortugas in 1810. Crew saved.

Acasta – British merchantman, Captain Parkin, from Jamaica bound for Liverpool; wrecked sometime before December 5, 1811 in the Dry Tortugas. Crew and most cargo saved.

.Sir John Sherbroke – ship, Captain Kennedy, from Jamaica bound for New York with general cargo and 60,000 dollars in specie; wrecked in 1812 on a reef off the Dry Tortugas. Crew and specie saved.

Granville Packet – British ship, Captain Curlett, from Baltimore bound for Pensacola with mail and specie; wrecked on the Dry Tortugas, September 23, 1814. All hands lost.

There it is in black and white! A Falmouth packet, named after my mother's family, carrying mail and military guineas to what was obviously a British garrison in Pensacola, Florida, ran aground on the Tortugas with a complete loss of life and cargo. Or so it is believed. Only I know differently.

DECEMBER 9, 1865

I was summoned to see the commandant this morning. His office, next to the sally port, reminded me of a porters' lodge I once visited in an Oxford college, full of pigeonholed keys, letters and ledgers and, with a freestanding stove, too hot for comfort.

My jailers march me into this cluttered room, salute, and leave me standing by a pile of shackles and leg irons gazing at a general who is sweating in his shirt-sleeves. He hears my chains rattling and looks up from his desk.

My first impression is of a heavily lined face and white hair. 'Grenfell, ain't it?' says he, rising to his feet and shaking hands warmly. 'Now where's that bell of mine? I'm always losing it.'

I see a small bell on the floor beneath his desk. 'Would this be what you're looking for, sir?'

'Indeed it is. Well spotted.' General Hill is obviously a man of kindly disposition, if somewhat vague. 'I'll ring for coffee,' he says. 'I dare say you'd like a cup.'

On looking around the room I am distressed to see that its brick walls need a good scrubbing. Hill follows my line of sight. 'Do you know how many bricks went into building Fort Jefferson?' he asks rhetorically. 'Well, I'll tell you: sixteen million. I believe this is the second biggest brick building in the world after the Great Wall of China.'

He pauses to let this fact sink in. 'We've also got the largest hot shot furnace which can heat twenty-four-pound balls in twenty-five minutes, and 175 cannons to fire them.'

It is my turn to say something. 'That's very impressive, sir. But why bother to build such a huge fort in the middle of nowhere?'

'Ah, Grenfell, you have failed to appreciate that this is one of the most strategic anchorages in North America. By fortifying this commodious harbour on one of the world's busiest shipping lanes, the United States acquired an operational base from which ships could be sent out on offensive sorties, although that is only part of the story. The fort's immense size is also a reflection of its defensive mission. After the war of 1812, when your people set fire to Washington, our political leaders became convinced of the need for a strong coastal defence system and a board of military engineers accepted Thomas Jefferson's idea for a chain of forts stretching along the nation's coastline. The largest of these, Fort Jefferson, was meant to be an indestructible gun platform, capable of destroying any enemy shipping that came within a three-mile range.'

'But that's no longer the case, is it, sir?'

'You are right,' he admits sadly. 'Its military usefulness has waned because of technological advances in warship design and the advent of ship-borne rifled artillery. That's why Fort Jefferson is now a military prison.' And that's why a two-star general like you is rotting away in this hellhole. I don't say this aloud, of course, but nod sagely and rattle my chains in sympathy.

Hill clears his throat. 'I am deeply disturbed by the barbarism of keeping a man of your age and distinction in leg irons and have made my feelings known to the War Department in Washington. Unfortunately, they insist on treating you as a state prisoner.'

'I am honoured you should speak on my behalf.' I muster a weak smile but inwardly I am seething. That swine Stanton hasn't forgotten how I misled him when we met in Washington. He stood behind his high bookkeeper's desk, glowering at me through steel-rimmed glasses, as I told my cock-and-bull story about leaving the Confederate army and wanting, as a British citizen, to do 'a spot of hunting' in the North.

'What did you do to deserve such harsh treatment?' Hill interrupts my brooding over the past.

'I was going to lead an attack on Camp Douglas to free Confederate prisoners of war but Colonel Sweet got wind of our plans and I was arrested before I could do anything.'

The general looks upset. 'As you may know, I played some part in that affair,' he says gruffly.

'Aye, and I don't hold it against you, sir.' I stiffen my upper lip. 'You were only doing your duty.'

'That's big of you, Grenfell, it really is. Tell me, who did you serve under in the recent conflict? Did you know my old comrade-in-arms Braxton Bragg by any chance?'

'I was his aide-de-camp at Stones River.'

'Were you indeed? I met him at West Point when we were cadets, back in '37. Such a long time ago,' he adds, all misty-eyed.

'And how did you find him?' I am genuinely intrigued.

'Never had much time for him, although he was definitely a bright boy, graduated fifth in his year, naturally disputatious, absolute stickler for regulations. Ulysses Grant used to tell a tale about Bragg doubling up as commanding officer and quartermaster at a frontier post and refusing his own request for company supplies. Braxton was a real ornery customer, a man who could pick a fight with himself. What was he like at Stones River?'

'Unpopular,' says I. 'Breckinridge's Kentuckians wanted to kill him more than the enemy.'

Hill laughs and slaps me on the shoulder. 'It can't have been fun being at his beck and call. Rather cramped your style, what?'

I grin and nod, wondering how best to take advantage of his charitable disposition. 'Begging your pardon, sir, but having to wear these chains is what cramps my style.'

'I know that, I really do, and it pains me to see such a valiant opponent brought so low, but my hands are tied by War Department regulations.'

Hill lapses into silence before realising what he's just said. 'Not that I'd want you to think I'm another Braxton Bragg. Supposing, for the sake of argument, the post surgeon expressed concern over your health and recommended physical activity to aid your recovery, I think we'd be able to remove your shackles on humanitarian grounds. What do you say to that, Grenfell?'

'I say thank you kindly sir. As it happens, I have quite a desire to do some gardening. I'd like to see what will grow in the thin topsoil on the parade ground. A spot of digging and planting – unchained of course and free from prison strip searches – would suit me well.'

The old general gives me a shrewd look, making me wonder whether I've been a bit too eager. 'It depends where you do your gardening. We can't have you digging up the entire parade ground.'

'Indeed not,' I reply smoothly. 'The best place for a small garden would be at the north end, near the officers' quarters and the hot shot furnace.'

'Why do you think that?' he asks.

'There are many reasons – the depth of soil, the angle of the sun, the shade offered by existing buildings make this the best growing area.' It was utter gammon, of course, but, as a non-gardener, Hill wasn't to know that. I'd chosen this area for one reason only: it was where the slaves had been digging when they unearthed the gold coins.

'Well then, that's settled,' says the general. 'You can garden unchained for two hours a day. Choose your plot, no bigger than ten square yards to start with, mind.'

That was only to be expected. I must demonstrate my green fingers before Hill will let me loose on his parade ground. Fortunately, I've always liked sinking my hands in the warm earth and enjoy propagating plant life.

'There's one problem though,' I say knowingly. 'Atoll soils are thin, sandy and highly alkaline. They require nutrients. We've got plenty of phosphorus here but not nearly enough nitrogen. I can compensate in part by growing legumes such as beach peas and garden beans, which add nitrogen to the soil, but what I really need is a substantial quantity of chalky clay.'

'Is clay really good for a sandy soil?' Hill sounds dubious.

'Oh yes, I grew up in Cornwall where the soil was sandy. Clay improves the quantity and texture of the soil, adds organic carbon and increases the soil's water retention, which is vital in this climate.'

'Well, you're in luck, Grenfell. We've just set up our own brickyard and kilns to save transportation costs and there's plenty of freshly dug clay drying in the sun. I dare say we can spare a couple of bags. Now, is there any other way I can be of service?'

I decide to chance my arm. 'Can you do anything to improve

the food? It's an unwholesome diet with no fresh vegetables.'

The commander's eyes began to twinkle. 'Well there you are, Grenfell, grow vegetables in your garden and we'll all benefit from it. Now, where's that coffee?'

Hoist, you might say, on my own petard.

DECEMBER 11, 1865

Isaiah 2:4: 'They will beat their swords into ploughshares and their spears into pruning hooks.' Be it known that I have replaced my sword with a shovel and rake. And if you are wondering what this lord of the gardening tools looks like, I can tell you he is dressed in Confederate grey with a conically pointed straw hat perched on his head; a cross you might say between your Southern planter and a scarecrow. My garb is widely commented on by the prison guards as I begin my first day's dig. The general view is that I've taken leave of my senses. Let them think that. I know what I am doing.

I choose a raised site between the officers' lodgings and the hot shot furnace, stake it out, and begin the spadework. The earth is a light brownish-grey colour which suggests there is roughly six inches of topsoil before I reach the white coral sand below, and it's to that depth that I must dig to stand any chance of finding the slaves' treasure. Two hours under the hot sun and I've had enough. All I unearth is a broken locket with a woman's picture in it. Perhaps I'll have better luck tomorrow.

DECEMBER 15, 1865

Digging is hard work in this climate. I have turned over several layers of soil in my patch and found nothing. I am disappointed but not downhearted. After all, I am hunting for a needle in a haystack. General Hill dropped by yesterday to enquire why I was excavating so deeply. I told him most plants need at least six inches of soil for their roots and that seemed to content him. 'Very well,' he said, 'and now you're going to do some planting.'

'No sir,' I replied. 'The next thing is to fork in the clay. Ideally, the soil should be given time to improve after that, but as we're both anxious to get on with the business of growing vegetables, I'll sow whatever seeds you can spare me.'

In truth, a soil as thin and lacking in organic matter should be left for three months before planting but neither the commanding officer nor I can wait that long. We have different agendas. He sees my garden as a test case for penal reform while I see it as a way of acquiring a fortune.

I try to remember what our wise old Cornish gardener told me when I was young. Pengelly believed in raised beds and well-timed planting. I know that peas and beans grow best in a sunny spot and ought to be planted in rows, but how wide apart should the seedlings be and how much water do they need to germinate?

I am on my way to the library to read the fort's only book on horticulture.

JANUARY 21, 1866

I was woken in the night by Samuel Mudd's wheezing. Our doctor is in a bad way. Never robust, he is now little better than a skeleton. I express concern about his condition and he admits to severe joint pain, swollen gums and shortage of breath, all of which are symptoms of scurvy.

'Given our diet, scurvy is only to be expected,' he whispers. 'The only vegetable we ever see is a potato, the meat is rotten and the bread is full of black bugs and dirt. Even the water we're given is full of wiggly things. My constant prayer is for death as that alone can set me free.'

'Don't give up hope,' I implore him. 'If your lawyer succeeds in getting a writ of habeas corpus you'll be out of here soon.'

Mudd tries to sit up. He is in obvious pain. 'It won't happen,

Grenfell. My foolish escape attempt put paid to any hope of an early release.' I have heard the others talking about how Mudd had concealed himself in the coal bunker of a troop ship but know no more than that.

'Do you want to talk about it?' I say.

'No, what I want to do is to write to my wife Frances but my eyesight isn't good enough for that. Will you help me?' I can hardly deny him such a request. I find our one remaining candle and light it with a safety match. Mudd takes the candle and holds it over the wooden bench. I kneel in front of it with quill pen, ink and paper. The letter he dictates is a harrowing one:

'My Dearest, Imagine being loaded down with heavy chains, locked up in a wet, damp room for more than twelve hours in every twenty-four, and working the rest of the time on stupid, pointless tasks. The atmosphere we breathe is impregnated with sulphuric hydrogen gas, which is highly injurious to our health. The gas is generated by the numerous sinks that empty into the sea beneath the small porthole that is our only window. My legs and ankles are swollen and sore, my shoulder and back are painful, and my hair is falling out. My eyesight is also bad. That is why my words are being written down by one of my comrades in misfortune, Colonel Grenfell. During the day, my eyes water to such an extent that I cannot view any object many seconds without having to close or shade them from the light. With all these handicaps, I have some difficulty in walking around the fort with bucket and broom to perform my menial duties under armed guard. This has been our treatment for the last three months, coupled with a bad diet, bad water and every inconvenience. But we struggle on.'

This was the pitiful letter that Sam Arnold took to the post room in the morning. I wonder whether it will be censored.

JANUARY 22, 1866

The letter has gone. I learn this from Sam Arnold when he returns from his clerking job with the post adjutant. Arnold shares my concerns for Mudd's health and mental state, and attributes his decline to the harsh treatment he has received since his failed escape attempt.

'Didn't he realise he was a marked man?' I ask. 'With a vindictive Secretary of War breathing down their necks, the prison officers couldn't allow a state prisoner to get away.'

'Yeah, he knew that, but he didn't like the idea of being guarded by black soldiers. Last September, before you arrived here, we were told that the New York Volunteers were about to be relieved by the 82nd Coloured Infantry. Old Sam Mudd wasn't prepared to stand for that. "It is bad enough," he complained, "being a prisoner in the hands of white men, your equals under the Constitution, but to be lorded over by a set of ignorant, prejudiced and irresponsible beings of the unbleached humanity is more than I can submit to." He was very strong on the subject.'

Mudd is a racist, I think, brought up to believe that Negroes are mentally and morally inferior to white people. 'So what did he do?' I ask.

'Well, he took off his prison clothes and put on a suit. Then, as bold as brass, he boarded a ship called the *Scott* that was moored at the wharf ready to take the Yankee soldiers home. He had bribed a seaman to hide him in the lower hold. But what Sam didn't realise was that no ship could sail from Fort Jefferson until the commander had accounted for every prisoner in his charge. He was missing at roll call and the *Scott* was searched until Mudd was found. The commander threatened to string him up by his thumbs if he didn't reveal his accomplice. He named a man called Kelly, who was thrown into a cell. Not that he stayed there long.'

'Really, what happened to him?' I try not to sound too interested.

'Kelly got away. He broke his chains, ripped the iron grating out of the window, dropped into the ditch, stole a small boat and sailed away. That was why they put sharks in the moat. And in case you're wondering, we all suffered for Sam's rush of blood.' Arnold's expression hardens. 'We were all chained up, thrown into this dungeon and forced to do hard labour. Not that we hold it against the doctor. He's a refined gentleman after all and it's understandable that his spirit should chafe under his imprisonment.'

I think Arnold and his colleagues are remarkable restrained. I am not sure I'd be so forgiving. Perhaps I can get them better accommodation. Thanks to my vegetable garden, I am General Hill's favourite prisoner. He might grant my request for a lighter, airier cell.

JANUARY 27, 1866

I am feeling proud of myself. My garden is a great success. The bags of newly dug clay have improved the texture of the soil but the real secret lies in achieving adequate groundwater conditions. Bush beans need two to three inches of water a week which is more than falls from the sky during this season. However, since I have chosen to garden beside the officers' quarters, I can store rainwater by simply placing a barrel under the downspout from the building's rooftop guttering while also siphoning off water from bathroom and kitchen waste pipes.

My bush beans will be ready for harvesting in three weeks' time and so will the beets. The English peas may take a little longer. Granted the beans are a bit straggly and the peapods somewhat wizened but they are growing vigorously, as is the cowpen daisy I acquired as a cutting from the post surgeon. He brought this flowering shrub to the prison to treat skin ailments: it's a tip he got from the Seminole and Chickasaw medicine men who cure venereal disease with this daisy.

If I achieve my target of thirty pounds of vegetables, General Hill has promised me twice as much land to cultivate and plenty of desalinated sea water from the fort's steam machinery. Everyone is benefiting from his good humour. Prisoners have been given a monthly credit of three dollars with which to buy food and tobacco. Not that the money goes very far – a toothbrush costs seventy-five cents!

Yesterday saw another change for the better. My fellow inmates and I have been relieved of our leg irons and moved into a more spacious cell with a proper window, albeit a barred one. Most of the credit for this goes to Dr Mudd's wife Frances who has been lobbying President Andrew Johnson on our behalf. Things are definitely looking up.

FEBRUARY 14, 1866

Our new cell is a place of decorative art and design. Spangler and Mudd are making jewellery boxes and cribbage boards in the carpentry shop and bringing them back at night so that we might admire their woodworking skills. As a qualified stage carpenter, Spangler is obviously in his element while, under his tuition, the doctor is proving remarkably adept with saw and chisel.

Today is Valentine's Day. I make myself miserable by yearning for Rose Greenhow and worrying about her young daughter. I get over my depression by planning what to do with my enlarged prison garden. Having exceeded expectations with a thirty-two-pound crop, I have been given a new plot between the officers' building and the powder magazine. I am thinking of sowing tomato, sweet corn and collard seeds. I keep reminding myself that I am only pretending to be a gardener and that the point of the exercise is to find buried treasure.

General Hill asks me whether I want any help with the digging. 'No, sir,' I reply quickly, 'I must do it myself for health reasons.' 'But there is nothing wrong with your health,' he responds. 'You may be a little thin but, apart from that, you look fine.' He's right of course. My stomach is taut, my arms and chest well-muscled. I am fit enough for whatever the future may hold.

FEBRUARY 16, 1866

I have been reading about the War of 1812 and now know a great deal more about the last voyage of the *Granville Packet*. The Falmouth boats were two or three-masted 10-gun brigs that transported mail and bullion from one part of the British Empire to another. In September, 1814 the *Granville Packet* sailed from Baltimore harbour, where Admiral Cochrane's expeditionary force was laying siege to Fort McHenry, with a year's back pay for the hundred or more British troops garrisoning the city of Pensacola in Spanish Florida.

Depending on rank, a British soldier's annual pay varied between two hundred and seven hundred guineas. One might deduce from this that the ship was carrying about thirty thousand guineas in gold coins when it sank in the Tortugas. However, the slaves talked about finding only one chest on Garden Key. Personal experience has taught me two men can lift about 150 pounds. Therefore, since each guinea contained a quarter of an ounce of gold, the two slaves would have struggled to move a chest holding more than nine thousand guineas. Although these guineas are no longer legal tender, their value has increased because of the rising price of gold. With an ounce of gold fetching upwards of twenty dollars on the New York Exchange, the buried coins could be worth fifty thousand dollars.

The prospect of becoming rich urges me on as I sweat over my enlarged vegetable patch. Fifty thousand dollars would buy me a decent country estate in England or a large plantation in Virginia. Rolling in imaginary blunt, I give no thought to how

I might escape from the island with a heavy treasure chest. One thing at a time is my motto.

FEBRUARY 27, 1866

The way General Hill favours me does not pass unnoticed. The guards call me a boot licker and an apple polisher but I pay no attention to them. I've been called worse things in my time.

Hill drops by while I am working on my allotment. 'They don't like you in the War Department, do they Grenfell?' the general says. Apparently, my charitable sister Mary, who married a vicar, wants to send me clothes, bedding and books but has been refused permission. 'Mrs Vyvyan is a most gracious lady. Why don't you write to her or indeed to other members of your family? The post adjutant tells me the only letters you send are to your attorney.' 'I am grateful for your concern, sir,' I reply, 'but I don't wish to hear from family or friends because it unsettles my mind. I am sure you understand. It's better this way.'

MARCH 4, 1866

The casual brutality of officers in the Fifth US Artillery is quite astounding. Earlier today, with many people watching, a black prisoner fell into the moat. The poor fellow couldn't swim and he splashed around desperately, shouting for help. But the officer of the day ignored his cries. The Negro drowned before the sharks attacked his body.

Today is a Sunday, when attendance at the Episcopal chapel is compulsory. Any prisoner who fails to attend is flogged. Worship at Fort Jefferson is hardly an uplifting experience. Guards roam the chapel aisles and anyone caught whispering is sentenced to three days' bread and water in close confinement.

I can only conclude that our over-zealous soldiers are looking for excuses to punish us. What with the hot, humid climate, the mosquitoes, the awful food and lack of fresh water, Fort Jefferson is, of course, a terrible military posting and new officers quickly learn that there are only two forms of amusement, getting drunk and inflicting pain on the prisoners. Consequently, there is a long list of rules that must be complied with. For instances, the penalty for failing to salute an officer is circuits of the parade ground carrying a heavy cannon ball. Some punishments are even more barbaric. Prisoners are roped and dunked in the Gulf, their flesh is whipped raw, or they are tied to tree branches by their thumbs. This used to be called 'strappado' in the medieval torture chamber.

There is one second lieutenant I particularly hate. His name is Aidan Murphy and he recently beat a prisoner to death with his rifle butt. I can see him now, standing on the parade field, arms akimbo, with little honest width between his eyes and a mouth set in a permanent sneer, glorying in his sadism.

Murphy and his cronies steal from the prisoners; parcels that arrive in the post room soon disappear. Then there's the intoxication that follows the arrival of the Cuban supply ships. Cases of liquor are opened and quaffed on the quayside. When stocks run low, officers raid the post hospital for alcohol and hold drunken orgies in which they take advantage of the female kitchen staff. I hear about this from Dr Mudd who plays the fiddle at these 'entertainments' in the officers' mess. Even the racist doctor doesn't like to see black women treated in this way.

I have changed my mind about General Hill. He should be ashamed to be in charge of such a slack garrison. He is either turning a blind eye to what is going on or he doesn't have the strength of character to stamp it out.

MARCH 17, 1866

There is nothing like a Florida sunset. The beautiful reds and oranges shade into coral pink and violet, colours to warm the heart of a prisoner peering through the barred window of his casemate cell. I look out to where the turquoise water laps against the powder-soft sand and remember the exploits of that intrepid but highly volatile eighteenth-century explorer Captain James Cook. He ended up on a coral island when his ship, the *Endeavour*, hit an outcrop on the Great Barrier Reef, but he still managed to sail south months later to claim Australia as a British territory. Like him, I struggle to steer an even course between hope and despair, a balance difficult to attain in a sea of human wretchedness and hatred.

I have to believe in something and that something is a chest laden with coins left on Garden Key after a shipwreck. Yet each day's unsuccessful digging makes it harder for me to cling onto my dream. I curse the doubt creeping into my mind but cannot undo the damage. Today was a major disappointment. My spade hit something solid in the earth and my heart leaped in hope. When all the soil had been lifted off the object I realised it was simply construction debris.

APRIL 4, 1866

Why is hope so much harder to sustain than despair? I am tired of digging. Tired of the tedium and futility of the diurnal round. The future is a long dark corridor leading to a bolted door. I must learn to accept that. But I cannot help wondering where the ship's chest might be. Perhaps the slaves buried it under sand that has since been built on. Another possibility is that the slaves lied about the chest's existence and actually stole the coins from a soldier who was guarding them. But what was an American militiaman doing with so many George III guineas? Was one of his ancestors a corpse robber? It hardly seems likely.

APRIL 23, 1866

'The miserable have no other medicine, but only hope.' Shakespeare died 250 years ago today but his words still ring true. The black depression that has been dogging me for weeks has finally lifted, leaving my senses sharp and clear.

The latest news from my attorney has buoyed me up. Robert Hervey has written about a recent United States Supreme Court ruling that it is unconstitutional for military tribunals to try civilians when civil courts are sitting. This landmark decision was delivered in the habeas corpus proceedings brought by a Southern sympathiser called Lambdin Milligan, who, like me, received a death sentence later commuted to life imprisonment. In *Ex parte Milligan,* the Supreme Court found that the appellant was a civilian and that his state, Indiana, was not in rebellion and, therefore, granted the writ of habeas corpus in accordance with 'the fundamental principles of American liberty'.

Hervey maintains that this decision completely vindicates the arguments he advanced at my trial. I too was a civilian, having left the Confederate army well before the commission of the crimes with which I was charged, and I was neither a resident in one of the seceded states nor a prisoner of war. Furthermore, as a British subject, I should have been protected by the same legal safeguards as an American citizen.

On receiving Hervey's letter, I write to Sir Frederick Bruce, the British minister in Washington, imploring him 'to lose no time in demanding from the Secretary of War an order for my release, seeing that the Supreme Court has finally settled the question as to the legality or illegality of my arrest, imprisonment, trial and sentence. As all the proceedings under which I now suffer are unconstitutional and illegal, they can be no reason to detain me any longer in this miserable fortress.'

But does *Ex parte Milligan* really settle the validity of my detention or will they come up with some kind of legal flummery to keep me here? We shall see soon enough.

MAY 11, 1866

Another loud night of drunken debauchery by the officer class ends in the destruction of my vegetable patch. Buckets of sea water have been poured over the tender young plants causing them to shrivel and die. And I don't have far to look for the culprits. Lieutenant Murphy and three of his toadies are standing nearby, puffing away on cheroots as they admire their handiwork.

I don't stop to think. Yanking a wilting cabbage out of the ground I march across to Murphy. 'Here, have this for your supper. It will help with the hangover!'

'Wow!' says Murphy in mock amazement. 'The worm has turned. Mr High and Mighty Grenfell is naw longer shiftin' arse.'

'You did this,' I rave, wild with anger.

'Prove it,' he sneers.

'I don't have to. Such a wanton act of vandalism carries your trademark.'

'Yer hear dat boys.' Murphy seeks the support of his acolytes. 'The English lord wants ter mess wi' me. Yer man doesn't realise dat Oi grew up in a New York gang where brass knuckles an' knives were dey order of the day. He's never been ter the Brooklyn Docks, 'tis a tough neighbourhood, let me tell yer. Murder is commonplace and dare are no convicshuns cos nobody talks in Irishtown, not if they want ter keep livin' dare.'

His boastful spiel draws grunts of approval from his followers who give me the Yankee glare, arrogant and full of menace. 'You can't intimidate me like you do the other prisoners,' I say through gritted teeth. 'One day I'll be out of here and I'll remember your ugly faces.'

'He's threatenin' us boys!' Murphy pretends to shiver with fright. 'Listen, slugger, nathin' would gie me greater pleasure than to duke it out witcha in the ring but dat ain't possible, waat witcha bein' a miserable worm an' me an army officer responsible for law an' order in dis 'ere compoun'. What is gonna happen is this: when dat eejit of a general's back is turned, my friends an' Oi are gonna pay yer a visit, teach yer ter show some manners. In the meanwhile, yer can keep your mouldy vegetables.'

He throws the cabbage in my face and turns on his heel to go, but I am not finished yet. 'Tell me, Murphy, are all bogtrotters addle-brained? You've ruined a bed of perfectly good vegetables which would have improved the wretched food you're given to eat. Isn't that a stupid thing to do?'

Murphy sneers at this. 'Thar's only one vegetable Oi ayte an' that's de potato, an' yer weren't growin' any. But what really upsets me is yer attitude. Yer should salute me an' call me sorr.'

'Over my dead body,' says I.

His voice rises and the veins in his neck begin to bulge. 'Dat can be arranged. Oi've just aboyt 'ad a bellyful ...'

Murphy breaks off. A figure is walking across the parade ground towards us. 'Here's de general ter save yer! Better shut your gob, if yer know what's good for yer.'

He and his toadies stalk off as General Hill wanders up to commiserate. 'What a pity, Grenfell, your vegetables are ruined. Some kind of blight, would you say?'

'A man-made one,' I mutter.

'What's that you say? Surely you don't think someone deliberately sabotaged your garden?'

'Look at the earth.' I point to the tell-tale layers of dry white salt lying on the soil's surface. 'Gallons of sea water were poured on my garden in the night in the knowledge that it would kill the plants.'

General Hill shakes his head. 'But who would do such a thing?'

'Well, your officers were having one of their nocturnal parties. You may have heard them. I certainly did.'

'No, no, you must be wrong. No officer of mine, however

271

drunk, would behave like a savage. I can't believe it.' Hill leaves with a worried frown on his face. He is an old man and this is his last posting. He cannot face up to the truth.

Of course I'm the ultimate loser. I'm left with a blighted garden and a general who has lost interest in me, leaving me vulnerable to attack by Murphy and his brutes. For the record, they are all second lieutenants in the Fifth United States Artillery and their names are Frederick 'Bull' Robinson, George W. Crabbe and Albert Pike. Like the old Chinese military strategist Sun Tzu, I believe in keeping my friends close but my enemies closer because one day they will come looking for me.

JULY 23, 1866

This hot, humid, rainy summer drags on and pleases no one apart from Fort Jefferson's most anti-social resident, the mosquito. Our prison is swarming with these biting bloodsuckers and swatting them is our daily exercise. They are a greater menace than our sadistic officers who have been held in check by General Hill's latest order banning torture. What our commandant cannot control are these loathsome insects. Mosquitoes should be wiped off the face of the earth.

I am feeling low. In days gone by, there was always the promise of something new in my life; the opportunity to visit a different country, the chance to reinvent myself. But that's gone now. As things stand, I'm locked up for good and any chance I had of finding a fortune in the earth has withered with the vegetables I planted there. The general asked me if I wanted to start another patch but I said I couldn't be bothered. That's the thing about depression; it saps your vitality.

Perhaps you'd like to know when my mosquito mood began. It was when we were told that the War Department had decided to release all civilians condemned by military tribunals who had served at least six months of their sentence, only to learn that this order did not apply to the political prisoners under sentence in the Dry Tortugas. It's as if I had conspired to assassinate Lincoln.

This is my reward for making a monkey out of Stanton. Why did I have to give him false information about Confederate troop movements? I remember his beady eyes gleaming as he took down what he imagined to be priceless military intelligence, only to discover later it was absolute balderdash. As far as the vengeful Secretary of War is concerned, I deserve to rot in hell, otherwise known as the Dry Tortugas.

And I am rotting away. My symptoms are fatigue, muscle pain and loss of appetite. Dr Mudd says I may be suffering from stage one yellow fever or from dropsy, brought on by malnutrition. That would seem a likely diagnosis, considering the quality of our food. Bread, rotten fish and meat, all mixed together, served on a tin plate, and cups of coffee lifted out of a dirty bucket with grease swimming on its surface. Yet I want to blame the mosquitoes for my condition.

OCTOBER 8, 1866

This is the anniversary of my incarceration here and I fear it will be the first of many. There has been talk of suing out a writ of habeas corpus but so far nothing has been done. My attorney tells me the British minister in Washington is working tirelessly on my behalf, but with Stanton at the War Department and President Johnson already fighting for his political life I cannot see how Sir Frederick Bruce can possibly get me out of here.

One thing I can report is the presentation of a touching petition from 'certain inhabitants of Cornwall' seeking my release, sent to Washington by the American ambassador in London. I have been shown Judge Advocate General Holt's reply. It makes bleak reading. 'The commutation of Grenfell's death sentence was an act of rare clemency,' Holt wrote. 'That exercise of the pardoning power, rescuing him from the gallows, to which his merited punishment had consigned him, is believed to have extended the extreme measure of mercy that can be asked on his behalf.'

This is what I would expect from Stanton's pompous lackey but it is good to know I still have friends at home.

DECEMBER 27, 1866

The year is winding down and I have received a belated Christmas present! A blistering editorial has appeared in the Memphis *Appeal*: 'Let the people of the South consider that the inhuman treatment of a gallant soldier who, for love of freedom, fought their battles, is not only a disgrace to the nation, but a burning, damning shame to themselves and their posterity forever.' These words were written by my old comrade Thomas Hines who recruited me for the Chicago venture. I have often wondered what happened to him after the Yankees learned of our plans and rounded up the rest of us. He must have got away. Good luck to him.

FEBRUARY 5, 1867

Prisons breed violence. They are full of suppressed rage and frustration. Such emotions can only be heightened when your jail is on a small island in the middle of nowhere. To stop soldiers from deserting while on shore leave, General Hill refuses to issue passes to Key West, which makes our guards feel like captives and ripe for mischief, particularly when Major MacConnell is left in charge. He is a handsome enough fellow, big and broad-shouldered with curly fair hair, but his cruel grey eyes give him away. After the Dunn affair, no one could have any doubts about his true nature.

The trouble began when a supply boat arrived and, as usual, prisoners were marched to the wharf to unload cases of liquor for the fort. One of these prisoners, James Dunn, became drunk on the job. When MacConnell saw his inebriated state, he flew into a violent rage and had Dunn hauled off to the parade ground to pick up an iron canon ball. The poor man didn't know what he was doing. He could barely stand, let alone carry a heavy weight.

I was passing by at the time and heard Major MacConnell order one of the guards, Edward Donnelly, to 'string this man up until he's sober'. Dunn was tied to a post by his wrists and left to hang there for four hours. Then, in mid-afternoon, he was taken down, still unconscious, and moved to an iron railing near the sally port where he was effectively crucified. It was a piteous sight, Dunn swinging to and fro like a carcass on a butcher's hook, the veins in his neck extended like cords and his whole weight resting on swollen and putrid thumbs.

And there he dangled until General Hill chanced by. 'What is this man doing here?' barked the general. 'He's drunk, sir,' replied the guard. 'Cut him down!' ordered Hill. 'No man in this condition is ever to be punished like this again.' Having given his command, the general disappeared into the fort. A senseless Dunn was dragged off to the guardhouse and thrown into a cell.

But it didn't end there. Major MacConnell was drunk at Retreat and ready to pick a fight, not least with his commanding officer whom he considers an incompetent weakling. 'Where's Dunn?' he shouted as the flag was lowered at sunset. 'Sobering up in the guardhouse,' replied Sergeant Donnelly. 'Bring him out and make him carry a ball.' But Dunn still couldn't do it. Two hours later, he tried again but his bleeding, swollen hands couldn't grasp the ball. 'I am doing my best,' he wailed. 'But I can't hold it.'

Sergeant Donnelly was unmoved. 'Sentinel,' he said, 'if he refuses to carry it, run him through with your bayonet.' Dunn had another go. This time he raised the weight to his knees and staggered a step or two, before crumpling to the ground. 'Sentinel, you are going to have to bayonet me,' Dunn groaned.

'String him up again,' Donnelly demanded, for want of a better idea.

Dunn's muffled cries for mercy during his third hanging had no effect on his captors but so annoyed Garden Key's lighthouse keeper that he complained to Major MacConnell. 'Can't you do something?' the angry man asked. 'You're butchering a convict outside my window and it's spoiling my supper.' Fearing the keeper might raise the matter with General Hill, MacConnell had Dunn taken to a dungeon behind the guardhouse where he was left until the following morning.

The rumour is that Dunn has lost the use of his left hand which may have to be amputated before gangrene sets in. I have seen plenty of wanton savagery in my day, but nothing to equal this.

FEBRUARY 22, 1867

I am a dead man walking. That's what the guards tell me when they throw me into solitary confinement. I am not too worried about such threats. We all have to die sometime. If I go to meet my maker at least it will be with the knowledge that I've exposed the prison system here.

Although I couldn't stop those sadistic bastards from torturing Dunn, I thought they should be named and shamed and wrote a scalding letter to a Richmond lawyer who had been a Confederate general in the Civil War. Bradley Tyler Johnson used his contacts to get it published anonymously in the New York *World*. Unfortunately, the newspaper was read by a Fort Jefferson officer on furlough. On his return to the fort, guards ransacked our cells. Under my cot they found a list of all the officers who had taken part in prison atrocities. But they cannot really harm me because of General Hill's decree about torturing prisoners. So they bide their time. And I wait to see what happens next.

MARCH 12, 1867

General Hill's tour of duty ended three days ago. While the fort waits for his replacement to arrive, that arch fiend Major McConnell is left in charge and my day of reckoning arrives.

The officers have been systematically starving me so that I can barely stand when they put me on sick call on Sunday morning. Despite my sunken cheeks and skeletal frame, I am passed fit for labour. Out in the yard, I am expected to move heavy lumber from one pile to another. I soon collapse from exhaustion, only to be yanked to my feet by the provost marshal who turns out to be the Irish lieutenant Bull Robinson. 'Why aren't you working?' he asks. 'I cannot bend my back,' I gasp. 'Oh yes, you can,' he sneers. 'Guards, take him down to the wharf.'

Here I am ordered to pick up bricks and load them onto a lighter. 'Look,' I say, 'I'll do any kind of work that doesn't involve bending. You can see my back is locked.' 'You're malingering, Grenfell,' Bull roars with ill-concealed glee, 'and need to be taught a lesson.' I am stripped of my shirt and my wrists are tied to an iron grating above my head. 'There you are,' says Robinson. 'Now you know exactly how James Dunn felt.'

They leave me hanging there for most of the day, naked to the waist and without water, exposed to the fierce rays of the sun and constantly bitten by mosquitoes. The pain is indescribable as the joints and ligaments in my arms gradually loosen. With my body pulled down by gravity, I cannot breathe properly and my heart feels as if it is being squeezed. I now understand how death comes from crucifixion. It's breathing that kills you because you cannot get the air out of your lungs. I am slowly suffocating. Robinson returns with Crabbe and Pike in the late afternoon. They inquire whether I am now prepared to carry bricks. I shake my head. This is what they have been counting on.

When they release me from the grating and bind my hands

together, I guess what will happen next. 'Do you intend to submerge me in the sea?' 'Yes' says Crabbe. 'Well, fuck you,' I croak and jump into the water, knowing I can swim quite well even with my hands tied. Seeing this, they haul me out, rope my legs together and throw me back into the sea. 'See if you can float now, you poxy Englishman,' Robinson bellows. And I duly do so. Shrieking with frustrated rage, my tormentors wade into the water to retrieve me. I am dumped on the quay to be kicked by Robinson while his colleagues fetch iron weights to attach to my feet. This time I will surely drown.

Famous people have delivered wonderful last words before dying. The composer Beethoven said the comedy was over, the philosopher Hobbes talked about taking a great leap in the dark, while General Stonewall Jackson wanted to sit in the shade of the trees after being shot by his own troops at Chancellorsville. My final utterance hardly measures up to this exalted standard. 'Gentlemen,' I say scornfully, 'if you intend to murder me, do it in a respectable way, and I will thank you for the act.'

'Damn you,' shouts Pike. 'You deserve to die for the crimes you have been guilty of.'

'God can judge who is the most evil, you or me.'

This provokes Robinson into adding further weights to my feet before dumping me in a rowing boat. But the way he lassoes my waist and holds onto one end of the rope before pushing me out of the boat into deeper water encourages me to think I am to be dunked rather than drowned outright.

Working on this hypothesis, I hold my breath after I've been dropped into the sea. Down I sink and after a minute my heart begins to pound and my lungs to burn. Then my mouth opens, seeking oxygen that isn't there, and the seawater rushes in. As I black out, my body is yanked to the surface. Gasping in air, I look about me and see a group of visitors disembarking onto the wharf. The Christian Welfare ladies are paying their annual visit to the prison. 'Murder!' I splutter. 'I'm being murdered!' The charitable women hear my yells, look away in horror and rush off into the fort.

Back into the water I go for a fourth time and am held down long enough to lose consciousness. When I come to I am lying on the dock like a beached sea creature with Bull Robinson once again kicking my defenceless body. 'You'll either work or I'll kill you!' he shouts. 'Then you'll have to kill me,' I gasp, 'for I cannot pick up bricks now you've cracked my ribs.'

I do not remember what happened next for I must have fainted away. But they didn't kill me. Instead they dump me in a dark cell with cockroaches for company. 'Why don't you write another letter to your lawyer?' a guard jeers as he brings me bread and water.

Today I receive a visit from our new prison doctor. Major Smith wants to check whether I have any broken bones. Having examined my scarred and badly bruised body, he excuses me from any labour for a fortnight and, at my request, brings me writing materials.

Better yet is the news that McConnell has been replaced as acting commandant by Major Valentine H Stone, one of whose brothers, Henry, fought alongside me in Morgan's Raiders. Major Stone is reputed to be a stern disciplinarian. Perhaps he will stamp out the brutality in this prison.

MARCH 27, 1867

I am summoned to Major Stone's office. He shows me a letter he's received from his brother, urging him to treat his old army friend Colonel Grenfell with every consideration. I am moved by Henry's kind words and glad to hear Major Stone's promise to treat everyone fairly. 'For too long,' he says, 'Fort Jefferson has been a badly run jail. The officers responsible for the maltreatment of prisoners are no longer with us. They have been transferred elsewhere.' Amen to that!

JULY 17, 1867

Major George Andrews, the new post commandant, arrived last Monday and immediately made a good impression by improving the food we eat. Fresh fish and beef, Irish potatoes, corn and beans have been added to our diet and we can purchase additional provisions with our prison 'wages'.

Andrews has been particularly generous to me. On grounds of age and health, he has relieved me of heavy labour. 'You are now the only Confederate officer of any prominence still in prison,' he told me. 'I will allow you to send and receive uncensored mail and you can spend your days in the library or revive the garden of which my predecessor spoke so highly. Think about it, Grenfell.'

Maybe he is right and I should start gardening again. While considering whether to grow peppers or radishes, a picture flashed into my head, one that should have been there when I started digging. What I see is a gang of convicts, myself included, marching across the parade ground towards an officers' building shaded by mangrove trees.

I have long considered that visual memories are triggered by the unconscious mind, by an unstated question rattling around in the brain. To wit, what would clever slaves like Jerry and Jack do if they unearthed a chest full of gold coins while digging the fort's foundations? The natural reaction would be to fill their pockets with coins and bury the rest out of sight. As not even a dog buries a bone in the ground without hoping to dig it up later, the slaves would choose a significant landmark, close to where they were working, such as a clump of mangrove trees.

This morning I told Major Andrews I would like to start gardening again on a piece of land in front of the officers' mess.

'But that's near the mangroves with their massive tree roots. Nothing will grow there,' said a frowning Andrews. 'You may be surprised to learn, sir,' said I, 'that that piece of land has more nutrients in its soil than anywhere else on the parade ground.' We treasure hunters know how to tell a tall story.

AUGUST 26, 1867

At last, I have been given the all clear to begin gardening. The prison doctor would not allow me to exert myself until the rainy season was over. We have had more than thirty-seven inches of rain in three months – almost as much as we get in a normal year – and a south-easterly wind has brought even larger swarms of mosquitoes than normal into the fort.

It could be that I have been kept waiting too long. A second yellow fever case was admitted to the garrison hospital today. The previous one proved to be fatal.

SEPTEMBER 4, 1867

A week has gone by and we have a yellow fever epidemic in the fort. The hospital is full of new cases and already there have been three deaths. If only we knew what caused the disease and, therefore, how to treat it. The prevailing view is that it is passed from person to person. The first four casualties were soldiers from Company K bunking in the same casemate on the south side of the fort. To check the contagion, Dr Mudd and Ned Spangler were ordered to bring hammers and wood from the carpenter's shop and board up the infected room where the soldiers had slept.

Everyone is in a state of panic about this outbreak. Yet there is still room for black humour. So far, only guards and officers have gone down with the fever and, as one prisoner put it, 'This is God's vengeance on a bunch of sadists.' With our officers falling like flies, I have been ordered to suspend digging outside their quarters.

The disease begins with a headache, followed by pains in the neck and back and a rise in temperature. Then the infection attacks the liver and kidneys, yellowing the skin and eyes like jaundice. In its more severe form, the mucus membranes rupture and the sufferer begins to vomit darker and darker bile. When the vomit turns black, the victim dies: all in all, a grim prognosis.

I have just heard that Dr Smith has contracted the disease. The fort is left without a physician in the midst of this fearful pestilence.

SEPTEMBER 5, 1867

I awoke this morning to find soldiers in our cell. Major Andrews wants Dr Mudd to take command of the post hospital until a regular surgeon arrives from the mainland. Dr Daniel Whitehurst, a civilian physician from Key West, will take over in due course. Ironically, this is the same Dr Whitehurst who was second in command at the fort when the slaves escaped twenty years ago. He had been expelled from Fort Jefferson at the start of the Civil War because of his Confederate sympathies.

What a topsy-turvy world this is to be sure! Who would have imagined a couple of Johnny Rebs being called up to save Yankee lives? Make that three. I have just volunteered to be a medical orderly and head nurse. No hospital can run efficiently without a proper nursing staff and the fort has relied thus far on voluntary help from soldiers' wives and the laundresses who do the washing. The efforts of these admirable ladies need to be coordinated. My immediate task is to nurse Dr Smith and his sick wife. She may recover but I doubt if he will.

SEPTEMBER 7, 1867

We have lost our first patient. Dr Smith died earlier today. He was a man of humanity and kindness who tried to protect prisoners from their abusive captors and worked tirelessly when the fever began to rage. Yet during the period of his sickness not a single officer or wife visited him.

The fort is run by a ghost garrison. Fear is etched upon every soldier's face, wondering when his turn might come.

SEPTEMBER 12, 1867

When the first victims succumbed to the fever, Major Andrews had them transported to Sand Key to keep the infection from spreading inside the garrison. Unfortunately, patients were often left lying on the wharf for several hours before facing an arduous voyage on the open sea. Dr Mudd has adopted a totally different approach, bringing all the patients together in the fort. He argues that the fever has already taken hold and cannot be dislodged until the poison has expended itself. It follows therefore that more lives might be saved by concentrating the nursing in one place.

The disease has now reached the inner barracks and is decimating Company K, particularly those soldiers who wore heavy cloaks during the frequent showers of rain we have experienced recently. With the fever spreading like wildfire, discipline is not all it should be. Soldiers act as stretcher bearers but show scant respect for the dead or dying. No sooner has the breath left a man's body than he is put in a coffin, which is nailed down and hurried off to the wharf. The coffin is rowed to a nearby atoll, a grave dug and filled, and the burial party rewarded with a bottle of whiskey. To speed things up further, coffins are placed alongside the hospital beds of those expected to die, only to be removed again by orderlies when a patient clings tenaciously to life.

Our supply of beds and bedding has given out and we have been forced to bring infected beds into what should be a sterile area. Our nurses began to fall sick shortly afterwards, as did the laundresses who washed the soiled bedclothes. Whatever we do seems to backfire on us.

SEPTEMBER 17, 1867

The most remarkable spread of the disease occurred last night in Company M, which is quartered immediately above our hospital. This coincided with a change in the prevailing wind. Within two hours, thirty men were attacked by the most malignant form of the disease. As all our hospital beds were spoken for, we decided to enclose the six casemates nearest the existing wards and to give up our own cots to the sick.

I managed to get a few hours sleep in the early morning. When I awoke it was to the sound of silence: no bugle call, no soldiers on drill or parade, only an all-pervasive gloom. By the time I reached the hospital the mercury stood at 104 degrees. It was truly terrible to be hemmed in by red-hot walls with not even a breath of air to fan the burning brow or the fever-parched lip.

Sweating profusely and feeling utterly helpless, I watched our chaplain's final suffering. The Reverend William Matchett had moved fearlessly among the sick, praying for them and anointing them with oil, until he contracted the fever. Never a robust figure, he was now skin and bone. 'Death straps me down,' he whispered in my ear. 'The miasma sits heavily upon my chest.'

Hearing this, I did a little praying of my own. 'Please don't let this good man die!' I muttered again and again to no avail. God wasn't listening to a sinner. But the minister heard me and made the sign of the cross on my forehead. Before the end came, he opened his eyes and reached beneath his pillow with a shaking hand. 'I have offended God because my mission has fallen far short of what it should have been. Here, take these copper keys: one opens the chapel and the other is for the communion cupboard. I give them to you in the hope that you will pray for my departed soul and for those of your fellow prisoners and guardians.' Then, with a sigh, he expired.

How strange it felt to be called upon to do God's work

when you are devoid of faith. Even so, I pocketed the keys with something approaching reverence.

News of the epidemic has reached the mainland and the supply ships have stopped coming. Fort Jefferson is cut off from the outside world. A cloud of despair has settled over us. We have been left here to die. As I wander down the vaulted passageway between the inner and outer brick walls of the fort I am reminded of Rome's Coliseum where gladiators fought for their lives. At least they died with sword in hand. I envy them that. The best I can do is wield a spade.

I might as well revive my hitherto fruitless search for buried treasure. With two thirds of the garrison laid low with the fever and the other third living fearfully behind closed doors, the parade ground is a deserted place at dawn. There is no one to check up on me. I will retrieve my wheelbarrow, gardening tools and gunnysacks from where I left them and begin work at first light. At least it will be good exercise.

I dig for digging's sake. The great affair is to keep busy in a time of absolute peril and, if possible, to survive.

SEPTEMBER 19, 1867

I hardly know how to begin this entry, my hand is shaking so. Perhaps I might start by saying that Fat Charley got it right. Charley is something of a prison character; a good-natured, seemingly indestructible rogue who acts as the ferryman of the dead, rowing the coffins of the newly deceased to their final resting place on an adjacent key and greatly enjoying the whiskey that comes with this miserable task. In his cups, Charley lets everyone know he thinks it 'mighty harsh' that he should be locked up in Fort Jefferson for 'merely obeying orders'. He claims his colonel ordered him to retreat at Bull Run. So he retreated to Vermont, and, finding his regiment had not followed him, waited there for further orders.

Anyway, shortly after dawn, I am wending my solitary way to the hot shot furnace to collect my gardening tools when I run into Charley emptying his bladder on the parade ground. 'Gardening again, Colonel Grenfell, you'll wear yourself out,' says he laughingly, resting his heavy frame against the prison whipping post. 'But as the good book says, "Blessed is he that tendeth the sick and tills the land, for he that seeketh findeth."' Charley's garbled quotation, a mixture of Matthew, Luke and Proverbs, turns out to be prophetic.

I have chosen to dig between the veranda surrounding the officers' block and a cocoa palm that towers above the evergreen mangroves. But as my spade bites into the fine Bermuda grass, I notice the sun's rays are slanting down in such a way as to cause the palm to cast a long shadow and decide to shift my digging to the shadow's edge where the sand is covered by two feet of topsoil. I have removed almost half this earth when my spade strikes something solid with a dull thud.

Drops of perspiration fall into my eyes and my heart begins to beat violently. Is this construction debris? A lot of masonry must have been buried here. Taking a deep breath, I attack the ground with renewed vigour. A loud ringing noise! The steel blade of my spade ricochets off what might be wrought-iron hinges. Another blow encounters similar resistance but makes a different sound.

Sinking to my knees, I feverishly scoop the soil away by hand, feeling almost frightened of what I might find. My searching fingers uncover a two-foot-long iron bound chest made of cypress with the royal coat of arms engraved on its lid. There is no mistaking the quartered shield supported by the lion and the unicorn. The Falmouth packet ships carried mail and money at the Postmaster General's behest. This must be the chest the slaves found all those years ago and, in their eagerness to open it, Jerry and Jack broke its padlock and iron hinges. I lift the lid with sweating palms and peer inside.

The coffer is divided into two sections. The upper one is stuffed with papers. And below that is a second compartment full of gleaming coins! I can only stare, transfixed by the sight of so much gold. Awaking from my trance, I move to take possession of the treasure, picking up handfuls of guineas and letting them slip through my fingers. How did I feel at that moment? I swear I was grinning like an idiot and could scarcely stifle the huge cry of joy swelling inside me. My luck had finally changed.

But greed is man's besetting sin. Like a miser, I look furtively over my shoulder, checking to see whether my actions have been observed. The wealth I now possess is my passport to power and influence, but only if I can get off this ghastly island and take my money with me.

The chest is too heavy to move, so I empty the coins into gunnysacks and lift them into my wheelbarrow. Then I replace the chest in the earth and cover it with loose soil, sprinkling seeds on the surface to create the illusion of an allotment, before pushing the heavily laden wheelbarrow across the parade ground to the prison chapel.

SEPTEMBER 20, 1867

Avarice is growing within me like a malignant tumour. I cannot wait to be free of my nursing duties so that I might further examine my sacks of hidden treasure. I labour through the night and well into the morning before that moment comes. 'It's time you had a break, Grenfell,' says the newly arrived Dr Whitehurst. 'You look all in.' I thank him and take my leave.

The chapel is always supposed to be open but I bolt the door behind me. The smaller of my two copper keys unlocks the communion cupboard which contains consecrated bread and wine, holy water, three flasks of oil blessed by the Episcopal Bishop of Florida, a spare altar cloth and four gunnysacks of guineas. The sacred and the profane on separate shelves!

I take the altar cloth and spread it on the stone floor. Then I tip the contents of the sacks onto the cloth and begin to count my precious coins. An hour later I am still breathing over them like a fiery dragon. There are almost nine thousand military guineas. I put them back in their sacks and turn my attention to the papers I'd removed from the ship's chest.

They are tied together with a red ribbon. On top of the pile is a sealed letter addressed to the Right Hon Earl Bathurst, Secretary of State for War and the Colonies. I break the seal and behold the looped cursive handwriting of a Major General Robert Ross, commanding officer of the British Expeditionary Force on the Potomac. Here is what he wrote:

August 26, 1814

Your Lordship,

Acting on Admiral Sir Alexander Cochrane's behalf, I have the honour to inform you that we have defeated an American army twice our numbers at Bladensburg, taken all their cannon, and destroyed the Baltimore Flotilla under Commodore Barney, before walking through the streets of Washington with as much safety as if we had been in London. Our arrival in the capital city two nights ago led to the hasty departure of President Madison from his White Palace, which we burned down along with the Capitol, other public buildings and military arsenals, before returning fifty miles through enemy country without losing so much as a single soldier on the march.

From ancient times it has been the privilege of the victorious party to loot and capture the enemy's property. In accordance with this international law of pillage, I allowed my troops to ransack the President's Palace before setting fire to it. A packet of papers was uncovered in the process which bore the presidential seal. Many of the enclosed letters were written by America's former president Thomas Jefferson and are of a remarkably frank nature, touching not only on Jefferson's personal relationship with the Madisons but also on the imperial ambitions that drove America into declaring war on us. Therefore, it may be that this correspondence is of some value to His Majesty's Government.

Motivated by a prurient curiosity, I arrange the letters in chronological order, starting with one Jefferson wrote in November 1801 lamenting the absence of the Secretary of State and his vivacious wife Dolley. Apparently the Madisons had been living with the widowed president in his Washington residence and the three of them had enjoyed romping around the place, taking part in 'foot races' and indulging in bedtime 'caresses', until rumours of their ménage à trois forced the Madisons to move out. What a lonely Jefferson seemed to miss most was the opportunity to rest his head upon the lovely bosom of the woman he called his 'First Lady.' At the opposite end of the spectrum was a letter written on June 11, 1812, a week before Congress declared war on Britain, in which Jefferson called for the 'conquest of Canada' and for the whole continent of North America to be associated in 'one federal Union'.

Now, I am no student of American politics but a cursory reading of these letters convinces me of the soundness of General Ross's judgement. Had they been delivered to London as he intended, the British government would probably have used their content to denounce America's leaders as debauchees and dishonest expansionists.

Someone is trying to get into the chapel. I drop the papers into one of the sacks and lock them up in the cupboard. Then I open the door and apologise to the soldier waiting outside. On returning to the post hospital, fresh doubts arise in my mind. How am I going to get off this island with four heavy sacks of gold? The obvious answer is by sea. This raises another question: can I sail a ship single-handed or will I have to recruit a crew and share my new-found wealth with them? Such matters must wait until the yellow fever epidemic has abated. That's if it ever does!

SEPTEMBER 24, 1867

There cannot be more than a dozen men on Garden Key who have not experienced the pestilence in some shape or form and yet the death toll is remarkably small. Of the thirty fatalities, only two have been prisoners. One of them is our cellmate Michael O'Loughlen. He was apparently convalescent when a sudden deterioration in his condition took place with yellowing skin, nose bleeding and delirium. Fearing his impending fate, O'Loughlen gasped, 'Doctor, doctor, you must tell my mother all!' Quite what he meant remains a mystery.

We are living through a nightmare, working around the clock in temperatures of over a hundred degrees, tending the sick. Today, during a short break, Dr Mudd told me how useless he felt. 'All I can do in most cases is offer the patient a few consoling words.'

I wince at the light and tell him he is mistaken. 'You have achieved so much with your medical knowledge.' He examines my no doubt haggard face. 'What's the matter with you?' he asks.

'Nothing,' I reply. Nothing is making me feel nauseous and light-headed.

'You're overdoing it George, you'd better have a rest.'

As I write this, the muscles in my back have begun to ache. Another nothing, another symptom of yellow fever and, I suppose, another nail in my coffin. I have cheated death so often on the battlefield. Has it finally caught up with me when, for once in my selfish life, I am trying to help my fellow man? There is an obvious irony here. My head is pounding and sweat pours off me.

No man is an island. John Donne's meditation enters my feverish mind. Yet we are all prisoners on a quarantine island with only this dreadful disease for company. How does Donne's meditation end? 'Any man's death diminishes me, because I am involved in mankind, and therefore never send to know for whom the bell tolls; it tolls for thee.' I can hear its sonorous chime.

OCTOBER 2, 1867

The darkness is tangible. It is heavy and threatening. I am trapped within its texture. My face is hot and yet my body is cold and immovable. Honest Abe Lincoln is lecturing me on the causes of the Civil War. And here's me thinking he was dead. I tell him it's the worst war in which I've fought, little better than mass slaughter, and what has it achieved? An end to slavery, he says. Ah yes, but that would have happened much earlier if you'd remained in the British Empire. We wanted our liberty, he replies. Do you remember what Thomas Jefferson had to say about liberty? He said that the tree of liberty must be refreshed with the blood of patriots and tyrants. Well, Abe, which were you?

Rose has just touched me. Touch is the threshold between the living and the dead. She is face upwards, swollen and blue in the water, her dress and petticoats billowing like a stately ship. I release her from the reeds' embrace and carry her to the hot coral sand. Kneeling over her, I open her pale lips and blow between them, mouth to mouth. But I am too late to save her.

I plunge into an abyss, my thoughts fragment and whirl out of control. The burgundy gown she wore at Morgan's wedding. How did that get in here? 'It's high time you knew something about the family business, George.' My father is talking in that calm, measured way of his. 'This here is a lump of Cornish cassiterite, it's a heavy ore, three times the weight of granite. Smelting is the process by which we extract the ore's tin content and it's done in one of these furnaces at a temperature of about two thousand degrees Fahrenheit.' *He's too hot. I am too hot. Sponge his forehead, nurse, he's burning up. I'm down in the dark. His temperature is still rising.* 'Tin mining is the most dangerous occupation on earth,' the little doctor tells me, 'hardly a miner lives to be fifty. Some die in accidents, the rest from lung disease.' He picks up a candle. 'And this is the culprit, the metal miners' canary. The bosses claim that if the candle burns then the air in the mine is okay. It isn't.' *You can stop sponging nurse, the fever is leaving him.*

Two days have gone by since then and I feel well enough to write down what I can recall of my delirious dreams. I was one of the last to catch the fever and received better care than would have been possible earlier in the epidemic. Dr Mudd puts my recuperation down to a resilient constitution; a recovery aided, no doubt, by knowledge of what is locked away in the communion cupboard.

OCTOBER 5, 1867

Still feeling a bit wobbly but I am out of bed at last. And not before time, now that Samuel Mudd has contracted the disease. In my eyes, he is a hero who has worn himself out in relieving the sufferings of the garrison and it is sadly ironic that he should succumb now, forty-seven days after the epidemic began, when the fever is running out of fresh victims.

Spangler, Arnold and I have agreed to watch over him. Although ignorant of the disease's pathology, I intend to adopt the methods of treatment practised during its prevalence: cooling the body with sponges impregnated in vinegar and camphor, administering ten grams of calomel and ten of Dover's Powder in the early stages of the fever, preparing herbal teas to quench the patient's thirst and giving him spirit of nitre whenever he is restless and his skin feels hot and dry.

OCTOBER 11, 1867

Great news! Samuel sat up today and drank a glass of porter. The worst is obviously over. Much of the credit for his recovery goes to Edward Spangler who saw to it that the patient received clean water and wholesome bread during his enforced confinement. Spangler continues to surprise me. He is the most faithful and solicitous of companions.

At the time of writing, no more than twenty men are fit for duty in the fort. A fever that causes headaches, muscle aches, vomiting, jaundice, kidney failure and bleeding is not easily got over. Yet the mortality rate remains amazingly low. Sadly, two of the kindest people I have ever known, Major Stone and his wife, have passed away.

Major George Andrews asked to see me today. He began by praising my conduct during the epidemic and promised me extensive privileges. One of these was the opportunity to resume my gardening. As if I would want to do any more digging! But Andrews did give me one good bit of news. That old stick in the mud Sir Frederick Bruce is to be replaced as British minister in Washington by Sir Edward Thornton, whom I knew when he was chargé d'affaires to Uruguay. With an old friend to plead my case I can once again entertain the hope of freedom.

Judging by recent newspaper publicity, my continued imprisonment is becoming an embarrassment to the government. I am receiving gifts from all over the South, including a trunk of clothes from Mrs Jefferson Davis. But I must put on weight to wear these suits with distinction.

OCTOBER 27, 1867

The fever has exhausted itself and will soon be stamped out, and with it, the need to pray for deliverance. When the epidemic was at its height a month ago, prisoners and guards knelt in their pews imploring mercy from on high. When men are frightened out of their wits, they will always seek divine guidance. Now they no longer need the chapel and this works to my advantage. My whole future lies in four gunnysacks wedged between sacramental offerings and sacred vessels in what is little more than a broom cupboard.

With no immediate prospect of a new minister being sent to the island, Major Andrews asked me to continue looking after the chapel. I accepted this task with a show of reluctance. 'I am prepared to offer a spot of spiritual guidance and to pray with anyone who needs my support,' said I, 'but I am not ordained and cannot hold services.' Actually, any Christian can administer communion but I wasn't going to tell him that. We agreed prayer sessions would take place on Sunday morning. Today was the first of these scheduled meetings and the whole thing was a frost. No one turned up.

I have been thinking a great deal about escape. There are numerous boats on the island and Cuba is only ninety miles away. Given a favourable breeze and the strong current of the Gulf Stream it should be possible to reach this Spanish colony in no more than a few hours. Indeed, I hear on the grapevine that it's been done before, although the prison authorities are reluctant to admit as much. Bolstered by such hopes, I have spent hours in the library constructing a navigational chart to show the shipping lanes in the Gulf of Mexico and the prevailing currents that might get me to my chosen destination.

Hard as it is for a man of my impatient nature, I intend to bide my time to see whether Sir Edward Thornton's diplomacy can gain my release. Meanwhile, there is a major problem to be resolved. Whether as a free man or a fugitive, I need to find some way of smuggling nine thousand guineas out of the fort without being detected. That means putting the money into something less obvious than a sack; a receptacle that is more appropriate to a house of God.

I lock the chapel door, open the communion cupboard and search for inspiration, finding it eventually in the stout wooden box in which the prison Bible is kept. That's what I require, Bible boxes, and I have an idea how to get them.

NOVEMBER 14, 1867

Although not yet fully recovered, Samuel is back in harness and, once again, he is acting as a replacement for an ailing army physician. We recently acquired the services of Dr Edward Thomas only to see him contract the yellow fever, weeks after the last case had been reported. These Yankee quacks are made of poor material.

Although his illness has left Samuel physically emaciated he is in a much better frame of mind, harbouring genuine hopes of getting out of here now that Fort Jefferson's military staff have petitioned President Johnson for his quick release. This citation is a handsome tribute to his skill and courage. It reads: 'Deprived as the garrison was of the assistance of any medical officer, Dr Mudd, influenced by the most praiseworthy and humane motives, spontaneously and unsolicited, came forward to devote all his energies and professional knowledge to the aid of the sick and dying.'

I ask the soldiers for a copy of their petition and take it to the valiant doctor in the post hospital where we are nursing the last of the fever patients. Samuel's face lights up on reading what they have said about him. 'That's quite a recommendation,' he chuckles.

'You deserve every word of praise and more besides,' I tell him.

Samuel gives me a hug. 'What about you George? Where's your reward? You've been a tower of strength. I couldn't have managed without you.'

'It doesn't signify,' I say breezily, which is a barefaced lie. 'But I wonder if I could ask a favour of you.'

'Ask away.' Samuel is still basking in the glory of the garrison's commendation.

'Do you and Spangler plan to continue working in the carpentry shop?'

'Sure, I'm there a couple of hours a day. Why?'

'Would you be able to make me five Bible boxes, do you think?'

Samuel frowns. 'That's a lot of work. What do you want them for?'

I have my answer off pat. 'You know I was left in charge of the chapel by the late Reverend Matchett. Well, I've found a pile of Bibles we don't need and I thought it might be a nice gesture to put them in boxes and send them as gifts to the chaplains of other military prisons. What do you think?' He is my friend but I can't tell him the truth. No one must know about my treasure.

Samuel claps me on the back. 'I think it's a capital notion. Those long hours of prayer in the chapel seem to have done you a power of good, George, and there I was thinking you lacked faith.'

'You are most perceptive,' I reply. 'I still wonder though whether I am posting letters to a non-existent address.'

'Yet you persist in the practice, which is altogether admirable. Tell me, did you ever pray for me?'

'I did when you were sick. My prayers may have done nothing to aid your recovery, but they gave me peace of mind.'

'Thank you, George. Consider your Bible boxes as good as made. What dimensions have you in mind and what timber would you like? The best hardwood in the shop is plantation-grown teak which is famous for its mellow colour and durability. Because of its strength and aesthetic ...'

I stop listening. My exit strategy is beginning to take shape.

DECEMBER 7, 1867

I have heard again from my attorney. Sir Edward Thornton has replied to Hervey's letter, assuring him he will do his utmost on my behalf when circumstances are more propitious. I take this to mean that nothing has changed. Escaping from the island seems to be my only option.

Not that I'm feeling very dynamic today as I lounge on a hammock strung between two mangrove trees eating a banana. This is the best time of year when the temperature drops and the fort's menacing brick walls are softened by jasmines, morning glories and cypress vines. Among the privileges I've been granted as a fort hero is the right to wear my own clothes and, in my pocket, a ticking watch reminds me it is time I visited the post hospital to check on Fat Charley's health. The good-natured boatman was the very last to contract the fever and it has hit him hard. His once plump amiable face is now as pale and drawn as that of an undertaker's mute.

'How goes it with you, my friend?' I ask in my best bedside manner.

'Bless you Colonel, I am feeling much better today. As the Book of Psalms says, "The Lord is my strength and my shield; He restores my joy and health." I will soon be ready to go sailing again.'

'That's the ticket!' say I. 'Tell me about that boat of yours. I hear she is properly trimmed out.'

'That she is. There be nothing better in these reef waters than the *Rosetta*. She is lapstreak like a Viking boat, gig-built and schooner-rigged, powered by sail and oar, long enough at seventeen feet to carry five passengers and marvellously seaworthy. I tell you, Colonel, she's a regular beauty. With her hull painted vermilion, and pure white inside, she is a gay object to behold on a blue sea.'

'What kind of freight does the *Rosetta* carry?'

'Out here in the Tortugas she's used mainly for collecting supplies and taking the mail. Busby and I sail her to Key West every Saturday and make the return journey the following day.'

Another part of my escape plan is slotting into place.

DECEMBER 15, 1867

The Bible boxes are ready. Made out of hard plantation teak, measuring fourteen inches by ten, with a padded velvet interior like a jewellery case, they are fit for purpose. I pay Samuel and Ned for their work with money I've been sent by friends and admirers.

Southern newspapers have latched on to the fact that I am the most senior Confederate officer still in prison and this has led to a show of sympathy for the 'gallant English cavalier'. I am particularly proud of the letter from Jefferson Davis, expressing outrage at my continued confinement and enclosing a packet of tobacco and twenty dollars. Another very civil note comes from an unexpected quarter: General Braxton Bragg writes to say I'd been an excellent officer, a man of chivalry and generosity. Well, I can't quibble with that, can I?

Not that these generous words will have any effect on my incarceration. Congress is still controlled by Radical Republicans who want to punish the South and Edwin Stanton is still Secretary of War. I await another letter from my lawyer to confirm this gloomy forecast.

FEBRUARY 26, 1868

The die is cast. I have no alternative but to cut and run. Better a watery grave than the slow death that awaits me here. We've just been told that when Major Andrews completes his tour of duty at the end of the month he will be replaced by Lieutenant MacConnell, the very man who was demoted and posted away from this fort after I denounced his sadistic behaviour in the New York *World*. Maybe I am getting windy in my old age but news of this inexplicable appointment leaves me panic-stricken, my mouth dry with fear. Once again, the fates have conspired against me.

'He'll kill me inch by inch,' I croak in a self-pitying way. 'You may be right,' Samuel Mudd replies, 'but I'd rather die than play the fiddle while drunken soldiers dance and fornicate with nigger girls.' Much as I admire him as a physician, I can't abide his racism. I guess it's bred in the bone.

I go to the library and pen a letter to my favourite daughter, Marie Pearce-Serecold. 'Our kind commandant, Major Andrews, is about to be relieved. This is a great loss to us all, but to me in particular. His successor has a deadly hatred for me.' She ought to know this. It might help to explain my subsequent actions. I also tell her I have been the worst of fathers and ask for her forgiveness.

Walking down one of the fort's arched passageways with its gun embrasures and powder magazines, I feel surrounded by evil. You might think I am in an almighty funk, and you wouldn't be far wrong, but my shivering stops once I am out of those claustrophobic corridors. Nothing has changed after all, apart from the speed with which I must launch my escape bid. I can't sail the *Rosetta* single-handed, no one could, so I need a couple of prisoners to share in the adventure and I have worked out whom to approach.

My prime target is Johnny Adair, a Union soldier court-martialled for striking a superior officer, who has come out of solitary confinement this very day. The other prisoners tend to give Johnny a wide berth because of his bad reputation and frightening appearance. I am over six feet tall but he tops me by a good six inches, and the width of his chest is in keeping with his height. But what interest me more are his daring and iron nerve.

Shortly before my arrival here, so the story goes, Adair and a Negro prisoner escaped on a plank and paddled for three miles through shark-infested waters to reach Loggerhead Key, where they stole a boat belonging to the lighthouse and rowed all the way to Cuba. Adair then made the mistake of trying to raise money by putting his partner up for sale in the local auctions, which led to the outraged Negro betraying him to the Spanish authorities. Brought back to Fort Jefferson in irons, Adair made another bid for freedom. Handicapped by his fetters, he still managed to swim to Loggerhead Key, only to discover that the lighthouse boat had gone. Another unsuccessful jailbreak you might think, but I look at it differently. I see an ideal travelling companion: a man mountain, ruthless and determined, if somewhat lacking in the brain department.

I find him lolling near the blacksmith's shop, enjoying the sunshine and gnawing on a toothpick. 'How goes it, Johnny?' I ask in a friendly sort of way.

His broad impassive face lights up into a toothy grin. 'I've been waiting to talk to you, Colonel Grenfell. We were on opposite sides at Cemetery Ridge. I was in Custer's Michigan Brigade and you shot his horse.'

'That's about all I managed to do that day. You fought us to a standstill.'

'That we did, sir.'

'Call me George. Something tells me we are going to be firm friends, Johnny.'

And that was all it took. A whispered conversation and I have my first recruit. Now that we are joining forces it seems only sensible that we should share a prison cell. I tell Major Andrews that Adair found God while in the hole and wants to pray with me. It's a less than plausible tale but Andrews is too busy thinking of hearth and home to bat an eyelid.

My erstwhile cellmates are not so easily fooled. 'You're up to something, George,' says Samuel Mudd winking his eye at me. 'Not that I blame you with that butcher MacConnell coming back and him so bitter towards you. Whatever you're planning, I'm sure we wish you luck.'

After handshakes all round, I take my leave of them and go off on another recruiting trip. My destination is one of the most disgusting places in the fort, the prisoners' mess, where meals are almost guaranteed to give you chronic indigestion. On entering the room I bump into a bevy of black girls in grubby overalls scraping congealed food off the floor before the next sitting.

'Where's Joseph Holroyd?' I ask the kneeling scullions.

One of the girls looks up at me with a trembling mouth. 'Boss is in dah kitchen, massa.'

Her servile words catch me on the raw. Haven't we just fought a four-year war to put an end to slavery? Fuming over this apparent hypocrisy, I swing open the kitchen door and find a curly-haired young cook swiping at black beetles as they scurry across his workbench. He registers my presence with a wave of his wooden spoon. 'These bloody beetles get into everything,' he snarls over his shoulder. 'We have beetles in the soup, the bread, even in the tea. I've asked for a decent insecticide until I'm blue in the face but they say they can't requisition pyrethrum.'

The angry cook lands a crushing blow on several winged insects before coming to a halt. He wipes the sweat off his smooth cheeks and gives me a grin of recognition. 'Colonel Grenfell, the military hero, isn't it? Holroyd's the name, killing bugs the game. How about lending a hand? Here, take this ladle. You should be good at this. It's said you've killed more men than you've had hot dinners. Although you won't get one of those here,' he chortles.

After violent activity with ladle and spoon, the kitchen's beetle population is temporarily reduced and Holroyd hangs up his trusty weapon on a nail above the sink. 'I'm sick of this job,' he says. 'No decent food to cook and constant complaints from the customers. I almost wish I'd died of the fever. I guess I've got you to thank for keeping me alive.'

I find this sudden change of tack quite bewildering but my fresh-faced companion hasn't finished yet. 'The word is you've found religion and become a Bible-thumper. Often happens that way. Spreading the gospel and piling up corpses seem to go together in the Christian mission.'

'How long have you been here?' I ask, anxious to change the subject.

'Since the spring of '65, but it seems longer than that and I've still got two years to go.'

'And what was your crime?'

'Oh, you'll laugh at this,' he says. 'I was found guilty of poisoning a ship's crew, all 130 of them. I was the head chef on one of those steam-powered ironclads, the *Milwaukee* she was called, fought in the battle of Mobile Bay. The master at arms found rat droppings in his stew and hysteria set in. I was put in irons and sent to a brig, which was very fortunate because the *Milwaukee* hit a mine and sank soon afterwards.'

'Did you do it?'

Holroyd gives me a sharp look. 'I'm not saying I did and I'm not saying I didn't. The prison officers thought my punishment should fit the crime and put me into this filthy kitchen.'

The cherubic chef spreads out his arms in mute misery. His kitchen is indescribably dirty and stinks of putrid pork and potato skins. 'I'm expected to cook in these surroundings! I tell you, Colonel, it can't be done. I'm not to blame for the rotting vegetables and the mouldy bread or for the size of the portions. It's the regulations, you see, two ounces of this and three of that, there's no room for improvisation. Some of the convicts get so hungry they end up eating candles and old poultices. Have you ever wondered why breakfast is at six and lunch at eleven thirty? I'll tell you why. It's to fit in with the officers' shifts. Prison bureaucracy, that's what it is.'

I nod in sympathy. 'That's scandalous. I don't know how you put up with it.'

'Nor do I.' Holroyd shakes his head sadly. 'What I'd give to get out of here and off this hellish island.'

This is my cue. 'Supposing some of us decided to form an escape party, would you be with us?'

'You mean *when* you escape. Of course I'll come along!'

I have to hand it to Holroyd; he's quick on the uptake and a cool customer. 'Now would be a good time to go,' he says like a seasoned conspirator. 'There are only two companies left on the island. The rest of the Fifth Artillery is putting down a riot in New Orleans. That means no more than four sentries on duty at night and only one down by the wharf. And the best way of getting there is through a window in the mess hall which is where I happen to sleep.'

'That's a capital notion,' say I, feigning surprise at the news.

'There's a problem though. The hall door is locked at night. You'd have to bribe a guard to open up.'

'Leave that to me,' I tell him. 'Be ready to move in a week's time. I'll give you exact details as soon as I can.'

We shake hands on the deal and I leave my new accomplice, the *Milwaukee* poisoner, to contrive an evening meal out of maggoty bacon and corn husks while I set off to find a corruptible soldier, ideally one rostered to be at Sentry Post Number Two on the night of Friday, March 6.

I've selected this date for three reasons: firstly, because I want to be off the island before Lieutenant MacConnell arrives and slaps me in irons; secondly, because the *Rosetta* will be anchored on the wharf that night ready for her weekend run to Key West and, lastly, because the fort's officers will be holding one of their drunken parties and making sufficient noise to cover our tracks.

The soldier I seek out is Private William Norveil, a bony, shambling youth with a badly pockmarked, hairless face. Bullied by the officers because of his ugliness, he looks ripe for the picking. All he needs to do is open a couple of doors once the corporal of the guard has gone to bed and turn a blind eye while we fix *Rosetta*'s oars and rudder. We'll sail away nice and easy and he will be the richer by ten guineas. You see, I've thought of everything.

I know Norveil often goes for solitary walks along the seashore when he's off duty. He's a loner. Something else I've learned about him is that he's fond of cheroots, those cylindrical clipped cigars made of cheap tobacco. That's why I've bought a packet with my prison wages. There are many ways of striking up a relationship but offering somebody a gift is one of the best.

Norveil is standing on the sandbank throwing pieces of reef rubble into the turquoise water lapping around his feet. I join him and silently watch the ripples he's creating in the sea. 'Like one of these?' I ask, fishing out my packet of cheroots.

Norveil goes red with embarrassment. I'm probably the first prisoner to offer him anything but abuse. 'Gee, mister, that would be swell, if you're sure you can spare one.'

We light our thin cheroots and the pungent smoke circles overhead, warding off some of the mosquitoes. Norveil swats at his face. 'God, I hate these little beasts. They feast on your blood and buzz around your ear like a fat man in a buffet line.'

'And they bite soldiers as often as they do prisoners. That's very democratic, wouldn't you say?'

'I'm as much a prisoner here as you are and just as badly

treated,' he replies bitterly. 'You're Colonel Grenfell, ain't you, I recognise you now, sir. You and I have something in common; we've both been tortured by the guards, only you lasted better than I did. I blacked out as soon as they forced water down my throat. I've a mortal fear of drowning.'

'Most of us do, son.' I couldn't help feeling sorry for the boy. 'Where are you from?'

'Cincinnati, Ohio. My parents were German immigrants but they died of cholera in 1851 and my brothers and I went to live in the orphan asylum near the waterfront, which weren't so bad as I met Betsy and we fell in love, only for them to drag me off to fight for Uncle Sam.'

A sad life story told in a single badly constructed sentence. My heart goes out to him.

'I was at Antietam and Gettysburg,' he says. 'From what I've seen of warfare, the idea is to kill everything that moves and set fire to what doesn't, but even that is better than being stuck on this terrible island with a bunch of sadistic perverts.'

'Look, William – I hope you don't mind if I call you that?'

'I'd be honoured if you would, sir.'

'Well, William, here's the truth of it. I will give you ten English guineas, which are worth about fifty dollars, if you will help us to escape during your sentry watch on Friday week.'

'And you'd take me with you?' he asks eagerly, his voice cracking with emotion.

'Of course I would but I can't guarantee your safety. You're risking death and disgrace.'

'I don't care a tinker's damn for that. All I want is to get back home to Betsy and your fifty dollars would sure come in handy.' To my relief, he doesn't ask where the money is coming from.

There's an old Irish saying about fear being a fine spur. The shock of Lieutenant MacConnell's imminent return has galvanised me into long overdue action. With Adair, Holroyd and Norveil on board, I have completed my escape party. All we need is good fortune.

Whether we succeed or fail in our enterprise, this will be the concluding entry in my prison diary.

WHATEVER CAN GO WRONG, WILL GO WRONG

He awoke to the sound of a bugle blowing reveille. Grenfell rubbed the sleep out of his eyes, rolled out of bed and donned his coarse prison shirt and trousers. As he did so, realisation dawned, and with that butterflies in his stomach. This was the eight hundred and eightieth day of his captivity in Fort Jefferson and, if things went well, it would be his last.

The sound of a key turning in a lock put an end to such reflections. Two armed soldiers grabbed his arms and began to march him out of the cell.

'Here, what's going on?' asked Johnny Adair, towering over them menacingly. 'That's my friend you're roughing up.'

'This ain't none a yore business, big man.' A guard underlined his point by poking a pistol in Adair's ribs.

'Ease it, Johnny,' Grenfell urged, trying to calm his racing heart. 'I'd best see what they want.'

They took him to the commandant's office near the sally port. The room hadn't altered much since his last visit: the same pigeonholed keys and ledgers, the same pile of shackles and leg irons. But what *had* changed was the man in charge.

Sitting with his booted feet on the desk, grinning at him, was Grenfell's arch enemy Lieutenant MacConnell, flanked by that other despicable brute, Second Lieutenant Murphy.

'Look who's here, Murphy,' MacConnell sneered. 'It's the great humanitarian, the one who tells lies about us in the newspapers.'

'Aye, an' he'll soon see de error of his ways, Oi'll be boun''

'Hold your horses, Paddy, let's not be too hasty. Grenfell is a different man these days. He's caught a religious fever, they say, and is now a Christian. Isn't that so?'

Grenfell was thunderstruck. MacConnell had arrived earlier than expected. Better answer his question though. 'You could say I've acquired a faith,' he replied defensively. 'I've come to believe in the power of prayer.'

His cold-eyed tormentor took his feet off the desk and leaned forward in mock solemnity. He was enjoying this game of cat and mouse. 'Really, is that all you've got to say?'

Right, Grenfell thought, if this smirking bastard wants old-time religion, I'll give it to him, both barrels. 'Praise the Lord,' he began. 'I have a mission to fulfil that transcends these prison walls. The hour of salvation is upon us. We must spread the good word around the world and bring an end to the confusion of languages from the days of Babel.'

MacConnell and Murphy looked at one another in astonishment. Their prisoner was either stark raving mad or a Bible-thumping evangelist.

'And how will this come to pass?' asked MacConnell, unconsciously adopting the language of the Old Testament.

'In small ways at first,' replied the visionary Englishman. 'Five Bible boxes are going to Key West tomorrow where Dr Whitehurst will pick them up and send them on to the chaplains of America's other military prisons. This was sanctioned by your predecessor. Later, when my days of captivity are over, I plan to become a missionary and carry God's teachings to heathen shores ...'

'What a load of shoite he's blatherin', ter be sure,' snorted an indignant Murphy.

'We shouldn't judge him too harshly,' said his commanding officer. 'He may be truly penitent.'

Why is he toying with me like this? Grenfell wondered. Then it came to him. MacConnell was on probation and couldn't afford to victimise the man who had publicly denounced him. His enemy needed an excuse to destroy him.

'I *am* truly penitent … sir.' The last word stuck in Grenfell's throat but it was a small sacrifice to make in the circumstances.

'Let us hope so.' MacConnell's voice was full of disbelief. 'You're dismissed.'

He rushed to the chapel, locked the door behind him, opened the communion cupboard and emptied the contents of the gunnysacks into the padded teak caskets. The sooner the Bible boxes were stored in *Rosetta*'s hold the better. Getting them there was the tricky bit as it entailed carrying the boxes, one by one, down to the wharf where the schooner was anchored.

It was with a profound sense of relief that he handed the fifth box to the ship's skipper Fat Charley. But his satisfaction was short-lived. Heavy steps on the gangplank heralded the arrival of two black soldiers followed by their commanding officer, holding a handspike. Lieutenant MacConnell grabbed the box and stuck the metal bar under its lid. 'I thought I'd take a look at these Bibles you're sending out, cully,' he leered.

At first, the solid teak resisted MacConnell's attempts to lever up the lid until, with a splintering sound, it finally gave way. There was a glint of triumph in the lieutenant's pale eyes as he ripped away the covering.

'My God!' he gasped. He was looking at a deluxe edition of the King James Bible bound in black leather with gold stamping.

'Do you want me to open the other boxes?' Grenfell asked meekly. 'I've got a key here.'

MacConnell's face reddened with rage and frustration. He took a deep breath before admitting defeat. 'No need for that,' he barked. 'Only checking for irregularities.'

Fat Charley waited until the soldiers had left the ship before laughing aloud. 'Well I'll be a vice admiral of the narrow seas,' he chuckled. 'I never thought to see that measly little pimp so put down and over a bunch of Bibles too!'

Grenfell smiled wanly and sank onto a bulkhead. Drops of

icy sweat trickled down his neck. He had deliberately mentioned the Bible boxes to MacConnell to get them on board ship and had gambled on the sadistic officer toying with him by staging a last-minute inspection. That was why he had placed a Bible in the final casket.

He watched as Fat Charley sealed up the cargo hold with wooden planking. 'Don't you worry none Colonel; the rest of your boxes will be safe and sound on tomorrow's trip.'

Thinking about a rather earlier voyage than the one his friend had in mind, Grenfell couldn't wait for night to come.

*

It was close to the witching hour when they heard footsteps outside their cell. Dressed in the warmest clothes they could muster, Grenfell and Adair rose from their cots and waited tensely by the door. The rattling of a set of keys punctuated the silence. 'Dammit! I've got the wrong one.' The lock was tried again and this time the cell door swung open. Private Norveil crouched outside. 'Sorry about that,' he muttered. 'It's difficult to see in the dark.'

The three of them ran down the steps and out into the courtyard where Norveil produced another key to admit them to the mess hall. Joseph Holroyd was standing on a table beneath the open window through which they planned to escape. 'You're a bit late,' he complained.

Grenfell cut him off. 'No time for explanations. Have you dealt with the sharks, Mr Holroyd?'

'I surely have,' the plump cook replied. 'I've dropped enough barbasco balls into the moat to stun the largest leviathan.' Barbasco was a creeper that grew in profusion on the island but no one had ever mentioned its stupefying effect on big fish.

'And how about the rope you promised?'

'I have that too.' Holroyd brandished a braided rawhide rope. 'There's about twenty feet of it which should be long enough.'

Grenfell took the rope, tied one end to the table leg and threw the other end out of the window.

'I'll go first,' he muttered. With surprising agility for a middle-aged man Grenfell leaped onto the table, grabbed the rope in both hands, levered himself up onto the window ledge, swung around and began to descend with his feet braced against the fort's outer wall. Such was his concentration that he was hardly aware of the thick buffalo hide biting into his hands. Soon he was down, dropping noiselessly into the moat.

Grenfell offered a silent prayer as he cut through the water with a powerful front crawl. The frightening outline of a shark floated past him, belly up. The *Milwaukee* poisoner had dealt emphatically with the prison's last line of defence.

A loud splash announced the cook's arrival in the water where he floundered until Grenfell swam to support him. Adair plunged in shortly afterwards and helped keep Holroyd's head above water. Having praised Holroyd for his inventiveness, Grenfell now silently cursed him. They were making too much noise. But the splashing didn't stop until three bedraggled figures finally pulled themselves out of the moat and lay exhausted on the far bank.

After only a moment's rest Grenfell stood up, cautioning the others to wait while he located Norveil. 'I'm over here, Colonel,' a voice whispered urgently. 'Just as well you went through the window. I ran into a group of drunken officers under the sally port, most of whom were armed. You wouldn't have stood a chance.'

'Have you checked the ship?' he asked.

'Yes, the ship is ready to go and the oars are where I said they'd be on the wharf.'

Something rustled behind Grenfell's head. He whipped around in fear of discovery, as a figure moved out of the inky darkness.

The light fell on the heavy, scarred face of Hank Woodward, an army deserter serving a five-year sentence for rape.

Norveil gasped in dismay but Grenfell kept cool. 'What are you doing here, Woodward?'

Woodward's deep-set eyes burned like coals. 'I coming with you,' he said, 'and if you don't agree, I'll blow the whistle on yer, see if I don't.'

Keep him talking, Grenfell thought instinctively. 'How did you get out?' he asked.

'Came through the wall, didn't I, loosened the bricks between my cell and the casemate next to it, crawled through and jumped out of a gun embrasure into the moat.'

'How did you know we were going to escape tonight?'

A very large shadow was creeping up behind Woodward.

'Because I told him, that's why.' The massive frame of Johnny Adair sprang forward and cracked Woodward over the head with a ship's oar. He fell like a stone with blood spurting from a head wound.

Adair picked the unconscious man off the wharf and slung him over his shoulder. 'I'll dump him somewhere safe,' he muttered before disappearing out of sight.

He returned a few minutes later. 'Sorry for the delay,' he said calmly.

'Why did you have to tell him we were going?' Norveil wailed. The young soldier was shaking with fright.

'I spoke out of turn,' Adair grunted. 'Big mistake but I've taken care of it, haven't I? Now let's stop jawing and be on our way.'

'Right,' said Grenfell, taking charge once again. 'Johnny, I'd like you to hoist the jib and ease out the main sheets.' Adair nodded but a loud rumble of thunder drowned his reply.

Lightning arced across the wharf as they climbed on board the *Rosetta*. A storm had come out of nowhere as it sometimes did in the Gulf of Mexico. The rain sheeted down horizontally and electricity encircled the small schooner. The self-appointed skipper shouted instructions but the rising wind whipped away his words. Taking hold of Holroyd, he yelled in his ear, 'I know you were on an ironclad but you can raise a foresail, can't you?' The normally cocky cook looked less than sure.

'Grab these ropes,' Grenfell bellowed. 'Don't forget to haul the throat and peak halyards at the same time and, whatever you do, keep the gaff horizontal!' Although no sailor, he knew that in a high wind and pounding surf a small gaff-rigged schooner was pretty much balanced with foresail alone. The greater the wind, the more the mainsail pushed the stern of the boat to leeward.

As the *Rosetta* left the harbour, Grenfell weighed up possible escape routes. He had originally planned to steer a course through the narrow channel between Garden Key and Bush Key before turning in a southerly direction. But with the wind blowing hard from the north he would be sailing into the teeth of the gale and then broadside to it during the crucial passage over the reefs, increasing the risk of the ship capsizing. Instead, he steered a southerly course with the intention of approaching the hazardous reefs from the southwest. But here too there was danger. To make this crossing on a pitch-black night during a violent storm meant navigating by instinct alone, with all landmarks blotted out. It would require skill, strength and a lot of luck to come through unscathed.

At first, everything went well. There was a brief lull in the storm and the little vessel ran before the wind, tearing through the water with everything flying. As visibility was down to a few feet, Grenfell detected the ship's urgent motion by her heave and thrust, the vibrating wood beneath his hand and the groan of cordage and canvas. Then the weather deteriorated with blinding rain, a shrieking wind and an angry swelling sea that tried to smash the small vessel to pieces. *Rosetta*'s gunwales had to ride high in the air to crest the waves and her decks were shipping too much water. He felt frustration welling up inside him, ready to explode into violence.

Shafts of lightning illuminated the plight of the crew who were hanging on to the lifelines for grim death. Above their heads, the sails were being ripped to shreds. They needed shortening. Someone had to go aloft. Grenfell looked for a volunteer. He could see that Norveil was petrified. Holroyd seemed to be nursing an injury while the ever-willing Adair was far too big and clumsy to mount the narrow ratline ladder that swayed and lurched with the ship's wallowing. No, he would have to do it himself.

He began to climb, his eyes stinging from the salt spray, clinging to the ratlines with each staggering roll, choking on flying water as the wind endeavoured to shake him from his precarious perch into the boiling cauldron below. Reaching the yardarm, he flopped forward over the wooden spar, with his feet braced on ropes looped horizontally beneath the yard, while his slippery fingers tried to gather in a thousand square feet of billowing canvas. Caught in a maze of rigging it felt as if every moment might be his last. Yet somehow the job got done.

The pressure on the rigging eased and the rolling of the ship changed to a viciously unexpected pitch that all but hurled him into space. It was like trying to break in a stubborn stallion, only much more dangerous. Descending rapidly, he sighed when his feet touched the deck, only to find an even greater menace awaiting him there.

Accompanied by theatrical bursts of thunder and lightning, a solid wall of water was rushing towards the bow. Not even a sturdy vessel like the *Rosetta* could possibly withstand the fury of the forty-foot wave driving towards her. Nature was about to have the last word. Grenfell braced himself for the *coup de grâce*.

He had time to yell, 'Tie yourselves to the masts, boys,' before the wave crashed over the boat. Gunwales broke, timbers tore apart, and something heavy hit his head. He seemed to be falling through darkness, sucked down into oblivion.

*

LIEUTENANT MACCONNELL'S REPORT TO
GENERAL HILL
MARCH 12, 1868
Private William Norveil of Company 1, Fifth US Artillery, who had been on duty posted as a sentinel over the boats within the boom, did between the hours of eleven o'clock pm and one o'clock am desert his post, taking possession of a small schooner called the Rosetta *and carrying with him three prisoners – G St Leger Grenfell, J.W Adair and Joseph Holroyd – while a fourth, Henry Woodward drowned in the moat. I am impressed with the conviction that Grenfell had considerable money in his possession with which he bribed the sentinel into joining his escape bid.*

The steamer Bibb *which was lying in the harbour volunteered to search for the fugitives at first light, although Captain Slott made no secret of his belief that it was a fruitless errand, as no small ship could have ridden out the night's storm. Setting out at eight a.m. Captain Slott criss-crossed the waters south and southeast of the Tortugas but found nothing – neither boat nor bodies. It is my opinion that the fugitives were drowned at sea.*

*

Where am I? That was his first thought on regaining consciousness, together with astonishment at being alive. Gradually he came to his senses. He had a raging thirst, a mouth that tasted of salt and a head that seemed to be splitting. Tentatively, he tried to open his eyes, contracting his pupils and blinking furiously in the bright sunshine. His last fuzzy recollection had been of howling winds and a mountainous wave about to upturn the *Rosetta*; yet now he could hear the lapping of water on a shore and scent the sweet smell of coconuts and the earthy green aroma of bamboo. Perhaps he was dead and had gone to paradise. He wanted to laugh at the notion but his head exploded. The thunderstorm was inside him, beating mercilessly against his skull. His stomach heaved in unison.

His sight began to return, albeit as a blurred double vision of the main deck of the *Rosetta* with scattered yards, sails, ropes and blocks of the foremast lying fore and aft. The ship was canted at an odd angle. She appeared to have run aground.

Grenfell made another discovery. He couldn't move. He had a dim memory of lashing himself to the masthead before the craft capsized. With fumbling fingers, he untied the rope, heaved himself upright and looked about him in amazement.

The vessel had washed ashore on a beach of dazzling whiteness fringed by gently swaying coconut palms, lush mangrove thickets and a collection of bright green trees and bushes that glittered in the blinding light. The only signs of life on this coral strand were the nesting sea turtles. There was not even a footprint in the sand.

How, he wondered, had the *Rosetta* managed to get here? And what had happened to his shipmates? He yelled out their names and waited for a response. The only sound to break the silence was the harsh cry of gulls hovering overhead. Fearing the worst, he tried again. Nothing. He was alone on his island paradise.

Like any mariner saved from the sea, he thanked God for deliverance before praying for the souls of his drowned comrades – the bold reckless giant, the sinister cook and the luckless young soldier who had wanted nothing more than to be reunited with his sweetheart.

Then another thought struck him and sorrow gave way to

greed. Those golden guineas, had they survived the shipwreck? He slithered across the deck to find out. To his intense relief, the cargo hold seemed intact. Taking a crowbar from the ship's tools, he prised open the wooden planking and looked inside. The Bible boxes were just where he had left them. So too was the wooden cask in which Fat Charley stored his fresh water supply. Lifting the lid of the barrel, Grenfell drank greedily to quench his thirst. There was a price to pay however. Almost as a reflex action, he vomited on the decking.

After his sickness subsided, he gingerly explored the top of his head and located a crusted lump on the crown. He must have been knocked out by a piece of flying timber and had lost a good deal of blood in the process. No wonder it felt as if a horse had kicked him.

He was also aware of the enveloping heat. Sweat was prickling his neck. His heavy suit was clammy and uncomfortable but he had nothing else to wear, and nothing to protect his head from the blistering sun. Necessity, they say, is the mother of invention. Panting like an old dog, Grenfell sifted through the wreckage on the main deck until he found a piece of torn canvas from which he could fashion a crude head covering.

Shaded from the sun's intensity, he forced his swollen eyes to focus on something other than sand. On the hazy horizon, limestone cliffs reared up with what looked like timber-built cottages clinging to their crevices. Judging by the amount of smoke curling above them, these wooden shacks must be occupied and, sooner or later, someone would notice that a ship had run aground on the beach below. Where he came from in Cornwall, shipwrecks were regularly ransacked by scavengers. Whatever kind of people lived here, they were likely to behave in a similar fashion, and the *Rosetta*'s cargo hold was the first place any looter would look for valuables. He had to find another hiding place for his boxes. He took off his shoes and clambered unsteadily out of the vessel to begin his search.

317

Incongruous memories of his Cornish childhood sprang to mind; what it was like to have sand between your toes and the waves whispering to you. Marazion beach had been his favourite playground. Here he had dug for clams and scampered between barnacle covered rock pools with a fishing net to trap sea snails and whelks. He had delighted in a beach's simple treasures. Now, as an adult, he lived in a material world where a different kind of treasure had to be concealed.

What he was looking for was a natural cavern and luck was on his side. Within half a mile of the boat was a limestone cave with dim recesses in the rock that could be used for storage. Returning to the *Rosetta*, he extracted thirty guineas from one of the Bible boxes for personal use before carrying the casket to the cave. Transferring the other boxes from ship to shore required four more energy-sapping journeys.

Grenfell felt dizzy and disoriented, overwhelmed by the enormity of the task facing him. For any castaway, the first steps were the hardest: quitting the safety of the beach to explore an unknown hinterland spelled danger. He was a reluctant Robinson Crusoe; not exactly in rags but dressed in a damp suit that was too heavy for the climate and a pair of hefty prison boots.

First, there was a cliff face to be negotiated and he was already perspiring freely by the time he reached it. The only track upwards was pitted with potholes and pieces of rock. Terns huddled in cracks and crannies while gannets and gulls circled overhead as if to warn him off. The higher he climbed the harder it got. His limbs ached and his heart rate rose with the effort.

Finally, he reached the top and was rewarded with the encouraging sight of a wide, gently undulating plateau of tall, coarse grasses and flowering shrubs shaded by cedars and huge feather duster palms. He could also see what might be a road glimmering in the heat haze. On closer inspection, it turned out to be little better than a footpath whose rusty soil revealed the presence of another crumbling sedimentary rock, sandstone.

For want of a better idea Grenfell decided to follow this primitive road, walking in a westerly direction. With flies buzzing around him and sweat getting in his eyes, he was beginning to have second thoughts when a wagon train appeared in the distance. Surely this was too good to be true? He had encountered mirages in the Moroccan desert, observed pools of water that were merely a reflection of the blue sky, but this had to be more than an optical illusion. A convoy of four ox-drawn wooden wagons, laden with freshly cut sugar cane, was steadily approaching him. The wagons were heavy and clumsy and their huge wheels cut into the friable surface of the track leaving deep ruts behind them.

The lead wagon was driven by a hardy little man with a sprouting beard. He was dressed in a poncho and a pair of grubby oiled linen trousers with a bright red kerchief wound around his head. 'Whoa,' he said to his oxen, before commanding the black slaves driving the other wagons to stop too.

Grenfell heard a voice, not unlike his own, croaking away in Spanish. An ability to speak several languages, slinging the bat in British Army parlance, had long been one of his more useful attributes. 'Perdona me señor,' he said apologetically. 'Seria tan amable de decirme donde conduce este camino? Estoy perdido, que se ve.' He was lost and would like to know where this road led.

The carter looked suspiciously at the dishevelled, emaciated figure standing in front of him. His small, wary eyes were set in a pinched face, wrinkled like a tobacco leaf. 'Quien quiere saber?' he grunted, asking a question of his own. The man spoke Spanish, but not Castilian for he seemed to eat the end of his words.

'Estas Cubana?' Grenfell asked hopefully. 'Claro que soy yo,' the man replied. '*Soy un carretero. Que pasa comparde?*' This roughly translated as 'Of course I am. I'm a wagon driver. What's up, man?' Like many people of peasant stock, the carter had an inbred dislike of foreigners.

He told the *carretero* he was a shipwrecked Englishman in need of assistance and, to his surprise, the man's mood changed dramatically. 'English, you say. God save the Queen!' he chuckled. 'I know all about your sceptred isle.' Grenfell was speechless. Not in his wildest dreams had he expected to find a Cuban wagon driver quoting Shakespeare.

'The sugar planter I work for, Señor Juan Pedrosa, teaches us all about your country. He was educated there.'

'That's good to know,' Grenfell said, opening his Spanish vowels and swallowing his consonants. 'Am I anywhere near Havana?'

'You're four leagues away and going in the wrong direction.'

The wagon train was carrying eight tons of cut cane from Señor Pedrosa's San Isidro estate to the sugar mill on his main plantation. 'Do you want a lift?' the carter asked. Grenfell nodded enthusiastically. 'But where's your luggage? Was everything lost in the shipwreck?'

Not quite everything, Grenfell replied, he'd hidden a few things on the beach. Would there be room for them on one of these wagons? The carter told him he worked long hours and was not well paid. Grenfell took the hint and delved into his coat pocket. 'Look at these!' he said, showing the driver what he was holding. 'Each of these shiny English coins has a gold value that's worth more than your weekly wage.'

It was only a guess but the covetous look on the man's face suggested he might be right. 'I will give you the first coin now and the second one when you load my luggage into your carts. The third one becomes yours when you drop me off in Havana Vieja. Is that agreed?'

The small, wizened *carretero* spat on his hand before offering it to him, '*Lo hacemos de hecho. Ernesto Sanchez a su servicio.*' They shook on the deal. 'And you are?' Ernesto asked.

He was about to identify himself as George Grenfell when he remembered he was an escaped convict believed to have drowned at sea. Better leave the wanted man in Davy Jones's locker. Casting around for a name, he thought of the letter he was carrying and who had written it. 'The name's Ross,' he blurted out, 'Major Robert Ross, pleased to meet you.'

Ernesto helped him up onto the driving seat and cracked his whip. The oxen lumbered forward. They were underway. He had stolen another man's identity yet he felt no shame. In fact, he enjoyed the theft. With this alias came a new version of himself.

They reached the beach where the *Rosetta* had run aground and the Negroes moved the boxes from the sea cave to a new resting place among the crates of sugar cane on Ernesto's wagon. He looked at them inquiringly. 'You are strange soldier, Robert, keeping your luggage in wooden boxes.'

'Ah, but I'm no longer a soldier,' said Grenfell, flown with inspiration. 'I'm a Christian missionary and these are Bible boxes.'

Ernesto lowered his voice in reverence. 'So you're a Catholic priest, are you?'

'No, the Episcopal Missionary Church.'

'Cubans are Catholic but my patron, Señor Pedrosa, does not accept our simple faith. He says we invented God to give our miserable lives some meaning.'

'So your planter is an atheist?'

'Sorry, I do not understand this word. Señor Pedrosa lives on the Constancia estate, where we take our sugar cane. Why don't you come too? I know he would like to meet an English gentleman, even if he's a missionary.'

Grenfell declined the offer, wondering how a humble

carretero could issue such an invitation. As the cart rolled onwards he reflected on the gamble he was taking. Johnny Adair had given him the name of a Señorita Martinez, seamstress, shoemaker and forger of official papers in the Calle del Obispo. She was quite literally his passport to freedom and he didn't even know if she existed. He hoped for the best. There was nothing else he could do.

The journey to Havana was punctuated by frequent stops to extract the wagons from ruts and craters in the track. What with Ernesto's blasphemies, the difficulty in getting the wagon train to work together, and the suffering of the animals it became almost too painful to watch. It was what logicians call a vicious circle – unwieldy over-laden sugar wagons getting stuck on a makeshift bridle path that was steadily deteriorating because of the pounding it took from heavy cart wheels.

But that wasn't the whole story. Nature also conspired to delay them. A creek had cut its way into the land to create a fresh obstacle for the wagons. Ernesto yanked on the reins, sat back on the headboard and pulled a thin cigar and an iron tinderbox out of his trouser pocket. He lit his stogie before speaking. 'This stream is little more than a muddy channel at low tide. Now it's almost two metres high.'

'What's that?' Grenfell pointed to the bleached bones of a skeleton floating in the brown water.

'Oh, that's a cow's backbone. All that's left of the animal after the turkey buzzards have feasted.'

'And how did that happen?'

'Grazing cattle come here for a drink and sometimes get stuck in the mud.'

Abrupt, unsentimental words delivered with that hissing noise of his; closed vowels, weak consonants and a lot of sibilance. They forded the stream eventually and reached a crossroads where their way was blocked by a fruit seller with a stall bulging with bananas, oranges and coconuts. The swarthy, sharp-faced trader looked hopefully at the new arrivals. Ernesto grunted and raised an open hand, with the palm outwards, bending his fingers towards the man. Grenfell took this to be a sign of rejection and was surprised to see a small coin exchanged for a coconut.

Ernesto took a knife out of his poncho and cut the coconut in half. 'Here, eat this,' he said. 'It's very good.' Grenfell found the skin no harder than that of a melon and gratefully sucked the milk and the soft white pulp out of the rind. It was refreshing and wholesome. He now knew three things about Cubans: they liked soft coconuts and soft consonants, and had a strange way of summoning attention.

His rough diamond of a driver stubbed out one cigar and lit another before whipping his oxen into action. Grenfell added chain smoking to his list of local customs.

They rumbled on along the dusty red coastal path. Their winding route took them into a tropical orchard, in which avenues of oranges and limes, bananas and pineapples, cocoas and plantains provided thick-leaved shade for the stubby coffee plants thrusting forth their dark red berries. The sight of this peaceful plantation, with its natural growth of fruit and berry, and the cerulean hills shimmering in the distance, filled Grenfell's heart with a kind of fierce joy. For that moment, at least, he could enjoy the sensation of liberty. He felt as free as the birds chattering in the thickets.

Ernesto broke the silence. 'There used to be lots of places like this when I was a boy. That was before our masters realised they could make more money out of turning Cuba into a host of monotonous cane fields. It's all sugar now. Raising and making sugar in the countryside; selling and exporting it in the towns. If this is progress, I spit upon it.'

'But satisfying the world's sweet tooth must have made a lot of people rich.'

'Only the dominant class are rich, the pure-born Spanish aristocracy who own the biggest plantations and have all the political power. Cubans are only good for fetching and carrying. Take me; I travel the length and breadth of the country, sleeping under my cart with only a sombrero to keep the mosquitoes away.' Judging by his body odour, Grenfell's companion also went days without changing his clothes.

'Do you feel you're exploited by your patron?'

'No, not at all. Señor Pedrosa does the best he can with his rundown estate but he can't afford to give me a full-time job so I must seek work elsewhere and other employers are not so kind.'

'And these sugar planters who treat you badly, they are all Spanish colonists?'

'Absolutely, we have no freedom or independence. Our tax system comes from Spain, as does our currency and our religion. Everything is imposed upon us. Cubans can't vote, attend political meetings, sit on a jury, bear arms or have any kind of public career. The laws that govern us are made abroad, and administered by a Spanish Captain-General through Spanish civil and military officers. When we reach Havana, you will see soldiers everywhere in the city, slum ruffians imported from the back streets of Córdoba and Madrid, who enjoy throwing their weight around. You need to look out for them, particularly if you haven't got a travel permit.'

Grenfell's heart sank on hearing this. 'They will want to examine my papers?'

'That's right, stop and search; they're very keen on that.'

'How do you obtain one of these travel permits?' he asked lightly.

'When foreigners disembark in Havana they are supposed to go to the port's customs house and hand in their passports and, if everything is above board, they are issued with a licence that permits them to stay on the island for up to three months.

It's this licence the soldiers want to see.'

Ernesto gave him a hard look. 'Forgive me, Señor Ross, but would I be right in thinking you do not possess a passport?'

'It was lost in the storm.'

'Well, you have a problem. Without a passport or a licence, you will soon be arrested. Don't worry though, I'll take you where you want to go but by a different route.' Grenfell expressed his gratitude by handing Ernesto another coin.

The path was curving now towards the coast and they could hear youthful laughter. Indian children were playing in front of a large circular building made of wooden poles, woven straw and palm leaves. 'That is a *bohios*,' Ernesto told him. 'It's big enough for several families.'

'Where do these people come from?'

'Cuba. The Taino tribe was here long before Columbus.'

'Are there many of them?'

'No, not many. The Taino were a gentle people without knowledge of evil. They didn't murder or steal and were no match for the Spanish conquistadors who brought fire and the sword to our island. That the culture survives at all is due to the number of mestizo children born out of wedlock.'

His companion tossed away another cigar stub. 'I'm part Taino myself and proud of it,' he said fiercely. 'They made our country what it is today, not the Spanish. Cuba is a Taino word and so too is Havana. We have also contributed to your language. Words like "tobacco", "hurricane" and "canoe" are Taino.'

Up ahead, Grenfell could hear hammer blows and the whistling of a whip. 'That's one of our chain gangs,' Ernesto explained. 'They're all over the island.'

A group of ragged convicts, fettered around waist and ankle, were hacking away at the roadside. Mongrel soldiers dressed in seersucker uniforms with red cockades in their straw hats watched over them. They carried bullwhips, ready to lash the back of any poor shirker. This brought back such painful memories Grenfell couldn't help but shudder.

Ernesto made use of his own whip to urge his oxen forward. The wagons were climbing now, up a steep hillside. On reaching the top, he took his hands off the reins and gestured proudly. 'Behold, Cuba's capital, the largest town in the Caribbean, or so I'm told.' Below them lay a forest of masts in a narrow-necked bay guarded by fortresses while, further off, an ancient city of white and yellow stone buildings, red-tiled roofs and baroque towers basked in the sunshine.

A few minutes later they were rattling through cobbled streets that seemed much too narrow to be urban highways. The houses were set close together, flush to the road, with large barred windows at ground level, mostly without glass. Through these windows they could see well-dressed women sitting in the cool recesses sewing and talking to one another. 'This is how rich females pass their time in Havana,' Ernesto said contemptuously. 'It is considered unseemly for a white woman to walk in the streets. She must go everywhere by carriage.'

And what strange carriages the wealthy used – ungainly contraptions called *volantes* that consisted of a pair of huge wheels joined by long shafts to an open chaise body, driven by mounted Negroes in large spurred boots and gaudy livery. Reclining in the upholstered seating were gentlemen in white linen suits or black dress coats and matching cravats while wafting fans and flounces of silk or muslin revealed the pampered and overprotected presence of the fairer sex.

Havana was waking from its collective siesta as the Pedrosa sugar wagons trundled through the old walled city. Ernesto picked his way through a maze of tiny streets where two-way traffic seemed impossible, yet vehicles somehow avoided one another, often scraping against stone exteriors in doing so. They passed the thick, gloomy walls of a convent, a lively tavern selling Bacardi rum, and scores of black girls on narrow pavements. The houses hereabouts were of contrasting shapes and sizes. Dilapidated one-storey hovels and disreputable drinking shops stood alongside beautifully preserved colonial mansions painted in pastel colours, with elaborate balconies and interior courtyards. The rich aroma of a spit-roasted pig wafted from one such garden causing Grenfell's stomach to growl.

Ernesto told his hungry companion that Old Havana was built on a grid system around four main plazas, one of which they were about to enter. The square was dominated by the unequal towers of the city's cathedral in which the great explorer Christopher Columbus was buried. Ernesto didn't stop to sightsee but pressed on down the Calle San Ignacio before turning right onto the Calle del Obispo, a street of almost identical shops with glass doors and windows, lit counter areas and stacked shelves.

'A lot of the shopkeepers around here are black,' Ernesto said. 'They are the sons and daughters of former slaves. Now, where do you want to get off?'

'Number twenty-nine, please,' Grenfell said with more confidence than he felt.

They stopped outside a shoe shop that seemed to be closed. 'I'll wait here for you,' Ernesto grunted as he helped the Englishman out of his cart.

Grenfell banged on the door and waited anxiously for an answer. After knocking twice, he heard someone shuffling around inside and a distorted face peered through a bottle glass window. It belonged to an old man with a black skin. '*Que deseas?*' enquired a nervous voice.

'*Me gustaria hablar con la señorita Alejandro.*'

'*Ella no está aquí.*'

With a sinking heart, he asked the old man what had happened to her.

'*Mi hija esta en la cárcei. Los soldados vinieron y se la llevaron hace quince dias.* Soldiers had arrested his daughter a fortnight ago.

'*Qué delito habia que cometido?*'

'*Se decia que habia estado vendiendo documentos fraudulentos.*' Alejandro's days of forging passports were over. She had been accused of selling fake documents and was being held without charge in the Castillo del Principe, Havana's main prison. Grenfell tried to persuade the frightened old man to open the door so that they might talk further but to no avail.

His situation was desperate. He was stranded in a city full of soldiers without any official papers. Yet he couldn't give up now. Passport control was still in its infancy and there must be plenty of document forgers in a cosmopolitan port like Havana. It was simply a case of knowing where to look. Meanwhile, though, he needed to lie low, preferably outside the city, and what better place to hide than on a suburban sugar estate run by an Anglophile planter?

'Do you want us to unload your boxes, Señor Ross?' Ernesto was asking him. The carter was anxious to be on his way.

'No, leave them where they are,' said Grenfell, fishing another guinea out of his coat by way of inducement. 'I've changed my mind and would very much like to meet Senor Pedrosa. That's if you'll take me to him.'

The Cuban driver pocketed the coin, told him to hop aboard and started off again. He was going to a part of town where his boss might be. The Plaza Vieja differed from the city's other squares in that there wasn't a church in sight. 'This used to be a covered market,' Ernesto enthused. 'Bullfights and public executions were held here. Now it's a coolie auction site.'

Having taken part in the Opium War and got a crossbow arrow in the shoulder blade, Grenfell tended to be rather chary of Chinamen but these ones looked harmless enough. Their heads were shaven, except for a tuft on the crown, and they were dressed in loose garments of blue and yellow.

A brutal-looking overseer was whipping them into line as they waited to be displayed on the auction block for the benefit of a rapidly growing crowd of bidders. Knowing something of the background to the trade, he was bewildered by this procedure. 'I thought these coolies were brought over as free men to work on fixed-term contracts. So why are they treated like this?'

Ernesto paused to light a cigar. 'The customers demand it,' he explained. 'They are looking for cheap slaves, yellow as well as black, and they want to examine the flesh.' Almost on cue the hapless Chinese were forced to remove their clothes before climbing onto the block to be poked and prodded by potential buyers. The cowering victims closed their eyes in shame.

Memories flooded back of being stripped in a similar fashion on his first day at Fort Jefferson and, sharing their humiliation, Grenfell averted his gaze.

'Just like a cattle market,' said the elderly fellow with mutton-chop whiskers standing next to him. 'These coolies should have been auctioned this morning but there was a problem with the ship they arrived on. There were so many dead bodies aboard, the vessel had to be fumigated before these beauties could be landed. A floating coffin, you might say.'

Grenfell imagined what they had had to endure: herded onto a boat in Macao, locked away in the ship's hold for a longer journey than the notorious Middle Passage, surrounded by rotting corpses, before staggering ashore in Cuba to be sold like pieces of meat to the highest bidder. What kind of welcome was that to the New World?

'Who'll give me four hundred pesos for this fine specimen?' the auctioneer yelled cheerfully. 'He's well muscled with all his own teeth and he's more intelligent than your average Negro.'

'Is that a good price for a coolie?' Grenfell whispered to Ernesto.

'It's a bit on the high side actually. Coolies are much cheaper than Negroes. Mind you, they do have drawbacks. You can't beat them like you can a slave and a lot of them commit suicide.'

'What's the death rate?' he asked.

'Three quarters die before completing their contract.'

'So who buys them?'

'Mining companies, sugar planters mainly. I thought Señor Pedrosa might have been here today. He needs more workers on his estate.'

'How much can a coolie earn cutting cane?'

'Four dollars a month, food and board, and two suits of clothes a year.' Not much in return for eight years of servitude – if they are lucky enough to last that long. Grenfell's heart went out to them.

'Have you seen enough?' Ernesto wanted to know. 'Then let's be going. We've got an hour's journey ahead of us.'

They clattered through more cobbled side streets, narrowly avoiding a silver carriage rushing in the opposite direction. As the vehicles swerved apart Grenfell caught a glimpse of a hawk-like face not unlike his own. 'George! George Grenfell?'

The shock was overwhelming. The man in the *volante* was his first cousin Henry Riversdale Grenfell! It seemed unbelievable until he remembered that Henry's branch of the family owned a copper mine in Santiago. He must have been on his way to the auction.

'That man seemed to know you. Do you want me to stop?' Ernesto sounded suspicious.

'No, let's press on. A case of mistaken identity,' he muttered, avoiding any further eye contact.

What if Riversdale approached the British consul to discover his whereabouts? Visions of capture and deportation back to the Dry Tortugas clouded his mind as they travelled through Havana's poorer eastern suburbs and out into the surrounding countryside.

'We're almost there now,' Ernesto claimed, strangling some more vowels. 'You'll hear the plantation before you see it.'

Grenfell tried to grapple with this gnomic utterance. What he could see were green pastures and a gashed red road in which the furrows seemed to deepen the further they went. Then the sound of slaves chanting in a distant field wafted across to him.

'What are they singing about, Ernesto?'

'They are offering prayers to their *orishas* or gods, and also to the souls of their ancestors. They chant in Yoruba because they come from West Africa. They sing to keep their spirits up.'

The wagons turned off the well-worn road onto a stony path and passed under an entrance arch. Ahead of them lay a sea of head-high sugar cane through which lines of reapers were cutting a broad swathe; black men and women slashing away at the stalks with long, thin-bladed knives. It was exhausting repetitive work which followed the same rhythmic pattern as their chanting. Two blows with one of these cleavers removed the outer leaves and a third cut off the stalk, near the ground.

'It's called a machete,' Ernesto informed him. 'You see how they leave the lower part of the plant in the ground because another crop will grow from the stubble. It's very cost-effective.'

As he spoke an ox cart rumbled up and the cut cane was loaded into it to be taken off to the mill. 'The oxen are worked in the Spanish fashion. See how the yoke is strapped upon the head, close to the horns, instead of around the neck as is the custom elsewhere.'

Grenfell raised an inquiring eyebrow. For a lowly wagon driver, Ernesto was remarkably well informed. 'I know about this,' the carter answered the unspoken question, 'because I am also the *boyero* on this plantation – herdsman, I suppose you would call it. We tend to double up here. Supervisors are a bit thin on the ground.'

A loud cracking sound introduced one of his white colleagues; a tall, muscular man with a hard face brandishing a long cowhide whip.

'That's Jordan Blackstock, he's a *contramayoral*,' Ernesto said. 'Every gang that's set to work must have an overseer. They watch over the slaves, make sure they're pulling their weight.'

'By use of the whip, I suppose?'

The disgust in Grenfell's voice was obvious and Ernesto reacted to it. 'Look, with the slave, the ultimate sanction is force. I'm not defending the system which is manifestly unfair, but what I am saying is that you could never run a sugar plantation without the threat of physical punishment. Mind you, some of these overseers are callous brutes.'

They watched Blackstock lashing a strapping young Negro with his knotted whip, laying a track of bloody welts across his shoulders.

'That man is foolish. He's only been here a week and already he's throwing his weight around. If he wants to whip a boy near to death, he should choose a worthless one rather than Kwasi who cuts more cane than anyone else. Still, what can you expect when you hire American trash?'

'You hire Americans?' Grenfell repeated in amazement.

'He came here from Louisiana. He'd been working as a field hand on a sugar plantation in New Orleans where the cane is picked before Christmas. They have a very short harvesting season. Our *zafra* is later and twice as long. Señor Pedrosa doesn't like Blackstock but he's short of slave drivers. Talking of the patron, it's time you met him. Leave your luggage in the wagon. No one will touch it.'

They jumped off the cart and headed towards a solid stone building with smoke-encrusted chimneys that seemed incongruous in this pastoral setting. The steady thunder of grinding machines reminded Grenfell of William Blake's poem about dark, satanic mills defacing England's green and pleasant land, and of a day he had spent with his father in a tin-smelting house in Penzance. The ten-year-old boy had found it a frightening experience.

As they approached the mill, sweating half-naked slaves rushed out carrying baskets on their heads. 'They are taking *bagazo*, that's waste cane, off to the fields to dry before using it as fuel,' Ernesto told him. Grenfell felt an unexpected longing for his childhood. He thought of the Cornish countryside and of raking hay into windrows before it was baled for winter feed.

Once inside the mill, the past was forgotten. He had entered a mechanised hell, a realm of fiery furnaces; a hideous bedlam in which the shouts of the slaves and their overseers competed with the clanking of the engine, the crackling of the fuel, the hissing of the steam, and the crushing of the cane as it passed between the giant cylindrical rollers that squeezed the juice out of the stalks.

It was an assault on the senses: the intensely sweet smell of the juice and the sugar vapour and the wild repetitive cries of the slaves who stoked the fires and filled the cane-troughs. '*A-a-b'la! A-a-b'la! E-e-cha candela! Pu-er-ta!*' they chanted. Grenfell's head was pounding and he felt giddy, which was hardly surprising as a half coconut was the only thing he'd eaten all day.

Everything seemed to be in motion, whirling around in utter confusion. Gradually he began to make sense of it. There was a rough assembly line that started with Negroes feeding dried waste cane into a furnace to make the steam that drove the machinery that turned the rollers that ground the newly cut cane. From the rollers, the juice fell through a large receiver into an open vat and flowed beyond that into a series of very hot copper cauldrons in which the liquid seethed and boiled.

Ernesto screamed in his ear. 'Those vats are called defecators in which the juice is purged and purified.'

'What happens to all the scum?' He yelled back.

'We give it to the hogs or simply toss it on the muck heap. It makes good manure. We're separating the thick brown syrup known as molasses from the crystallised sugar. It's a long and laborious business.'

Grenfell knew all about molasses. Morgan's Raiders had been fed on black treacle. Here though they were trying to get rid of it in a complicated procedure that involved large shallow pans, holed storage barrels warmed on open flames, copper receivers and thousands of draining moulds of sugar. Ernesto showed him the final product, a sugar cake that was yellowish-white because of its remaining impurities.

'The quality is bad today. As you can see, Señor Pedrosa is not a happy man.' He pointed towards a figure in a white linen suit talking in animated fashion to a bunch of sheepish-looking subordinates. Because of the background noise level Grenfell couldn't hear what was being said but those near the owner felt the force of his words.

Pedrosa caught sight of Ernesto and walked over to join him. '*Me alegra ver que estas de vuelta,*' he said. '*Y que es esto, entonces?*'

'*Permitame presentarle al Señor Robert Ross, que viene de Inglaterra.*'

'I am delighted to make your acquaintance Señor Ross. My name is Juan Pedrosa and, as Ernesto has no doubt told you, I love your country very much.'

Here was a Cuban who spoke perfect English. He noticed

the laughter lines around the edges of Pedrosa's shrewd eyes, how his dark hair was swept back and brushed into horns behind his ears. A trim moustache added gravitas to a rather fleshy effeminate face.

'Tell me, what do you make of my little *ingenio azucarero*?'

'It's certainly memorable.' This was the kindest thing Grenfell could find to say.

Pedrosa laughed at this. 'Yes, as the divine Dante says, *lasciate ogni speranza, voi ch' entrate*.'

'My Italian is a little rusty, but aren't those the words inscribed on the Gate of Hell? "Abandon all hope, you who enter here."'

'Bravo, Señor Ross! You are a linguist. What, if I may ask, is a man of learning doing in Cuba?'

'I'm afraid my visit is an involuntary one. My ship was caught in a violent storm and washed up on your shore this morning where I was lucky enough to run into Ernesto and his wagon train.'

'Poor old chap, what a terrible experience. Have you anywhere to go in Cuba?'

'I can't say I have.'

'Then you must stay with me. Did you save any possessions from the wreck? Good, good. Ernesto will drop your luggage off at my home. Right, that's decided. Where's Sukey?'

A pretty black girl answered the call. 'Go to the big house and tell Betsy Ann I want the guest room made up for the night and ask cook to fix dinner for seven o'clock. Have you got that, my dear?'

Sukey nodded her head and smiled shyly before running off.

Pedrosa watched her go. 'That girl has lovely legs ... not that I've designs on her,' he added hastily. 'I am not like my neighbour Burr Ashby who has several slave concubines.'

This shared confidence appeared to cement their relationship for the planter put an arm around Grenfell's shoulder and suggested they took a walk together. 'It's much cooler out here,' he said, stating the obvious. The sky was turning from azure to salmon pink as the sun slowly began to set over the countryside. 'I love these huge skies, the sense of peace that comes with twilight.'

Grenfell doubted whether Pedrosa's slaves shared his fondness for the great outdoors. But he noticed how the planter's presence in the cane fields wrought a change in them. The pace of work had quickened since his arrival. Even a benign master was a figure of fear. Should a slave displease him, he could be deprived of food and sleep, given the lash or left in solitary confinement.

The man who had fought so furiously for a slave-owning Confederacy was now wholly convinced that the system was morally wrong. It corrupted everyone, particularly the owner who couldn't afford to be kind. If he was too gentle with his slaves, they would get the upper hand and gradually destroy the plantation economy. Equally, those who enforced discipline usually fell into violence and depravity. It was an almost impossible balancing act.

Pedrosa watched the sunset. His mood was mellow. 'Spain abolished slavery fifty years ago but it still operates here because we need cheap labour on our sugar plantations. *Necessarium malum.*'

'Ernesto says you were educated in England. Is that where you developed a taste for Latin?'

'Indeed so. My father was a Spanish grandee who sent me to Harrow Public School when I was thirteen. Latin was my favourite subject.'

Grenfell tried to envisage his host in a black tailcoat and boater fagging for the school bully, having to play compulsory games and quoting Horace at every opportunity.

'I went up to Oxford and got a first in Classics at Corpus

Christi. What I didn't like was the college's excessive piety. It was full of clerics reminding you of how their distant predecessors had written the King James Bible. Many of my college friends succumbed to this brainwashing and found God, whereupon they ceased to be fun. Why couldn't He have stayed hidden?'

His voice had a magnetic quality. The way he resisted the rising pitch of a question until the final word, the slight lisp that turned an 'r' into a 'w' sound, and the upper-class air of certainty with which he delivered his thoughts. It was the voice of authority.

'Personally, I believe in liberal humanism. I foresee a future of incremental material and social progress built around the emerging sciences and a reassertion of our classical roots.'

Grenfell wanted to know what he made of a former slave's observation that no man puts a chain about the ankle of a fellow human being without finding the other end fastened to his own neck.

'Advocates of slavery see themselves as the head of a great family, a benign father figure who looks after and disciplines his wayward children. I have no time for such talk, Señor Ross. The kind master and the docile slave are figments of the imagination. When I first came here to replace my dead father I hated the sound of the whip. Now I wouldn't be without it. You cannot run a sugar plantation without retaining the threat of punishment. A master has to keep his revolver and rifle loaded. He needs dogs at his gate, trained to give the alarm when a stranger comes near the house. He must guard against the encroachments of thieving Negroes and poor whites from other plantations, breaking down hedges, trampling cane and setting fire to it. We had two fires in our fields last year that cost me twenty thousand pesos. There is little law and order in these parts but, in the fullness of time, things will change. Now here's the paradox. To create a better society, the country must grow richer, yet Cuba's wealth depends on sugar's slave economy. But why am I talking about my problems when yours are so much greater? You must think me a poor host, Señor Ross. I am most anxious to hear about your shipwreck.'

Grenfell improvised wildly. Major Robert Ross had fought for the Confederacy in the American Civil War before returning to England to run the family mining company. He had been on his way to New Orleans on business when his schooner was caught in a dreadful storm and he had only survived by lashing himself to the mainmast. A good fiction should always contain a kernel of truth and it certainly impressed his host.

'Terence limned your epitaph: *fortes fortuna adiuvat*, fortune favours the brave.'

'I don't know about that. It was simply self-preservation.' He tossed a Latin proverb back at Pedrosa. '*Dulce bellum inexpertis.*'

'War is sweet for those who haven't experienced it,' the sugar planter translated. 'You're right, I haven't.' Their laughter was interrupted by the clanging of a bell and work stopped in the fields.

'"The curfew tolls the knell of parting day!" You see I am conversant with your English poets. Come, it is time we went up to my house.'

The slaves were also on the move. They were forming an orderly queue outside a large shed. 'They are waiting to be served by our *mayordomo*,' Pedrosa explained. 'He's the storekeeper. He gives them food to cook, mainly yams, plantains and boiled chicken.'

Grenfell asked how long the slaves worked each day and was told it was a twelve-hour shift from six in the morning to six at night with short breaks for breakfast and lunch. Many of Pedrosa's fellow planters forced their field hands to work through the night, sometimes with no more than four hours sleep, but this was a self-defeating policy because so many slaves died in the process and each one represented a thousand-peso investment.

They passed a row of stone buildings, including a storehouse and a jail. Beyond this lay the mud huts of the Negro living quarters where families gathered around cooking fires in a most companionable fashion. As Grenfell watched this open-air ritual a little boy knelt in front of him saying, '*Buena noches, Señor.*' Imagining this to be a request for money, he reached into his pocket, only to see the planter bend down and pat the child's curly head, saying '*Dios te haga bueno.*'

'You must be wondering what an atheist is doing bestowing a blessing,' Pedrosa whispered. 'Most of these slaves are Christians and they expect me to be their priest. I do not want to deny them the solace of their simple faith.'

They walked up a curving driveway towards a white three-storey plantation house. Even in the gathering dusk Grenfell could admire the perfect symmetry of its graceful Palladian columns, arched windows and long veranda. A short flight of stone steps led to the front porch. Waiting there was a tall black woman. She was wearing a matching skirt and head-wrap and moved with a languid grace as she came down to meet them.

'Everything is ready,' she said in a warm, engaging tone. 'Dinner will be at seven and we have placed Señor Ross's luggage in his bedroom.' 'Thank you, Betsy Ann,' Pedrosa replied, offering her his arm, prompting the thought that they might be husband and wife rather than master and slave.

Once inside the hall, she smiled coyly at Grenfell, showing gleaming white teeth. 'If you will excuse me, I have things to attend to.' He watched her go with mixed emotions, delighted to have aroused the interest of this husky-voiced beauty and worried in case his host had noticed how openly he had stared at her.

Pedrosa had other things on his mind. 'Forgive me for asking this,' he began, 'but does your luggage include a change of clothes for dinner?'

'No, I'm afraid not, my trunk was lost at sea,' Grenfell couldn't look him in the eye. He hated lying to this decent man. 'Only a few personal possessions were saved.'

'My dear fellow, you should have said.' His appraising eye sized up the Englishman. 'You are somewhat taller and thinner than I am but I'm sure we can find you something to wear. While we are doing so, perhaps you would like a bath.'

Grenfell thanked him for the offer and was ushered into a large upstairs room. Lit by wall mounted torches, the chamber contained a four-poster, bedroom furniture and a cast-iron roll-top bath. He was relieved to find his Bible boxes under the dressing table.

Black servants arrived with buckets of water heated on the kitchen range. What a pleasure it was to be rid of his stained suit and grubby shirt and luxuriate in the warm water. He stayed in the tub for almost half an hour before reluctantly getting out. As he did so, there was a knock at the door.

Wrapping a towel around his dripping body, he opened the door. Betsy Ann entered the room carrying a pile of clothes and a pair of riding boots. 'Perhaps you can change into these,' she said, dropping them on the bed. He noticed a soapstone necklace had been added to her appearance. She turned to face him, aware of his attention.

'I love your skirt,' he said. 'It shimmers in the torchlight.' Strips of green, blue and purple cloth had been intertwined and bound together to give the garment an uneven weave.

'It is a Yoruba fabric. It reminds me of my home in Benin.'

'May I call you Betsy Ann?'

'You can call me what you like. I am a slave and that is my slave name.'

'What is your real name though?'

'I was born with the name Akugbe. It means togetherness, unity.'

'I shall think of you as Akugbe. It's a lovely name.'

This cool, remote creature seemed disconcerted. Her eyes wandered to the boxes under the dressing table. 'Are you a man of God?' she asked pointedly.

'Not really. Only one of those boxes holds a Bible.' How refreshing it was to tell the truth. He hadn't done that for a while.

'But Ernesto tells me you intend to be a missionary. Is that not true?'

'I'm thinking of it.' Suddenly he realised what lay behind her questions. 'Whatever gave you the idea that missionaries were celibate?'

'Well, they were where I came from in West Africa,' she said defensively.

Something passed between them. Grenfell was acutely aware of his nakedness beneath the towel and she fingered her beads in a distracted fashion.

'The master hopes you will join him when you are ready. Goodnight, sir.'

Her sudden departure felt like a rebuke. Grenfell dressed hurriedly in a cotton shirt and a white linen suit, and looked at himself in the mirror. Staring back at him was a gaunt, heavily bearded individual with a scabbed cranium and skin that had been flayed raw by the sea storm.

On entering the dining room, he was confronted by a very large dark mahogany table and two Chinese waiters in black dress coats standing to attention. The master of the house sat in a carver chair at the top of the table looking out of a window at the gathering gloom. Grenfell coughed to announce his presence and Pedrosa turned to greet him. He too was dressed in a white linen jacket and pants with a richly embroidered waistcoat adding a splash of colour to his overall appearance.

'Come and sit down my dear fellow. We're dining alone tonight.'

'What a magnificent table. Is it a family heirloom?'

'No, tropical heat and humidity took its toll of my father's soft furnishings so I ordered a local craftsman to create furniture out of the island's hardwoods. Not that I could afford it. But I didn't know that then.'

'You were in the dark about your financial situation?'

Pedrosa stared up at the ceiling. 'Absolutely. As a young man, I lived in a fool's paradise; doing the Grand Tour, visiting the Orient. Then my father died and I returned to Cuba, an overeducated playboy with no desire to be a sugar planter, only to discover that papa had gambled away the family fortune and we were seriously overdrawn at the bank. It has taken me ten years to pay off his debts, but as Cicero rightly judged, *Vitam regit fortuna, non sapientia.*'

'Fortune, not wisdom, rules our lives,' Grenfell construed.

Pedrosa clapped his hands and the coolies left the room. 'What do you think of my Chinamen?'

'They look a lot better than the poor wretches I saw at the coolie auction. They've let their hair grow for one thing.'

'I bought them because they were cheap. I got three of these chaps for what it costs to buy a black slave. They come from Shanghai. And what is Shanghai famous for, I asked myself? Why, Benbang cuisine, the most delicious Chinese food imaginable. So, I thought my coolies would be better employed as cooks and waiters than as cane cutters.'

The waiters returned with silver tureens of food. 'I hope you like this.' Lids were lifted off dishes to reveal savoury pearl balls and stir-fried vegetables. 'Have you tasted this kind of Chinese food before?'

'As a matter of fact I ate several such dishes when I was in Shanghai back in '59.'

'Really, what were you doing there?'

'Soldiering in the Second Opium War; part of Palmerston's gunboat diplomacy which led to Admiral Hope trying to force a passage at the Taku Forts.'

'My word, you have got around Major Ross, or may I call you Robert?'

'I would be delighted, Juan.'

One of the waiters appeared with a decanter. 'We'll let the wine breathe for a while, Li Wei,' Pedrosa ordered. 'This is a Tempranillo, Robert. It's a Spanish grape that ripens early in the Pinar del Rio vineyards and, in a good year, it makes a full-bodied, spicy wine. The name means "early little one" and it's just about the *only* one as far as I am concerned. The white wines in Cuba are almost undrinkable.' For a man with financial difficulties, he certainly lived well.

The rest of the meal arrived. It consisted of pork and ham stew, a tasty crab dish and fried rice in which individual grains were cooked in an egg and soy sauce. Grenfell ate ravenously and the food was soon polished off. 'Thank you, Wang,' Pedrosa said, wiping his mouth on a napkin. 'Present my compliments to Zhang Tao in the kitchen.'

The waiter bowed. 'It has been our pleasure to serve you tonight,' he said.

Grenfell waited until Wang had left the room. 'He has a good command of English.'

'Yes, he's a quick learner.'

'You seemed quite angry earlier today in the mill,' Grenfell said. 'Wasn't the raw sugar up to standard?'

'No, it was very poor. To get a purer product I need modern machinery but I can't afford to buy it.'

'What kind of machinery would that be?' he asked, scenting an opportunity.

'Well, for a start, I need a better hydraulic mechanism to

improve the grinding process and with Derosne's advanced vacuum boiler I'd be able to produce a finer, whiter sugar that would attract a much higher price on the open market.'

'As a matter of interest, how much money do you need?'

'It would cost thirty thousand pesos to install Derosne's technology, complete with steam clarifiers, filters and charcoal reburners. The introduction of crushers and shredders to increase the liquid extraction rate from the cane would also be costly. In all, you're looking at a figure of at least forty-five thousand pesos.'

'Have you tried borrowing from the bank?'

'Of course I have, but our Cuban banks are useless. They are run from Madrid and act only in the interests of Spain. They are not prepared to advance large sums of money to small planters. The only people you can turn to are Havana's merchants but they want your next harvest as collateral. It's exasperating! I've read all the latest science on cane strains, irrigation, fertilisation and the treatment of crop pests, I know exactly what to do but, without the necessary cash, I can't put my ideas into practice.'

Juan Pedrosa's frustrated sense of mission throbbed in the Englishman's ear like a battle cry. 'Can you tell me what the dollar exchange rate is in this country?'

'A Cuban peso is supposed to have parity with a dollar but in practice that isn't so. The dollar is a much stronger currency.'

Waving away the waiters, his new friend picked up the decanter to pour out the rest of the wine.

The moment had come. Grenfell crossed his fingers under the table. 'Supposing someone was prepared to invest fifty thousand dollars in your business, what would you do for them?' He tried to make this sound conjectural, but had a feeling it hadn't come out right.

Pedrosa stopped pouring and stared at him open-mouthed. 'Are you saying what I think you are saying?'

There was a pause as Grenfell pondered how best to reframe the question. 'Believe it or not, I have the gold equivalent of fifty thousand dollars at my disposal. If I give this money to you, what will I get in return?'

'My undying thanks and a partnership in my business,' Pedrosa replied instantly.

'That's a most generous offer.'

'Then let's shake on the deal.'

The sight of the planter's hand stretching across the table brought him to his senses. He couldn't start a life-changing relationship weighed down with deceit. 'Look, there's something you need to know about me and, once you've heard what it is, you probably won't want me as your partner.'

Pedrosa's eyebrows shot up. 'That appears ominous, but as Horace said, *vitiis nemo sine nascitur*. Let's go outside and get the night air while you tell me your terrible secret.'

They moved onto the veranda and sat in long-armed planter's chairs beside a mahogany and cane table on which two tumblers and a bottle of spirits had been thoughtfully placed. 'You must try some of this, Robert.' Pedrosa poured the transparent liquor into his glass. 'It is a white rum distilled from fermented molasses and filtered through charcoal by the Bacardi brothers.' He took a swig of rum, smacked his lips, sat back in his chair and gestured for his companion to begin.

Grenfell took a tentative sip of the spirit and cleared his throat. He could hear his blood thudding in his chest. There was no other sound. A full moon created an eerie half-light in which the tall palm trees were silhouetted against the evening sky. The plantation seemed to drift away on the heavy stillness of the night.

'My real name is George St Leger Grenfell and I am an escaped convict.' He waited for a reaction but, in the shadows, his companion's face was impossible to read.

'Amazing as it may seem, I was in a Fort Jefferson prison cell yesterday.'

The dam broke and the words came tumbling out. He told his host about enlisting in the Confederate army as a cavalry colonel and how he had been arrested and convicted of treason for his part in the Camp Douglas conspiracy. He ran through the brutal years on the Dry Tortugas and what had convinced him there was buried treasure on the island. He described what it felt like to open the ship's chest and find thousands of George III guineas inside. He outlined his escape plan and what had happened when he sailed away on the *Rosetta*. He talked for the best part of an hour without interruption, hardly stopping to draw breath.

During this long narrative Pedrosa sat impassively, fingers steepled under his chin. 'So where is the money now?' he asked finally.

Grenfell couldn't help grinning. 'You don't have far to look. The guineas are upstairs in my bedroom.'

What he didn't anticipate was his host's laughter. 'My God, you are a cool customer and no mistake.'

'Maybe so,' he replied. 'But how do you react to what I've just told you?'

The chuckling ceased. 'You have honoured me with the truth and in doing so you have placed your life in my hands. You have trusted me not to betray you. You are the most resourceful man I've ever met and you are my friend for life. And to answer your question directly, yes, I'd be proud to have you as my partner.'

Grenfell's spirits soared. He had found a new home. The two men embraced like brothers and toasted each other in rum.

'Mind you,' Pedrosa added, 'I think you should keep the name of Robert Ross for now.'

'I think so too, particularly as I had the misfortune to run

346

into my cousin Riversdale Grenfell at the coolie auction. He's a director of a Cuban copper mine and could well ask questions.'

Pedrosa shook his head in sympathy. 'What appalling luck,' he said. 'If your cousin contacts the Chief of Police's office it won't be long before orders are issued for your arrest. We must move rapidly, George, so here's what we are going to do. I will take you to Havana on Monday morning to meet an acquaintance of mine. Antonio Fontanella is a merchant banker who is as greedy as hell's mouth. With gold bullion in short supply here, he keeps his own goldsmith to melt down any coins he comes across and he will give us a better exchange rate than we can get at the banks. Fontanella also employs a crook called Claudio who is an expert forger. Robert Ross will have a passport and the necessary travel documents by the end of the week. Then we'll call in at my law firm, Campos and Castro, and get a partnership agreement drawn up. Next, we'll visit my tailors and have you measured for some clothes, before enjoying a celebratory lunch in the Hotel Plaza. How does that sound?'

'As if I've found the ideal partner.'

'In the words of Horace, *nunc est bibendum*,' Pedrosa said, pouring out the rum.

The drinking went on well into the night. Finally, bidding the planter goodnight, Grenfell lurched unsteadily into the hall and was about to go upstairs when a door opened and Betsy Ann floated into sight. The sight of her gave him goose bumps.

'I thought you'd gone to bed,' he said feebly.

'No, I'm just locking up for the night.'

'I will be staying here for a while. Señor Pedrosa and I are going into business together.'

Her dark eyes stared at him solemnly. 'Now that you're residing here, Señor Ross, what do you want done with your money?'

That stopped him in his tracks. 'What money?' He tried to sound puzzled.

'The money you've got in your bedroom. Forgive me for mentioning this, sir, but those boxes are far too heavy to have clothes in them. Besides which, Ernesto dropped one of them and I'm pretty sure I heard coins rattling around inside.'

She registered the sheepish look on his face. 'But you don't have to justify yourself to me; if the master trusts you that's all that matters in this house.

'However,' she added with a sly look, 'I think you are probably a very wicked man.'

'That's right,' he retorted, tantalised by the closeness of her slim body. 'Just how wicked, you cannot imagine.'

Her face creased and he saw what a beautiful smile she possessed. 'Perhaps I may find out in due course.'

'You can count on that.'

'*Buena noches.*'

The most extraordinary day in his life ended a great deal better than it had begun. And with a new name, Robert Ross.

EXTRACTS FROM THE DIARY OF MAJOR ROBERT ROSS

JULY 23, 1871

The great ship dips and rises, rhythmically, in the light swell and freshening early morning breeze. I have my sea legs now and move in keeping with the vessel, feeling as much at home on the water as any Homeric hero. I wonder what my good friend Juan Pedrosa might say if he could see me now. It would probably be in Latin. He would remind me of my former aversion to seafaring and I would have to admit that first-class travel on this Cunard Line steamship has been a therapeutic experience.

These last few days of fresh air, good food and gentle exercise on the *Calabria*'s spacious poop deck have restored my flagging spirits to such a degree that I am looking forward to the challenge awaiting me when we dock in New York this afternoon. Señor Robert Ross, the Cuban sugar planter, is about to make his debut on the international stage, having already achieved an unexpected notoriety on board ship.

One thing I've discovered about voyaging with the idle rich is their propensity for gossip. Our luxury liner is a veritable rumour mill. Whether this grows out of a need to feel superior, a desire to buy attention, or the repetitive boredom of life at sea where everything is done for you I cannot say, but the *Calabria*'s upper deck hums with intrigue, some of it about me.

This grapevine became apparent last night. I had settled down in my customary place on deck to do some reading before dinner when two middle-aged women stopped near me. They were attired in the latest fashion, fussy layers of ruffles and flounces adorning their narrow-fronted skirts and huge bustles behind them, so that it appeared as if their dresses might swallow them up at any moment. 'I don't know what these boats are coming to, my dear,' one of the ladies said in a high-pitched nasal whine. 'We're not safe with him around.'

'I've heard he has a holstered revolver under his dress shirt,' the other one whispered in a shocked voice. 'Molly Peabody, she's one of the Peabodys of Fifth Avenue, always wears bombazine, well, she swears he's the gunslinger mentioned in Beadle's dime novels.'

That was when I realised they were talking about me. It was too good an opportunity to miss. Looming out of the shadows I gave them a narrow-eyed grin. 'Ladies,' I drawled, tipping my Stetson, 'I am mighty pleased to make your acquaintance.'

'Oh my goodness, it's him, Mabel. Come away quickly.' With that the gossips fled, no doubt to tell stories about their close encounter with Wild Bill Hickok. One thing they were right about was the sidearm strapped to my vest.

I am wearing it now as I sit down for my final breakfast in the ship's saloon. I admire the starched linen tablecloth and the gleaming silver cutlery. Nothing is too good for the passenger with money to throw around. A waiter brings a menu and I order smoked red herrings followed by a broiled rump steak. He wants to know whether I desire tea, coffee or cocoa with my meal. Normally, I drink tea but this time I ask for coffee. 'Turkish or Ariosa?' the steward enquires. I opt for the American brand, partly because I can't stand the taste of thick, black Turkish coffee but mainly because Ariosa happens to be the roasted coffee marketed by the tycoon I will be meeting later today.

Six years ago, an ingenious Pittsburg grocer called John Arbuckle patented a process for roasting coffee beans and coating them with a sugar-based glaze to lock in the flavour and aroma, and followed this up by inventing a labour-saving machine that could grade, fill, weigh and seal the coffee beans in one-pound bags. With his Ariosa coffee sweeping the country, Arbuckle is now one of the largest importers of coffee and sugar in the United States. I sent him some of our refined sugar a few months ago and he was sufficiently impressed with its quality to invite me to his Brooklyn Bridge warehouse to discuss a supply contract. A deal that ought to make my partner and I rich men.

Investing in a sugar plantation has proved a huge success. Annual output on the Constancia and San Isidro estates has more than trebled from three hundred to a thousand tons in the last three years and the acquisition of Derosne's advanced vacuum boiler has enabled us to produce a much purer and drier form of sugar. As a consequence, we are achieving an annual yield of twenty per cent on sales and Robert Ross has become a highly respected businessman in Havana. There is of course an irony in this. My fortune changed as soon as George Grenfell ceased to exist.

It happened like this. Because of my precarious status, Juan arranged for back copies of the *New York Times* to be delivered to us by American merchant ships visiting Havana. Months went by before I saw my name in print and then it was to announce my demise. The *Times* headline read 'War Department Declare George Grenfell Officially Dead'. A smart New York lawyer called F.F Marbury Junior had persuaded the American government to issue a death certificate. My estranged wife Hortense wanted to know whether she was legally a widow and therefore free to remarry. And good luck to her. She will be much happier with a Frenchman.

I am halfway through my smoked herring when a silvery, bell-like voice interrupts my daydreaming. 'Is that seat taken, sir?'

In front of me stands a smiling girl, as beautiful as only a high-bred octoroon can be, with high cheekbones, arresting violet-blue eyes and long black lashes.

'No, I've been keeping it for you,' I reply gallantly.

'How very kind of you!' she trills, arranging herself daintily on the seat opposite me. I notice she is wearing an almost diaphanous day dress that shows off her figure to perfection.

'My name is Cassandra Brown.' She takes off her crocheted lace gloves and holds out a pale white hand for me to kiss, before talking to me in French. '*Merci, monsieur, il est une joie de trouver un bel home avec qui je peux parler.*'

'Where did you learn to speak French like that?' I can't help asking.

'In a convent in Paris,' she retorts, very demure.

We talk of many things, cruising on the Seine, walking through the Louvre, tackling frog's legs on the Ile Saint-Louis. She is intelligent and entertaining and I am so enchanted I forget to eat my broiled steak. Then, not to put too fine a point on things, she gets down to business.

'Now that we've established common ground Robert, I am anxious to know whether you *are* a gunfighter, as the gossipy women on this ship seem to think.'

'Well, what do you think?' I say, wondering what comes next.

Cassandra lowers her lids; her lips quiver in amusement. 'I think you are quick on the draw and have got a lovely weapon.'

I don't shock easily but this double entendre takes me by surprise. Does this captivating creature mean what she's just said? She waves away a menu-bearing waiter and hands me her calling card. 'If you're staying in our city do visit my establishment on Seventh Avenue. I'll take good care of you.'

Having delivered this invitation, she gives me a look that is pure whore and slips away, leaving me in total turmoil. Lust and guilt, aroused by Cassandra Brown's sin and impudence. She cannot be more than twenty. I think of another girl brought up in a Paris convent and wonder whether she too has fallen into prostitution. Rosie must be eighteen now. My hired investigators traced her to the Convent du Sacré Coeur but the trail ended there. The poor orphan had left the cloister and simply vanished. Where had she gone and what was she doing? The thought of her living in degraded poverty haunts me still. When Rose Greenhow sacrificed our love for the Bonnie Blue Flag I reacted badly, throwing myself into the Camp Douglas conspiracy and getting arrested. Languishing in a Yankee prison, I could do nothing to help her abandoned daughter.

Where women are concerned, I seldom get things right and rather envy my Cuban partner's lack of passion. It doesn't stop him from having a warm and generous heart. I think of Juan's good humour as he smokes one of his interminable cigars or gets drunk on the veranda. No one could have treated me with greater tact or sympathy, particularly over my sexual desire. They say time heals all wounds. I don't believe that. Wounds remain, red and raw, covered with scar tissue.

'Can I get you anything else, sir?' The waiter's polite question reminds me that I am sitting at a breakfast table in the *Calabria* saloon scrunching my serviette into a tight linen ball, with an uneaten meal in front of me. 'No, you can take that away.' I point to the steak. My appetite has vanished and I want to be alone with my bitter thoughts.

I managed to keep my feelings for Betsy Ann in check while we lived under the same roof. Then Juan asked me to supervise the cane cutting on his other sugar estate. I agreed to do so but took the opportunity to point out that San Isidro's rundown plantation house needed a woman's touch. Could I take Betsy Ann with me? On seeing how she favoured the idea, he readily agreed. And we were happy together, finding pleasure and comfort in each other's company. But it didn't last. She contracted cholera. Fearing the worst, I rushed through the paperwork to make her a free woman. But why had I waited until she was dying to end her slavery? I torture myself with that question.

By changing my name and earning an honest living off the

land, I have tried to be a better person. But even as Robert Ross, I am the same selfish egotistical man. We aren't born good or bad but goodness is difficult to achieve. Juan says I'm depressed and a trip to America will do me a power of good. He could be right but for the wrong reasons.

We are within sight of the Battery on the southern shoreline of Manhattan Island and will soon be docking in New York. I go back to my cabin intending to do some last-minute packing for what promises to be a long journey. After concluding the Arbuckle sugar deal, I intend to cross America by train. A two-thousand-mile trip fuelled by the ragged need for revenge. For hate, like love, is a powerful emotion and I have an old score to settle.

Sitting in my cabin waiting to hear the ship's bell announce our arrival, I look again at the yellowing newspaper cuttings I carry with me. The stories are all clipped from back issues of the *New York Times*. I read the first of these reports three weeks ago and thought nothing of it. Mind you, I was drinking heavily at the time. But when the newspaper printed a second story I sat up and took notice. After all, the *Times* is America's journal of record, a newspaper that can be trusted to get its facts right.

WYOMING TRAIN ROBBERY
WELLS FARGO GOLD STOLEN FROM UNION PACIFIC EXPRESS

Cheyenne, June 12 – The Union Pacific passenger train, bound westward, due here at 7 am, arrived at Hillsdale, a small station 23 miles east of Cheyenne, on time. Just as the train was starting from the station, three masked men boarded the express car. The conductor and two brakemen rushed forward to apprehend them but were fired upon and forced to retire. Whereupon the robbers decoupled the engine and the express car from the main train, locked the fireman and the express messenger in a mail room, and forced the engine driver to continue down the track. Stopping the train some five miles from Cheyenne they broke open the express boxes and stole about 40,000 dollars in gold coin before escaping into the countryside where horses were waiting for them. All Western Union telegraph wires were cut in the vicinity.

TRAIN ROBBERY SUSPECTS NAMED
WELLS FARGO OFFER REWARD FOR CAPTURE OF SHANKS GANG

Cheyenne, June 14 – All the talk upon the streets today is of the great robbery on the railroad near Cheyenne and of its similarity to an earlier train robbery in Wyoming. Back in May, three masked men boarded another westbound Union Pacific passenger train at the Medicine Bow depot. They made their way to the express car, held a gun on the messenger, and stole 10,000 dollars in greenbacks. Because of the smoke and fumes coming from the engine, the robbers lowered the black kerchiefs covering their faces. Behind the masks were John T Shanks and his accomplices Floyd Long, Nat Cannon and Cherokee Jones. Working on the hypothesis that the same outlaws carried out the more recent robbery, Wells Fargo has offered a $5000 reward for recovery of the stolen money and the arrest and conviction of the Shanks Gang. Citizens are warned that Shanks is an experienced gunfighter who has killed at least two men in cold blood.

Seeing Shanks' name in print stirred me into action. I saddled up my horse and rode into Havana. I hadn't held a gun in my hand for six years but the city armourer seemed to know what I needed. The latest Colt revolver is a lightweight affair with an eight-inch barrel that can fire six rounds in ten seconds. Back on the plantation, I practised shooting leaves off sugar cane stalks at twenty paces. 'Take that, you bastard,' I yelled incoherently, sending our slave labour scurrying for safety. They had never seen their master in such a violent mood.

'You frightened the field hands,' said a reproachful Juan Pedrosa at dinner that night. 'Our overseers are concerned for your sanity after seeing you shoot our sugar cane.' 'I'm awfully sorry, perhaps I was a tiny bit unhinged,' I said apologetically. 'But anyone going to America needs a firearm.'

Juan let the subject drop but he knew I was hiding something. I didn't want to share the reasons for my irrational behaviour, particularly when he was bound to counsel me against seeking vengeance. The case for which became even clearer after reading the following article in the *New York Times*.

THE LEGEND OF THE WESTERN OUTLAW
By James D McCabe

We live in an age driven by make-believe, full of tall tales and dime novels about lean-jawed gunslingers with snake eyes who take to a life of crime in cowboy country. That this satisfies a need in us is hard to explain. Perhaps there is a dash of tiger blood in the veins of all men; a latent disposition even in the bosom of the most law-abiding East Coast city dweller to admire the reckless outlaw who rides the open ranges of the West.

Take the case of John T Shanks, named only a week ago as the instigator of two daring train robberies in Wyoming Territory. Is he content to disappear into 'them thar hills' with his ill-gotten gains? No sir, not a bit of it, he has other things on his mind, like sending a letter to the Cheyenne Leader in which he portrays himself as a victim of press persecution. Remember that these protestations come from a glory hunter who admits to having committed more than one murder. 'I never killed a man that did not need killing,' he claims in his own defence. When asked to explain why he bought a cowboy a steak dinner before shooting him in the Bucket of Blood saloon, Shanks is alleged to have said, 'I didn't want to send him to hell on an empty stomach.'

Gun-packing in the West has become a kind of moral law while robbing trains is regarded as a form of medieval knight-errantry. It is a strangely warped perspective that finds romance in the quick reflexes of a gunfighter and chivalry in crime but that is how legends are made nowadays.

Let us return to the hero of this present hour, John T Shanks, and see what he says for himself. In his letter to the Cheyenne Leader Shanks writes: 'Some newspaper editors call the Shanks Gang thieves. We are not thieves but bold robbers and proud to be known as such. Some of the greatest figures in history were bold robbers such as Alexander the Great, Julius Caesar and Napoleon Bonaparte. It hurts me greatly to be called a thief when I fought bravely for the Confederacy in the Civil War.'

Well, John T, I have been delving into your murky past and find no redeeming feature to your character. Yes, you fought in the Confederate army but only to get out of a Texas penitentiary where you were imprisoned for forging land warrants. Later, you betrayed your colleagues and perjured yourself in several courts of law. In 1865 you changed sides and obtained a captaincy in the Fifth United States Volunteer Infantry, otherwise known as the Galvanised Yankees, which was sent out west to protect the railroad and settlers from Indian attacks. You ended up in Fort John Buford but deserted in 1866. Since then you have moved around Wyoming Territory stealing money wherever you can find it. You are, in short, an unmitigated scoundrel who one day soon will get his comeuppance.

Well said, James D McCabe, whoever you are! Shanks's judgement day is surely coming and, when he's finally laid to rest, I hope it will have been my doing. It is said that life is too short to be spent in nursing animosity but those that say that have never encountered a devil like Shanks. Yes, I can see the paradox. My desire for vengeance makes me dependent on my foe, believing that his death might allow me to live in peace. Not as George Grenfell but as Robert Ross.

AUGUST 3, 1871

It is eight a.m. and our Union Pacific Overland Express has reached North Platte in Nebraska where, I am reliably informed, the train will be stationary for at least half an hour. If there is one thing I've learned during these long weary days of rail travel, it is that steam locomotives have an insatiable thirst for water and need to make frequent stops under towers and hydrants.

According to the railway timetable we will reach Cheyenne in twelve hours' time but, for the moment, I must content myself with examining North Platte. Out of the smeared carriage window it looks like an end-of-the-tracks town that has put down more substantial roots. Glowing in the early morning sun are several church spires, rows of newly built stores and shops, a courthouse and two saloons that are doing a roaring trade even at this hour.

The reason for North Platte's rapid development suddenly becomes obvious. In a cloud of dust and collective mooing, hundreds of longhorns are driven through the streets. One of the Texas trails ends in North Platte's railroad stockyards where freight wagons wait to run the cattle into Wyoming, the Dakotas and Montana. These breeding herds have been rushed up north to replace the now largely defunct buffalo on the rich grazing lands of the Great Plains.

In keeping with the timetable, we set off again at 8.30. Clanking and hissing, our train sways around a bend in the track. The scenery is spectacular. The tall pines and firs of the great forests, the vast carpet of colour created by prairie clover and purple sage, the soaring white peaks of the Rockies far away to the west.

The iron horse is binding the nation together, bringing the arteries of civilisation to this wild and wonderful land. Many people see this as a symbol of American democracy and progress but I beg to differ. The trickle of wagon trains that once crossed the empty prairie has turned into a deluge of hopeful humanity seeking a better life out West. But before these settlers moved, millions of buffalo roamed the Great Plains and were hunted in a sustainable fashion by Indian tribes like the Sioux. Now, with so many extra mouths to feed and a growing demand for meat and hides back East, buffalo hunting has become wholesale slaughter. Armed with long-range rifles, Civil War veterans make a living as professional hunters, killing scores of animals a day.

Angry and bewildered by this overwhelming attack on their food supply, the Plains tribes took to the warpath, which brought in trainloads of soldiers, who killed even more buffalo in the mistaken belief that they could starve Indians onto reservations. Now where's the democracy in that? Surely no one can claim that the Indians are getting a fair shake.

'Like any democratic institution the railroad is a force for good and evil. But so long as there's good coffee in the world, things can't be too bad, can they?' The philosophy of John Arbuckle, the coffee tycoon I'd met in New York ten days earlier. As a member of the Plymouth Church, he is implacably opposed to slavery. 'Aye, Robert, the ancient Greeks were slave owners,' he declared. 'They invented democracy but relied on slaves to do everything for them but their thinking.'

It seems an age since I heard his laughter as we sat in a warehouse on the Manhattan waterfront sipping mugs of his famous Ariosa blend. I was only just off the ship and struggling to get the measure of this good-natured mogul with his long beard and rasping voice. For a start, he had more philanthropic concerns than you could shake a stick at. 'New York is an exciting city no doubt but it's an unhealthy place with all the overcrowding and the bad air.' To combat this, he planned to hire ships and have them towed out to sea to give underprivileged city dwellers the benefit of fresh ocean breezes. He also talked, rather surprisingly, about funding a campaign for better dental hygiene. 'We are encouraging folk to have a sweet tooth, Ross, by putting sugar in hot drinks. Shouldn't we also try to protect their pearly whites?'

I suggested that the refined nature of our Cuban sugar might do less damage to American molars. 'I come from Pittsburg where almost everyone has bad teeth,' he replied. 'It's an obsession of mine, I'm afraid. But you needn't worry Ross, your sugar is first-class and I want a three-year deal for half your crop. I've had a legal agreement drawn up. I think you will find it a fair price.' I took one look at the contract figure and signed before he could change his mind. Arbuckle added his signature and we shook hands on the deal. I had never met anyone who held so unflinchingly to what he believed in or possessed greater clarity of purpose.

'How about a wee dram to celebrate?' he asked, revealing unexpected Scottish ancestry. Arbuckle didn't wait for an answer, producing a bottle of Old Bushmills from a desk drawer. With a bottle of Irish whiskey in front of us we settled down to do some serious drinking. Arbuckle showed a lively interest in Robert Ross's career and had to be eased off the subject and onto the safer ground of coffee processing. Speaking with a controlled passion, he told me how he and his elder brother Charles had filled dull hours in the family's grocery store in Pittsburgh by experimenting with ways of improving the freshness, flavour and aroma of roasted coffee. His eureka moment came when he coated his roasted beans with an egg and sugar glaze. That was the first stage; next came grinding and storage, which saw measured amounts of still warm ground coffee poured into metal containers and wrapped in airtight one-pound packages.

He reached into the top drawer of his desk and produced a yellow packet on which a flying angel hovered above the words 'Ariosa Coffee'. The flying angel was both a smart piece of advertising and a declaration of intent. Not content with the market he'd achieved on the East Coast, Arbuckle had set up supply depots in Tucson and Abilene to bring his superior coffee blend to the rest of the country.

I noticed the gleam in his eye when he spoke of the cowboy's plight. Out West, coffee beans were still sold green in general stores and range riders had to roast them over their campfires. If so much as one bean got burned in the skillet, the entire batch was ruined and with roasted coffee deteriorating rapidly in the open air the cattle hand ended up drinking a vastly inferior beverage.

When I told him about my rail trip to Cheyenne, Arbuckle jerked in his chair as if I'd electrocuted him. 'Will ye do me a favour, laddie?' he asked. 'Perhaps you'll take some coffee samples with you and give them away to any cowboys you meet. You should meet plenty up there in Cheyenne. Texans drive their longhorns along the Goodnight Trail to connect with the railroad in Wyoming.' Arbuckle would arrange for a wooden crate containing a hundred packages of Ariosa to be placed in the baggage car of the train I was catching from Union Station.

That was when I saw the beauty of the arrangement. My best chance of getting close to Shanks was by travelling incognito. Having a passport in the name of Robert Ross was an obvious help but for Ross to arrive in Cheyenne as a coffee salesman was an even better disguise. 'Why don't we take this a stage further?' I said. 'Give me a letter of authorisation and I'll peddle your coffee for you. It's a sure-fire winner.'

'What a brilliant idea,' he said. 'Let's drink to it! Sorry there's no Scotch malt.' The genial Arbuckle opened another bottle of Bushmills and we got drunk together.

That was ten days and two thousand miles ago. It hardly seems possible I have come so far. From New York to St Louis to Omaha and on to Cheyenne, more than a hundred station stops, and now, finally, I am about to reach my destination and first impressions are far from favourable. The wild beauty of North Platte has been replaced by scorched plains supporting neither tree nor bush, across which strong winds blow ominous grey clouds that blanket everything in a thick dust.

What with the smoke and steam it is hard to see through the grimy windows of my coach as the locomotive grinds to a halt with hissing brakes. Cheyenne seems to consist of three or four blocks of frame houses and low, flat-roofed wooden shops with a scattering of tents and shanties on its outer perimeter. A large frame hotel belonging to Union Pacific hugs the side of the track and men in stovepipe hats and ladies in crinoline dresses stand in its portico entrance. Only the spluttering engine breaks the silence. Cheyenne's dust seems to swallow sound. Expecting a rip-roaring community full of cowboys, buffalo hunters and quarrelsome outlaws, I am disappointed by the apparent lack of urgency or excitement.

But on getting off the train I quickly change my opinion. It is a true frontier town after all. Swarthy, buckskin-clad teamsters and tanned range riders in broad-brimmed hats and chaps lurk on dark street corners with the high-pitched wail of hurdy-gurdies cranking away behind them. What is less engaging is the unfinished look of the place. Only a few houses have painted exteriors; rubbish tips are scattered around and there is a total absence of gardens or greenery to separate urban dwellings from the boundless prairie beyond.

I have booked into Cheyenne's second best hotel which is a couple of blocks away on Sixteenth Street. With my carpetbag in one hand and Arbuckle's wooden crate in the other, I weave my way past a party of bedraggled Indians carrying 1866 Winchesters, before stepping smartly aside to avoid being run over by a drove of longhorns escorted by horsemen in hooded coats and high boots, armed with six-shooters and repeating rifles. Everyone I meet seems to be expecting trouble.

Cheyenne has a bad reputation. It's said the only law here is supplied by 'Judge Lynch' with a quantity of rope. I can't help wondering whether I am on the road to perdition. Time will surely tell.

AUGUST 6, 1871

This is my third day in town and already I'm the Pied Piper of Cheyenne, followed wherever I go by coffee drinkers and drifters hoping for a free packet of Arbuckle's magic beans. My sales drive has taken me into hotels, saloons, billiard halls, even a brothel, to demonstrate the dark and flavoursome taste of my roasted beverage. The hardest part of the job has been locating the hot water to go with it.

While waxing eloquent on coffee's unique properties – its caffeine content helps cowboys stay alert to protect their herds at night and improves the speed and accuracy of their shooting – I also encourage locals to talk about Cheyenne's violent nature and what can be done to clean it up. I learn that its citizens have taken matters into their own hands by forming a Vigilance Committee and that notorious outlaws like the Shanks Gang have been warned to keep out of town.

The news comes as something of a blow. I have travelled thousands of miles only to find that my quarry is lying low. The silver lining is that John T is somewhere in the vicinity, waiting to be gunned down by me. But how do I get to him? I am thinking about this when a note is thrust under my bedroom door while I am shaving. The Cheyenne *Daily Leader* wants to interview me about the amazing coffee I've brought to Wyoming. And why not? I know that Shanks reads about himself in the papers so I persuade my obliging hotelier to telegraph all the local newspaper offices announcing a press conference at five o'clock in Cheyenne's Bucket of Blood saloon.

At the appointed hour, I step onto the dusty boardwalk and swing open the pair of butterfly doors. Inside, I see a long oak bar with a brass foot rail and barstools that is a perfect replica of the saloons I'd read about in cheap novels. But apart from a bartender washing dirty glasses and a poker game in which a high roller is fleecing a bunch of drunken teamsters, the place is totally empty. I feel rejected. Nobody has turned up to interview me.

'Excuse me, sir, would you be Mr Ross?' An earnest, shaggy-haired youth in a shabby suit is standing behind me. 'Sorry if I'm late. I was waiting outside for my friends to arrive.' He points to two other cub reporters who have sidled into the saloon as if expecting to be greeted by gunfire.

'And you are?' I ask briskly.

'The name's Billy Starr of the *Daily Leader* and this here is Chuck Wyman of the *Sentinel* and Lee Ryder of the *Tribune*.'

I shake hands all round and point to a table and four empty chairs. The first thing they want to know is how my coffee got its distinctive name. I explain that the first 'A' in 'Ariosa' is for Arbuckle and that the rest of the word is an amalgam of Rio de Janeiro and Santos, Brazil's leading coffee ports. Then I explain how my firm has revolutionised not only the production process but the way the coffee is distributed and sold. Why, I say, warming to my theme, we have a machine that can fill, weigh, seal and label coffee bags, and coffee packets will soon contain sticks of peppermint candy and coupons that can be redeemed for razors, scissors, even wedding rings.

'Will more of your coffee be coming out West?' This is the question I've been waiting for.

'Absolutely, I've wired Mr Arbuckle about the success of the Cheyenne trial and I can promise you he'll be shipping out several hundred crates of Ariosa on the Union Pacific in a week's time. Now, that's all I can tell you, boys, save to say that I'll be travelling on the train to keep an eye on such a valuable cargo.'

Billy Starr rises to the bait. 'How much is it worth?' he asks.

'Why, upward of fifty thousand dollars,' I reply, exaggerating wildly.

'Aren't you concerned about the possibility of a train robbery, Mr Ross, seeing we've had a couple recently on this stretch of the line?'

'You mean the Shanks Gang? Nah, I'm not worried about them. I'm pretty sure we've seen the last of them now that there's a price on their heads.'

I bring the interview to a close and buy each of the boys a shot of Kentucky whiskey at the bar. They are sure their papers will give my interview plenty of 'column inches'. I fervently hope John T Shanks reads one of their stories and reckons that robbing the express of its expensive coffee shipment will further enhance his fame and fortune.

AUGUST 13, 1871

It is not quite dawn. Two men pace up and down the station platform, waiting for the train to arrive. They are wearing long, loose canvas coats that flap around their ankles in the high wind. These coats are worn to protect horsemen from trail dust but they can also conceal an arsenal of weapons within their folds. The duster is an ideal garment in a violent, raw community where living is always on the edge.

The two men bend like trees as they are hit by an even stronger gust of air wailing down from the mountains. There is something primeval about this force. Long before the railroad was built carboniferous forests rose and fell on the land, decaying under the winds, layer upon layer, to be pressed into coal. But the wind came first. Like death and taxes, it is a constant factor.

The wind drops away. There is a peculiar moment of silence before one of the men lowers the bandana covering his face and yells to his companion, 'It's gone!' I have grown accustomed to shouting to make myself heard.

'Yah, noticed that. Happens once or twice, I hear tell.' This laconic observation comes from Dick Winscott, a small, unobtrusive cove who looks lost in his long coat. His modest bearing belies the fact that he is the local railroad agent and, as such, the nearest thing to law and order in these parts. Winscott made his name as a Pinkerton agent. Working undercover as a bartender in Indiana, he played a key role in the capture of the notorious Reno Gang, the first outlaws to rob a train back in '66. As one train robbery followed another in a wave of copycat crimes, the railroads hired big, burly bruisers as security guards. Wiry Dick Winscott was the exception to this rule; employed by Union Pacific for his brains rather than his brawn. Yet, as I've discovered, this soft-spoken, unassuming man will not shirk from a gunfight. That's why he's here now; waiting for the Omaha train that is already carrying two armed guards.

There is a strong possibility that we'll need our six-shooters to protect the so-called 'Coffee Express'. The newspaper stories about Arbuckle Brothers freighting hundreds of crates of coffee out West have had the desired effect. Shanks has taken the bait. Two days after publication, the Cheyenne *Daily Leader* received an anonymous letter attacking me as an Eastern tinhorn who underestimated a bold robber's grandeur of mind and fixity of purpose.

'I think we've got us a train thief,' was Winscott's assessment of the situation. 'You say you're coming along for the ride,

Mr Ross, but how good are you with a gun?' I tell him I'm a reasonable shot. I've practised with my Colt revolver until I can put all six shots into a five-inch envelope at ten paces. For as all real gunslingers know, most 'kills' are made at close quarters and accuracy is more important than speed.

Cheyenne's station platform is showing signs of life. Ghostly figures are moving around with shaded oil lamps. The railway track begins to vibrate and we know our waiting will soon be over. The locomotive arrives five minutes later, hissing and steaming until it comes to a halt. Once the smoke has cleared, doors are flung open for people to get off and on. The passenger cars are in the middle of the train. They are preceded by an engine and tender and a locked-off baggage-express car, while two coal-carrying flatcars and a caboose bring up the rear.

We board the train and make our way forward through the crowded coaches. And that's when I spot a familiar face. He is sitting opposite a Mexican woman with a baby. He too is dressed like a Mexican in a sombrero and poncho but his eyes give him away. They are narrow and furtive. They belong to John T Shanks, the man I have vowed to kill!

He is already on the train and the half-breed sitting next to him must be his sidekick Cherokee Jones. My body tenses. But there is no need to draw. Shanks hasn't recognised me. Why should he? I'm a dead man shrouded in a cowboy's duster.

The baggage-car door opens and we step inside and have two rifles pointed at our heads. Winscott's men look a mite nervous but they are certainly ready for action. 'Where do you think they are going to hit us, boss?' a strapping young man in a bowler hat wants to know. 'Could be almost anywhere on the line between here and Laramie,' Winscott replies. 'It all depends what Shanks' plan might be ...'

I have to interrupt. 'He's on the train with Cherokee Jones, seats three and four in the next carriage.' There is a stunned silence as the railroad agents come to terms with this startling development.

'Never thought he'd do that,' says Winscott amiably. 'Wonder what his game is?'

His colleagues scowl and shrug their shoulders. That leaves me, itching to express an opinion. 'I don't think he'll *do* anything until the other members of his gang have stopped the train somewhere up ahead. It will be their job to immobilise the engine driver and attack us from the front while Shanks and Jones come at us from the passenger car. It's going to be a two-pronged attack.'

Winscott takes off his Stetson and scratches his thinning hair. 'Reckon Ross is right. The key question is where they intend to stop the train. Granite Canyon might be the best place for a derailment. There are sections of fill in that gully where the rails are actually unsupported. It would be plumb easy to tear it up.'

I reach into my duster for some Cuban cigars and hand them around. We light up and reflect on what Winscott has just said. It makes a lot of sense. The race to extend the railroad through Wyoming led to sloppy construction work and nowhere is worse than Granite Canyon where stones meant to support the track have already sunk into the soil. During my week in Cheyenne I've covered every inch of the railroad between here and Laramie and checked out all the possibilities.

'I'm betting Floyd Long and Nat Cannon have created some kind of barricade up ahead and are waiting there with the getaway horses. That being so, don't you think Granite Canyon is a bit exposed? The engine driver can see a blocked track miles away. There's no element of surprise and no easy escape.'

'He's got a point, Dick,' says bowler-hatted Lennie, waving his Winchester rifle in my direction. 'Where's a better site for a hold-up, Mr Ross?'

'My guess would be Dale Creek Bridge, just beyond

Sherman's Pass. It's a timber viaduct with a span of 650 feet that sways in the wind. The speed limit there is only four miles an hour. You come round a bend in the canyon and there it is. Any obstruction on the line and the train has to stop dead.'

'I can see how that works,' Lennie agrees.

Dick Winscott pulls out his pocket watch. 'Right, so it's either Dale Creek or Granite Canyon which gives us twenty minutes to get ready. Lennie and Joe, I want you on the engine footplates with long-range rifles, ready to shoot on sight. Mr Ross and I will deal with Shanks and the half-breed when they come a-calling.'

Suddenly the car jerks and the locomotive clanks and spits into life as the engine boiler delivers sufficient steam to push the pistons back and forth. The big driver wheels begin to move faster; the train picks up speed and the whistle blows. We are on our way to what I hope will be a final showdown. I stub out my cigar butt on a wooden coffee crate and think about my telegraphic exchange with John Arbuckle.

I had told him about my promise to deliver a much larger consignment of coffee by rail which could lead to the train being robbed of its valuable cargo by the Shanks Gang. What did he want to do? *I am sending the coffee as requested*, he wired back. *What better advertisement could there be for Arbuckle's Ariosa than a bunch of outlaws staging a train robbery to get their hands on it. My old friend Jimmy Batterson will insure the cargo. His Connecticut insurance company sells accident policies to train travellers. So, no worries!*

But I still have doubts about what I am doing. That wise old bird Confucius believed that anyone embarking on a journey of revenge should dig two graves, one for his enemy and one for himself. And in any case a packed train is not the ideal place for a shootout. Bullets go all over the place and passengers get hurt. A single .44 slug can ricochet off a brass fitting or go through several upholstered seats. So, what should I do? Let evil go unpunished? No, I have come too far for that. Retribution used to be the cornerstone of our legal system and revenge is a wild justice for those wrongs for which there is no remedy in law.

It is stiflingly hot in the baggage car. I try to light another cigar and drop the match. Why do fingers become thumbs in times of stress? Lennie is perspiring freely. He stands his rifle against the crates and wipes the palm of his hand on his trousers. 'Hot in here,' he says. Dick Winscott nods in agreement. 'Sure is. Best to keep the passenger door locked though or the conductor will be in asking for our tickets.' Which isn't a great joke but it helps to relieve the tension.

Lennie picks up his rifle and opens the forward door that leads to the engine. 'We'll be off now. Granite Canyon can't be more than a couple of miles away.' 'Shoot to kill, lads,' are Winscott's parting words. But there is no need for them to do anything as the train hurtles unimpeded through the gully and into Sherman's Pass.

'What do you think, Dick?' I ask dry-mouthed.

'It's coming,' he says. 'I can feel it.'

The train is moving slower now as the line follows the contours of the bluff ahead. We hear Lennie's startled voice. 'Ambush up ahead!' he yells. Shots ring out. Bullets smack into the engine cab. One shell strikes the coal, splattering the tender with tiny pieces of graphite.

Then all hell breaks loose. The baggage-car door is blown off its hinges and Cherokee Jones lunges into the empty space to be met by a blast of gunfire which thumps him against the wall of the cab. Shanks looms up, shooting wildly. A bullet grazes my leg but I steady myself to return fire.

There is smoke everywhere. The acrid clouds clear sufficiently to reveal a wounded Dick Winscott and a very dead Indian. This leaves Shanks unaccounted for. Screams are coming from the next railcar. The connecting door has been left open and I see my enemy, pistol in hand, staggering down the corridor as passengers dive for cover beneath their seats. He is bleeding profusely. I limp after him in what is a slow-motion chase. He reaches the end of the second compartment and crawls out onto an open-air platform.

'Stop right there, Shanks. I've a gun on your back and am entitled to shoot you if you so much as move a muscle.'

'Hell, I know that voice,' he says through gritted teeth. 'But it can't be you, Grenfell, you're a dead man. I read about it years ago.'

'You shouldn't believe everything you read in the newspapers. Now I'm putting my gun down and inviting you to turn round. I want this to be a fair fight.'

Shanks swivels around, cocking his pistol as he does so. 'You're a hard man to kill,' he snarls.

'But you're not,' I reply, pumping him full of lead.

For an instant, he clings to the platform, his face twisted in a grimace of shock and pain, before toppling over the side and disappearing beneath the train.

I go out onto the platform to make sure he's dead.

'Bravo, sir,' says a timid voice behind me. I have been joined by Billy Starr of the *Daily Leader*. 'I came along to report on an attempted train robbery but I never thought it would end like this with a coffee salesman gunning down our most ferocious outlaw.'

'He wasn't much of a gunslinger, son. Shooting people in the back was more his style.'

'You may be right, Mr Ross, but once my eye-witness account appears in print all our readers will be talking about you. You'll be an absolute hero. See if I'm right.'

'I hope you like publicity.' A bloodstained Dick Winscott is grinning broadly. 'They'll be featuring you in those Penny

Dreadfuls, inventing all kinds of stories about the man who shot John T Shanks.'

Train passengers gather around to add their congratulations and I feel a slow joy spreading within me. I am free at last. Free of the past. It is time to go home.

MAY 17, 1875

Waking up in new surroundings can be a confusing experience. I stretch languidly beneath the bedclothes, too warm and lazy to open my eyes, trying to remember where I am. With a hot sun playing on my eyelids I could be in Cuba, lounging on the veranda of my plantation house; only I don't live there any longer. Equally, I might be in San Francisco, in one of those colourful adobe houses in the Bay Area near the Arbuckle coffee warehouse. Then it comes back to me. I'm staying in Louisville's most expensive hotel, Galt House, playing the part of the successful businessman.

Not that there's anything wrong with this. A man who has made a fortune out of soft commodities might be expected to take his ease in such surroundings. And I'm here for a specific purpose. I am going to the race track today to watch what promises to be a turf classic. That's what the Louisville *Commercial* is calling it anyway. 'St Louis has her fair,' the paper gushes, 'Cincinnati her music festival, New Orleans her Mardi Gras and our fair city can gain equal fame for her races.'

Set up to rescue thoroughbred racing from its post-war doldrums, the Louisville Jockey Club is celebrating the opening of its new track at Churchill Downs with the first running of the Kentucky Derby and such is the interest in this event that there's hardly a bed to be had in the city. The hotels are crammed with owners, trainers, breeders and punters. On arriving at Galt House last night, I found the lobby full of people wanting to place bets on the big race and had to fight my way to the reception desk where the clerk informed me that a telegraph wire had been strung between the hotel and the track so that guests could get the race results immediately.

In truth, everything about Galt House speaks of money, starting with the crystal chandeliers in the entrance lobby and moving upwards, by a severe craning of the neck, to the eight steel beams that support its second-floor Grand Ballroom and several higher floors. Yet however plush they may look; American luxury hotels are very similar. They have the same basic layout: a ground floor that is a public thoroughfare, with a much grander mezzanine or second floor and, above that, the bulk of the bedrooms arranged on floors that are virtually identical. If the hallway in your hotel corridor features, shall we say, a fruitwood coopered jardinière containing aspidistras then you can be almost certain that the same jardinière and flower arrangement can be found on each of the other floors. The Americans pride themselves on their individuality yet seek uniformity in hotel architecture and furnishings. How different this is from the crooked landings and nooks and crannies in your average Cornish coaching inn. But where American hotels score over their English rivals is in advanced hygiene. The practice of attaching a bathroom to every bedroom to create a hotel suite has yet to reach our part of the world.

I lie back in my hot tub to contemplate the day. It is all planned out. Breakfast downstairs followed by a visit to the race track. I know remarkably little about American horse racing. In England, it is a gambling sport for the well-to-do. They call it 'the sport of kings', with the doffing of top hats to Queen Victoria's son, but it won't be nearly so class-ridden over here. My white linen suit is probably the right kind of smart, democratic attire.

Throwing open the bedroom window, I can feel the heat building up outside. It's barely nine o'clock and already the day is close, the air heavy with moisture. There is talk of a thunderstorm later and anyone going to the races may need an umbrella more than a mint julep. A pair of stout boots might also come in handy if the going gets soft in the paddock.

On entering the hotel's dining room, I am reminded of Mark Twain's recent novel, *The Gilded Age* in which the satirist contrasts America's obvious wealth and dazzle with its inner corruption and poverty. Everything here glimmers with gold but the overall effect is superficial and somehow tawdry. Gilded columns support an ornate plasterwork ceiling; gold velvet curtains drape the tall Gothic windows and giltwood chairs frame the tables at which guests eat.

I am shown to a table beneath a gas-lit chandelier and asked whether I want coffee or tea before being pointed towards the 'buffet'. Guests are supposed to serve themselves from the silver chafing dishes displayed on a long sideboard. A head waiter in livery helps me make my choice. I accept scrambled eggs, some rashers of bacon, grilled tomatoes and a couple of Belgian waffles with maple syrup and take a heaped plate of food back to my table, where another waiter pulls out a chair, seats me, shakes out the folds in my starched linen napkin and wishes me a hearty appetite. This is service Kentucky style, friendly, polite and almost apologetic, where the chamber's solid stone walls muffle the guests' clamour to a respectful murmur.

To eat well in America you should have breakfast three times a day. An English wit said that and he could be right. It is certainly my favourite meal. I open a copy of today's *Commercial* and find that the latest race results have knocked the political scandals of the Grant Administration off the front page. A mahogany grandfather clock is striking ten as I finish eating and sit back with a cup of coffee to await the arrival of an old friend.

And here he is, former Confederate General Basil Duke, a slightly built figure with dark hair, trimmed moustache and beard, exuding an air of massive probity. Once he sees me, his long, somewhat mournful face breaks into a broad smile. 'My, you've changed, George,' he says in that deep voice of his. 'You're not the burly chap I remember.'

'No, I'm two stone lighter. There is nothing like a prison diet for losing weight and I never put it on again. It's my disguise, along with the grey hair.'

'Yes, of course, you're no longer George Grenfell, are you?'

'Right again, Basil,' I reply. 'I am now called Robert Ross.'

Duke does a double take. 'You're not by any chance that character from the dime novels, are you?'

'That's me, I'm afraid, but it's all a lot of nonsense.'

'But you must have done something pretty spectacular to acquire such fame?'

'I managed to stop a train robbery in Wyoming a few years back. But let's talk about you. I understand you're chief counsel for the Louisville and Nashville Railroad which is an odd turn of events, wouldn't you say?'

Duke bellows with laughter. 'I would indeed. The L & N Railroad was one of our favourite targets when we were riding with Morgan's Raiders but times change and I've changed with them.'

'I guess we all do that.'

'Yes, well, I never would have figured you for a sugar planter or a coffee magnate. How did that come about?'

'Pure happenstance, but tell me, how did you become a veritable pillar of society?'

'No, you first Robert, if I must call you that.'

I tell him about my prison break and the treasure I'd taken with me and how I'd used the gold to buy into the prosperous sugar estate I now owned. Tragically, my partner Juan Pedrosa died in Cuba's civil war, leaving me his share in the business, to which I have added a directorship in Arbuckle Ross, a West Coast conglomerate trading in coffee and sugar.

My old friend shakes his head in amazement. 'Your luck has certainly changed for the better,' he says, stating the obvious.

'Put it this way,' I tell him. 'I have learned what kind of good luck your bad luck can create for you. Now it's your turn.'

A waiter arrives with coffee on a silver tray and pours each of us a cup while Duke talks about moving to Louisville after the Civil War. 'Kentucky could never make up its mind whether it was for the Confederacy or the Union. I was able to exploit the state's Janus-faced view of its recent history to make myself a respected citizen while also defending the principles on which we fought the war. I am both attorney for the Fifth Judicial District and a leading light in Louisville's Southern Historical Association.'

'So it's possible to have your cake and eat it in Kentucky.'

'I believe so. Now, I have a little surprise for you. Unless my eyes deceive me, we are about to be joined by a mutual acquaintance, Tom Hines. When he heard you were coming to Louisville, he insisted on paying his respects.'

Striding purposefully towards our table is a slim man in a smart suit. Captain Thomas Henry Hines still has a droopy moustache and soft, wary eyes. He holds out a well-manicured hand. 'I hope we can be friends, despite what happened in Chicago,' he says. 'I got the message you left for me by the way. I reckon it saved my life.'

'So you *did* return to O'Brien's livery stable. I asked Billy Pettigrew to tell Mr Hunter that the cat had got kittens.'

Basil Duke chortles. 'I don't remember that phrase in the Confederate code book.'

'No, I improvised. To have kittens is to feel fear. But how did you get out of town, Tom?'

'I rushed back to the safe house and hid under a mattress with the owner's wife lying on top of me. She told the Union soldiers she had a contagious illness and they kept well away from the bed.

376

When it rained next day, I sneaked out under an umbrella and left Chicago in a hurry. I felt really bad about leaving you behind, particularly when they sentenced you to hang ...'

Duke interrupts. 'You may not know this George, but Tom here paid your legal costs, using the money he'd been given to finance his uprising. Not that it did you much good in front of that military tribunal with those arch traitors Shanks and Langhorne lying through their teeth.'

'I applaud the intention, Tom, and many thanks too for the stirring article you wrote in the Memphis *Appeal* while I was in prison. The master spy has become quite a journalist.'

'I'm a lawyer now and a county judge,' says Hines, 'leading a staid existence in Bowling Green with my wife Nancy whom, mark you, I had to spirit out of a Catholic convent in Ohio.'

I think of little Rose orphaned in a Paris convent, waiting for someone to get her.

Hines sighs. 'Those heady days of full-blooded cavalry charges with John Hunt Morgan seem a long time ago.'

The mention of Morgan's name creates an awkward pause in the conversation. 'I was sad to hear of the death of your brother-in-law,' I say to Duke. 'Shot in the back in Tennessee, wasn't he?'

'Yeah, he was only thirty-nine. Poor Mattie hardly got to be a wife before she was a widow. Their wedding in Murfreesboro must have been the last time I saw you George, when you put all our noses out of joint by capturing the attention of that gorgeous Confederate spy Mrs Rose Greenhow. She died in '64 too, just like John Hunt, a martyr to the cause.'

We stop to consider the injustices of life and an attentive waiter takes the opportunity to fill our empty coffee cups. Hines is the first to speak. 'The nearest I came to death was in Detroit when I was mistaken for John Wilkes Booth. He was on the run after the Lincoln killing and no one knew exactly where he was. I had to jump over several fences and commandeer a ferryboat to escape being shot.'

'I actually met John Wilkes Booth. He was one of Rose Greenhow's agents.'

'Was he by God? What was he like?'

'Charismatic, hyperactive, overdramatic, convinced he was cut out for greatness, on and off the stage, but intensely superstitious. A Romany fortune-teller told him he was destined to die young with everyone's hand raised against him. You might say John Wilkes lived up to the gypsy's prophecy.'

'And made things more difficult for the rest of us by killing Lincoln,' Hines says grimly.

Duke looks at his pocket watch. 'I think we should be going now. There's a carriage outside.'

We are shown to a four-wheeled landau and climb into the passenger seats for the trip to Churchill Downs. The driver cracks his whip and the two black horses canter off down First Street. We are not alone in making this four-mile journey. Scores of private carriages are rattling off in the same southerly direction, travelling through a well-to-do suburb of Italian villas and Queen Anne houses. Then we are out into the lush countryside, skirting the woodlands through which the Nashville railroad runs and keeping well clear of the mule-driven streetcars carrying crowds of rowdy racegoers to the Jockey Club gates.

As we approach the entrance, Basil Duke hands out passes. 'These are for the grandstand enclosure and for the post-race reception. They'll also get us into the paddock.'

'These tickets must be like gold dust,' Hines says. 'How did you manage to get them, Basil?'

'By being well connected, I'm attorney to the Jockey Club President. You'll meet Colonel Meriwether Lewis Clark in due course.'

The first race on the card, a six-furlong sprint, is already underway. Hundreds of carriages spill onto the infield, making it almost impossible to follow the horses. I am told the winner is a filly called Bonaventure. Our carriage is waved into a reserved space and we step out onto the hallowed turf. This is the famous blue grass of Kentucky, a strain of lawn seed that produces bluish-purple buds when grown in the state's rich limestone soil.

On cue, a bluegrass band strikes up with banjos, fiddles and guitars to play 'Barbara Allen', an English ballad with an Appalachian twist. My spine begins to tingle as I listen to this sad love song. I think of all my dreams and ambitions, the millions of choices I've made that have brought me here today. I am no longer in bondage to the past and can choose my destiny. It is just around the corner. And for once I feel lucky.

We are met by a tall man with an anxious face. This is the mercurial Colonel Clark, the founder of the Louisville Jockey Club. 'Good to see you, Duke,' he begins. 'I thought we were going to have a thunderstorm but God has relented, it's a perfect day, and we've got a fast track and a huge turnout, ten thousand people all told.' Clark hands us an information sheet about the runners and riders. Then he leads us to a grandstand packed with well-groomed gentlemen and ladies in costly dresses. I catch sight of a beautiful chestnut-haired young girl flirting with an Adonis in a blue blazer and feel a sudden, irrational stab of envy.

No sooner have we found our seats than a bugle blows to announce the appearance in the paddock of the thoroughbreds contesting the second race of the day, the Kentucky Derby. By the time we get to the parade ring the horses are already saddled. Almost all the jockeys are black. Is this a sign of emancipation or simply another form of slavery? On reflection, I guess it's a bit of both. Before the war, plantation owners had slaves working as stable grooms and riders. Now that they've got their freedom, it is only to be expected that they will seek employment on the Southern race circuits.

Colonel Clark wanders over and introduces us to one of the owners, Hal Price McGrath, who has two horses in the race. McGrath is a raucous red-headed fellow with a ready smile. 'You know what they say about me, gentlemen,' he began. 'That I'm a war profiteer and a professional gambler and not to be trusted but I know about horses. Let me give you a tip; whether you take it is up to you.'

'Go ahead, sir,' says Hines, eager for inside information.

'Back my big bay Chesapeake. He's the pre-race favourite and a really fast finisher.'

But my eyes are on his other horse, a gleaming chestnut stallion with a white star and two hind stockings. 'What about Aristides?' I ask.

'He's got no chance,' McGrath replies curtly. 'Aristides is a speedball but at fifteen hands he can't stay the distance. He's in the race to be the hare. I've told his jockey Oliver Lewis to set a fast pace so that Chesapeake can come through with a late run.' The owner has it all worked out in his head but I'm not sure he's right. Acting on impulse, I put ten dollars on Aristides to win at twenty to one.

The fifteen starters are led out to the post and marshalled into two ranks by the starter who, I'm told, is the President of the Blood Horse Association. Back in the stand Duke hands me a pair of binoculars and I train them on Colonel Johnson just before he drops the flag. Fifteen thoroughbreds thunder off down the dirt track.

The green and orange silks of Aristides are the first to show, closely followed by McCreery who takes over the running at the furlong mark. Behind them, I can see the red colours of Volcano and the black and white stripes of Ten Broeck but McGrath's bay horse is nowhere to be seen. As they reach the quarter, little

Aristides goes to the front again and begins to pull away from the field.

Hines whistles through his teeth. 'He can't keep this up. You heard what his owner had to say.'

'McGrath is wrong about that stallion,' I tell him. 'He's bred to win. You can see the determination in his eyes.' But it's the chestnut colour that attracts me – first the girl, now the horse.

Duke has a stopwatch on the race. 'He's run the first mile in one minute forty-three. That's awfully fast, surely?'

'He can win from here!' I have to shriek to make myself heard above the cheering crowd.

Aristides' jockey doesn't think so. Following pre-race orders, he begins to rein in his horse as he waits for Chesapeake to overtake him. My binoculars focus on a red-headed man at the head of the straight waving his arms furiously. Hal McGrath is urging Lewis on.

Horse and jockey respond immediately. Off they go again, racing like the wind, and hold off a late challenge from the fast-finishing Volcano. The gallant Aristides gallops under the wire in what is said to be a world record time for the one-and-a-half-mile distance. Hats are tossed in the air, including my Stetson, for I have won two hundred dollars.

There is a further opportunity to celebrate at the Jockey Club reception afterwards. Over several glasses of champagne, I explain the importance of breeding to my bemused comrades. Aristides was sired by the great English stud Leamington and his dam was Sarong who came from the Lexington-Glencoe bloodline. 'Racing is terribly inbred,' I tell them. 'I learned this when I was in Morocco. Believe it or not, ninety-five per cent of all thoroughbreds are descended from an Arabian colt that a bankrupt English merchant bought from a Bedouin tribesman back in 1704.'

'But that's absurd,' says Duke. 'It defies all logic.'

'No, it's true. What's more, Thomas Darley's Arabian never ran a race but his offspring have won thousands of them.'

Aware of a throaty laugh behind my head, I turn around to see that girl again. She is responding to something said to her by an elderly man in a frock coat. He is obviously trying to impress her, and why not, for she is a vision of loveliness in a coral silk dress. With her beautiful face and silky skin, I think every red-blooded male should be desiring her acquaintance.

I try to pull myself together. It hardly becomes a man in his fifty-eighth year to have such thoughts. Yet the idea of her continues to excite me. She seems so familiar. Is it the chestnut hair, the emerald eyes, the pointed chin or that dry husky laugh that echoes in my memory?

Suddenly I have the answer. My lost girl has grown up. The room begins to spin as I move towards her. I take a deep breath and touch her gently on the sleeve. 'Hello Rosie,' I murmur.

She swivels around at the sound of my voice and the colour leaves her cheeks. Her mouth opens and she seems to lose her sense of balance. I think she is about to faint and put out a hand to steady her.

'But you can't be George,' she gasps.

'No, I'm not George,' I whisper, pleading with my eyes. 'My name is Robert Ross. But I used to have a friend who called me La Longue Carabine, remember?'

A light dawns in Rosie Greenhow's bright green eyes. 'Of course. How have you been, Robert? I've *really* missed you.'

'There hasn't been a day ...'

'Who is this, darling? Introduce me to him.' Her beau has arrived and put a protective arm around her shoulders. I realise he is defending his territory.

Rose frowns but does his bidding. 'Clay Birmingham, Robert Ross,' she says in a perfunctory manner.

The young man flashes a smile in my direction. 'And what

do you do for a living, Mr Ross?'

'I am West Coast representative for Arbuckle Brothers.'

'Oh, a coffee salesman,' he sneers. 'Wait a minute though, didn't I read about an Arbuckle agent who was a gunslinger in his spare time? Wasn't he called Robert Ross?'

'You've been reading too many cheap paperbacks, Clay. That isn't you, is it Robert?'

'I'm afraid so, although Beadle's dime novels wildly exaggerate my prowess with a gun.'

'It's time we were going.' Birmingham takes Rose's arm. 'We're having afternoon tea with the Crittendens. It was a pleasure to meet you, Ross.'

I watch her go with a keen sense of loss. Suddenly she breaks away from him and hurries back to me. 'Where are you staying?' she whispers urgently.

'At Galt House Hotel,' I mumble, 'on the corner of First and Main, by the Ohio River.'

'Good. Order dinner for two in the hotel for eight o'clock. I will be there as soon as I can.'

With that she turns on her heel and glides out of the room leaving me speechless. Once she has gone, astonishment gives way to elation. I am going to see her again.

Hines jogs my elbow. 'Who was that delightful girl you were talking to? Anyone we know?'

'Actually, yes, she was at the Morgan wedding in Murfreesboro. She's Rose Greenhow's daughter.'

'You mean the pretty little thing with the ringlets.'

'You see, you do remember.'

'Sorry to interrupt,' says Duke, 'but once Robert has collected his winnings I think we should be going.'

On the way back I ask about Clay Birmingham and learn that he's the playboy son of a Louisville bourbon distiller. I can't decide which I dislike more, bourbon or the Birmingham offspring. We also chat about the war. Duke describes how he escorted Jefferson Davis out of Richmond before it fell, but all I can think about is Rosie and how attracted I am to her. One of the deepest pits in hell must be reserved for a man who first sleeps with the mother and then covets the daughter.

The carriage reaches my hotel and I invite Duke and Hines to visit me in San Francisco. It's a big house and I could do with some company. Hines chuckles at this. 'Judging by the way Rose Greenhow's daughter was looking at you, you may not be alone for much longer.'

I tell him he's mistaken, I'm old enough to be her father and then some, but secretly I hope he's right. There's no fool like an old fool, they say.

*

The grandfather clock strikes the hour. It's nine o'clock. I push aside my bowl of barley broth and gaze miserably at the silverware and crested china. Rosie isn't coming.

A waiter brings the menu card to my table. 'Would you like to order your main course, sir?' he asks with a meaningful glance at the empty seat next to me. I take the card and pretend to study it – lamb hot pot, roast chicken with bread sauce, rolled ox tongue. My appetite has disappeared.

'I'm sorry I'm so late.' Rosie is wearing a cape over an apple-green silk-taffeta dress. She looks flustered and out of breath but the words come tumbling from her lips. 'I was in such a state in case I missed you. I've been waiting so long for this day. I read you'd drowned at sea, like my mother, but I couldn't bring myself to believe it. Something told me you were alive and that we would meet again. Now here we are.'

I want to cry out for joy. Instead, I ask her whether she had any problem in getting away.

'Not half,' she replies, 'Clay behaved like a spoilt brat. Just because I agreed to stay at his father's home for the Derby, he seems to think he owns me. Bad things were said, so I packed and left.'

'Where are you staying now?'

'Here, with you. I had my luggage put in your suite. I told the concierge we were married.'

It takes an effort of will to stay silent. Words like 'wonderful' and 'perfect' spring to mind. When I can trust myself, I say very slowly, as if speaking in a strange language, 'I am trying to lead a better life and seducing a young woman who could be my daughter cannot be part of that, can it? Besides, there's your reputation to think of.'

'I don't care a fig about reputation!' How like her mother she sounds?

She sits in the vacant chair and takes off her cape. Her green dress has a low neckline. 'You are talking to a divorcee after all.'

Rosie had married a young West Point army officer, Lieutenant William Penn Duvall, when she was eighteen and got divorced two years later. 'It was a big mistake. Serves me right for trusting a Yankee but I got tired of waiting for you, George.'

'Long after the war, when I was a sugar planter in Cuba, I hired a French detective to search for you in Paris. All he could tell me was that you'd been living in the Convent du Sacré Coeur but had left.'

'That's right. Mother left me in the convent when she sailed back to America. I couldn't stop crying when I heard of her death. That was a terrible time. I asked to be baptised so I could pray for her soul, even had thoughts of becoming a nun. Then, when the war was over, my elder sister Leila collected me and brought me back to Washington.'

'I wish I could have been there for you Rosie, I really do.'

'I kept hoping you'd show up at my cell door but it never happened.'

'No, by then I was in a different kind of cell, a prison one, waiting to be hanged.'

'That must have been terrible. When we got back to the capital Leila went to the British Legation and they told her a military tribunal had sentenced you to death but that your sentence had been commuted to life imprisonment on the Dry Tortugas. After that I heard nothing, until the news broke of your escape and supposed death at sea, George.'

'Yes, George Grenfell was declared dead six years ago so that his wife could remarry. That's why I'd prefer you to call me Robert Ross. It's the name on my passport. You do understand, don't you?'

'I don't care what you call yourself. Actually, Robert is quite appealing. It was my father's name, you know. He died when I was a baby.'

The waiter is hovering over her. 'Yes, I'd like the mutton chops with mashed potatoes, green beans and mint, if you've got any.' She signals for an empty glass to be filled with claret and shakes out her heavy linen napkin.

I order the roast chicken and another bottle of wine. We look at one another but say nothing. The silence lengthens and grows weighty, but neither of us can find the right words. What we're about to tell each other must be perfectly expressed.

'Look, Robert, I've been wrong about many things but never about you. My mother should have married you. Now I will. That's if you'll have me?'

Her proposal changes everything. It fills the gloomy dining room with light. My heart is singing but my head still finds grounds for objection. 'You know it wouldn't be right. You're twenty-two and I'm almost fifty-eight. It's too big an age gap. Marry me and you'll come to regret it.'

'Stop it, George, Robert, whoever you say you are!' There are tears in her eyes. 'My mind is made up. I couldn't be without you again. And if you're so worried about the passing years, we'd better not waste any time. Find a priest and take our vows. What do you say?'

Rosie looks radiant as she holds out a slender hand to me. I am almost suffocated by the intensity of my longing for her. This is my second chance and, whatever the consequences, I am determined to take it.

*

There is a gas lamp outside my window and it casts a fitful light on our naked bodies as we lie exhausted on the bed. Her flesh is smooth, supple and firm while mine seems to be hanging off me. That's the problem with old age – you no longer fit your skin. I sit up and an extra fold of flesh gathers around my stomach. I pull the bedclothes over us before kissing her awake. There is something I need to say.

'The thing is … the thing is …' I begin.

'Yes, Robert, what is the thing?'

'I don't know where I belong. I've lived in so many countries and not really settled anywhere.'

'Haven't you worked this out yet? You belong with me, Robert. As long as we are together, it doesn't matter where we are. We're wanderers, you and I. We need adventure in our lives.'

She slides on top of me, bending forward to cover my face with her copper hair.

'I'm here for you, my darling girl, now and forever,' I vow passionately.

'My goodness, you are too,' she murmurs. 'There is so much to look forward to.'

POSTSCRIPT
JUNE 12, 1903

'He's waiting for you Mrs Ross, in the Residence.' Ike pushes a button to summon the White House elevator. 'There used to be steps here,' he adds. 'This was Mr Lincoln's favourite stairway.'

The electric contraption comes to a shuddering halt and its gates open to reveal a young boy and a piebald pony. 'What are you doing, Master Quentin, taking Algonquin upstairs in the elevator?' Ike sounds exasperated.

'Don't be angry, Mr Hoover, Archie's not well so I brought Algonquin into his bedroom to cheer him up. You won't tell Father, will you?'

'Well, that depends on whether you take your pony back to the stables.'

I am ushered into the elevator which now smells of horsehair and the gates close behind me. 'Those Roosevelt children are allowed to run wild,' my guide grumbles as we begin our ascent. 'There are five of them youngsters and they get into every nook and cubbyhole in the building. They treat the White House as if it was a family home. They roller-skate and bicycle-ride through the state rooms, even when foreign dignitaries are here.'

This is my first experience of an elevator and I can't say I enjoy being locked inside a rattling, swaying cage. 'How long have you worked here, Mr Hoover?' I ask to take my mind off things.

'Since '91. I came here as a telephone operator to install electric lights in the executive mansion and stayed on. Now I'm a sort of general factotum, I help around the place.'

The cage opens and we are in a bright, newly-painted

corridor. A regal-looking woman wafts towards us in a summer blouse and flared walking skirt. 'Morning, Mrs Roosevelt,' Ike says.

The First Lady shakes her head. 'The president's not here. You'll find him in the West Wing.'

On the way down, Ike explains that the West Wing is one of President Roosevelt's many innovations. Presidential staff had worked on the second floor of the Executive Residence until Mrs Roosevelt objected to it. She needed more room for her large family. To respect her wishes, the President had added a temporary office structure to the west of the mansion on what had been the site of some dilapidated old greenhouses.

'My mother used to water President Buchanan's tomatoes in those greenhouses,' I tell him.

Ike Hoover's eyebrows shoot up. 'Who was your mother, Mrs Ross?'

'Rose Greenhow. She often acted as President Buchanan's hostess at White House receptions.'

'My knowledge of history is hazy but wasn't she imprisoned as a spy during the Civil War?'

'She was indeed and, as a matter of fact, so was I.'

We reach the president's office. Huge oriental jars guard either side of closed double doors. The disconcerted usher knocks loudly. 'Come,' says a high-pitched voice and in I go. Sitting behind a large mahogany desk is a stocky man with a bull neck, closely cropped brown hair, a droopy moustache and pince-nez spectacles perched on a large nose. He looks up at me. 'Glad to meet you, Mrs Ross. I understand you've brought me something your late husband thought I should see.'

This is the first time I've seen Theodore Roosevelt and I am struck by his myopic china-blue eyes. 'Yes, Mr President, confidential papers belonging to the White House.'

'If that is so, how did he come by them?'

'That's a long story, Mr President. Can you spare the time to hear it?'

'Probably not, Mrs Ross, so let me be candid with you. There are more than eighty million Americans and I am sure you appreciate I don't have time to talk to all of them individually but I've made an exception where you are concerned because of your husband. Was he the Cuban sugar planter who also made a fortune out of selling Arbuckle's coffee in the West?'

'The very same,' I reply, somewhat apprehensively. I am not easily impressed but I find myself somewhat in awe of this supremely confident, pugnacious politician with his clipped tones and extravagant hand gestures.

'Then I do have time for you. Excuse me a moment.' He takes a desk telephone out of its cradle and dials a number. 'Clarence, delay this morning's labour meeting. Put it back until lunchtime. Oh and get the kitchen to bring in the tea trolley. Thank you.'

He gives me a knowing look. 'Perhaps I should start the ball rolling by explaining my interest in your husband. I've just returned from a two-month tour of the American West where he's quite a hero. When we stopped for lunch at the Arbuckle ranch in Wyoming, I was taken into a den full of photographs and old newspaper cuttings about an attempted train robbery in which a coffee salesman called Robert Ross gunned down a fearsome outlaw. Then, later that day, after one of my inspiring speeches on the stump, I visited Cheyenne's most famous saloon, the Bucket of Blood, where there is a brass plaque dedicated to his memory. It said he was the fastest gun in the West. I asked the barman about this inscription and he told me what happened after the train shootout. The two surviving members of Shanks's gang had come into town looking for trouble. Ross was drinking at the bar when they burst into the saloon with their rifles at full cock. But he still outdrew them, firing both his revolvers simultaneously. Now I'm a great lover of Western mythology but the two-gun sharpshooter is beyond belief. The notion of a shooter whipping out two pistols and firing them accurately in different directions has to be codswallop. I said this to the barman in the Bucket of Blood and he looked me straight in the eye and drawled, "Well, Mr President, you're a bright man, you figure it out." The trouble is I can't.'

'Robert seldom talked about those days in Wyoming, sir. He was very embarrassed by the way the dime novels lionised him. What I can't understand, he would say, is why the public is so in love with the idea of a gun-slinging coffee salesman. I think he was genuinely bemused by the attention paid to his prowess with a gun when there were much better tales to be told about him.'

'And what would they be?' The president's head jerks to and fro as he speaks.

Theodore Roosevelt is America's youngest and most energetic chief executive and everyone knows he loves tales of courage and adventure. I am reeling him in like a big fish. Even so, I need to be careful.

'How about the story of a man who was given a death sentence for a crime that was never committed or the story of an English soldier of fortune who was declared officially dead by the United States government only to reappear as a Cuban sugar planter with an American passport or, better yet, the story of how he acquired the papers I'm now carrying, which were taken from the White House before the British set fire to it in 1814.'

There, I've said it. The truth can't hurt you now, George.

Roosevelt's fist pounds the surface of his desk. 'I am in the mood for a good story,' he exclaims. 'You have my attention, Mrs Ross, pray continue.'

A knock on the door indicates the arrival of the tea trolley pushed by a smiling black lady. 'I've got your favourites, Mr President,' she announces proudly. 'Turkey sandwiches, cookies and some of your wife's hot biscuits.'

'Bully for you, Cleopatra. The gang hasn't been bothering you again? No more snakes in the cake tray or water bombs dropped on your head?'

'No, sir, your kids have been just fine.'

'That's a relief. Do you have any children, Mrs Ross?'

'Yes, a boy called George, named after his father. He's at Harvard now.'

'My alma mater,' he says wistfully. Then his eyes harden. 'But your husband's name was Robert?'

'He was George before he was Robert. Didn't I mention that?'

'No, you didn't. Look, it's a lovely day. Why don't we continue this enthralling conversation outside? Cleopatra can follow on with the trolley.'

'That would be delightful, sir.'

He opens a French window in his office and we stroll between the colonnades of the West Terrace out into a parterre in which paisley-shaped flower beds are framed by low boxwood hedges. 'What do you think of my dear wife's creation? She calls it her colonial garden.'

Daisies, irises, roses, peonies and daylilies fill the garden with colour and blue and red geraniums are allowed to tumble through the borders to give the design a careless, old-fashioned charm. I congratulate him on Edith Roosevelt's landscaping. We find a bench seat. Cleopatra trundles after us with coffee and cakes. Apparently, the president has a sweet tooth and is particularly partial to what she calls 'fat rascals'.

'Now, Mrs Ross,' he says, 'why don't you start at the beginning? Tell me how you met George who later became Robert.'

I take a deep breath and begin my story. 'I first met George St Leger Grenfell at General John Hunt Morgan's wedding in December 1862. George was one of the ushers and ...'

'My good friend Basil Duke was the best man,' Roosevelt

adds. 'I met Basil at the Filson Club in Louisville. We're fellow historians, you see.'

'I'm surprised to hear that, Mr President. Duke was a Confederate general and wrote his history from a Southern point of view. I wouldn't have thought you'd have much in common.'

'Ah, there's a lot you don't know about me. Were you aware, for instance, that I had two uncles who fought for the South in the Civil War? No, I thought not. The Bulloch brothers were brave men and I admire them far more than the mollycoddled Roosevelt bankers and businessmen who never lifted a finger but to count their money! Forgive me, I interrupted you. Please continue.'

'Yes, Basil Duke was Morgan's brother-in-law and second in command of the Thunderbolt Raiders. George was a colonel in the brigade. As he was Cornish by birth and had fought all over the world, I guess you would call him a mercenary but he joined the Confederacy on principle rather than for profit. In fact, when I first met him, he had never received so much as a nickel for his services.'

Roosevelt peers at me in his short-sighted way. 'You can't have been very old when that meeting took place.'

'I was a precocious nine-year-old and I was at the wedding with my mother.'

'Was she connected to the Morgan family?'

'No, she had come to Murfreesboro with Jefferson Davis. He was inspecting his Tennessee troops. At the time she was something of a celebrity. Have you ever heard of Mrs Rose Greenhow?'

'You bet I have. She's the enchanting woman who went from being de facto First Lady to an imprisoned Confederate spy in a single year. The fortunes of war, you might say. But what happened to you when she was behind bars?'

'I was with her. Men used to pay our jailers to come and leer at us.'

'That's disgusting!' I hadn't realised how prudish this flamboyant, outspoken man could be when it came to sex. 'I hope Lincoln put an end to that.'

'Our imprisonment got to be such an embarrassment to him that he let us go to Richmond on the understanding that we would never return to Washington.'

'As I recall it, your mother became Jeff Davis' envoy in Europe and was drowned on a sea voyage to America. She was a lady of great courage and resolve.'

I nod sadly. 'But she gave her life for nothing. Her diplomatic mission was a failure.'

The president bristles. 'There is no disgrace in failure, Mrs Ross, only in a failure to try. But let's get back to George Grenfell, what kind of man was he?'

'He was a tall, handsome Englishman with an air of danger about him. I thought he was a figure out of a romantic novel. And he was so charming. You've got to remember I was an impressionable nine-year-old girl. I wanted him to be my special friend but there was a complication. He became my mother's lover. They planned to get married as soon as he could get a divorce from his French wife. At least, that's what I was told.'

Roosevelt takes a sip of coffee and stares reflectively over the rim of the cup. He wants to ask me whether I welcomed the idea of George as a stepfather but good breeding and natural reticence stop him from doing so.

'Not that they spent much time together,' I gabble on, trying to cover my tracks. 'The war saw to that. George was all over the place, fighting with Bragg and Breckinridge at Stones River, with Jeb Stuart at Brandy Station and Robert E Lee at Gettysburg. Then Mother got her diplomatic appointment and off we sailed to Europe. I didn't see him again for twelve years.'

The president offers me the last cookie and looks pleased when I decline. 'What happened to him in the meantime?'

'He was caught up in what became known as the Northwest Conspiracy which sought to liberate Confederate prisoners from Northern prison camps. The first blow was to be struck at Camp Douglas in Chicago and George was to lead this raid. But he was arrested before he had actually done anything and tried by a military tribunal who sentenced him to death, even though the war was over.'

'I find this hard to believe. You can't hang a man for a crime he never committed.'

'That's not strictly true, Mr President. Guy Fawkes was hanged, drawn and quartered although he failed to blow up the English Parliament.'

'But that was in the seventeenth century,' Roosevelt rumbles. 'We're more civilised these days.'

'I think it was a question of timing. The verdict was delivered four days after Lincoln's murder.'

'Ah, that might explain it. There was a positive blood lust after Abe's assassination. Poor George, he had no luck at all! How did he escape the noose?'

I tell him about the British ambassador persuading President Johnson to commute George's sentence to life imprisonment and how he was sent to the Dry Tortugas where he shared a prison cell with the Lincoln conspirators. I describe life in Fort Jefferson. The way he was tortured, the yellow fever epidemic, and how he discovered treasure in the parade ground; a ship's chest full of British guineas and President Madison's confidential papers.

Roosevelt finishes the last cookie and wipes the crumbs away from his mouth. 'This is beginning to sound like *The Count of Monte Cristo*, Mrs Ross. Are you sure he didn't make it up?'

'No, sir, I've seen some of the guineas he found, they're military ones dated 1813, and the Madison letters are also genuine, as you will see when you read them.'

'This is capital! New source material. I wrote a book about the War of 1812, you see. Tell me, how did George get his treasure trove off the island?'

I talk about his escape on the *Rosetta*. How he was the only one to survive a terrible storm in the Gulf of Mexico and was lucky enough to be cast ashore in Cuba where he used his money to buy a partnership in a sugar plantation. With that went a new identity. He became an American citizen called Robert Ross.

'Where did he get the name from?' Roosevelt asks.

'From a signature on the documents I'm carrying. Major General Robert Ross led the British expeditionary force that sacked Washington.'

The president smites his forehead. 'Of course he did. I knew there was something familiar about the name.'

He wants to know why the sugar planter became a coffee salesman and what he was doing in Wyoming. I explain about Shanks' villainy and George's determination to take revenge on the man who had ruined his life, even if it meant crossing America and tricking Shanks into staging a train robbery.

'You mean to say he set the whole thing up. I cannot condone his actions, no God-fearing Christian could, but I admire his determination to bring a bad man to book. Robert, as we must now call him, was certainly a daring fellow.'

'He was a changed man after that. George had led a charmed existence without ever realising how precious life was. Now, as Robert Ross, he had a second chance and expressed his gratitude by becoming a philanthropist. Most of the money he made out of coffee and sugar went into caring for other people's welfare. He supported funds to educate former slaves in the South and he also set up a Cornish charity to put gas lighting into mining villages.'

'When did he die?'

'On January 2, 1900. Almost his last words were that he didn't belong in the twentieth century.'

Roosevelt laughs loudly. 'What an epitaph that is. I wish I could have met your Robert Ross.'

'Robert was a great admirer of yours. He was a bedridden eighty-year-old when you set off for Cuba with your Rough Riders. On hearing about your plans, he got dressed and asked me where the nearest recruiting office was. Thought he could tag along as a cavalry adviser. It took two doctors to restrain him. Anyway, he was thrilled to read about the storming of San Juan Hill. They've given those Spanish grandees a bloody nose, he told me.'

'By jingo, we did,' Roosevelt roars. 'We had a duty to intervene on behalf of Cuban independence. It was a splendid little war.'

'Was that really what it was about?' I ask him. Unlike the president and, indeed, my beloved late husband, I am not much moved by machismo. The short Spanish-American War may have been exciting while it lasted but I can't understand why it had to be fought at all, unless of course it was to protect American interests in the island's tobacco and sugar. What it did do, though, was to enhance Theodore Roosevelt's standing. Taking a small hill in Cuba turned him into a national hero.

'It was our duty to wage war, ma'am, more as a matter of honour than gain,' he says emphatically. This mercurial man seems to be able to read my mind. That must be what makes him such a clever politician.

'When great nations fear to expand, shrink from expansion, it is because their greatness is coming to an end. Are we, still in the prime of our lusty youth, still at the beginning of our glorious manhood, to sit back among the weak and the craven? That cannot be!'

'I think you will find that your illustrious predecessor Thomas Jefferson expressed very similar sentiments before the War of 1812.' I take the Madison papers out of my handbag and hand them to him. 'It was Robert's dying wish that these letters should be returned to the White House.'

He shuffles through the pile of papers, extracts the relevant letter, and, after a moment's hesitation, begins to read aloud. 'I have known no war entered into under more favourable auspices. It is thirty years since the signature of our peace with England in 1782 and what a vast course of growth and prosperity we have had since then. And I do believe we shall continue to grow, to multiply and prosper until we exhibit an association, peaceful, powerful, wise and happy, beyond what has yet been seen by men. As for France and England, with all their pre-eminence in science, the one is a den of robbers, and the other of pirates. Their empires will surely wither while ours will grow to replace them. We must strike while the iron is hot: first, to make ourselves predominant on land, and then to use the war to strip our enemy of all her possessions on this continent by adding Canada to our confederacy. I salute you with unchanged affection and respect, Thomas Jefferson.'

Roosevelt places the letter back in the pile on his knee, before removing his pince-nez and rubbing his nose. 'Well, glory hallelujah! I'm often accused of being a warmonger who is prepared to sacrifice the flower of our youth to my imperial ambitions, and now we find that the Sage of Monticello was not nearly as peace-loving as he was made out to be. He too had thoughts of empire. I cannot thank you enough, dear lady, for bringing this letter to my attention. I will study the rest of these papers at my leisure.' He ties them up with red ribbon and slips the packet into his coat pocket.

It is time to speak out. 'I should warn you, Mr President, that some of the earlier correspondence covers a period in Jefferson's presidency when he was sharing his residence with the Madisons, playing what he called "games" with them, and indulging in bedtime "caresses" with Dolley.'

Roosevelt sticks out his bull neck. 'This will never do,' he harrumphs, donning his pince-nez again in displeasure. 'It's not in the interests of the American people to have such goings on publicised. These letters may have to be burnt. History is not to be trifled with!' Which, I think, is exactly what you are about to do; choosing which bits to reveal and which to suppress.

Aware of my silent censure, he changes the subject. 'You know, Mrs Ross, God may move in a mysterious way but He does so with perfect symmetry. A Robert Ross steals these papers and a Robert Ross retrieves them. But after digging them up on the Tortugas, what did he do with them?'

'He left them in a safety deposit box in Havana's National Bank, along with the deeds to the sugar plantation. I had to go to Cuba to get them back.'

'The nation owes you a debt. Can I do anything for you in return?'

I had been hoping he might ask me that. 'Yes, there is one thing sir. Can you file an antitrust suit against the American Tobacco Company?'

'That's a bolt out of the blue,' Roosevelt says slowly. 'What have you got against ATC?'

'ATC has a stranglehold on the American market and is using its power to reduce the purchasing price of tobacco. Small farmers are being ruined as a consequence. It's actually costing them more to plant the crop than they can make by harvesting it. You promised to give ordinary people a square deal and ATC is a trust that needs busting.'

My words have a strange effect on him. His shoulders go back and his head pitches forward as he studies me anew. I am used to men looking at me but not like this. Having completed his inspection, he gives me a wide toothsome grin.

'You do well to remind me of my responsibilities, Mrs Ross. The corporate consolidation of our nation's business

399

is destroying economic opportunity for the little man. The government is us; we are the government, you and I, and it is up to us to restrict the power of big business for the general good. I will get my attorney-general to establish whether ATC is a monopoly and therefore in violation of the Sherman Antitrust Act. But you haven't explained why you are concerned about tobacco farmers.'

'It's like this, Mr President: during what was a truly wonderful marriage, Robert and I never really settled in one place. Now that he's gone I want to put down roots. So I've bought the farm where my mother grew up. It's called Conclusion, a 560-acre plantation near Ten Mile Creek in Montgomery County, Maryland. The climate is warm and dry and the soil drains well. I'm planning to grow tobacco. So you see I have a vested interest in getting a fair price for my crop.'

A throat is discreetly cleared. Ike Hoover hovers near our bench. 'Can I remind you, Mr President, that you have a cabinet meeting in five minutes time?'

Roosevelt shakes my hand. 'I have really enjoyed our conversation, Mrs Ross. You are a remarkable lady and I hope we meet again.'

He rises to his feet and I realise for the first time that he is no bigger than I am. But size doesn't matter. The United States is lucky to have such an intelligent and decisive man in the White House.

Ike shows me a short cut through the gardens to the main gate. I say my farewells and cross the wide expanse of Pennsylvania Avenue, narrowly avoiding an onrushing tubular-framed motor car.

I haven't got used to the speed at which these petrol-powered vehicles travel yet, and I hear the Ford Motor Company is about to market a car that is twice as fast as anything on the roads now. I guess that's what they mean by progress, George. Talking of which, I am about to catch one of these motorised streetcars to go to the railroad station to meet our son. Young George is coming down from Harvard to spend the weekend with me in Washington. He's grown as tall as you and just as handsome. He's thinking of making a career as an academic. I hope you approve.

But you may not like what else I am going to say. Having told President Roosevelt your full story, I reckon your son should hear it too. He has a right to know the truth about his father. George Grenfell may have done some bad things, but he was the man I adored as a child and with whom I had so many happy years of marriage. He's as much a part of our family history as Robert Ross. You were lucky enough to get a second chance in life and you turned things around. In case you haven't noticed, my darling, I'm fifty now and I too want to make a fresh start.

No more lies or half-truths.

The path to redemption lies in remembrance.

FACTUAL BACKGROUND TO THE NOVEL

I first heard of Colonel George St Leger Grenfell on visiting Fort Jefferson, a huge brick fortress built on a small atoll in the shark-infested waters of the Dry Tortugas that became a top security prison in the aftermath of the Civil War. Here we were shown the actual cell that Grenfell shared with the so-called Lincoln conspirators. Our tour guide waxed lyrical about Dr Samuel Mudd, the Maryland doctor who had had the misfortune to set John Wilkes Booth's broken leg after he'd assassinated President Lincoln, while dismissing Grenfell as a Cornish spy whose well-merited death sentence for treachery had been commuted to life imprisonment. Coming from Cornwall, I wasn't satisfied with this explanation. To commit treason, you either had to betray your country or murder someone to whom you owed allegiance. The guide said Grenfell had been arrested before he could lead a raid to free Confederate soldiers from a Chicago prisoner-of-war camp. So, he hadn't betrayed his country or murdered anyone and, more to the point, he had been sentenced to death for a crime he never got to commit. Where was the justice in that?

Later research revealed that Colonel Grenfell was an immensely courageous but deeply flawed mercenary who joined the Confederacy in the Civil War. A hero to Robert E Lee and a legend to the gullible hillbillies under his command, 'Ole St Lege' claimed to have defended bullet-strewn barricades in the Indian Mutiny, charged with the Light Brigade at Balaclava and to have hacked his way through South American jungles with Garibaldi. Yet the charismatic figure who told these tales of derring-do had a darker side to his character. He was a wanted criminal, a fraudster who had bankrupted his own father, seeking some form of redemption by fighting in one foreign war after another.

Grenfell also had an eye for the ladies. As far as I know he never met Mrs Rose Greenhow but he should have done. She, too, is a historical figure. An American femme fatale who went from being the de facto First Lady in President Buchanan's White House to an imprisoned Confederate spy in little more than a year. Sent to Europe on a diplomatic mission, Rose drowned at sea in 1864. She is still regarded as a heroine in the South.

There are two views about Grenfell's eventual escape from Fort Jefferson in 1868. The official one is that he drowned in a storm in the Gulf of Mexico but neither his body nor the boat he'd commandeered were ever retrieved. On the other hand, he was frequently sighted in Cuba and on the American mainland in the years ahead. I have imagined Grenfell leading a second and far more successful life under an assumed name.

Anyone interested in the history of this period should visit my website, www.davidftaylor.co.uk.